Peter Mark May was born in Walton on Thames, Surrey in 1968. Married with two young sons, he has been writing as a hobby since he left school.

After the sudden death of this brother in 2004, he decided to take voluntary redundancy from an eighteen year Civil Service career and completely changed his life emphasis. Taking two years off work to enjoy life with his family and working on getting his latest horror novel finished.

He is writing a new personal horror novel entitled 'Kumiho', set during the Korean War.

# DEMON

# PETER MARK MAY

# DEMON

Vanguard Press

VANGUARD PAPERBACK

© Copyright 2008

**Peter Mark May**

The right of Peter Mark May to be identified as author of this work has been asserted by him in accordance with the Copyright, Designs and Patents Act 1988.

**All Rights Reserved**

No reproduction, copy or transmission of this publication may be made without written permission.
No paragraph of this publication may be reproduced, copied or transmitted save with the written permission of the publisher, or in accordance with the provisions of the Copyright Act 1956 (as amended).

Any person who commits any unauthorised act in relation to this publication may be liable to criminal prosecution and civil claims for damages.

A CIP catalogue record for this title is available from the British Library.

ISBN 978 1 84386 398 4

*Vanguard Press is an imprint of*
*Pegasus Elliot MacKenzie Publishers Ltd.*
www.pegasuspublishers.com

First Published in 2008

**Vanguard Press**
**Sheraton House  Castle Park**
**Cambridge  England**

Printed & Bound in Great Britain

# Dedication

For my brother Tony, he would have liked this one.

Acknowledgements:

**Debbie Meer** for all her typing skills.

**My loving family** for their patience.

**The Necronomicon** published in 1980 by Avon Books of New York for some of the incantations.

# CHAPTER 1

It was half 'n hour before 'chucking out time' so the streets were desolate, dark and deserted. It was early January and sleety-snow fell solidly from the dark heavens above. It had rained earlier that day, so the snow was only settling on a few cars. The pavements were slick in the yellow glow of the intermittent street lamps.

Napier Road was one of the longest in the area, with houses and flat conversions on either side. Turning into Napier Road from Green Street brought into view the entire length of the road disappearing into the distance. Until it met a slightly more busy B-road that led into town.

Only one such person was walking down the right-hand side pavement of Napier Road tonight and was half way into his trek. He was dressed in a long black coat that flapped at his ankles; a black cap, scarf and gloves which hid away most of his remaining features. It was bitterly cold, two degrees above freezing, but the chill icy wind made it feel much colder. The man trudged on, his head bowed, only glancing up now and again to check on his progress along the dark and silent road.

As the man walked along he fiddled with the bus fare in his pocket, he had chosen to walk home instead, to give him a chance to think. Leaving his change alone for a moment he paused to stroke a black cat that had sidled up to him, after jumping on to a knee-high brick wall. He leant down and gave the cat a tickle under the chin. The cat seemed to like it, probably because they seemed to be the only living things out tonight.

The man in black managed to get a purr out of the cat before the feline suddenly arched its back and ran off down the road.

"What's the matter cat?" the man asked quietly to the disappearing rear end of the moggie. The man straightened up, shrugged and began walking along the pavement towards home again. But the night seemed different now and he couldn't understand why. He was still alone on the street and his breath still puffed out in a cloud before him, yet he felt an uneasy chill eat deep into the marrow of his bones. Carrying on regardless, as that was all he could do, he approached a road that led up the hill to a cul-de-sac.

Then he became aware of the sound of footfalls coming towards him at a loud and hurried pace. At first he wasn't sure where the sound of running was coming from. He realised his hand was hurting because he was gripping his change so hard, even through his glove. Then a streak of white through a bush caught his eye and running down the side road came a black woman, dressed only in a white blouse, short black skirt and black ankle-high hugging boots.

The woman was in some distress and was emitting a low moan as she ran. The man stopped dead in his tracks as the woman reached the T-junction that led into Napier Road. She skidded to a halt on the frosty pavement using the pole of a road sign to keep her vertical. Her head shot left and right, like a fox being chased by hounds searching for a way of escape.

The frightened woman finally focused on a man dressed in all black, but she could see his white face between the tip of his cap and the top of his scarf-covered mouth. Pushing herself away from the signpost with a glance up the road she had just escaped from, she covered the distance between herself and the man in black in a couple of seconds.

"Please help me, he's after me," she cried and the man could see in her eyes she was scared witless. "Don't let him get me!"

"Don't worry, I'll protect you." The man sounded young but reassuring. "How far is he behind you?"

"Only a few seconds," the woman gasped with exhaustion.

"Trust me and do as I say if you want to see the light of another dawn." The man's words were strange, but oddly reassuring.

"Okay," she replied nervously, this being the last decision she could ever make. The man's eyes flicked to the hedge, as he thought he saw movement out the corner of his vision.

Suddenly he grabbed the woman and spun her around, pinned one arm behind her back as his other black gloved hand went to her throat.

"Hey, what are you doing!"

But the conversation stopped there as a shadowy figure, attired in a hooded long black cloak emerged from the side road into Napier Road, about twelve feet in front of them. Both the man and the woman gasped, because the figure seemed to be surrounded by his own personal darkness, even under a street lamp. His complexion under his shadowy hood seemed grey, his features were oddly elongated, but unusual and most frightening of all were his glowing hellfire red eyes.

"I have her," the man stated, finding his voice. "What is thy bidding, my master?"

The ghostly dark figure was taken aback and obviously had not seen any Star Wars films lately.

"Unexpected," he hissed, "a kindred spirit." The figure flowed a foot closer without even taking a step.

"Give her to me and I will reward you with my mark of everlasting protection, as a helper of dark forces." The man noticed the snow was still coming down, but not within a five foot radius of the burning-eyed figure.

"Get ready to run," he whispered to the girl, as he released her pinned arm. The man, still shielded by the woman, reached down into his outside coat pocket and grabbed three of the coins there. The man released the girl and moved around to stand just in front of her and to her right, but more importantly, between her and the unearthly figure that had been chasing him. The man slowly raised his gloved hand, showing the three coins to the burning-eyed figure ahead.

"These are the coins of the sovereign of this realm, they bear her head as the Queen of this Kingdom of Light. I am her servant and bow down in worship of her and have sworn my everlasting allegiance to her and my unworthy life. These are her symbols of rulership and power. I believe in them, I believe in their power."

With that the man threw them as hard as he could at the burning-eyed figure in front of him. Two of the coins found their mark, while the other disappeared into the night. The burning-eyed figure cried out in pain as the coins hit. As they did they hissed and burned into his body, sending tiny clouds of hellish red smoke into the air. The dark figure staggered back as his wounds shone like fiery holes in the side of a furnace, glowing intensely in the unnatural darkness that surrounded him.

The man put his left arm across the woman and grabbed a handful of her blouse as he pushed her into movement. With his arm protectively across her, he began to edge them on to the grass verge adjacent to the pavement and next to the empty road.

"Who are you that knows the dweomer craft of old?" spat the injured crimson-eyed figure.

"I know well enough not to tell you my name!" the man replied, his gloved hand in his pocket again searching for more coins.

"And worthy adversaries are so rare in this wanton, unbelieving age." The burning-eyed man moved forward quickly, but the girl was amazed at her saviour's speed as he flung two more coins at the unearthly man. More puffs of red smoke appeared as the coins once again found their mark. Two lava-coloured wounds had appeared now on the fiend's chest and right thigh. The unearthly figure fell to his knees, his eyes burning bright in agony.

They both backed a few more steps around the kneeling fiend attempting to find a place from which they could flee for their lives.

"Back demon! You are defeated this night. You will not take this girl back to Gehenna tonight!" the man shouted, while collecting the last three coins from his pocket and placing them in his left hand. The demon stared back at them in a rage: the faint smell of sulphur was in the air.

"I will hunt you down and rip out the old knowledge from your brain and devour it!" the fiery-eyed demon screamed.

"With a nice chianti, eh?" the man spat back. "Maybe we could share a bottle of red wine and cast the battled figures across the chequered board."

The rage seemed to go out of the demon's voice at this. "You are cunning for one so young. I bow to your wisdom again and your victory over me." The demon opened his arms out wide and he bowed from his kneeling position.

"We will share wine and play chess, but that will only spare you for one night. From then on you're fair game." The demon chuckled, low and throaty, sounding like he had a throat cancer and gargling with treacle at the same time.

"If indeed you are the victor." The demon roared and leaped towards the man and woman. While he and the demon had conversed, the man had clasped the last remaining coins between the fingers of his right fist. The man's gloved fist came up just as the demon was upon him, his punch catching the demon slap-bang in the face.

The woman gasped as the demon exploded and vanished in a large sulphurous cloud of red smoke, which shrank and disappeared like a snake into a crack between two paving stones.

"Shit!" the man cried, hastily ripping off his burning glove and blowing on his burnt hand. "Come on follow me." The man grabbed the woman's hand and they turned and ran hand in hand down Napier Road. They reached the end of the street that came to a T-junction which was the main B-road that led in and out of town. Both the man and the woman looked back nervously at the dark, silent street behind. Only the noise and white glare of a passing truck brought them back to reality.

"Quick put this on!" the man offered, unbuttoning his coat, as he led her down Hove Road away from the dreaded Napier Road. The woman followed silently as they headed for a Pelican crossing. "We'll head for my house, it's not far." The man finished taking off his long black coat and handed it to the now shivering woman. "You'll be safe there. Come on, we better hurry."

The woman put her arms through the sleeves of the coat and just buttoned two middle buttons before they set off hand in hand again across the crossing and down another street off Hove Road, called Churchill Lane. The woman was exhausted, but kept running as she wanted to get as far away from the night's horror as she possibly could. They were half-way down Churchill Lane when she croaked "Dela!"

The man slowed to a brisk walk and turned his head towards the woman, "What?"

"My name's Dela, Dela Robinson," she gasped, her teeth and eyes the main features he could see of the woman, but those bits seemed very attractive.

"Oh, sorry," he smiled, "my name is Nathaniel Whitworth Alexander Le Meuille," he replied as they dropped to a slower walking pace.

"Thanks," gasp, "for saving my life," she managed to finish before gasping another breath.

"That's okay, but the task's only half done, we'd better start trotting along again if you can manage it. I'll feel much safer when we've reached my place."

"I'll try."

"That's the British spirit." They began to jog along the empty lane. Churchill Lane led off to a curved row of flats called

Cole Street which ran up an incline on it and into Cole Road. The man kindly slowed to a walking pace as they reached the top of the hill. Dela noticed a very large, odd-shaped house silhouetted by the sky on the corner where Cole Street and Road met. The sight of the place sent a chill down her spine – it looked like Dracula's fortress on top of some Carpathian mountain.

"Here we are then," Nathaniel spoke for the first time in five minutes, "home safe and sound." Nathaniel had stopped by a six foot wooden gate cut into a seven foot high brick wall that was continued by dense fir trees, dotted with holly bushes.

"You live here?" Dela asked incredulously, looking up at the narrowish three-storey house, "alone?"

"Yes," he replied, pulling a rather large iron key from his back trouser pocket and inserting it into a lock unseen by Dela because of the dark.

The key turned and Dela heard a loud clunk, as Nathaniel pushed the door inwards, "Come on, let's get you inside."

"Why do you want to get me inside so quickly?" Dela was just having second thoughts about her saviour; thoughts that would have sprung to mind earlier if she hadn't been distracted by other weirder events.

"Because it's freezing cold and you're wearing my coat," Nathaniel replied from the doorway, "and it's got my door keys in it."

"Good point." Dela searched about in the pockets of his coat as she followed him through the door into a small garden, with a paved path cut into the side of the hill with steps up to a back door.

Nathaniel closed and locked the garden gate behind her and led her up the garden path to a door in the side of the odd – looking house.

With a jingle, Dela fished a key ring full of the keys from his inside pocket and handed them to him.

"Thank you," he replied politely and sincerely. Quickly he undid the two Chubb locks at the top and bottom of the back door, then inserted a Yale key in a middle lock next to the handle on the door. Nathaniel pushed the door open and stepped aside to usher Dela in while keeping his eyes on the shadows in his small confined garden.

Dela hesitantly edged forward until she could see inside the house – a long hallway stretched forward that seemed to run the entire length of the place.

"Quickly!" Nathaniel prompted with a smile.

Dela quickly glanced at her saviour. She had a sixth sense with people in her game and all her instincts told her that he was okay. She stepped into the hall, to her left the room opened up into a very large kitchen, with what looked like every kitchen utensil anyone could ever want.

Nathaniel followed her in, shut, locked and bolted the door behind them. He then unclipped a small blind and rolled it down the window part of the door, and secured it before switching on the hall light. He quickly moved past Dela, leaving her standing where she was to cover the same type of glass panel on his front door. Then he was back past Dela again into the kitchen, with a quick explanation of a smile, to pull down the long roller blind covering the kitchen window. Dela's head whirled as her tall, busy hero finally returned to stand next to her.

"How are you doing?" he asked kindly, putting a cold hand on the arm of the coat he had lent her.

Dela exhaled. "Numb," was all she could reply, but it summed it up accurately.

"I bet you could do with a drink, I know I could."

"Yeah."

He took her hand again through habit rather than any other motive, and led her down the hall. There was a door in the right wall, and she passed two on her left before coming to the foot of stairs leading up into the gloom.

"I keep all the best spirits upstairs in my study, otherwise Cerberus gets them and he isn't allowed upstairs." Nathaniel chatted on like nothing supernatural or scary had happened at all that night.

"Cerberus?"

"Oh, he's my dog." Nathaniel moved toward the right-hand door putting his hand on the knob, "He should be in here."

"I don't like dogs!" Dela exclaimed.

"You don't?" Nathaniel looked back at her with a little bit of hurt in his voice.

"Or rather they hate me. In fact, they scare the shit out of me." Dela smiled thinly.

"But Cerberus isn't like any dog you've ever met, he won't bite." Nathaniel pushed the door open wide, but all Dela could see was the faint outline of a gloomy; well-furnished dining room. Then from deep inside the dark room came a deep guttural growl, like it was being resonated through a bass bin.

Slowly out of the shadows came one of the most enormous dogs Dela had ever seen. As he reached the light of the hall, she could see he was some sort of Alsatian mix, mixed with a wolf or horse, Dela thought.

The wolf/dog stared straight at her. As she backed away she bumped into the stair banister. Her legs were like rubber and her heart was pounding again. After all that had happened to her tonight, she was amazed her heart hadn't given up the ghost and stopped.

Cerberus gave a bark and the whole house resonated with his echoing sign of ferocity.

"Cerberus, bad dog!" Nathaniel commanded and with one glance at his master Cerberus fell to the floor in submission, mewling like a chastised puppy. "If you can't behave in front of guests, you'll just have to work. I want you to patrol the hall. No one comes into this house without me knowing," Nathaniel ordered.

Cerberus made a small barking sound in his throat, as if to say "yes" and sloped off down the hall towards the back door, his eyes fixed firmly on the floor.

"Sorry about that."

"It's okay," Dela whimpered.

"Let's get you upstairs and get you that drink." Nathaniel took her hand again and led her upstairs away from the dog. Dela took his hand again without hesitation; it was now a comforting contact. He led her upstairs to a small landing which had five closed wooden doors. The house was obviously years old, Edwardian, Victorian, something like that, Dela thought. There was one door dead ahead and two each left and right. Nathaniel opened the first door on the left and switched on the light as he entered.

"Excuse the mess," Nathaniel said as he let go of her hand and walked into his study and went over to stand by the window.

To Dela it seemed she had walked straight into an old antiques shop. A large antique desk with a green leather top stood against one wall, with a modern swivel chair pulled up to it. There were various shelves; sideboards and cupboards choc-a-bloc with objet d'art; crosses, books, crucifixes, drawings, test tubes, a shield leaning up against a wall, piles of paper, maps, parchments, scrolls, box files, a computer and many other things besides.

Dela continued to scan the room as Nathanial came away from the window and opened the top of an old wooden globe, which revealed four bottles of spirits and four glasses.

"Have a seat," Nathaniel nodded towards an old-looking high backed solid leather chair. He meanwhile walked his fingers over the bottles: Drambuie, Glenlivet, Remy Martin, but finally stopped and pulled up a bottle of Glenmorangie.

Dela sat down and looking up found a tiger head was staring down at her from above. Mystical pictures and mezzotints covered the rest of the dark green wallpaper, which covered the room where the wood panelling finished.

Nathaniel turned and handed her a double Glenmorangie and he sat down opposite in his modern computer chair. They both took long sips of whisky. Nathaniel closed his eyes and savoured the aroma as it wafted up his nose. When he opened his eyes he saw that Dela's glass was empty.

"Want a refill?"

"No," she shook her head, "I want to know what that was?" Dela's eyes were wide and pleaded to Nathaniel for answers.

"Glenmor- " Nathaniel stopped, catching her drift, "oh, that outside you mean?"

Dela nodded.

"That was a demon," he replied matter-of-factly.

Dela wanted to shout at him. 'Are you mad?' but then she would only be incriminating herself with the same lunacy if she did. "How did it get here and how did you know how to defeat it?" she asked, trying to distance herself from the fact that she might have gone completely mad.

"It could have got here a number of ways," Nathaniel explained, "pagan rituals, summoning, some black magic gateway, I can't tell 'til I have more facts, really." Nathaniel sipped at his whisky, "Can you tell me what happened before you came running down the road into my life?"

Dela gazed at his smile and even though he seemed uncool and not her preferred type or colour, she noticed that he had a delicate way with words that put her at ease. Dela felt if pushed she could sit here all night and tell him her entire life story, or at least tonight's part anyway. Dela went to have another sip of whisky for Dutch courage, but found she had finished her drink, so swallowed hard and began.

"I'm a masseuse," she began, staring intently into Nathaniel's green eyes for a flick of disapproval. There was none, so she continued, "Well, a travelling masseuse. People ring my number and I come over to their houses, homes, places of work and give them a massage." Dela spoke fast, she become very nervous and defensive about her line of work.

"It sounds ..., well ..., dangerous," Nathaniel commented, "you work alone?"

"I haven't got a pimp if that's what you're thinking. I do massage. If the punters want me to go topless it'll cost fifty pounds extra, but that's as far as it goes. They ain't allowed to touch me. I have a black belt in karate, if any mother-fucker touches me I kick them in the balls. I ain't no ten quid a shag slapper. I have a flat, a mortgage and more importantly, my pride." Dela finished her thousand mile an hour story with a sigh.

"So what happened tonight?" Nathaniel asked, ignoring her outburst with a blink of his eyelashes.

"Oh!" Dela was taken aback, normally a man would be shouting or apologising about now. This was a new response.

"Dela, please, this is important. I don't care what job you do, if I'm going to keep you alive for your next massage, I must know what happened tonight!"

Dela was amazed at the passion and ferocity her tall handsome hero could project with his low, sharp words. "I'm sorry."

"Go on," he egged, with a softish voice and a glint of a smile.

"Well, I got a call at six for a job in this area, a house a couple of streets away from where – " Dela thought for a moment, "where we met. The client's name was Ashley Maddy. I was to come to an address he gave at nine o'clock to give a massage. I said it was way out of my area, I live in Balham, but he said he would pay me two hundred quid for a massage only, no extras." Dela paused to rub her sleek brown nose. "I arrived at ten to nine at the house by taxi: it was in a quiet street. So I knocked on the front door and this tall, tanned gentleman with jet black hair and a little pointy beard answered, he looked in his late thirties, but fit, you know," Dela explained and Nathaniel nodded in return.

"The place was spanky, well up-market. I mean, I can tell an up-market place because the hall carpets didn't reach to the wall, like on purpose." Dela smiled for the first time and Nathaniel was hard-pressed to remember a woman with a more engaging smile.

"So he led me upstairs into a small room which only had a small table and chair and a proper massage table, you know, the ones with the hole to put your head in. The guy was good-looking, but weird, doesn't say a word. He gets out two hundred pounds and puts the notes on the small table then strips off completely. I'm ready to punch the guy's lights out, but he just hops on the table and lays down on his front." Dela realised she had been doing punching motions with her hand, so she put the glass down on the carpet. "So I put the money in my holdall, get my oils out and take off my coat, putting them all on the little table."

"Then what happened?" Nathaniel asked, sipping at his whisky.

"Well, I start rubbing him down and apart from his silence being a little odd, I calm down a little and get into me work. Then," Dela paused, "could I have another drink please?"

"Not a problem." Dela reached down and handed him her glass. "Same again?"

"Sure, babe," Dela replied matter-of-factly. Nathaniel refilled her glass and after draining half of it Dela began again.

"I was working away and I was getting hot, not in the panties area either – the whole room was very humid, the sweat was dripping off me like piss, you know. So I reapplied some oils to his back and continued, but his skin was getting hotter and hotter. I thought the guy was having a heart attack, so I stepped back. It was like his skin was changing colour and the oil on his back started to sizzle like bacon fat, man." Dela sipped again from her drink. "I must have backed away because I was in a corner next to a window and the oil on his back had caught fire. I remember screaming, then he got up, how I dunno, he was on fire, but not in pain and his eyes were pits of fire".

Nathaniel noticed that Dela's hands were shaking badly now. So he knelt before her, took the whisky glass out of her hands and placed it on the floor. "Go on, if you can."

Dela sniffed in trying to hold back tears, "Well I did what I always do, booted him in the nuts. But he didn't go down or anything, he just smiled. I couldn't get past, he was blocking my way to the door, so I pulled up the sash and jumped out the window."

" 'Fuck'!" Nathaniel exclaimed, "excuse my French."

"Fuck indeed! Luckily I landed on a patio-type thing over the back door to the house. I jumped down and pegged it out of the back garden into the street and just ran for it. But he followed wearing some sort of monk's gear. I couldn't believe the streets were so empty – not a person or bleedin' car in sight 'til I found you." Dela reached down and picked up her drink, "so that's my horror story. Now tell me about your life and how you knew how to kill that devil?"

"Demon," he corrected.

"Whatever," she replied, showing her open palms to him, "what's the difference?"

"Horns," he replied tartly. "What I'm about to tell you, I have never told anybody in my life. Probably because they would never believe me, but after what you have witnessed tonight I think you may," Nathaniel began.

"My ancient relatives on my father's side were knights of old and each eldest son from one generation to the next was the King's Paladin. A sort of religious knight-errant who was the King's Champion, but he also would defend the Regent of the time against demons and witchcraft. The King's Paladin was also the keeper of an ancient Latin text on Dweomer craft, demon lore and rites and spells for banishing demons. This went on 'til 1832 when my great-great-great-great-grandfather was the King's Paladin. Our family had held the book since 1639 and he decided to translate it from Latin into English. This took over ten years, but something went wrong. The original book was lost and a girl in the service of the Queen was killed. Our family was stripped of much of its land, wealth and title and the King's Paladin title was amalgamated and given to the King's Champion of the time," Nathaniel pointed at Dela, "that still exists today."

"Nice history lesson," said Dela. "If your family was shamed and the title and book had long since gone, how do you know so much?"

"I'll show you," Nathaniel replied, getting up from his swivel chair. He walked over to the wall behind Dela, whose eyes followed him around the room. Nathaniel stopped under a moose's head, reached up and poked in the long-dead beast's left eye. Dela blinked as a door-sized section of the wall suddenly moved, slowly showing two feet of a dark hidden room behind.

"Impressed?" Nathaniel asked.

"Someone must have put some E in my coffee this morning, because I've seen some real weird shit today!" she replied in a lush Caribbean accent. "Anyway, it takes a lot more than a hole to impress me!" she added.

"Really?" Nathaniel replied with a smirk and a raised eyebrow. "Come on," he urged, holding out his hand to her again. Dela rose and took his hand and let herself be led into the darkened secret room.

The room was small, dark and dirty and only a small blue light directed down on to a lectern illuminated the room. An ancient-looking leather bound book lay on the lectern, covered by a glass box. The only other item in the room was a long chest, half-hidden in a dark corner.

"This," Nathaniel said, lifting up the hinged glass case, "is the translation into English from the original Latin book that my great-great-great-great-grandfather made in 1832."

"Worth a bit is it?" Dela asked, inclining forward.

"Priceless," Nathaniel replied in a far-away voice.

Dela's eyes were becoming accustomed to the dark. She noticed that a strange magic circle was painted on the floor and the lectern was in its dead centre.

"Come closer," Nathaniel beckoned.

"Why?" Dela asked, not sure if she wanted to join him in the magic circle.

"Because this book should be able to tell us what type of demon attacked you."

"Why do you want to know that?" Dela asked, shuffling into the circle on her toes. Maybe if she didn't put her full weight down nothing could happen to her.

"Before he can return we have to find a way to defeat him forever," Nathaniel said absently.

"Back up! Back up!" Dela said loudly, "Return, but you killed him!"

"I only vanquished his corporeal form. I defeated him in combat three times so he had to return to Hell in defeat. I only killed his human self, he, depending on what he is, can return to kill us."

"What do you mean, what he is?" Dela asked. The fear of her earlier encounter began creeping into her bones once again.

"What type of demon he is. This will tell us how long he is banished from this earth – usually three months – and when and how to defeat him before he gets his revenge," Nathaniel explained, putting his hands on her shoulders. "So it is vital that we find out what type he is!" Nathaniel left one arm on her shoulder and turned her towards the old leather-bound and silver-clasped book.

"What type?" Dela looked bemused, "what do you mean, regular or king size?"

He smiled in the dimly-lit room, making him appear so much better looking, "Kind of. There are three types – " he began.

"There's that number three again," Dela butted in.

"Yes, it's a biblical demonic number. Lucifer's number is six, six, six, his demon's number is three, three, three. There are lesser demons, demons and the three, again High Demons or Demon Lords."

"How does someone your age know all this?" Dela asked rhetorically.

"I read it in a book," Nathaniel replied, tapping the book on the lectern.

"What name did he give you again Dela?" Nathaniel asked as he unclasped and opened the book.

"Ashley Maddy," Dela replied. A cold shiver ran up her spine, like someone was walking over her grave.

"Right," Nathaniel said finding the chapter he had been looking for. "Shit!"

"What is it?"

"Ashmadi is the Hebrew name for the Demon Lord Ashmodaios. We are in deep shit, Dela!" Nathaniel explained, looking scared for the first time since Dela had met him.

"Why?"

"Because he's a Demon Lord, one of Satan's three Arch-Lords, anti-Angels if you like," Nathaniel replied in a stressed, raised voice. "And he knows your name."

"That sounds bad," Dela stated the obvious.

"Bad! Bad?" Nathaniel shouted, "in three days' time Ashmodaios could be knocking on my front door asking for our blood!" Nathaniel turned away, his hands on his head.

"I thought you said we had three months!"

"So did I, but this guy's shit-hot, he can recover quicker than any normal demon." Nathaniel turned to face her, putting his hand on her shoulder "You'd better stay here tonight, it'll be safest 'til I figure out what to do next."

"Well, I don't want to be alone," Dela replied, staring deep into his eyes for meaning. "You do live alone, don't you?"

"Yes. Well, there's Cerberus," Nathaniel shrugged.

"No girlfriend, then?"

"Not since I broke up with my fiancée tonight, no." Nathaniel replied sharply, turning away and heading out of the secret room.

"No chance of a reconciliation, then?" Dela pushed, following him out of the room.

"Never." He turned and looked down at her, as if to say 'don't ask any more personal questions.'

"Why?" she asked with a feminine grin.

"You ask a lot of questions," he replied, trying to put her off the scent.

"Yeah, I'm a mouthy bitch, ain't I?" she laughed.

Nathaniel grinned in spite of himself. "Because I didn't want to leave this house, because I lived in the past, I have no real desire for bags of money, fancy cars or furthering my career, etcetera."

"Oh. Are you good in the sack?" Dela asked straight-faced.

"Fantastic!" he replied straight-faced, getting used to Dela's shock tactics.

"Sounds like a right stuck-up stupid cow!"

"Like Laura Ashley on Acid, very pretty of course, but the brains and charisma of a small *petit-poi.*"

Dela laughed and Nathaniel joined in. It was a temporary relief from the terrors of the night.

"What'll we do now?" Dela asked as the laughter died.

"We?"

"You – Batman, me – Batgirl, savvy?"

"Well, we have to prepare," Nathaniel began "Ashmodaios can't return for three days, but he might send a couple of his minions round."

"What would this Demon Lord have done, raped me?" Dela moved forward and took his arm as she asked.

"Possibly, for starters, then eaten your heart, possessed your body or taken your soul most likely," he answered sincerely.

Dela gulped, "What now?"

"Well, we'll visit this house where you were attacked in the cold light of day and retrieve your stuff. Have a snoop around the house, see who owns it, then take a look at the spot where I banished him," Nathaniel explained, "but we better prepare our defences for tonight first."

"Against the minions?" Dela asked scornfully.

"Yep," Nathaniel replied, "I've just got to pop downstairs to the kitchen to get something and I'll be back."

Dela watched her saviour run from the room; she sucked at her bottom lip then sat down in the leather chair. She was alone for the first time since the attack, and now that she had time to reflect on the night's strange events, she began to cry.

Nathaniel found her weeping to herself as he returned to his study and placed a large plastic container of salt on his table. Kneeling down he put his arms around her and she uncharacteristically buried her head into his neck. "Hey, I can't leave you alone for one moment, can I?" he reassured her. "A woman with a face as beautiful as yours should be happy and smiling all the time. If you had a face like mine, then you'd be miserable!"

A choked laugh came from his neck and Dela pulled back, wiping away the tears from her eyes. "Nathaniel, what's the salt for?" she asked after she had got her tears under control, "I prefer pepper myself."

"Ah!" he cried, standing up with a click of his kneecaps, "This, dear Dela," he picked up the salt container, "will ensure a good night's sleep."

"I use Nytol myself," Dela quipped, sniffing up her tears.

"We have to put it across every portal of the house: windows, doorways etcetera. You see a demon cannot cross a threshold if there's an unbroken line of salt there. That's not as easy as it sounds, so I need the old Blue Peter favourite." Nathaniel picked up a large roll of sticky tape from his cluttered desk.

"Sticky tape?" Dela inquired.

"Double-sided sticky tape. It'll keep the salt in place, especially in this draughty old barn." He smiled again, a quite magical feat in the circumstances thought Dela.

Nathaniel bent down and reached out his hand, and Dela took it. "You really are my white knight."

"And you're my black beauty."

Dela laughed at him.

"I meant to imply you were beautiful, and not a horse!"

Dela, with his help, pulled herself up, "Don't worry Nathaniel, I've been called worse."

"People can be so petty and colour blind," Nathaniel stated.

"And you're not?" she asked scornfully.

"No, I have only problems with people with grey skin and red glowing eyes," he replied, "come on, let's get to it."

Dela put her manicured hand on his shoulder, noticing she had lost a couple of fake purple nails. "You're a nice guy, Nathaniel."

"Thank you, miss," he replied, doffing his hair like an invisible hat.

"Nathaniel. A bit of a mouthful, can I call you Nath or Nat?"

"Nath will suffice." Catching Dela by surprise he bent over and kissed her forehead, "Come on, time is of the essence."

Smiling like a cross between a loon and a happy puppy, she followed him to the window.

Nathaniel put his double-sided sticky tape from one side of the window-sill to the other, cutting it with a sharp three inch penknife he pulled from a drawer in his desk. He then carefully removed the backing tape so that a sticky length was ready for the salt. Nathaniel, under Dela's watchful eyes, painfully poured the salt in an unbroken line, slowly, from one end of the tape to the other.

"That's this room done, let's do the master bedroom. We'll do the window first, then move on to the doorways."

Dela was quite shocked by the interior of the master bedroom. It looked like one of those exhibited rooms in Hampton Court Palace. A large queen-sized four-poster bed was the main eye-catching piece of furniture. The walls were panelled in mahogany, the painted upper and lower thirds of the walls were a deep red, with gold leaf trim. Thick claret curtains covered the large windows and the room was richly furnished with a mahogany dressing table, wardrobe and chest at the end of the bed. Even the four-poster bed had scarlet segregating curtains and several old dark portraits adorned two of the walls.

"Well, will you look at this place?" Dela exclaimed, just staring round the room in wonder.

"You like the place then?" Nathaniel asked, moving over to draw the curtains, salt and sticky tape in hand.

"You bet, babe. It's, it's beautiful." Dela had never been in such an ostentatious room before.

"You can sleep here tonight then," Nathaniel offered, applying the sellotape to the large mahogany window sill.

"Yeah," Dela said, jumping at the chance to live like a fairy princess, even if it was only for one night. "Don't you want to sleep here?"

"Tempting offer, but I always sleep in another room, this is a bit much, don't you think?" Nathanial gazed quickly over his shoulder as he ripped off the sticky-back strip.

"No. Ever since I was a little kid in my mum's tiny flat, I've always dreamt of sleeping in a bed and bedroom like this." Dela thought back to those cold dark nights, sleeping in her grotty stark room.

"Well, tonight Princess Dela will get her wish," Nathaniel said, drawing a line of salt along the sticky tape.

They continued from room to room upstairs, doing Nathaniel's messy bedroom next, a jam-packed book-filled library, another spare bedroom and the bathroom. Nathaniel left the library and spare bedroom doors open and put a line of salt in their respective doorways. Nathaniel went downstairs and completed a few rooms, then returned upstairs to make a line on the top step where it met the first floor landing. By the time that he had finished it was five past one in the morning.

"We better get some sleep, we've got to be up early tomorrow to continue our investigation. We'll go in to the master bedroom and I'll salt us in, so to speak." Dela followed Nathaniel into the bedroom. "There's some old nighties of my mum's in that chest over there, if you need one."

"I never wear anything in bed except a smile," Dela replied and moved over to the bed and began to undress.

Nathaniel turned away quickly and busied himself with sticky tape and salt. Nathaniel took his time, but found it extremely difficult to be a gentleman and not have a peek at Dela.

"You can turn around now, it's safe," Dela called from the bed.

Nathaniel picked himself up and the tape and salt and walked over and put them on the dresser. Dela sat up against the headboard, the eiderdown at her waist, white sheet up covering her assets.

"Where are you going to sleep?" Dela asked, as Nathaniel rooted through a drawer to find a blanket.

"Oh, I'll just crash on this chair," he replied, tossing the blanket he found on a mahogany chair in the corner of the room by the windows.

"I don't want to sleep alone," Dela pleaded in a quiet voice from the bed.

"I'll be right here, there's nothing to worry about," Nathaniel turned towards her and pointed at the chair.

"I don't want to sleep alone!" Dela stated in a firmer voice and let the sheet slip to expose her attractive, firm breasts.

Nathaniel moved closer to the bed, "Er, that's not necessary you know, er, you don't have to because I saved your life," he stammered, showing his kind, shy nature and not the action hero side from earlier. Dela liked the fact that Nathaniel was not conceited.

"Come here Nath," Dela beckoned, "and shut up."

"Okay," Nathaniel replied and moved to her side of the bed, his masculine side soon reasserting itself with the help of the huge erection in his pants. Nathaniel bent down and Dela craned her neck up as they kissed each other's lips. Their mouths opened quickly and the kissing soon became urgent as their tongues explored the inside of each other's mouths. Nathaniel boldly put his hand on Dela's right breast; Dela responded with faster French kisses and her hands went to his black jeans and deftly and urgently undid his fly buttons. Dela turned towards Nathaniel and sat up on her knees a little, making their kisses easier and her hands delved into his boxer's and freed his enormous erection. Dela freed herself from his ardent kisses to gaze upon it, "That's a nice big surprise!"

"Thanks," Nathaniel replied, "so what are you going to do with my big surprise?" Dela couldn't answer, because her mamma (god rest her soul) told her never to speak with her mouth full.

Later as they lay cuddled up after their passionate lovemaking, in several orifices and positions, Dela asked him "What do you do for a job - sex instructor?"

"No, I work for the Home Office, actually. I have to really, to keep up the tradition as King's Paladin I have to work for Her Majesty's Government. I only work Mondays to Wednesdays anyway and that's one reason why my fiancée and I broke up. She didn't see the point of me working when I didn't have to and I couldn't really tell her the reason either." Nathaniel kissed Dela's smooth brow. "Oh, and she also accused me of being secretive," he raised his eyebrows and smiled. "Can't really blame her for that though."

"So was I better than your fiancée, then?" Dela asked with a twinkle in her eyes. She knew the answer already, because she had had the best sex ever with Nathaniel. Streets above all the other selfish losers she had shagged in the past.

"I don't know what I had before, but it wasn't sex, what we've just done is the definitive description of what sex should be like," he replied.

Dela lifted herself up a little over his chest – the feel of her breasts caused creases in the sheets half-way down the bed. "Good answer," she replied.

"Do you think we got carried away a little?"

"I let you put your dick in me and you haven't even taken me to a club or dinner yet. Yes, you could say we got carried away, but it was fantastic." Dela leant forward and kissed his lips tenderly.

"We better get some sleep," Nathaniel replied. His cheeks felt hot and red with embarrassment.

"Can't argue with you on that," Dela said and they snuggled up and finally, after the most eventful night of their lives, each drifted off into uneasy dreams.

# CHAPTER 2

Even though they wanted to be up early, neither of them woke up until ten the next morning after the previous night's exertions. Nathaniel sat up in bed and rubbed the sleep from his eyes. The room was still dark because of the heavy velvet drapes, but he could still see Dela lying on her front next to him, her beautiful naked back exposed.

He eased himself out of bed, then noticed the time as he put on his wrist watch. "Damn!" he cursed in a whisper. He headed out of the room naked, leaving the sleeping Dela and his clothes behind. He popped into his bedroom and quickly pulled on his old dressing gown and took a quick check out the window. The morning was grey and the trees and roads outside were wet from the night before, but it wasn't raining at that moment. Nathaniel had a quick look round the windows upstairs. Finding nothing, he padded downstairs to put the kettle on and feed the ever ravenous Cerberus.

Nathaniel checked the downstairs rooms and petted Cerberus while the kettle boiled. Then he made two cups of tea and put them on a tray with some sugar and took them upstairs to the master bedroom. He tried to put them carefully on the bedside cabinet, but the noise caused Dela's eyes to flick open.

"Morning," she murmured dreamily, with a half-asleep smile on her face.

"Tea?" She nodded.

"Sugar?" He asked again.

"One please," she replied, wrinkling up her nose, "I'm sweet enough as it is, you see."

Nathaniel acted as mother pouring the tea, as Dela sat up in bed, the sheet tucked under her armpits, and they drank their tea together.

"Fancy a shower?" he asked politely.

"Why, do I smell?" she retorted.

Nathaniel just chuckled in reply. "I've got some shirts and jumpers if you want a change of clothes, after your shower."

"Got any knickers or skirts?" Dela ventured.

"Funnily enough, no."

"You jump in first babe and I'll finish me tea," Dela said, wrinkling up her nose.

"Okay. If you want breakfast just pop into the kitchen and root about, see what you like," Nathaniel said, getting off the bed.

"What about that dog of yours, where's he?" Dela asked, her eyes shrinking to slits while her lips pursed.

"I'll put him out into the garden before I take my shower, okay?"

"You're too kind," she replied and sipped at her tea.

Dela peered out through the blinds of the kitchen window and was thankful to see Cerberus doing a large dump on the middle of the back garden. Dressed in her thong and the shirt Nathaniel had worn last night, she started to look into cupboards and drawers in search of cereal or bread for toast. She had just found a box of Shreddies when the front doorbell went, giving her a start.

She froze: the box of cereal in her hand, her heart beating like a toy rabbit with a drum and a long-life battery stuck up its arse. Slowly she found herself moving towards the front door, cereal still in hand. She peered through the rippled window in the door and she could make out only dark reflective colours of a person standing in front of the door.

"Nathaniel!" she cried as she reached the foot of the stairs. She waited patiently for a reply, but got only another attack of the doorbell in her ears. Trying to be brave, she approached the front door and peered through the spy hole. A short, attractive blonde woman in a flowery dress stood at the door, with a fur coat draped over her shoulders. She looked cold and annoyed, but no real danger to Dela. Taking a deep breath, Dela opened the front door and peeked her head round, keeping her body and bare legs away from the cold air. The young woman took a step back in shock.

"Can I help you?" Dela asked, looking out on the large, walled front lawn for the first time.

"Who -," the woman mouthed, then clicked her leather gloved fingers, "you must be Nathaniel's new cleaner. Is he in?"

"And you are?" Dela countered, not giving anything away.

"Cordelia Dean-Stanley. I'm Nathaniel's fiancée, didn't he mention me?" Cordelia asked in crisp-sharp Queen's English.

"He mentioned you'd split up," Dela replied with an amused look.

"Did he?" Cordelia looked shocked. "Well, that was a silly misunderstanding, can I come in?"

"Could be interesting," Dela said softly to herself.

"What?"

"Nothing," Dela replied and pulled the door in. "You'd better come in outta the cold."

"Thank you," Cordelia said, but Dela could tell she didn't mean it. Dela let her in and closed the door behind her. She turned round to find Cordelia staring at her attire.

"Oh," Cordelia looked in shock, "Where is he?"

"In the shower," Dela grinned, "you stay here and make yourself at home and I'll go and get him outta the shower." Dela didn't wait for a reply, but trotted upstairs as Cordelia stared up at her naked legs and backside visible under the shirt as Dela bounced up the stairs.

Dela knocked on the closed bathroom door, but walked in without waiting for a reply. Nathaniel stood before her naked, towelling his hair dry.

"Hi, couldn't wait, eh?"

"No, your fiancée Cordial, or whatever she's called, is downstairs and is waiting to talk to you!" Dela pursed her lovely lips and raised her eyebrows, an amused look on her face.

"Shit!" Nathaniel exclaimed with a shocked look on his.

"Shit, indeed, Nath, deep shit possibly." Dela's frown had turned into a scowl now.

"What does she want," he said rhetorically and he reached for his underpants, which lay behind him on the toilet seat.

"She says your split was a silly misunderstanding. Was it? Because I gave everything to you last night and if you let me down now white boy, I'm gonna kick your skinny little ass all round this bathroom," Dela explained succinctly in a Caribbean accent.

"Well, now I know how you feel," he said, reaching for a t-shirt. "I can go downstairs and prove to you how I feel, okay?"

Dela stepped aside, Nathaniel didn't look like a hard man, but he had a crisp way of explaining things that when someone looked into his eyes, they didn't want to argue with him.

Nathaniel grabbed his jeans and pulled them on, "Come on Dela, let's go talk to my ex-fiancée."

Dela went to say something, but just closed her mouth again and followed Nathaniel out of the bathroom. She couldn't remember a man ever shutting her up before; maybe she was falling in love.

Nathaniel trooped down the stairs in his bare feet, only pausing to zip up his fly, with Dela following at a slower pace behind him.

"Darling!" Cordelia said, "I've come to forgive you."

"That's big of you," Nathaniel replied, reaching the bottom of the stairs.

Cordelia looked up and copped an eyeful of Dela coming downstairs. "Can we talk in private, you know, not in front of the staff," Cordelia leant forward and whispered.

Nathaniel looked at Dela, then back to Cordelia and burst out laughing. Dela reached the bottom step with a frown on her face, not knowing what was going to happen next. Nathaniel put his arm around Dela.

"Dela's not my employee, she's my lover."

"What? But, but she's..." Cordelia trailed off, "she's ..."

"She's great in bed, I know," Nathaniel finished for his ex-fiancée.

"So you've been cheating on me, with, with this!" she finally finished, flinging her arm in Dela's general direction.

"No, we broke up last night and Dela and I only met after that and we've had a night to remember, I can tell you," Nathaniel smiled.

"Better close your mouth girl, there a lotta flies around dis time of year," Dela added, giving Nathaniel's bum a squeeze.

"You monster!" Cordelia exclaimed at Nathaniel and pulled open the front door and rushed from the house in tears. Nathaniel followed her to the door and stopped at the doorway.

"If she thinks you're a monster, what would she have thought of that dude we met last night?" Dela commented, but Nathaniel didn't really hear her.

"Do you think she'll be okay?" Nathaniel asked nobody in particular.

"You're too nice, Nath. She'll be fine," Dela reassured him. "Unless you'd rather be with her rather than me," she added in a weak voice.

Nathaniel sighed loudly and closed the door with a bang. Dela stood in silence behind Nathaniel a little fearful of what he would do next, maybe even hit out at her. Hell, she had only known him half a day.

"Come here," Nathanial commanded, his voice strong and unwavering. Dela, under his spell, walked forward, feeling for only the second time in years, not in total control of herself.

Nathaniel leant forward, his hand going to the back of her neck, and kissed her, their dry lips pressed hard against each other. Their mouths soon moistened as their kisses became more urgent and soon their tongues were entwined deep in each other's mouths.

They crouched and kneeled as they pulled at each other's clothes; Nathaniel lay back on the carpet and caressed her breasts as Dela leant over him. Nathaniel only had enough time to free his erection from his trousers before Dela pulled aside her thong and lowered herself onto his large member. Their love making was faster and more furious than the night before. They both came within moments and Dela lay panting and spent astride him. Nathaniel could not deny the fact that he was already falling deeply in love with her.

"What do you do for an encore?" Dela asked as they sat sprawled up the first five steps of the stairs, naked and entwined.

"Make your breakfast," Nathaniel replied, "then we must go and investigate the corner where we were attacked and that house that you went to."

"Will it be safe to go there?"

"He might have human minions under his sway," Nathaniel replied thoughtfully, "we better take Cerberus with us."

"I don't like dogs, but that sounds a good idea because Cerberus scares the hell outta this girl."

"Come on, let's get some clothes on," Nathaniel said, sitting up and flexing his legs, "I'll lend you a jumper and my coat, it still feels cold out there."

They dressed quickly and ate a quick fry-up to replenish the energy they had both lost since they had met, last night. With Cerberus trotting next to them, they set off along the frosty streets back to where they had met.

"Are we safe during the day?" Dela asked five minutes into their walk.

"Should be, but this is a Demon Lord we are dealing with, and one we humiliated and pissed off severely last night," Nathaniel stated authoritatively. "We must be vigilant."

Fear rose in Dela as they turned the corner into Napier Road. Everything seemed normal; the road didn't look like it had witnessed a supernatural event last night. It looked cold, grey and much like a thousand other roads around the country. Even Dela and Nathaniel looked normal enough; a couple out walking their dog, nothing sinister in the scene at all, but they knew different!

"It looks so different in the day time, so, peaceful," Dela said, breaking the silence. "Last night seems like a dream, or a nightmare," she added.

They crossed the road, with Cerberus now walking ahead towards the spot on the pavement where Ashmodaios was despatched. They approached the spot and looked around for prying eyes, as Cerberus sniffed at the very crack the Demon Lord had vanished down. With another glance above, Nathaniel crouched, pushing Cerberus away. His hands reached into his pockets and produced a petre dish and a pen knife.

Nathaniel chipped away at the blackened edge of the paving slab, then dug yellowed soil from the crack itself and put both sets of samples in his petre dish. Closing the lip of the dish he popped it and his penknife back into his pocket.

"That's that!" Nathaniel stated, standing up as someone opened the front door of a block of flats a little way down the road, on their side.

"What now, Sherlock?"

"Now we visit that house," he replied, "lead on McDuff."

"The name's Robinson, actually," Dela replied seriously.

"Dela."

Dela Robinson could tell from the sound of Nathaniel's voice that this was no time for prevaricating.

"Okay, okay. This way." Dela retraced her steps of the night before. Even though it was daylight and the street held no visible dangers, Dela felt a heavy burden of dread on her with every step she took.

Nathaniel must have had a sixth sense, or great empathy, because he reached down and took her hand and gave it a reassuring squeeze. Dela gave him a little thank you look and they strode on, Cerberus leading the way. The roads looked different in the daylight and she stopped a couple of times to check her bearings. The post-it note with the address for the house was in her coat pocket somewhere, wherever that was. They finally turned into a tree-lined cul-de-sac with only six detached houses in the street. Down at the end on their side of the street stood the house.

"How did you get here last night?" Nathaniel asked, "I can't remember if I asked you before."

"Tube, train, then taxi from the station," Dela replied. "There it is, the one on the end," she pointed.

Nathaniel, Dela and Cerberus walked slowly towards it. Most of the house was obscured from view behind tall bushes and overgrown trees.

"Notice anything peculiar about this street?" Nathaniel asked, looking around.

"No, why?"

"All of the houses we're passing are lifeless. That one's boarded up, that one has no curtains in any of its windows."

"It weren't like that last night," Dela explained. "There were lights; cars in the drives."

"Come on, let's have a look at the house you visited." Nathaniel and Cerberus led the way, with Dela close behind.

When they reached the house they found it too looked long deserted. The front door was closed and the windows showed shadowy, empty rooms inside. The front garden was overgrown and the gate to the garden hung only by its top hinge.

"This is bloody strange, man!" Dela stated.

"The whole street is strange, all these empty homes in an affluent town like this. Some property developer would have bought the lot of these ages ago. These seem like they've been like this for six months at least, maybe years." Nathaniel physically and mentally scratched his head. "Let's have a look, eh?" Nathaniel bent down and patted the dog briefly on the head. Nathaniel walked up the overgrown path to the front door. Dela hesitated for a second or two, then followed.

Nathaniel reached forward and knocked on the door with his fist. The seemingly unlocked door swung in a couple of inches.

"What are you doing?" Dela shrieked, "if someone's there they will know we're here!"

"I had thought of that," Nathaniel replied, pushing the door open fully, "but entering a house without knocking is still breaking and entering and against the laws of the land."

Dela stood dumbfounded as Nathaniel entered the house and pulled a Maglite torch from his coat pocket.

"A demon from hell tried to kill us last night and you're worried about breaking into an empty house? Man, you've got some weird ideas on law and order," Dela said loudly, following him and Cerberus in.

"Ssshh," Nathaniel hissed, reaching back and putting his finger on Dela's lips, "let's go for silent running, it could get dangerous from here on in." And before Dela could object, Nathaniel shot off sideways into a downstairs room.

They found nothing downstairs after a recce of a dining room, kitchen, front room, a terrifyingly funky downstairs lavatory and two or three totally empty and unidentifiable rooms. A search of the rubbish and broken furniture revealed nothing of the true nature of the house.

"Let's go upstairs," Nathaniel finally said to Dela, as cold fear gripped her.

"Normally that's a phrase I like to hear," Dela laughed nervously.

Nathaniel leant forward and kissed her left temple, "Don't worry, I will protect you."

"I know," Dela whispered and reached out and stroked his right bicep.

Nathaniel led the way upstairs with Cerberus just before him. Dela followed, her eyes darting downstairs, half the time waiting for a demon to jump her from behind. They reached the landing with no such attack.

"Which room did you go into?" Nathaniel hissed at her.

Dela just pointed to a slightly ajar door at the far end of the landing. Nathaniel crouched and whispered something inaudible in Cerberus's ear. The dog turned and licked Nathaniel's face then trotted off to the nearest of six doors and disappeared inside the room. Dela was convinced that the dog's eyes and demeanour denoted that the dog was saying goodbye. Nathaniel nodded her forward and they set off in a different direction to the dog and the room that Dela had escaped from the previous night.

The first door they came to was closed and Nathaniel pushed it open with the butt of his torch; it swung in easily with a long drawn out squeal. There were dirty curtains, half pulled at the only window, so Nathaniel flicked his torch round in the gloom. Seeing nothing threatening he proceeded inside with Dela close behind him, her hands pressed against his back.

A stained mattress lay in one corner of the room, and there was the wooden frame of a chair by the door. Flicking his torch down, Nathaniel and Dela saw that the floor was without a carpet and that a circle had been painted in scarlet on the floor. The circle had an outer and an inner ring four inches apart, and the whole thing was four feet in diameter and thirteen faint mystic symbols were inscribed equally between the two circles. A small black pot sat plumb in the centre of the circle; the wood underneath and near it was scorched black.

"What is it?" Dela whispered in his right ear.

"It looks like a circle of invoking." Nathaniel moved closer to the edge of the circle and knelt down. He stretched out his arm and with the torch in a finger tip grip pushed the pot over. A dark reddish liquid oozed from inside over the floor.

"What's it for? Black Magic?" Dela asked.

"Yes," Nathaniel replied curtly, rising to his feet and going round to the opposite side of the circle. "Don't enter the circle," he hissed as he noticed Dela was edging towards it.

"Okay, okay, keep your hair on man!" Dela replied, coming to a dead stop.

Nathaniel shone his torch into the pot and could see the smallest of white human-looking bones at the bottom of the ooze. It looked very much to his eyes that one was an infant's tiny skull.

"Stay where you are," he said to her. Taking a small digital camera from his coat pocket he began to take pictures of the whole thing, careful to get each individual symbol in focus. When he had finished he noticed a door in the wall next to him. It ran over the stairs so it could be a walk-in cupboard.

Putting his camera in his pocket, Nathaniel reached out and pulled the door open quickly. A huge black form sprung from behind the door and knocked him to the floor, winding him. Nathaniel saw a brief flask of large incisors and a hot, foul-smelling breath on his face. Then the creature, heavy on his wounded chest, reached forward and licked his nose.

"Cerberus!" Nathaniel exclaimed with embarrassed relief. "Get off me!"

Cerberus licked his master's face then clambered off him and barked at Nathaniel. Cerberus wagged his tail in excitement as Nathaniel retrieved his torch and composure.

Dela came round and helped pull Nathaniel to his feet. Nathaniel noticed that she was laughing at him – the great King's Paladin.

"Bloody dog," Nathaniel cursed to cover his embarrassment.

"My old granddad had a saying: Don't shit your pants, fly by them!"

"Thanks," he replied sarcastically and shone his torch into the doorway Cerberus had jumped out from. Originally it must have been a walk-in cupboard or wardrobe that ran over the stairs. Someone or something had knocked some of the dividing wall down which now linked up with another cupboard/wardrobe in another room. Dela followed him through the hole in the wall into the cupboard and the room beyond.

This room had worn badly like it had been unused and open to the elements for years. There were a couple of armchairs and a table with its Formica top peeling up at the sides. The room smelt damp and brown things were growing on some of the wallpaper.

They left the room quickly and explored a dank white bathroom, toilet, and a couple of bare rooms until only the one room remained. This had been the one which the Demon Lord had brought her to for the massage session of her life (or death). They slowly approached the white door.

"Ready?" Nathaniel whispered, and Dela nodded in reply.

She nearly pissed her pants when Nathaniel booted the door open without a word of warning. Cerberus rushed in as the door clattered against the inside wall of the room. Nathaniel shone his torch about the place, but found it was empty and daylight shone through the room's one open window. Nathaniel snapped off his torch and entered the room with Dela close behind.

"Hey, my stuff!" Dela exclaimed in delight, seeing her bag and coat lying on the floor. She bent down and examined it thoroughly.

"Is everything there?" Nathaniel asked, noticing the room had no massage table or any other furniture.

"My stuff is, but the two hundred quid he gave me ain't where I put it. I guess he took that back," Dela replied, stuffing her coat into her holdall to carry back with her.

"It probably didn't exist at all. Like this place, it was one of the demon's elaborate illusions." Nathaniel turned and helped Dela to her feet. "I've seen enough, let's get out of here."

"I ain't arguing with dat!" Dela replied in her mother's West Indian accent.

They were back at Nathaniel's house an hour later, drinking coffee and analysing the digital pictures from his camera on his P.C. Nathaniel used the mouse to click up another file to sit beside the pictures.

"What's that?" Dela asked, sipping her black coffee in the seat next to him.

"Oh, I scanned the Book of Demons into here, you know, the one I showed you last night."

"Your family's horror book from way back? Uh-huh, I remember it," Dela nodded.

"Well, I'm going to look through it and see if anything correlates to what we saw in the house today," Nathaniel explained, his eyes not leaving the monitor.

"Right," Dela nodded. 'Where's my dictionary when I need it?' she thought.

Nathaniel scrolled down one side of the screen. Dela watched as rows and rows of text and drawings scanned down in front of her eyes.

"There it is," Nathaniel gesticulated, pointing at the screen, "just as I thought, a circle of demon summoning. In fact, this is one of the most powerful you can possibly do, if you want to summon a Demon Lord!"

"Why would anyone want to do that?" Dela asked, turning to look at Nathaniel's worried brow.

"Why do men rape? Why do people murder?" He shrugged. "Power, morbid curiosity. Maybe their own lives are so hellish they want to transmit that terror on to someone else. I dunno."

Dela continued to stare at Nathaniel, 'You say you don't know, but I think you've hit the nail right slam centre on the head,' she thought. "What do we do now Nath?"

"Firstly, we've got to find out who drew that circle. I'll start with that house, see who has lived there or owns it now." Nathaniel moved his arrow cursor with his mouse and clicked on an icon to connect to his broadband provider.

"What you doing now?" Dela pulled her chair closer to Nathaniel and put her long fingers on his knee.

"A bit of background checking." Clicking some other icons, including 'favourites' a Home Office website popped up on the screen, with a password prompter. Nathaniel typed his name into one slot then a six-figure password that just showed as xxxxxx on the screen.

"What are you in now?"

"A classified Home Office/Police website, where I can do a few checks on that house," Nathaniel winked.

"Sounds a bit illegal to me," Dela said, raising her plucked thin eyebrows.

"Well, I don't just work in the Home Office for the pay you know, it has to have some perks." Nathaniel paused, "Oh God, what number house did we visit?"

"Hang on," Dela said, digging into her side pocket in her holdall, "here's the address I took down over the phone." She handed Nathaniel a yellow post-it note.

Nathaniel stared at the address on the paper.

"Something the matter?" Dela asked, "I bet I spelt something wrong. I'm shit at spelling,"

"Not really," Nathaniel said, "you've got exquisite handwriting, that's all."

"Thanks," Dela beamed.

"Did you notice the address?" Nathaniel asked, showing her the post it note again.

"Three Manes Close, that bloody number again!"

"And Manes means spirit of the dead or demon. This is not a random event. This invasion of our plane has been meticulously planned for many years. Let's put the address in the computer and see what it shows." Nathaniel typed in the address and clicked the search button on screen. Suddenly the screen flashed into life and data began to screen up in front of Nathaniel and Dela's eyes.

"The plot thickens," Nathaniel stated, tapping the screen with his index fingernail. "The Catholic Church owned all the houses up to two years ago. The houses were built on an eleventh century church which was destroyed during the Blitz. The Church decided to build their new church nearer to town and not up a bloody hill I suppose. The Church leased the land to a developer to build luxury post-war houses on. Two years ago the lease was sold to a developer named The Idiminu Corporation. The occupants were paid double the market value to leave and the houses have been unoccupied and unused for the past six months."

"You better get some info on this Idiminu Corporation. Sounds a bit Japanese to me," Dela offered her two-penneth worth.

"Or fishy," Nathaniel whispered, "let's just see what the book says." He clicked onto his ancestors' book and searched the text for 'Idiminu'. The hourglass cursor flicked off after three seconds at a page of the book.

"Well, well, the book says Idiminu is another word for demon," Nathaniel stated.

"What does that mean, you know, to us?" Dela asked, trying hard to keep up.

"That someone or something owns a corporation that owns houses, that demons are being summoned to and that corporation's name means 'demon'. This has been planned meticulously for ages, but why?"

"It's too hot in hell and they fancy a good old English winter for a change," Dela joked.

Nathaniel smiled, "Let's find the address of this Idiminu Corporation and who own or runs the place."

After twenty minutes search Nathaniel had found the London address of the Corporation and the home address of a Mr John Telal, the company's director, who lived in Tewkesbury, Gloucestershire.

Nathaniel stretched and rubbed at his eyes, "That's enough of that for a while," and set his computer to print off the information he had found. "Fancy some lunch?"

"Well," Dela smiled, moving closer to Nathaniel, "I do feel hungry," she purred.

"Excellent," he replied, leaning forward and kissing her passionately on the lips.

"What are we going to do now?" Dela asked as they stood in Nathaniel's kitchen that afternoon.

"Try and get to see this Mr Telal and ask him what his company is doing with those houses," Nathaniel replied, cutting a cheese sandwich in half.

"And how are we going to do that Nath, make an appointment?" she scoffed, sipping her coffee.

Nathaniel turned to her and smiled, "Exactly."

"I should have guessed you'd say something stupid like dat!" she exclaimed.

"Look, it's easy. You ring up first as my secretary, asking to speak to Mr Telal. I come on and ask to buy the land from him. Easy," he shrugged.

"What if he asks us to make an appointment?"

"Then we go and see him," Nathaniel smiled back.

"It could be dangerous, Nat," Dela implored, reaching out and grabbing his nearest hand.

"It's Nat now, eh? What happened to Nath? You'll be calling me Na next," Nathaniel replied light-heartedly.

"Be serious, man. I don't want to die yet. I'm too young and beautiful," she begged.

Nathaniel took her in his arms and kissed her. "I've only known you a couple of days and you've turned my life upside down. I won't let anything harm you and I will be around forever."

"'Forever'?" Dela's brown pupils widened, "but you don't know anything about me, my past, the bad things I've done."

He kept her in his arms. "That doesn't matter to me. What does is the present, now and the future, and I won't let you go." He pulled her close again and they kissed the softest and most tender kiss she had ever experienced. Dela's head swam and her knees turned to jelly. How had this man got to her so quickly?

"So, are you with me?" he asked, swaying her lightly in his arms.

"Well, if we do go to London to meet Mr Telal, at least I can pick up a change of my clothes," she grinned back at him.

"I'll buy you new ones," he smiled back.

"I'll hold you to that, mm-hmm," and Dela lent forward and they exchanged saliva once more.

"You ready?" Nathaniel asked as they sat in the front room by the phone.

"Yes," and before she lost her bottle Dela picked up the receiver and punched in the telephone number they had gotten off the Internet.

"Hello, can I speak to Mr Telal please?" Dela said into the receiver, "Okay, they're putting me through to his number," she whispered, her hand covering the phone. "Can I speak to Mr Telal, please?" Dela asked and listened. "I'm Mr White's personal assistant from TLC Construction. Mr White would like to discuss a sizeable offer for some property your company owns."

"She's put me on hold, his Pee-Ah," she whispered, hand over the phone again. "Yes, okay, I'm putting him on now, please hold," Dela said in her poshest voice and passed the phone to Nathaniel.

Nathaniel waited as he was put through to Mr Telal. "Hello, it's Daniel White here of TLC Construction and I'm interested in buying some property your company owns," Nathaniel spoke in clear, positive Queen's English. "Splendid, splendid. The properties in question are a number of houses in Manes Close," Nathaniel paused, "so you are aware of the properties? Come now Mr Telal, I'm sure we could come to some arrangement. I'm prepared to pay the going rate," Nathaniel blustered. "My interest? Well, I was going to bulldozer the buildings and build two sets of luxury flats." Nathaniel frowned, things weren't going his way. "You're not prepared to sell at any price, eh? May I ask why? I understand, but – Shit!" Nathaniel spat as the phone call was terminated at the other end.

"What-did-he-say?" Dela asked at full speed.

"He didn't want to know, or sell for that matter," Nathaniel sighed.

"What do we do now?"

"Pop up to London and check out this Idiminu Corporation and get you a change of clothes."

"Or some new ones," Dela ventured.

"Or some new ones," Nathaniel repeated in defeat.

That night Dela lay sprawled across Nathaniel after another fantastic round of love making. It was just after half-past twelve and the bedroom light was on, at Dela's insistence.

"What do we do when the sexual spark goes?" Dela asked his right nipple.

"We keep shagging 'til it turns into an inferno again, I think," Nathaniel replied.

Dela sat up in bed and faced him, "What are we going to do after this is all over?"

Nathaniel was going to give a jokey reply, but he could see that she had a serious look on her face.

"If we survive this, I want you to give up your job and we'll fly out to the West Indies for a couple of months' holiday," he answered earnestly.

"What if I don't want to give up my job mmmh?" Dela whined.

"Then we'll have a massage table fitted in the house, you can go legit and Cerberus can sit in all the sessions and bite the testicles off any man who dares to touch you, okay?" Nathaniel's strong and melodic voice seemed to ease the worry lines from Dela's forehead.

"You have a knack of saying all the right things, Nat, at the right time." Dela's face softened as she kissed him.

Nathaniel responded and pulled Dela's athletic body onto his body, their hot skin and passion fused together.

THUD!

Nathaniel sat up and Dela slid off him and turned her head to the ceiling, from where the loud intruding noise had emanated.

"What was that?" Dela hissed.

"Shush," Nathaniel hushed her up, his index finger going to his mouth.

THUD!

The noise was was quieter this time and appeared to be coming from the attic somewhere above the door to the bedroom. Naked as Adam and Eve, they both jumped out of bed and moved hand in hand towards the bedroom door. Nathaniel opened it in one fluid movement and they both rushed out on to the landing.

Nathaniel flicked on the landing light as they moved towards the stairs and the library door. They moved along to the bathroom door, heads cocked upward, ears straining to hear even the slightest sound. Downstairs they heard the muffled bark of Cerberus.

THUD! The noise sounded in the landing ceiling just next to the entrance hatch to the attic.

"This is like the fucking Exorcist!" Dela babbled, scared out of her wits again and realising they were both starkers.

A fiery red fist exploded through the entrance to the attic from above.

"We're in trouble," Nathaniel shouted.

"Let's run back to the bedroom," Dela screamed at him.

"No time, we're blocked off, it's too risky to run under it."

"What are we going to do?" Dela screamed in his ear, just as the hatch to the attic was ripped off its hinges and thrown back down the hole it covered, on fire and in pieces.

"Quick into the bathroom," he ordered, pushing Dela before him.

Nathaniel just caught the sight of two scaly red legs appearing through the attic hatch as he slammed and locked the bathroom door. Nathaniel anxiously looked around the room for a plan, eyeing the window, but dismissing it quickly. The thought of him and Dela jumping naked into the garden sounded painful.

"What now?" Dela cried, grabbing his arm painfully tightly.

"Get into the bath and lie down." He pushed her gently, "When he comes through the door I want you to turn on the taps to the shower full blast."

"What will that do?" Dela asked as she deftly hopped into the cold bath.

THUD! came the demon's first attack on the bathroom door.

Nathaniel clambered in after her as she lay down next to the taps and turned the control from bath to shower. "The cold water on his super-heated body should kill him." Nathaniel hoped so, glad now that he never had that proper shower done.

"But the rain didn't hurt the Demon Lord," Dela shouted at him as another THUD! hit the door causing it to splinter. Nathaniel noticed the unmistakable funk of sulphur wafting in from under the door. Nathaniel stood astride Dela in the bath, taking the flimsy showerhead in both hands.

"These lesser demons are carved out of fire and brimstone, the very source of hell itself." Nathaniel was interrupted by another wood cracking THUMP on the door as the white paint began to smoulder and turn black and the cracks in the wood largened. "They are not as powerful as a Demon Lord nor are they as intelligent or as well created."

The door was struck again sending a burning two-foot section of the top panel flying across the room to land in the open toilet with a hiss.

"Get ready with those taps, Dela," Nathaniel shouted, his voice quavering somewhat as he saw the burning red eyes of the demon through the hole in the bathroom door.

A final hammering on the ruined door caused the bolt to detach from the wall as 'demonic attack' probably wasn't part of its design specification. The door and the demon came lumbering in towards them, its evil eyes intent on unholy murder.

"Now!" Nathaniel screamed at Dela, who turned the cold taps on to full as fast as she could manage. Yet it wasn't fast enough, because Nathaniel had forgotten that it took a second or two for the water to shoot up the pipe to the shower head.

The demon moved forward and took a long roundhouse swipe at Nathaniel with his fiery left arm. In a slight slice of luck the demon's clawed hand snagged in the shower curtain and only connected with a glancing blow to Nathaniel's right shoulder and head. The blow didn't injure him too much, but Nathaniel overbalanced trying to duck back from the blow. He fell into the bath and knocked his head against the back of the bath and lay still.

The shower head now spraying icy cold water, landed on Dela's head as the demon turned his attention from Nathaniel's naked, inert figure to Dela, who was cowering at the head of the bath. His large head and body lowered down as Dela tried to shrink in to the bath, all the while her hands scrambled for control of the shower head as her eyes locked with the fiery demon's scarlet pupils, now only inches from her face. The demon opened its mouth and laughed, its foul breath causing a lump of vomit to rise in Dela's throat. Finally she got purchase on the shower head and brought it along her body, soaking her, until she eventually turned it full into the face of the demon.

"Take that, barbeque breath!" she hissed through her tightly clenched teeth as the icy water blasted into the demon's face, eyes and open mouth.

The demon roared in agony as the icy water ate into his flesh like acid. His claws went to his face as his scream turned to a piercing wail of agony. Dela sat up in the bath and continued to spray water over the head, arms and torso of the Mane from Hell. Its skin, once bright red like a thousand scaly rubies linked together, was turning to grey as the water found its mark.

Dela knelt forward now. "Take that, fucker!" she screamed as the water did its job.

The demon took its grey hands away from its face and Dela jumped back with a scream. Half the fiery fiend's head had been dissolved by the water and the demon leant back what was left of its head and screamed again, from somewhere deep in its throat. Behind her a couple of window panes blew out and a glass on the sink, with two toothbrushes in it, exploded into tiny shards.

The demon sank to its knees. Now only its legs were fiery red and glowing. Feeling brave, Dela leant over the bath and covered all of the body of the fiend with water. The demon's head bowed in defeat and all his visible crazy-paving skin had turned to charcoal grey. The remains of its head dropped into its lap and shrunk and collapsed down into itself. The whole demon, once over six feet tall, had now dissolved to the size of a football.

Dela dared a glance at Nathaniel, who lay at the end of the bath eyes closed and unmoving. Dela looked at the water-logged carpet and thought herself glad she wasn't the cleaner. The demon had shrunk now down to the size and colour of a clinker. Dropping the still spurting shower head into the bath, she hopped over the diminished demon and began to pull a wad of toilet paper into her hands. With such insufficient protection she grabbed the grey clinker demon and lobbed it into the toilet bowl with a loud plop. She swiftly pulled the chain and watched intently as the demon rolled in a circle, then disappeared down the U-bend and down the pipes to the sewers.

"That should fucking sort you out!" Dela spat at the toilet as she flicked the seat cover down. She then turned her attention to the prone body of Nathaniel.

"Oh, Nat," she whispered with concern as she nimbly got back in the cold slippery bath.

She put her hand to his naked chest and felt it rise and fall and his heart beat. "Nat, wake up," she said in his ear, but he did not move. "Nathaniel Le Meuille, please wake up!" she said louder now into his face. "Wake up because I've only just found you. Come on, wake up!" she pleaded, lines of concern across her brow.

Reaching back, she grabbed the shower head once more and said "Sorry" before she set the freezing water shooting into his pale countenance.

"The sword, the sword, we must get the sword!" he exclaimed as the freezing water woke him from his unconscious state in a second.

Dela grabbed him by the shoulders as the shower head slipped down sending the icy water onto her bare legs.

"You're okay Nathaniel, you're safe," she shouted at him as he thrashed about in a confused state.

"What the Holy Mother of God happened?" Nathaniel asked, his eyes squeezing up in pain, his right hand going to the rapidly rising bump on the back of his head.

"You're safe," Dela comforted him, "it's me, Dela, okay?"

"The demon!" he shouted, trying to get up, but only managing to slip in the wet bath into Dela's fumbling embrace.

"It's okay, I killed him. I used the shower to kill him." Dela flung the still jetting showerhead behind her.

"It's gone!" Nathaniel calmed himself. "Where?"

Dela let go of Nathaniel and turned behind her to turn off the taps to stop the icy water jetting up her crack. "There!" she said triumphantly as the taps were finally turned off. "I blasted him with the water and he shrunk away 'til he was the size of a bar of soap."

"Where is he?"

"I flushed him down the bog!" Dela beamed.

"Shame, I would like to have had the chance to examine it." Nathaniel looked downhearted as he rubbed his head.

"Shall I get the plunger and get him back?" asked Dela, sarcastically.

"Better not, eh? Let's let sinking demons lie, eh Dela?" Nathaniel slowly rose to a crouch and said, "Well done, by the way."

"Is that all the thanks I get for saving your life?" Dela stood up indignantly, her hands on her hips, feeling cold and only registering for the first time since they left the bedroom that she was stark naked.

"God, Cerberus, we heard him barking, I hope he's all right," Nathaniel said to himself as he bent down and grabbed a bottle of bubble bath.

Dela watched as he strode through the wrecked bathroom door, unscrewing the top of the bubble bath.

"You're worried abut the dog? I don't believe it!" she called after him. "I nearly get fried by a demon and I, at great risk to my silky black skin, save your pale, skinny arse and all you're worried about is the dog?"

Dela realised that he wasn't in sight and wasn't listening to her either. She carefully stepped out of the bath, looking where to put her bare feet and grabbed a towel from the rack to tuck around herself. She could see Nathaniel's backside through the door. He was pouring the contents of the bubble bath over the burning remains of the attic hatch, to extinguish them.

"What'll we do now?" she asked from the demolished doorway.

"Get dressed, then check on Cerberus and the rest of the house." When he had finished with the extinguished remains, Nathaniel padded off into the bedroom to get dressed.

"He must have hit his head harder than I thought, thinking about a dumb dog, while I stood naked in the bath. Not looking too shoddy for a chick who's killed a demon," Dela babbled, looking at herself in the bathroom mirror.

"Stop talking to yourself and get your beautiful behind in here, we've got work to do," he said, popping his head round the bathroom door.

"Slavery was abolished you know," she retorted, but headed for the bedroom anyway.

Nathaniel had already pulled on a pair of jeans and was just putting a sweatshirt over his head, when Dela walked in. As she approached he pulled the sweatshirt down and rushed past her with only a brief pause to kiss her cheek.

"I better check on Cerberus and the rest of the house," he told her as he snatched a pile of coins from an ashtray on his cupboard and headed downstairs.

"Nat, be careful!" she hollered after him, but she wasn't sure if he had registered her voice. Realising there could be more demons abroad, Dela dropped the towel and scrambled quickly into her clothes again. She would be glad to get a change of clothes and a fresh pair of knickers soon.

Dela hurried downstairs, turning lights on as she went, for her own comfort. She found Nathaniel in the kitchen hunched over something on the kitchen floor.

"Is your dog all right?" she asked, pretty sure that its name was Cerberus, but she didn't want to embarrass herself by pronouncing its name incorrectly. Just then the dog (cum-wolf) appeared from round the corner of the kitchen where his water bowl and basket were.

"He's fine," Nathaniel replied, getting to his feet, "not sure I can say the same for this chap."

Dela came up to Nathaniel's shoulder to see the body of a faint red demon on the kitchen lino. Its head, with a rather surprised look on its ghastly countenance, lay a foot away. The demon seemed to have grown out of the lino, where in fact it had just melted the plastic where it fell. Nathaniel went over to the sink and drew a washing-up bowl of water. Dela and Cerberus retreated a few yards as Nathaniel poured the cold water over the body and head of the demon. This caused the body to grey and shrink away as per the demon in the bathroom.

Dela realised that she had had her hand over her mouth in revulsion for the last five minutes and let it drop to her side. "Your dog bit it's fucking head off!" she exclaimed in disbelief.

"He's a brave dog, aren't you Cerberus?" Nathaniel replied, looking from Dela to his dog.

"But the dog, it's not burnt round the gob or anything, how?"

"He's a clever dog," Nathaniel smiled as the demon continued to shrink away at his feet and Cerberus barked his approval.

"A clever dog!" Dela repeated in disbelief.

"He's got the brains of three dogs," Nathaniel smiled and walked over and petted his pet. Cerberus gave a sheepish grin then farted very loudly and pungently.

"Yeah, and the arse of thirty-three dogs," Dela cursed, pinching her nose.

Nathaniel laughed and Dela followed and even Cerberus gave a jovial bark.

"I better go and check out the rest of the house," Nathaniel said after a while.

"You're not leaving me here alone with that. I'm coming too," Dela replied.

Cerberus barked his agreement and all three of them trotted around the house looking for further intruders, while the demon dissolved in the kitchen.

After checking out the attic, that being the last place to look, Nathaniel and Dela sat down on the top step of the stairs with Cerberus on guard behind them.

"So, we're even now," Dela said to break the silence.

"'Even'?" Nathaniel looked at her quizzically.

"That bad-assed demon I bagged in the bath, remember?" Dela emphasised her point by prodding a thumb at what was left of the bathroom door.

"'Even'? I mean thanks for the help, but 'even'?" Nathaniel retorted, "I saved you from a Demon Lord of Hades, you've got a lot more to do to make it 'even'!"

"Like what?" Dela asked indignantly.

"Like staying around for fifty years or so to pander to all of my sexual needs," he smirked.

"You git!" she smiled back and cuffed him around the side of the head.

"Ow!" he exclaimed, rubbing the bruise he had received from bashing his head on the bath.

"Sorry, sorry!" Dela apologised and reached forward, placing her long delicate fingers on his cheeks and pulling him forward to kiss him.

Behind them Cerberus growled loudly.

"Jealous?" Dela spat at the dog, as they kissed again. This time the dog barked loudly in their ears.

"Okay, I get your point dog, we don't have time to kiss, we've got to get dressed and get ready to get out of here at first light." Nathaniel's face turned grave again at the thought of two demons invading his family home.

"At first light, eh?" Dela mused, "sounds early to me!"

"I know," Nathaniel nodded, "but this place has been compromised now and it won't be safe to stay here another night."

"That's okay, we can crash out at my place for a while." Dela put her arm round Nathaniel, "and I can get me some clean underwear," she whispered.

"Right," said Nathaniel, standing up, "Cerberus, you're on guard, so go and patrol the house from top to bottom." Cerberus squeezed past Nathaniel's legs and moved downstairs off on his first patrol.

"And me?" Dela asked, fluttering her eyelashes.

"Get washed and dressed while I pack a bag of stuff, my laptop, and the book." Nathaniel stomped off along the landing to his study, leaving Dela alone on the stairs. She looked around sheepishly then got up and headed for the bedroom.

# CHAPTER 3

At first light they were ready to go. Nathaniel had a backpack and a holdall full of clothes, while Dela carried his laptop on a shoulder strap. The plan was to go into town, get some money from the cash machine and get train tickets to Dela's flat in Balham. Cerberus was going too, but all he had to bring was himself.

Nathaniel locked everything up, hid his valuables in the secret room and left a message out for the milkman to cancel his daily pint of milk. They set off once it was fully light so they had to wait until half past eight to be sure.

It took fifteen minutes to stroll into town, where Nathaniel drew out five hundred pounds from his building savings account as well as the two hundred and fifty pounds limit from his bank card. They proceeded to the station, caught the next available train to Waterloo, which pulled in to platform seven at ten-thirty. The journey took a little longer than usual, because there had been a crash two weeks' before. One of the new carriages had gone and caught fire. Only two people had escaped as none of the windows or doors could be opened; thirty people had burned to death. So all of those types of carriages had been taken out of service and replaced with old standard rolling stock that had only just been phased out.

They had a quick burger each (even Cerberus) sitting outside Burger King on the concourse, then headed down the tube to Balham.

"How far is it to your place then?" Nathaniel asked as they left the crowded confines of the tube system behind and entered the cosmopolitan streets of South West London.

"About ten minutes in stilettos and seven in flat shoes," she replied, sniffing a lungful of carbon monoxide tinged air. "It's good to be home."

"Mm," Nathaniel replied, looking round the dirty streets suspiciously.

"Let's go back to my pad, Nat," she smiled and pointed her elbow at him. He took her arm and they walked down the busy street towards a block of flats with Cerberus' nose sniffing new smells, in the rear.

Nathaniel hadn't really thought about the flat where Dela lived, well, he did now. It was seven storeys high, pimpled with satellite dishes and made from decaying grey concrete. A couple of smashed-in cars were parked/abandoned in the small car park in front of the flats. Three lifts and stairwells were stuck on to the building, one in the centre and one at either end, connecting the concrete balconies that gave access to each flat's front door.

"I think we'll take the scenic route," Dela said, leading him past a group of bored teenagers on bikes towards the nearest set of stairs.

"Why?" Nathaniel asked, looking around the place with interest.

"Mainly because the lifts never work," Dela replied. "Come on, it's only on the second floor."

They trotted up the concrete steps to a second floor balcony and walked past some front doors to Dela's flat.

Her place had a steel outer door, locked with two padlocks which she undid before opening the front door proper. Nathaniel and Cerberus followed her in and he was pleasantly surprised with its spick and span decor, which was in complete contrast to the exterior.

Nathaniel put his things down in the hall and ordered Cerberus to 'Stay' as he followed Dela into the earthy-coloured living room.

"Very nice place you have here," Nathaniel said earnestly and politely, looking around at the large wide screen TV, black leather sofas and a large Bison hide that was attached to the largest wall.

"It's not quite your mansion," Dela said, putting his laptop on the sofa, "but it's home and it's all mine."

"It's lovely," he smiled back at her. Dela cocked her head and put her hands on her hips.

"I need to change my dirty undies, fancy helping to cleanse myself in the shower?"

"Cerberus, lie down and keep guard, daddy's taking a shower," Nathaniel bellowed into the hall.

"Baby," Dela approached him and put her arms around his neck, "you have a way with words," she crooned.

"Come to pappa," he replied, crushing her to his manly physique and passionately fusing lips with her.

"What's the time?" Dela asked as they dried themselves off and got dressed again.

Nathaniel grabbed his watch from the side of the wash basin. "Half one," he replied, "we better get going."

"So we're going to this Idiminu Corporation, then?" Dela asked, slipping on a new bra.

"I am. It's safer if you and Cerberus wait here." Nathaniel started buttoning up his shirt.

"Safer for who? Nah, man, I'm coming with you," Dela stated in no uncertain terms, tapping him on the shoulder. "We're Batman and Robin remember?"

"I don't want to upset you; I just don't want to see you get hurt, okay? This will be dangerous."

He pulled her to him and looked deep into her clear brown eyes.

"Who says the demons won't turn up here when you're gone? And anyway you'll need my help to get in," Dela winked.

"Demons are nocturnal creatures so you would be safe, but you could be useful as a diversionary tactic."

"I've never been one of those before, is it well paid?" she smiled wickedly and pulled him closer.

"I doubt it," he frowned, "the pay's lousy but the perks are nice." Nathaniel smiled back at Dela.

"But the dog stays here!" she said bluntly.

"Cerberus stays here," he nodded, and they kissed quickly again.

Out in the hall, sprawled on the carpet Cerberus growled to himself.

By a quarter past two they were standing in a pub opposite the Idiminu building a drink in each of their hands. The building was tall and grey and seemed clean and relatively new and stretched at least ten storeys into the London sky.

Dela and Nathaniel watched as suited people and motor bike couriers passed in and out of the glass main entrance to the building, blissfully unaware of the owner's real agenda. The entrance and reception area was glass-fronted so they could see the reception desk and the lifts next to it.

Nathaniel noticed a crowd of suits, obviously on their way back from lunch. "Come on, we're going."

Dela just had time to put her drink down before he grabbed her wrist and led her out of the pub.

Dela took off her coat as they ran across the road to reveal a small, tight crop top that showed her assets to the world.

"You know what to do?" he asked as they reached the kerb in front of the electronic glass double-doored entrance.

"No probs," she said, approaching the door alone. "Good luck," she mouthed and turned away and sauntered through the automatic doors.

Nathaniel meanwhile tucked himself behind a support pillar as the group of executives approached the doors.

Dela cat-walked up to the reception desk and leant forward, her boobs nearly tumbling out of her top. "Can you help me, boys?"

The two security guards, who were lounging around looking bored, both jumped to attention (in more ways than one) and fought to get to the front of the desk first.

"Can I help you, miss?" they both asked in unison, trying hard to look at Dela's face.

"Now, can either of you guys tell me if this is the Idiminu building?" Dela pouted, leaning even further forward.

The reception guard barely registered a group of executives walk past heading for the lifts, but as they had passes so the guards quickly returned their attention to Dela.

"Yes, it is," drooled one guard.

"Can we help you?" asked the other.

"No, I just wanted to know, that's all," and Dela whirled round, her coat on her shoulder and wiggled out of the building again. The eyes of the guards followed her out, across the road and back into the pub again.

"What was that all about?" one guard asked the other when she was out of sight.

"Dunno. She probably fancies me," the other replied.

Nathaniel had sneaked off into the stairwell before the group of executives heading for the lifts wondered who he was. The plan had worked perfectly. As he bounded up the stairwell he took his mobile phone from his coat pocket and dialled Dela's mobile.

In the pub opposite, Dela fumbled for her phone. Luckily enough she had got her old table back and their half drained drinks were still on it.

"Hello?" she asked cautiously.

"It's me," Nathaniel spoke from the stairwell in a whisper.

"Is everything okay?" Dela asked.

"At the moment yes. I'm working my way up to the top floor on the assumption that Telal's office will be up there," Nathaniel whispered as he walked slowly upstairs.

"You be careful, lover," she said with emotion.

"I will," he replied. "Remember if you don't hear from me in one hour go to plan B and call out the fire brigade, police and ambulance services. I should be able to escape in the mayhem."

"Call me soon," she pleaded.

"If I'm able," he said "and by the way, you're a splendid diversion!" he added.

"You know it."

"I love you Dela, bye."

"You do?" she replied in shock as the phone line went dead. Dela put down her mobile phone and looked around the pub nervously. An attractive small woman in her early thirties and a slightly taller, brown skinned man with mixed race Chinese-type features entered the pub and went over to the bar. Neither of them had the slightest interest in her. Why would they know or care what her telephone conversation had been about? Dela mentally slapped herself and took a sip of her drink, trying to stay calm and in control.

Nathaniel had said he loved her and now, knowing he was in danger made her wish she had said the 'love' word too. It was unreal, their situation. First chased by demons from Hell, now she and Nathaniel getting together. If they had met in a club she would just have ignored him. This was her first mixed relationship, she wondered if they were all as exciting as this, she doubted it. If they both survived life after this should be a breeze in comparison.

The pub was thinning out now as lunch time ended. The couple who had come in earlier had bought their drinks and come and sat at a table across the Saloon from her. With nothing else to do, Dela sipped her drink again, checked her mobile was still on and working, then stared out at the Idiminu Building anxiously.

Inside the Idiminu Building Nathaniel continued his ascent in the stairwell. Luckily the building's workers were a lazy lot and he had only had to stop once as someone used the stairwell two floors above. It had given him time to hide his coat behind a fire hose on the stairwell. Now, dressed in his finest Home Office work suit and holding a briefcase, at least he looked like he belonged. By the time he had reached the top of the stairwell he was feeling exhausted and his calves were throbbing.

"I need to get in shape," he whispered to himself. The doors in front of him said 'Maintenance Staff Only', and he realised he must have come up too far. After a little nervous rest he trudged down the stairs until he reached a door with '10-EXECUTIVE FLOOR' written on a gold plate beside it.

Nathaniel took a deep breath and pulled at the door handle. It wouldn't budge. He tried it a couple more times then gave up. "What now?" he asked himself.

Without waiting for an answer he clicked his fingers and went upstairs again to the top of the stairwell and the red 'Maintenance Staff Only' door. Nathaniel tuned the handle and found out, to his surprise, that it wasn't locked.

He pushed forward with the door and found himself in a dimly lit room with bare walls. The room was devoid of life so he stepped inside and closed the door behind him. His eyes became accustomed to the half-gloom and he found he was in an engineering/control room for the four lifts in the building. Pipes, machinery, fuse boxes, control panels with faint lights, gauges and switches adorned each wall. Nathaniel walked across the grimy floor to the centre of the room trying to find anything useful. In the wall to his right was a hatch, half the size of a normal door.

Nathaniel went over to it and bent down, a metal handle locked it into place. Putting on his leather gloves which he got from his jacket pockets, he pulled the locking lever up and slowly swung the metal hatch towards him. The space behind the half door was better lit than the Maintenance Room. Crouching down, Nathaniel slowly put his head through, trying not to touch the floor and get his suit dirty.

The hatch led into a large space over the four lift shafts of the building. Only one lift was up at the top, the rest left a gaping abyss down to whatever floor the lifts were on. Only one metal crawl-way bolted to the ceiling lead across the tops of the moving lifts, with a flimsy looking fake ceiling separating the two sets of lifts.

Leaving his briefcase behind and taking his life in his hands Nathaniel crawled partway on to the metal crawl-way. Trying not to look down, he looked around the lift ceiling for possible entrances to the Executive level. Across the lift shaft to his left he spotted a man-size grille and a duct behind it that might be of use. The only problem being, he would have to step on to the roof of the lift to reach it.

Nathaniel crawled back into the Maintenance Room, took out his mobile phone and dialled Dela's number.

A robotic voice answered "We are unable to connect you to the network of your choice, please redial later."

"Bugger!" he said, popping the phone back in to his jacket pocket. "It must be all this machinery," he said to himself looking around the room. Nathaniel stood there in the semi-dark glow of the machinery's switches trying to decide what to do next. While he was still deciding he scrambled through the hatch and on to the crawl-way again. Pulling his wrist from his jacket and shirt sleeve, he looked at his watch. Pressing bleeping buttons, he put the stopwatch feature on, as lifts rose and fell gracefully below him.

Nathaniel waited patiently as the lifts went about their business until the lift to his left came right up below him to the 'Executive floor'. The instant it stopped he started his stopwatch and timed how long it remained there.

The lift descended, he checked his stopwatch – twenty seconds. 'Damn, that's not long enough,' he cursed in his mind.

Two minutes later it returned and he timed it again, thirty seconds went by, then a minute. Finally after two minutes, three seconds it descended into the gloom below. It was obviously pot luck if it was called quickly, otherwise it just hung around indefinitely.

"What a horrible place to die," he whispered as he swung his legs off the crawl-way and dangled them off into the abyss, waiting for the lift to arrive. The lift started ascending and Nathaniel tensed himself to jump the foot gap on to the top of the lift. Up and up the lift came, as his fear rose with it, but suddenly it stopped short of its goal. Nathaniel cursed silently to himself as the lift paused on the ninth floor. He didn't have time to wait or worry as the lift rose quickly to meet his dangling feet. He waited for five seconds in fear, then jumped on to the top of the lift, luckily getting a good grip on the hot tensile steel cables. He skirted the edge of the lift top and his inner head-count had already reached two seconds by the time he had reached the grille.

His fingers quickly went through the grille and gripped. He pulled at the metal grille cover, but it wouldn't budge. His head count was lost at fifteen seconds as he reached into his pockets and pulled out his Swiss army knife. Nathaniel had spotted a screw on the top of the grille holding it in place. Scared out of hit wits that the lift could descend any second, he opened the screwdriver attachment and went to work on the screw. The head of the screwdriver kept slipping out of the screw head and nervous sweat accumulated on his forehead and under his armpits.

Finally the screw turned and he hurriedly unscrewed the grille top with the odd nervous fumble. He pocketed the knife and pulled down the grille as he heard a 'ping' and noise from the inside of the lift.

Suddenly the lift disappeared from beneath his feet and Nathaniel was left dangling from the grille, his fingers intertwined through each side of it. The shock and pain in his fingers and arms was incredible as he looked down the shaft watching the lift descend a couple of floors and then stop. Nathaniel could now also see the back of the lift doors to the Executive level, but there was no chance in hell of reaching them. Looking down again he saw the lift was still stationary two floors below; there was no other way, he would have to try to pull himself up into the shaft above.

"If Bruce Willis can do it, so can I," he whispered through gritted teeth. 'But Bruce Willis has a stuntman and a safety net,' he thought darkly as the pain in his fingers increased by the second. Nathaniel tried to pull himself up on the grille, but unlike the wall-bars at his gym, the fall and stakes were a little high.

He had hung on for too long, all the power had drained from his arms and the smooth shaft above provided no handholds. Nathaniel suddenly realised that he might have very little time left; his fingers were slipping and the power in his arms ebbing away. He closed his eyes and pictured Dela, trying to draw extra strength from her image. He felt his grip give a little and his arms go numb, and he suddenly realised he was less than ten seconds from falling when the lift suddenly appeared beneath his feet with a start. Without looking down he springboarded himself into the air conditioning shaft and pushed along the cramped space until his entire body was safely inside. Nathaniel just collapsed as best he could, trying to breathe normally as the reality of his near-death escapes hit him with a horrifying realisation.

After two minutes he said "Thank you God," and began to push himself along the shaft to see if the drama of getting into it had been worth it. He didn't have to go far before he reached a grille on the side of the lift shaft. Looking through he could make out the outlines of a room below. Nathaniel contorted himself to free his Maglite from his jacket, pointed it through the grille and switched it on. It showed a small storage cupboard; this was Nathaniel's exit point.

Nathaniel flicked his torch to the inside of the shaft. The grille was fixed to the shaft's side, so that meant the screw holding it in was on the outside. Nathaniel wriggled his hand into his jacket pocket and retrieved his penknife. He extended the screwdriver attachment so it was only half out like a small L-shape. Using his thumb and forefinger he pushed the penknife through the grille and tried to reach the screw on the other side. But as he tried in vain to accomplish this he lost his grip on the screwdriver and it tumbled to the floor and skidded under some stationery racks. Nathaniel hissed a curse and smacked the grille in frustration with the pad of his fist. To his surprise the grille swung open on its hinges and clattered loudly against the wall below.

Nathaniel shuffled back until he was out of view from the open grille and froze, waiting for someone to investigate the noise. A minute passed; there was no noise at the store cupboard door, so Nathaniel peeked through the grille again.

Dela waited patiently in the pub. Time was moving fast for Nathaniel, but for Dela it dragged on. She had already fended off two advances from guys in the pub and used all her change in the fruit machine. Dela sighed, drained her drink, grabbed her phone, coat and bag and headed for the loo. The bar was empty now with only a couple of old men and the odd couple in the corner. God, she hoped Nathaniel was okay, because she was dead without him.

Nathaniel brushed himself off with a box of Kimwipes and had a look around the store cupboard. On one shelf he found a box of blank passes he had seen the workers wear as they entered the building. Finding a pair of scissors and some sellotape he set to work providing a pass for himself. He found that his Home Office pass picture was in the exact same place as the Idiminu Corporation passes, so he cut a square hole from the

Idiminu pass, put his own pass behind it and taped them together. Once it was slid into its pass holder and clipped on to his lapel, it looked the part.

The store cupboard could only be opened on the outside by a key, but inside, for safety reasons, there was a release knob so no one could be locked in by accident. Giving himself one last smarten and replacing the grille, Nathaniel grabbed a box of folders and opened the stationery cupboard door. Nathaniel knelt and jammed the folders in the door to stop it closing shut behind him.

He found himself in a bright corridor at the corner of a crossroads. Someone at the end of the corridor came out of an office and started to walk towards him. Nathaniel steadied his resolve and headed towards the man who was engrossed in a file he was carrying. Nathaniel looked each way at the crossroads and decided to head in the direction the man had come from. Thankfully, the man went past without even a glance and Nathaniel sighed with relief as he reached the end of the corridor, which turned right. Nathaniel decided to head in that direction.

As he reached the centre of the corridor there was another, smaller, corridor heading to an open plan office where a sharp-looking secretary sat. Yet more interesting to Nathaniel were the huge double doors behind her with a black marble effect. That had to be Telal's personal assistant and office. Just then the P.A. looked up at him and he moved off just as two suited men entered the corridor behind him.

Nathaniel moved off, heading for a window at the end of the corridor, with three sets of doors on either side of the corridor his only means of escape. He could almost feel the eyes of the men boring into his back as he walked along studying the doors for a sign of escape. The first two doors, parallel left and right, had lights shining through their frosted glass windows. He skipped them and carried on walking as the two large men closed the gap behind him. The next two doors were only a pace away – the one on the left had a light on, the one on the right was dark. He went for the dark one. His hand on the doorknob when the men caught up with him. He turned the handle, convinced that it was locked, but then it turned and he pushed and followed the door in. Behind him the men laughed at some joke and carried on down the corridor to another office. Nathaniel dropped the stationery he was carrying on a nearby chair and closed and locked the door behind him.

The small office had two desks and chairs with computers and trays, although there was not any work on either desk. Nathaniel walked round one desk and had a nose about. He found what he was looking for on a notice board attached to the adjacent wall. There was a wall planner, and this week had been coloured in with orange highlighter and someone had written 'Hols' on it.

"Have a nice trip," Nathaniel whispered to himself, examining the notice board thoroughly.

His eyes strayed to the empty desk and the white phone with twenty touch dial telephone numbers printed next to twenty brown buttons. Nathaniel smiled, picked up his mobile phone from his pocket and rang Dela's number.

Dela had returned to her seat with a tall glass of Diet Coke when her mobile range.

"Nathaniel?" she asked as she answered it.

"Who, girlfriend? Is that your latest client, baby?" came a familiar woman's voice.

"Merline! Sorry, I was expecting an important call," Dela replied, slightly flustered and annoyed that her friend had chosen now to ring her.

"Well, you got one baby," Merline purred, "where you bin lately? You bin harder to find than Michael Jackson's balls!"

Dela laughed in spite of herself. "What you want girl?" Dela asked, lapsing into Merline's fake American, half real Caribbean tones.

"Last week you promised to relax my hair and I haven't heard from you yet."

"Sorry, I've been kinda busy," Dela faltered.

"Busy getting busy I suspect, girlfriend, you-know-what-I-mean?" Merline screamed with laughter. "So I'll be round tonight at eight and you better be there 'cos I ain't taking any more delaying shit from your good self!"

"Merline – I..." Just then Dela noticed her message box flashing on her phone's screen.

"See ya tonight, Dela," Merline stated.

"Yeah, okay, bye," Dela said absently, cutting off her call to listen urgently to her message.

Dela pushed buttons and they beeped in response as she accessed her mail message. "You have one message, press one to ..." Dela pressed one to hear the message and shut up the squeaky automated voice on her phone.

"Dela, it's Nathaniel. I've made it to the Executive level. I'm gonna try and get into Telal's office. By my watch I still have half 'n hour left before you start diversionary tactics. That should be ample time. Don't call me, I'll call you, got to go, love Nat." The message ended and Dela lowered the phone, worried about her man and cursing because she didn't get to speak to him.

In the office Nathaniel picked up the receiver of the desk phone and pressed the button for Mr Telal's direct line. Nathaniel prepared to lower his vocal tones as the phone was answered only a few feet away, as the crow flies.

"Mr Telal's office."

"Can I speak to Mr Telal?" Nathaniel asked.

"He's out of the office today, can I help? I'm his P.A.," she responded with an aloof tone.

"Yeah, I've got a package here for him at main reception."

"Get one of the guards to sign for it and send it up by the internal mail," she ordered.

"Sorry, but my chitty has to be signed by, and personally collected by Mr Telal," Nathaniel stated, enjoying being bloody-minded.

"He is not here this afternoon, I am his Personal Assistant, I will come down and sign for it," the P.A. stated in no uncertain terms.

"I dunno, it says Mr Telal only," Nathaniel gambled, trying to keep up the act.

"Then I'll forge his signature!" the P.A. spat back, becoming very agitated.

"Mmh?" Nathaniel paused, putting his amateur dramatic skills to good use.

"Well?" the P.A. nearly shouted down the phone.

"Okay, then," he relented.

"I'll be down in five minutes," the P.A. advised him and slammed the phone down.

Nathaniel quickly put down his receiver and crept to the door, opening it slightly to peek out. The corridor was empty and he kept the door an inch ajar to see the P.A. coming. Nathaniel saw a shadow in the peripheral vision of his left eye and ducked back into the room. He waited two seconds and opened the door again to see the P.A.'s shapely behind disappearing round the corner and heading for the lifts.

That was Nathaniel's cue. He ducked out of the room, closing the door behind him and walked quickly down the corridor and left into the passage to Telal's P.A.'s outer office. Nathaniel only glanced around the P.A.'s office and headed for the imposing eight foot high black marble-effect doors. He pulled at one of the brass rings that were the door handles, and with a little effort one swung open enough for him to enter.

Nathaniel knew he had only 5 minutes maximum to look about the place and he wasn't even sure what he was looking for in Telal's plush, yet minimalist black marbled office. There was a distinct lack of paper in the office, so he walked swiftly over to Telal's desk and sat down. Telal's desk was virtually empty except for a black blotter, pen holder and pens and a phone. So Nathaniel turned his attention to Telal's computer terminal, but it was switched off.

"Damn it!" Nathaniel said, hitting the desk with his right fist. Then he remembered that the P.A.'s P.C. was on and he rushed out of Telal's room into the P.A.'s office and seated himself behind her P.C. Grabbing the mouse, he quickly moved it down to 'Start' and accessed 'Search Files'. Quickly he tapped in Manes Close, then different files appeared in a separate window, as a result of his search. Nathaniel realised time was short and went to print them out, but that would take too long. Quickly he rooted around in the P.A.'s drawer, he got lucky in the second one which had a box of CD discs marked 'formatted'. Nathaniel stole one and put it into the P.C.'s 'D' drive, highlighted all the Manes Close files and downloaded them.

Nathaniel nervously looked up, the P.A. would be back any minute now, as the files slowly downloaded. Finally it was finished and pushing his luck and time, he searched for the word 'Ashmodaios'. Only one file came up and Nathaniel double-clicked it and glanced up anxiously. It was a calendar entry for 30th January and it stated 'Project Ashmodaios commences' and the time stated was 12 a.m.

Nathaniel frowned as he shut down the files he had been looking at and returned the P.A.'s screen to the state he found it in. Nathaniel ejected the CD disc, closed the P.A.'s drawer and sprinted out of her office, only slowing to a walk at the end of the corridor. Nathaniel forced himself to calm down and started walking normally along the corridor. It was time to get out!

Nathaniel rounded the corner and nearly stopped dead in his tracks when he saw the P.A. and a tall, Japanese-looking man stomping along ahead of her. Nathaniel forced himself to continue walking slowly down the corridor towards the Japanese man, who he assumed was the infamous Mr Telal. As they closed, Nathaniel could see that Telal wasn't in the best of moods either.

"Unbelievable, Miss. Hastings, only an imbecile would leave my office unattended while going on a wild goose chase," Telal shouted behind him to the following, grovelling, P.A.

"I'm sorry, Mr Telal, it will not happen again." The P.A.'s prim voice wobbled as she apologised while they approached Nathaniel.

"If anything is missing it will be your last error, Miss. Hastings." Telal spat at his P.A. then turned to glance absently at Nathaniel as they passed.

Nathaniel didn't like the way he had said the last sentence, or the yellow look of Telal's deep-set eyes. Nathaniel held his breath until at last Telal and his P.A. had gone past. Nathaniel exhaled. He could breath, he could see the crossroads ahead and the slightly ajar stationery cupboard.

"You there! Stop! Who are you?" came Telal's voice from a few feet behind, but Nathaniel didn't stop. He pretended not to hear and carried on walking.

"You! Who are you?" Telal screamed from behind him and Nathaniel ran. He hoped he would catch Telal off guard as he rounded down the corridor to the stationery office.

The corridor was empty and Nathaniel pushed the stationery cupboard door open, skidding to a stop as soon as he could. He quickly pulled the folders from the door. Nathaniel then half-turned, half shoulder-barged the door closed. Grabbing the nearest metal cupboard, he pulled it near the door and pushed it over on to it. The noise of the racks and stationery falling could be heard as Telal and his P.A. arrived.

"Get the key, you stupid bitch!" he screamed at the P.A., who, in tears, rushed off to a nearby room to get a spare copy of the key.

Meanwhile inside, Nathaniel toppled a couple more stationery racks and headed for the grille and duct behind it. Nathaniel pulled a table underneath the grille and scrambled in head first. He thought about the grille, but didn't have time to pull it shut, even if it would have stayed shut.

Nathaniel pulled and pushed himself along inside the cramped, confined passage, his elbows and knees soon feeling the pain of his hasty escape. Nathaniel pulled out his phone and turned it on, then dialled Dela's number as he scrambled his way along.

"Hello, Nat?" came Dela's enquiring voice.

"Plan B! Plan B!" came Nathaniel's voice through a hail of static, then the line went dead.

Dela suddenly panicked, grabbed her belongings and headed out of the pub as she dialled 999 on her mobile phone, hoping Nathaniel was going to be all right. Dela went down an alleyway next to the pub, which widened out to the rear of the pub car park and was divided by three concrete bollards. For the first time in her life Dela dialled 999 and waited impatiently and with curious interest in what would occur.

"Emergency Services, which Service do you require?" came an efficient, sharp voice down her mobile.

"Er," Dela paused in thought, "all three, I think."

Nathaniel dialled Dela's number again as he reached the end of the tunnel, but only got static. The heavy machinery and electrical junction boxes near the lift motors must be interfering with his phone again.

Nathaniel heard a grunting and banging from behind him and realised that someone was actually coming after him. Pushing his mobile into his pocket, he looked out of the tunnel as the lift ascended to the top floor giving him an escape route.

Quickly he pulled himself halfway out of the duct, grabbed the sides of the hanging grille with both hands and pulled/pushed his legs out. Nathaniel was in good physical shape so his legs came over the back of his head and shoulders and he flipped down on to the roof of the lift. He felt a stinging pain in his left hand as he steadied himself and saw that the grille had cut his hand and it was starting to bleed. He realised his time was short so he ignored the pain and blood. He made his way quickly and carefully along the edge of the lift holding on to the steel cables for support.

The noise like a lion making its way along the duct grew louder behind him, but he forced himself to ignore it and finally he came in reach of the Maintenance crawl-way. Nathaniel reached up and grabbed its supports, which were fixed to the ceiling and ignoring the screaming pain in his left palm, pulled himself up to safety. Grunting, he got his torso on to the crawl-way and swung his legs across, 'til he collapsed on the grilled crawl-way from his exertions.

Suddenly there came a terrible scream from the duct and Nathaniel turned his head in horror to face his chaser.

It was Telal; or had been Telal. His skin and facial flesh had split in places to reveal a red skin underneath. His eyes were now feral and glowing red and long black nails had split the skin of its finger tips. The features were still human-ish, but blood-red and oily. Telal was something Nathaniel had not seen before, some sort of half-human/half-demon. The actual idea of the two species mating made bile rise up to Nathaniel's Adam's apple.

"I'm going to make you pay in blood, thief!" the Telal/demon screamed as he squeezed himself out of the duct.

Nathaniel was frozen in fear, and he knew that he was weaponless and staring death in the face. The Telal/demon jumped down on to the lift and started to edge round the roof of the lift towards Nathaniel. Suddenly the lift began to descend and the Telal/demon rose his arms frantically towards Nathaniel in anger.

Nathaniel leant over the crawl-way and watched as the lift and Telal disappeared into the darkness of the lift shaft below.

"You won't escape me thief-f-f-f," came the wail of the half-demon somewhere in the darkness below.

Nathaniel exhaled and made his way out along the crawl-way and back into the Maintenance Room. He quickly closed and locked the hatch to the crawl-way, noticing again that his hand was bleeding. Nathaniel took his white handkerchief from his top jacket pocket and wrapped it over the cut. Then he retrieved his gloves from his pockets and stuffed them on again. He bent down and grabbed his briefcase with his good hand and made his way with all haste into the fluorescent-lit world of the stairwell again.

Round and down Nathaniel went until he reached, unseen by anyone, the fire hose where he retrieved his coat and put it on. Standing up, he noticed a fire alarm on the wall. He lifted up his briefcase and jammed the edge of it into the glass and was rewarded with the ear-splitting peeling of fire alarm bells.

Even though he was out of breath, Nathaniel ran down the stairwell, jumping the last five steps at each corner. He'd managed to get to level four before others appeared from their floors to flee down the stairwell.

"What's going on?" asked a teenager in a suit, with two women appearing behind him.

"Fire on the top floor, everyone out!" Nathaniel shouted at them as he ran past at full pelt. Seeing the speed Nathaniel was going the man and two women followed him in panic.

The stairwell soon rang with the clatter of hurried shoes and the voices of worried Idiminu workers. When they reached the third floor at least ten people were coming out on to the stairwell before them. By the time they had got down to the second floor there was a crowd of people walking down the stairs. Nathaniel slowed to a gentle walking pace trying to catch his breath as he mingled in with the exodus.

By the time they began piling out into the ground floor lobby, the Fire Brigade had arrived and their sub-officer was talking to the guards on the reception desk. Nathaniel ghosted anonymously out with the throng as the Firemen directed them across the way and out of harm's way. Nathaniel trotted across the road avoiding the traffic, and spotted Dela hanging round the corner of the pub.

Nathaniel rushed up to her, grabbed her arm and pushed her round the corner and out of sight. Then he crushed her to his chest and kissed her hard and long.

"Miss me?" he asked, kissing her nose.

"Like I never thought possible," Dela replied in earnest.

"Come on, let's cut through here to the tube station," Nathaniel said, beginning to walk down the alleyway to the pub's car park. The people were really beginning to pour out of the Idiminu building now.

They hurried past the bollards, away from the street noise into the car park. There was a gate in the corner of the place which they made for, when a white van pulled up in front of them. They came to a stop and Nathaniel grabbed Dela's arm and backed away from the van. A man with a grey beard, aged in his fifties, stared at them from the driving seat.

Nathaniel pulled Dela round and started off towards the alley and stopped dead when the young woman and man from the pub came racing towards them.

Nathaniel and Dela looked at each other, then left and right respectively. Dela pulled at Nathaniel's hand and they headed for a gap between two parked cars.

"Don't run Mr Le Meuille, we just want to talk," came the woman's light, yet menacing voice.

Nathaniel turned to see the small brown man and the old bearded guy from the van coming towards them with pistols in their hands.

Nathaniel thought about running, then looked at Dela's questioning face and he knew he couldn't risk her being harmed.

"What'll we do?" she whispered.

Nathaniel raised his hands in reply, "Surrender it seems."

"Quickly! Into the van," ordered the man with the grey beard in a thick Northern Irish accent, and he flicked his gun, beckoning them towards him.

Nathaniel and Dela walked towards the van and the woman and other man closed ranks behind them. The Irishman then pulled a side door in the van open to reveal two rows of seats, but no windows.

"In you get," the Irishman ordered, "into the back seats."

"Quickly now," the attractive dark-haired woman added.

Nathaniel and Dela got in as instructed and sat down. The Asian-looking man got in next, sitting half turned on the seats in front to keep the gun trained on them. The Irishman handed his weapon to the woman, who got in next to the Asian man. The Irishman, as quickly as he could, shut the sliding door behind them and got into the driver's seat.

"Where are you taking us?" Nathaniel asked the woman.

"Somewhere safe," she answered honestly, "we just want a little chat, Nathaniel."

"How do you know my name?"

"Let's go Mr Green," she said to the driver.

"Right-ho," he replied and the van left the pub car park and the Idiminu building behind.

"The man asked you who the fuck you are," Dela raged, "so fucking answer?"

"Please tell your friend to shut up," ordered the Asian man in gruff, but perfect Queen's English, as he aimed his gun at Dela's head.

"Dela, for now I think discretion is the better part of valour." With that he shot her a withering look.

Dela went to speak again, then shut up. Her gran always said her mouth would get her into trouble one day. Looking at the pistols trained at her head, today could be that day, she thought.

So they sat in silence as the van threaded its way through the London traffic.

Nathaniel took Dela's hand a minute later and she gazed at him, thanking him with her eyes for his thoughtfulness. They could see dead ahead in between their captives' heads quite well and knew they were travelling east.

Five or so minutes after they had driven past Upton Park Station and twenty minutes into their trip, they pulled up to a garage set into the arches of a railway or tube bridge. The driver jumped out and unlocked the doors, which he pulled out to open, then jumped back into his seat and drove the van into the darkness beyond.

When they were inside Mr Green got out again then shut the doors behind them, leaving them in near darkness until he turned on a set of overhead fluorescent strips.

"Mr George," the woman and obvious leader of the trio said to the Asian man. He responded by opening the side door of the van and climbing out. Once he was out he beckoned for Dela and Nathaniel to join him.

Dela and Nathaniel clambered out into the garage, which was completely bare except for an old three-seater sofa.

"Have a seat," the woman said congenially, getting out of the van behind them.

Dela looked round and saw the pistol pointing at her, "Do we have a choice?"

"You could stand," the small lady with long dark locks replied sweetly.

"We'll sit," Nathaniel answered for both of them and led Dela to the sofa.

"What were you doing at the Idiminu Corporation building today, Nathaniel?" the woman asked, handing her gun to the tall Irishman.

"You can call me Mr Le Meuille, Miss?" he asked, trying to glean some information from her.

"You can call me Mrs Dawson if you wish Mr Le Meuille," she smiled, her red lips going thin.

"Just doing a spot of business for the Home Office," Nathaniel smiled in return, enjoying the sparring between them.

"While your young lady waits in the pub across the street from you?" Dawson stood, her legs apart and arms crossed.

"Half day's leave. My companion and I were going shopping in Knightsbridge afterwards."

"A very apt place for you to go, you being a descendant of the King's Paladin." Dawson's lips and smile widened as she played one of her trump hands.

"You seem to know a lot about me, and I, so little about you. Who are you people and why are we being held captive here?" Nathaniel was tired of games, he wanted some answers.

"They must be working for Idiminu, why else would they kidnap us at gunpoint!" Dela exclaimed to Nathaniel, ignoring her three captors.

"We don't work for Mr Telal or Idiminu. We are, in fact, staking the place out and want to know why you were there?" Mrs Dawson seemed to lose her cool now as she pushed for answers.

"You're pigs!" Dela exclaimed, which brought laughter from Mr George, who was standing to her left.

"No. We're the ones with the guns asking the questions, luv. Now spill the beans – why were you there?"

Mrs Dawson clicked her fingers and both Green and George pointed their pistols at Dela's head.

"I know who you are now, you're that Society group, S-F-S-R people who tried to recruit me two years ago!" Nathaniel exclaimed standing up now, the guns switching to his head.

"S-S-R, Mr Le Meuille," Mrs Dawson corrected him. "So now we know who we all are, tell us why you were there!"

"No. This isn't right. The Society is a bunch of old duffers playing Ghostbusters, they don't kidnap people or carry guns." Nathaniel cast his arms wide in exasperation.

"We've moved on, we are no longer the silent watchers, Mr Le Meuille. If action needs to be taken to save the ignorant majority, we will," she said, taking a bold step closer to the King's Paladin.

"I can't believe your precious Inner Circle of Seven would sanction murder, Mrs Dawson," Nathaniel tempted, towering over her.

For the first time Dawson's eyes wavered, not sure how to proceed.

"I work for the Home Office, visiting companies is part of my job. Now I wasn't personally interested in the Idiminu Corporation, but now I am!" Nathaniel stood, legs apart, hands on hips and dominating Mrs Dawson with his charisma and presence.

"He could be telling the truth," Mr George said, worried he might get put in jail for kidnapping.

"I am," Nathaniel replied. "Now tell me why a secret society of spook-hunters is staking out an international corporation's London H.Q.?"

Mrs Dawson looked at his shoes and thought for a while. "We could work together you know, share information?"

"At gunpoint!" Dela exclaimed.

"Let's start again shall we?" Dawson said and pointed to her two male companions who put their guns away. "Why were you at the Idiminu building today?"

"On official government business Mrs Dawson. Why were you there?" Nathaniel smiled, knowing the battle was going his way.

"You just couldn't play ball could you?" Mrs Dawson smiled back.

"There's me, there's the beautiful Dela here," he pointed behind him, "and my dog. I don't need anyone else."

"Shame," Mrs Dawson smiled wickedly back, which Dela didn't like at all.

"Here's my card, if you change your mind."

He took it. "Here's my backside, now watch it walk through that door." Nathaniel waved at Dela to follow him and nervously she edged towards him.

Nathaniel reached out and took her hand as she approached and they walked towards the door without looking back.

"Are we just going to let them go?" Mr Green asked, exasperated at the situation.

Nathaniel pushed open one of the unlocked doors and he and Dela disappeared into the fading twilight of an East London dusk.

Mrs Dawson sighed, "What do you expect me to do Allan, shoot them in the back? We chase ghosts remember, not make them."

"Come on, Mr Green, let's get ready to go back to base," Mr George ordered, clapping the Initiate on the shoulder.

"Do you know where you're going?" Dela asked as they tramped through the rapidly darkening streets.

"No, but if we keep walking I'm sure we'll find a bus stop, tube station or taxi rank soon," he replied as he led them through the East End streets.

"What then?"

"Then we download the information I stole from Telal's computer," he said, pulling a CD disc from an inside pocket, "on my laptop."

"Who were those weirdos who kidnapped us?" Dela asked after they had walked on a little further.

"Some secret society. A bit like the Masons, but they chase ghosts and vampires and all that. They tried to recruit me a couple of years ago but I refused. It seems they have strong suspicions about Telal and the Idiminu Corporation too." Nathaniel stopped talking as they rounded the corner and found themselves across the road from Plaistow tube station.

"Voila!" Nathaniel exclaimed, pleased as punch at finding the tube station by accident.

"Are you always this lucky?" Dela asked, looking up at him.

"I've got you, haven't I?" he replied.

"Nat, sometimes you say the corniest things, but I like hearing them." Arm in arm, they crossed the road and disappeared into the tube station.

# CHAPTER 4

They got back to Balham at five and night had already fallen. They walked along past the shops towards Dela's place.

"I hope Cerberus is all right!" Nathaniel said as they walked. The night had brought an icy chill wind with it.

"I hope he hasn't chewed my carpets," replied Dela, but when she looked around to find Nathaniel he wasn't there. Looking around she saw a door close on a WH Smiths, so she went to investigate. She could see the back of Nathaniel's head disappear behind a stack of book shelves inside. Frowning with annoyance, she pushed open the door and followed him in. She walked along two aisles where books and magazine were on show before.

Nathaniel turned to face her as she approached and he smiled widely.

"What the hell do you think you're doin' disappearing like dat? I was scared shitless something had happened to you!" Dela chastised loudly, her brow furrowing in anger.

"Travel-chess anyone?" He smiled wickedly, knowing it would both confuse and frustrate her more.

"What are you on about?"

Nathaniel lifted the box containing a travel-chess game for her to inspect.

"Why, I thought you had chess on your laptop." Dela said, her anger diminishing slightly.

"Back up, my love," he said, shaking the box to emphasise his point. "Can't be too careful with these demon types you know."

Dela stood aghast as he walked past, giving her a peck on the cheek as he did.

"Come on, let's pay for this, then get home in the warm, eh!"

"I give up," Dela exhaled in defeat.

"Never give up, Dela, you make life worth staying alive for." Then he was off to the counter to pay for the travel-chess before she could reply.

"There you go again, saying all the right things at the right times," she muttered to herself as she trotted after him.

Cerberus had been sleeping in the living room and woke when the front door to the flat opened. Nathaniel had only just enough time to turn the light on and walk into the hallway before Cerberus came rushing up to him and knocked him on his arse.

"I'm pleased to see you too, old fella," Nathaniel said, fending off licks from the dog's rasping tongue.

Dela shut her door behind her and took off her coat. *'I'm not,'* she thought to herself.

Ten minutes after the kettle boiled and Nathaniel leaned against the doorway looking at her admiringly.

"So this Telal guy is a demon?" she asked, putting teabags into two mugs.

"I think he was more of a half-demon, some sort of human-demon hybrid and that scares me."

"Sugar?" Dela asked.

"Yes," Nathaniel replied.

"No," she smiled, "how many sugars in your tea?"

"Oh sorry, one," he chuckled.

"Sweet enough as you are, eh?" Dela muttered.

"Yep."

"You said the half-demon type things scare you, but the thing that scares me is I could have been one of their mothers if that Demon Lord had fucking caught and raped me." Dela shivered as she spooned sugar into the mugs.

"I'm not sure that was his intention. Procreation with a demon or even an incubus is naturally impossible, the poor woman would die during the act, for various reasons too squalid to go into now. No, something like Telal is the product of ancient evil and modern science and technology, I fear."

"Let's hope that disk will be helpful," Dela said pouring the boiling water into the mugs.

"Me too. You finish off the tea, while I go and turn on my laptop, if you don't mind excusing me." Nathaniel finished politely.

"I don't mind, go on," she nodded to him. "Man, he's so polite," she whispered after he had left the room.

Dela brought in the two mugs of tea and a packet of penguins. Nathaniel had set up on her coffee table, so she put the teas on the other side of it, safely away from the laptop.

"So what do you think you'll find?" Dela asked sitting down next to him.

"Hopefully, some 'info' on Manes Close or where the half-demons are coming from!"

Della collected her tea and blew on the surface, before getting closer to Nathaniel. Cerberus, meanwhile, was snoring away in front of Dela's electric fire, dreaming of chasing demons.

The laptop chirred into readiness, so Nathaniel inserted the CD and double-clicked the 'My Computer' symbol. A window opened and he highlighted the D drive, then went to the file and opened it.

Several word documents appeared, and Nathaniel clicked the first one. It was a letter from Telal to an estate agent on the sale of number One Manes Close. The next two were on similar lines, but the next one was different. It was to a Fertility Clinic in Pershore in Worcestershire to a Doctor Geial.

It explained how Manes Close was now fully owned by the Idiminu Corporation and the last family were moving out on 31 August last year. Mr Lord would be round to visit on schedule and that he should continue with the D.H.I. project at full speed ready for 30th January and the completion of the Ashmodaios Project.

"This is getting more confusing by the minute," Dela stated. "What is the Ashmodaios Project?"

"Something leviathan in terror, I fear." Nathaniel shook his head in disbelief.

"What?" Dela asked, putting down her tea after seeing the look on her lover's face.

"A demon can only remain on Earth for seven hours at a time and only in the hours of darkness. I saw a calendar entry for the thirtieth of January for Project Ashmodaios, and I fear it can only mean one thing, the invasion of our world by the demons."

"How? You said it yourself, they can only stay during the night."

"Somehow I suspect this Doctor Geial has found a way to splice demon and human DNA and Telal is the result. A demon hybrid that can walk around camouflaged in daylight. Only then could Ashmodaios rule this world during the day and night!"

"Shit," Dela exclaimed, rocking backwards onto the settee, "so how do we stop them?"

"Where to start?" Nathaniel said, thinking aloud. Then after a few seconds of silent thought he picked up a pad and pen from the coffee table, which Dela used to make shopping lists.

"May I?" he asked as he put the pad on his knee and removed the cap from the biro.

"Be my guest."

"One, the Demon Lord, Ashmodaios is after us and hates us more than hell." He wrote as he spoke. "Two, Telal knows someone fitting my description is investigating him and the Idiminu Corporation. Three, 'The Society' know something about Idiminu and vice-versa. Four, the Demon Lord must know about our visit to Manes Close and the desecration of his invoking circle, stroke portal." Nathaniel paused to sip his tea then continued.

"Five, the Idiminu Corporation and this Fertility Clinic are in cahoots about human/demon DNA splicing and an invasion." Nathaniel exhaled.

"So how do we stop all these things happening?" Dela asked.

"We have to stop Ashmodaios; stop Telal, destroy any further half-demons being made, and stop an invasion which would enslave all mankind." Nathaniel smiled thinly.

"And we do this by?" Dela asked, turning her face towards him.

"That's the difficult part at present." His smile thinned a little more.

"In other words, you don't know!" Dela exclaimed.

"No," he said putting his hands up in submission, "but don't despair, we're intelligent, handsome and wise beyond our years, I'm sure we will think of something."

"Right," Dela exhaled lowering her head, "while you think, I'll get some dinner on. Hungry?"

"Ravenous." He looked up at her, an apologetic look on his face.

"I have faith, you'll think of something," Dela said as she made for the hall.

"You do?" Nathaniel asked, feeling the faith rise in him also.

"Yeah, because we're dead otherwise!" she called back.

"That was lovely," Nathaniel smiled, pushing his now empty plate forward a little onto Dela's dining table.

"It was only Spag-Bol, Nat," Dela replied, still eating the last third of her meal.

"In fact, that was the most splendiferous Spaghetti Bolognaise that I've ever tasted," he said in a bad Italian accent. "Better than Mamma uses to'a make." He finished it off with a kiss of his fingers and a wild gesticulation.

"Did your mum not cook you pasta then?" Dela asked lightly, but it was a loaded question to bring up his parents and past.

"Cannot remember, both my parents died when I was eight, I was brought up by my grandmother in Gloucester."

"I'm sorry," Dela sympathised, "how did they die?"

Nathaniel looked down at his sauce-stained plate. "Khristoff," was all he whispered.

"Who's Khristoff?" Dela probed, putting down her spoon and fork. All interest in dinner had vanished.

"A vampire," Nathaniel sneered, "the oldest, cruellest and most powerful Prince of the Undead that ever walked on God's good earth."

Nathaniel took a deep breath. "My Father, the King's Paladin before me, had been hunting him for years because he had killed one of our distant relatives centuries back. Father was obsessed with hunting and destroying him, it was his undoing. My father had slain five of Khristoff's loyal vampire guards." Nathaniel paused to rub a psychosomatic itch on his hand.

"Khristoff got his revenge by coming to the house and killed my mother and older brother Stephen before my father's eyes, then tied my father up, slit his wrists and let him bleed to death. The coroner reckoned it must have taken him over an hour to die, looking down at my brother and mother." Nathaniel's speech slowed, his eyes watered a little.

"What about you?"

"My sister Eleanor, Cerberus and I had been on two weeks' summer holiday with my grandmother when it happened. She brought us up after that."

"I'm so sorry Nat. So where's your sister now and what happened to this, vampire?" Dela reached out and touched his arm.

"Eleanor lives in the States now, California, she's a film producer."

"And Khristoff?"

"Still," he paused, "around somewhere I suspect."

"And you've never thought of revenge?"

"For a few years I thought of nothing else, but where did revenge get my father? No, if I ever come across him I'd slay him, but I won't risk the ones I love by chasing death." Nathaniel looked up at her now, tears welling in his red eyes.

Dela put her right palm against his cheek. "We have enough trouble with demons after us, eh?"

Nathaniel smiled, "I love-"

Just then the doorbell rang!

"Who's that?" Dela exclaimed, fear gripping her as she wondered who or what waited outside in the dark.

Nathaniel pulled some change from his pocket and mouthed a blessing over them as he rose. Dela grabbed a vase of flowers and threw the roses in the bin as she, Nathaniel and Cerberus moved slowly towards the door.

The front doorbell chimed again and the two humans and one dog froze for a second before continuing on.

Nathaniel flicked on the hall light and nodded for Dela to open the door. Nathaniel and Cerberus stood before the door, ready to attack as Dela thumbed the lock and quickly pulled the door in towards her.

Cerberus barked at the figure standing at Dela's door, who gave a very un-demonlike, girly scream.

Dela looked around the door to see her friend Merline, back up to the balcony wall, her hands up to her face.

"Merline?" Dela asked sheepishly.

"Who'd you think it was, Denise Lewis and who'da fuck is the man with the Werewolf?" Merline ranted, her fear giving way to anger now.

"Get in here, girlfriend," Dela said grabbing Merline roughly and pulling her into the safety of the flat.

Cerberus padded back into the living room after a disdainful sniff of Merline's perfume.

"Dela, what the hell is going on?" Merline screeched at her best friend. Then she turned and looked Nathaniel up and down. "Do you know you have a white man in your hall?"

"Yes." Dela replied, patiently waiting for Merline's motor mouth to slow down.

"So, you a paying client?" Merline nodded her head towards Nathaniel with her hands on her hips.

"Er, Dela," he paused, a la Hugh Grant, "I'll let you handle this, I think." He then slowly moved from the hall to join Cerberus in the living room.

"Merline, get your ass in here," Dela pulled her friend into the hall and closed and bolted the door behind her.

"What's going on girlfriend, you in some kinda trouble?" Merline asked, bemused.

"Yes," Dela frowned, "what are you doing here?"

"I called you re-mem-ber!" Merline said the last word slowly. "You-were-gonna-relax-my-hair?"

"Shit, sorry Merline, I forgot," Dela explained. "I'll do it for you now, okay."

"Okay," Merline beamed. "So what trouble has that guy been givin' you?"

"Nat," Dela said looking left into the living room, "he's not trouble, he saved my life the other night. We're close," Dela said closing her hands together and entwining her fingers.

Merline looked at Nathaniel sitting, stroking Cerberus. "You and him have gone horizontal?"

"Several pleasurable times," Dela laughed saucily. "Come on in an' I'll introduce him."

Dela led the way and Nathaniel stood up as the women entered the room.

"Merline, this is Nat, Nat this is my best friend, Merline." Dela introduced the two of them to each other.

"I am honoured to meet you," Nathaniel took Merline's right hand from her side, lifted it and kissed it.

"Hi," Merline squeaked, at a loss for words for the first time in her life.

"Merline came here to have her hair done," Dela said, "but I'm sure we can rearrange it for another night."

"No need, darling," Nathaniel raised his hand, "I'll take Cerberus out for a walk."

"You're gonna to take your dog out for a walk, here, at night?" Merline said, aghast at the naivety or foolishness of Dela's new boyfriend.

"Will you be all right?" Dela asked, concerned. "It can be dangerous around here at night."

"Ah, but I've got Cerberus, remember." Nathaniel winked and kissed Dela's cheek as he walked past to get his coat, Cerberus at his heel.

"See ya, baby." Dela smiled timidly and watched him and his dog leave.

"Well, girlfriend, you've got some explaining to do, big time." Merline ordered, crossing her arms and leaning slightly to the left.

Nathaniel and Cerberus got some funny and sometimes scary looks from the residents. He got a few gestures and was spoken at a couple of times, but a roar from Cerberus soon silenced them. He had been out for nearly an hour and was heading through some high rise estates, when he was confronted by three teenagers.

"Where do you think you're going, Mother fucker?" The shortest and ugliest of the bunch asked.

"Back to my friend's flat, so could you please move out the way?" Nathaniel smiled eyeing the youths, who all had sneering poker faces on.

"This is our patch, cunt, didn't you see our markers?" The squat leader gesticulated at a graffitied wall.

Nathaniel walked a step closer, "All I see is graffiti."

"Fucking hell," one of the other thugs said loudly from under his hoodie.

"You come in here, cross our territory, make fun out of our markers." The youth spat on the floor in front of Nathaniel. "Now you have to pay the price!"

Nathaniel stepped back, leaving Cerberus between him and the now blade-wielding tearaways.

"Cerberus," he commanded loudly, "play with the lads a bit."

All of the youths laughed and then advanced on the dog and Nathaniel. "First, we're gonna gut your dog, then cut off your balls!"

Clyde Goyle awoke with a start and found himself on a pile of rubbish-filled black bin liners. His mind was swirling, his throat dry and he had a cold sensation in his groin where he had pissed his trousers. He couldn't remember how he got there, or night falling. In fact, he couldn't remember much since his last hit at eleven o'clock that morning.

A loud roaring, growling shocked his dulled senses into action and he squinted down the alleyway he was in, to see what was occurring. A street lamp somewhere out of his vision cast silhouettes onto the alley wall to the right of him. He could make out three figures together, then another smaller figure and some sort of animal by his side. He could hear voices, but could not make out what they were saying in raised tunes.

Clyde sniffed and blinked at the same time as he noticed the three figures menacingly approaching the other. The heroin in his withered veins must have kicked in again as he saw the animal double in size and apparently grow two extra heads. There came a deafening roar and three screams as the three figures began running away from the beast. Suddenly, the three figures (young men) came running into the alley past Clyde without noticing him. Even though they looked like teenagers, each of the youths had totally grey hair.

"Must be the new trend," Clyde said as he lay back on the bin liners and fell into a dreamless sleep that hypothermia would never allow him to awake from.

"Oh, hello," Dela said as she walked from the bathroom to the kitchen when Nathaniel and Cerberus opened the front door, with the keys borrowed from Dela. "Nice walk?"

"Okay," Nathaniel smiled secretly and looked down at Cerberus, who was staring back up at him.

"We've just finished," Dela stated and disappeared into the kitchen. "Go on in, she won't bite."

Nathaniel strode into the living room to see Merline sitting on the sofa, reading 'Woman's Own', her hair now long and straight to her shoulders.

"Your hair looks nice," he said politely and it did look better than her earlier look.

"Thanks," Merline said, not looking up from her magazine. Nathaniel stood beside the sofa, as the embarrassing silence continued on too long.

"Dela says you work for the Civil Service, as do I?" Merline decided to play ball and be nice, for the time being.

"Yes," Nathaniel hurriedly replied, taking that as a cue to sit down. "I work for the Home Office."

"Really?" Merline said with a wicked smile. "I work for the Foreign and Commonwealth Office, as assistant desk officer, how about you?"

"Oh, I'm the head of the IT section," Nathaniel replied.

"Oh, pretty high up the ladder then?"

"High enough for me and I only work part time."

"Anyone for a coffee?" Dela asked, appearing at the living room door.

"Yes," Merline replied.

"Yes, please," Nathaniel replied, getting to his feet, "I'll help you." And he followed Dela out to the kitchen. Cerberus looked disdainfully at Merline and faded into the hall to fall asleep by the radiator.

"You two getting along?"

"Not as well as you and me," Nathaniel replied, closing the kitchen door behind them.

"Why did you close the door?" Dela asked as she pulled three mugs off her mug hook.

"So I can do this," Nathaniel answered by coming up behind her and cupping her breasts, his lips sucking at her slender neck.

"Good enough reason," Dela panted as she reached around her backside to unzip his fly. Dela half turned as Nathaniel hurriedly pulled up her short skirt and they kissed feverishly. Dela freed his erect cock from his pants as Nathaniel pulled aside her g-string and entered her from behind.

Merline had a very short attention span and looked around Dela's flat while she waited for her coffee. She looked at Nathaniel's laptop which was showing a starfield screensaver. She tapped the spacebar and the standard Office Windows menu glowed back.

Suddenly the small laptop beeped softly and a windows box appeared saying: Doctor Solomon's Virus checking. A large bug appeared with a warning sign next to it, 'Warning Virus Detected.'

Merline looked around, but no one was in sight.

Another message appeared on the screen: 'Warning, Demon Virus detected, switch off or face possible file corruption.'

Merline was getting worried now, she didn't want to bust Dela's new boyfriend's computer.

The screen was suddenly filled with static, then went blank for a second, then an orangey-red screen appeared. Flames graphics danced at the bottom and edges of the screen, and a voice as sweet and gentle as an angel spoke: "Come closer Merline."

Merline was hypnotised by the angelic voice and leaned in closer to the screen. As she did she swore she could feel the heat of the flames and smell the smoky burning funk of bad eggs.

"Touch the screen, my love." The voice tempted her.

Merline found herself reaching forwards and pressing the tips of her fingers against the screen.

"Now. My sweet, where are you? For I wish to send my arch-angels to worship your presence and bask in your beauty."

"Who are you?" Merline asked, trying to pull her fingers away from the increasingly hot screen.

"Your lord and master." The voice growled, not sounding angelic any longer.

"Let me go," Merline hissed, but her fingers were fused to the screen.

"Never. Your soul's mine now, bitch!"

Merline would have screamed, but an orangey-red light shot from the screen up her fingers, hand, arm and into her brain – her caring soul was sucked into the planes of Gehenna.

"Now," said her-master's-voice, "where are you?"

"Did you hear that?" Dela asked, wiping herself with a wad of kitchen roll.

"It's probably Merline wondering where we are," said Nathaniel, pushing his spent cock back into his trousers.

Dela disposed of the wet kitchen roll in the swing bin and readjusted her knickers and skirt to a more respectable position.

"What about the coffee?" Dela said, realising they had been in the kitchen ten minutes and done nothing but boil the kettle.

"You see to your guest and I will make the coffee, and if she asks why it's taking so long say that the kettle blew a fuse," Nathaniel offered, busying himself with the mugs, coffee and spoons.

"I'll have to watch you," Dela said, opening the kitchen door.

"Why?" Nathaniel asked, turning to face her.

"Because you tell the most convincing lies," she beamed and walked into the hall, past the sleeping Cerberus to the living room.

Merline sat staring at Nathaniel's laptop, and Dela noticed that the screen was going haywire and small frills of smoke were drifting up out of the speaker grill.

"Merline, what have you done?" Dela asked rushing over to unplug the laptop at the switch.

"Huh," Merline said, shaking her head. "It was an accident, I was looking for solitaire and it started going mental."

"Nat, come in here," Dela shouted. The screen began to blacken as she held the laptop's plug aloft.

Nathaniel came rushing in, "What's happened?"

"Your laptop's decided to fry itself," Dela explained, trying to keep Merline's involvement a secret.

"Is it okay?" Merline asked, moving along on her bum on the sofa to let Nathaniel sit down.

"It's just fused itself. I had the same thing happen to my home PC two years ago." Nathaniel picked up the laptop and took it into the kitchen for safety.

Dela followed him. "You couldn't do this just by tapping a few keys could you?"

"No, it's a hardware, not a software problem. Anyway, this laptop is now well and truly fucked and the CD has melted inside," Nathaniel explained with a curse.

"So we've lost all the info from Telal's office then?"

"We would have," Nathaniel pulled another CD from his pocket, "if I hadn't taken a copy earlier."

"Aren't you a clever man?" Dela smiled and leaned forward, hands on his shoulders, giving him the briefest peck on the cheek.

An hour later, they were sitting in the living room watching television and eating biscuits, but not talking. Dela was wondering when Merline was going to leave, but she knew she couldn't just throw her out.

"Anyone want a drink?" Dela asked, trying to bridge the conversational abyss.

"A cup of tea would be lovely," Nathaniel replied enthusiastically.

Merline just sat there unblinkingly watching the television like her life depended on it.

"Merline, what's-wrong-wid-you-girl?" Dela asked her friend as no reply was forthcoming.

"Huh," Merline said sleepily, turning to face Dela.

"Are you okay?" Dela asked, rising from her seat at the far end of the sofa.

"Yeah fine," Merline smiled thinly, then stiffened as there came a sharp knock at the door of the flat.

Cerberus stood suddenly from where he had been lying by the feet of the armchair Nathaniel was sitting on. Cerberus raised himself up on his haunches, the hair on his back standing on end.

As Dela moved to answer the door, Nathaniel stood up and held his palm up to her, stopping Dela in her tracks. "I'll answer it. Come on Cerberus." And the dog led the way out of the living room into the hall.

All of a sudden, Merline grabbed a vase of flowers off a pedestal next to the sofa, jumped up and smashed Nathaniel over the head with it. He staggered, water saturating his head and shoulders, then he collapsed sideways onto the armchair he had just vacated.

"Merline! What the fuck-" but Dela's cry died in her throat as Merline turned to face her, the pupils of her eyes glowing incandescent orange.

If that wasn't bad enough, a fiery red arm came thrusting through the small window of her front door, searching for the lock.

Cerberus barked at the arm loudly, then turned his head to face Dela, in three minds what to do next.

"Cerberus, deal with the front door," Dela shouted at the dog. "I'll deal with this!"

"Join me Dela in Ashmodaios' warm embrace." Merline opened her arms wide and smiled at her friend.

"Merline, snap out of it please." Dela pleaded as her possessed friend advanced on her.

"Merline is mine now you black bitch and you're going to join me in hell!" Came a throaty, familiar voice from the foul depths of Hades.

"Bastard!" Dela screamed, jumping up and sending a flying kick to Merline's throat. Merline's head was whipped back hard and she flew back and cracked her head against the living room doorframe. Merline collapsed in a heap on the floor, adjacent to where Nathaniel lay.

Dela just had time to draw breath before the front door gave an almighty crack and two fiery red demons entered. Dela swallowed hard in fright. These guys were bigger, tougher and much smoother looking than the demons that attacked them at Nathaniel's house. Dela leant over and began to shake Nathaniel, trying desperately to wake him and save them.

Yet Cerberus had other ideas. Dela's eyes widened even further as a shimmering gold haze enveloped Cerberus. Inside the magical mist the dog began to grow in size, not only in body size, but head wise too.

Cerberus grew to such a size that he took up most of the hall. His three barking heads turned themselves towards the two advancing demons. With one bound Cerberus' two great paws felled the startled demons and his heads soon made mincemeat of the pair.

Seeing the immediate battle was won, Dela glanced at the unconscious Merline, then returned her attention to arousing Nathaniel. Finally, her shaking and cajoling paid off and Nathaniel groggily came round.

"I'll never drink again," he moaned as his eyes flickered awake, "what hit me?"

"Merline did, with a vase. I think she's been possessed or something," Dela tried to explain.

"Some friends you have," Nathaniel winced as he tried to get to his feet with Dela's help.

"It ain't her fault."

"I know," Nathaniel staggered, rubbing his sore head, "the door!" His eyes flashed in concern.

"Two demons," Dela nodded, "but Cerberus's dealing with them, look!"

Nathaniel skirted the chair, holding onto Dela and saw Cerberus mopping up the demons.

"Grab some stuff quickly, we must be out of here before the police arrive," Nathaniel ordered, leaning against a wall for support.

"You okay?" Dela asked concerned.

"I will be, now get cracking, go, go, go," he urged. Dela finally went and Nathaniel slid down the wall to examine the unconscious Merline. Cerberus who had finished off the two demons and had returned to his normal size and number of heads, padded up to Nathaniel. The dog licked at Nathaniel's free hand and he in turn leant on the dog for support, while ruffling his fur.

"Thanks pal," he said to the dog, then turned his attention to Merline, "better go guard the door," he told Cerberus.

Nathaniel felt for a pulse in Merline's neck. There was a faint one, but her skin was burning hot. He carefully moved her head to one side and saw her hair was matted with blood where she had hit the doorframe.

Nathaniel got up gingerly and put on his coat and grabbed his rucksack. He came into the hall at the same time that Dela did.

"Get your coat on, we're leaving," Nathaniel ordered, pulled her coat from the rack and handed it to her,

"But what about Merline, we can't just leave her?" Dela took her coat, but resisted Nathaniel's attempt to drag her from her own flat.

"I'm sorry Dela, but she's gone." Nathaniel's gaze followed a bark from Cerberus where he could see the blue flashing lights now illuminating the dark car park outside.

"You mean she's dead?" Dela asked, staring at her lifeless friend on the floor.

"Not physically dead, but she's lost her soul to Ashmodaios and is possessed by his evil spirit. She's as good as dead. Now come on, the police are here." Nathaniel grabbed her arm this time and pulled her stunned body towards the front door.

"You have to save her, Nat," Dela cried, trying to comprehend the tragedy that had unfolded before her eyes this night.

"That's beyond my powers." Nathaniel pulled her towards the front door and spun her so she was face to face with him.

"The police are on their way up. Now, I don't have an explanation for them regarding the unconscious woman in your living room, the smashed front door or pieces of demon strewn around the hall. We have to escape and live to fight another day, so we can prevent this happening to someone else." He shouted forcefully into her face.

Dela looked at him, then at Merline's body, then slapped Nathaniel hard around the face and exited the flat, carrying her coat and holdall.

When they got onto the balcony they could see the police were already out of the two cars that had arrived and were making their way towards the main centre stairwell.

"Come on," Nathaniel urged as they ran towards the same stairwell.

"But the police are down there," Dela called after him.

"Yes, but we're going up." With that he sprinted up the stairs with Dela and Cerberus following behind. After a breathless minute's slog they were at the top floor of the flats. Nathaniel turned right and ran across the balcony towards another stairwell at the side of the building. Without talking, they began to descend this stairwell until they reached the third floor. They heard a police radio blare out below, so they headed left along the third floor balcony until they reached the centre stairwell and lift.

Nathaniel pressed for the lift to go down and then led Dela and his dog down the stairwell to the second floor.

"Go Cerberus," Nathaniel ordered, pointing down the stairs.

Cerberus obeyed and continued down the stairwell while Nathaniel grabbed Dela's hand and led her across the second floor balcony, continuing to the left until they reached another set of stairs. This they descended at an alarming rate until they reached the ground and car park. They looked around the corner and saw a couple of bobbies chasing Cerberus away from their position, into the car park.

"Let's go," Nathaniel ordered as he and Dela ran for it towards the street and the safety of a brick alleyway. They slowed to a jog and hid behind a wall and rested, trying to control their breathing.

"What about the dog?" Dela asked after she had caught her breath.

"Don't worry he'll find us, he has a great nose."

"Nat, your bloody dog had three noses, on three heads! I've seen him change and grow big and he chewed up those fucking demons like dog biscuits, what is he?"

"Wow, slow down," Nathaniel gently held and lowered her gesticulating hands. "You've seen his true self?"

"When you were sparko, yes. What is he?"

"A very old friend of the family." Nathaniel saw her angry look, and added, "I'll tell you later, I promise."

Before Dela could interject, Cerberus came padding around the wall and gave them a loud sniff.

Outside Dela's flat, two policemen stood either side of the door facing each other. They both then turned into the door and with their truncheons drawn, entered the flat. Their polished black shoes crunched on something that felt and crushed like bath salts. A red ooze also stained the carpet and the smell was like a thousand sprout-induced farts.

"What is this crap?" One PC said to the other.

"What happened to the front door? It looks like a bazooka's hit it!" The other PC replied.

They ventured slowly into the living room, which apart from a broken vase and one of the windows being wide open, didn't contain any answers, only more questions.

"What do we do now? Dela asked as they trudged down the alleyway, away from her block of flats.

"We need to lose ourselves for a while, bright lights, noise, lots of people," Nathaniel explained. "You know, lose yourself in the crowd."

"There's a club I used to go to." Dela spoke her thoughts aloud, "it's always packed and goes on 'til five in the morning."

"Sounds ideal," Nathanial mused, "let's go."

"What about the dog?"

Both Dela and Nathaniel stopped and looked down at Cerberus.

"Old friend," Nathaniel said, bending down to look the dog in the eyes, "it's time for you to disappear 'til dawn."

Cerberus barked twice at his master and wagged his enormous tail.

"We'll be fine, I have the whistle anyway."

Cerberus barked again and Nathaniel stood up. The hairs on Cerberus's neck started to stand on end and on the backs of Dela's and Nathaniel's necks also. Then, slowly, the air around the dog shimmered and he slowly faded away to nothing before Dela's astonished eyes. Dela walked forward and leant forward with her right arm, but nothing was there.

"What happened to him? Where did he go?"

"Cerberus, as you now know, is a special dog and has been in the Le Meuille family for over two hundred years. One of my ancient relations, a King's Paladin, saved his life and Cerberus swore he would serve the Le Meuille family until there comes a time when the last King's Paladin dies." Nathaniel spoke with an airy voice, his mind thinking of bygone family heroes.

"But where's he gone now?"

"Cerberus, sorry, comes from a different plane of existence. A dimension ethereal in conception; he is bound to earth by the tether of his oath only. He has just returned to his home for a while," Nathaniel mused, sounding like he was on a different plane himself, "the break will do him good."

"Oh, right!" Dela said, shaking her head in disbelief.

"Let's go boogie on down at this disco then," Nathaniel said excitedly.

"Boogie? Disco? What's the last CD you bought?"

"Charlotte Church. No, tell a lie, Britney Spears."

"Oh, my God, I'm sleeping with the musically retarded!" Dela grabbed his arm and lead him down the alleyway.

"I suppose you haven't got any Destiny's Child or 50 Cent or Puff Daddy CDs at home, then?"

"I've never heard of any of them," Nathaniel replied honestly.

"Dat's what I thought babe; that's what I was very much afraid of." Dela shook her head again, "You're in for a real treat tonight, then!"

They walked down to the end of the alleyway into a larger street and headed off towards the club. Behind them, in the shadows, a pair of orange incandescent eyes followed their progress.

# CHAPTER 5

"I'm sorry," Dela apologised as they walked down the street towards the club she had mentioned.

"Eh? What for?" Nathaniel asked, looking behind him to see if they were being followed.

"For slapping you," Dela explained, "I hope you can understand how I felt at the time."

"Yeah, I understand completely," Nathaniel nodded, rubbing at his cheek

"This is the place," Dela stated as they rounded a corner to find a queue of youngsters outside double doors manned by two bouncers. They were both dressed in tight-fitting suits and looked like they had just stepped out of the WWE.

"Hey, Clarence, how's it going?" Dela asked as she and Nathaniel approached.

"Hey, Baby, whatsup?" Clarence smiled showing off his gold tooth display.

"Me and my lover wanna dance," Dela said, grabbing Nathaniel's arm and pulling him into the conversation.

Clarence looked Nathaniel up and down and then smiled. "Sure thing, in you both go." Clarence turned to his fellow bouncer and gave him a questioning look, as Dela and Nathaniel entered the club.

"I dunno," Fat Larry replied, "maybe white is the new black!"

Clarence's mouth opened and a deep laugh resonated.

Across the street in a darkened alleyway someone or something watched with evil intent.

Dave Judd thought he was It and the only thing he loved more than himself was his bathroom mirror at home. Dave was thirty-seven going on seventeen. He lived for the weekends and the chance to show off his fake tan in the clubs and pubs around Balham.

Dave headed down the alleyway, which was a shortcut to one of his regular haunts in the area. Even through his Raybans he could see a girl standing at the end of the alleyway peering into the street beyond. Dave pushed his sunglasses up on to his head and walked up to the woman and rubbed his hand up her backside.

"Fancy some action sweetcakes?" he asked with treacle charm.

"Yes!" Merline hissed and turned and pounced upon the poor unsuspecting Dave, whose fine Italian shoes would never grace a dance floor again.

Nathaniel had never been in such a loud place before in his memory, but he was glad he was with Dela, because she seemed to know half the people there. They hit the floor after off-loading bags and coats in the cloakroom and the man serving them leaned over and kissed Dela's cheek. Dela had a Southern Comfort and lemonade, while Nathaniel settled for a medicinal Chivas Regal. Dela chatted to her friend the barman, while Nathaniel scanned the crowd, trying not to look out of place. The loud, pulsating rhythms affected his concentration as he tried to think of their next course of action.

Eventually Dela dragged him into a freshly vacated booth on an upper level, away from the dance floor.

"How long does this club stay open to?" Nathaniel barked in Dela's ear, trying to be heard over the loud music.

"About five a.m." she replied.

"It'll still be dark," Nathaniel said to himself.

"What?"

"It'll still be dark then," Nathaniel repeated, louder.

Dela leaned closer, "That's OK there's a Greasy Spoon round the corner, we can sit in there 'til dawn."

"What'll we do 'til then?"

"Come here." Dela grabbed his collar and pulled him close to receive a long, wet, passionate French kiss.

Clarence put his arm out to stop a woman jumping the queue, when he noticed it was Dela's friend Merline.

"Hey, sorry girl!"

"Is Dela inside?" Merline turned her sunglass covered eyes up towards the tall bouncer. Her tone was flat and emotionless, but the bouncer didn't notice.

"Yeah, she's inside," Clarence replied, "how's about you and me hooking up later?" the bouncer winked as he stroked her upper right arm.

"Drop dead!" she stated and walked inside.

Clarence started to laugh and Fat Larry joined in as the double doors to the club swung shut. Clarence coughed then continued chuckling, but the cough persisted and the look of mirth faded from his countenance. Clarence bent over and began to cough violently into his fist.

"You okay?" Fat Larry asked.

"Help!" Clarence whispered, the word just escaping his closing windpipe.

Fat Larry moved his big frame over to his friend as Clarence fell to his knees, his hands clawing at his throat and his eyeballs bulging from their sockets.

"Somebody call an ambulance!" Fat Larry shouted at the revellers in the queue.

"God!" Clarence managed to gasp before he fell to the pavement unconscious.

"Clarence! No mate! No!" Larry shouted, putting his friend on to his back, "Wake up!"

Fat Larry pressed two fingers against Clarence's neck as he had been trained to do, but there was no pulse. Larry started to give his friend CPR, but Clarence was dead before a girl in the queue could finish dialling for an ambulance.

"Where's the toilet in this place?" Nathaniel asked loudly in Dela's ear.
"Upstairs and to the left," Dela replied with hand signals.
"Back in a sec," Nathaniel shouted and headed off up some metal stairs to another smaller balcony and spotted the toilet in the west wall.

Merline cruised between the heaving throng of revellers, ignoring anyone who spoke to her. She made her way to the back of the place where she and Dela normally hung out. It took a minute to get through the throng, but Dela was nowhere to be seen. She then headed back to the bar to enquire there where Dela was.
Feeling a bit out of place, Nathaniel went to the toilet in a cubical, which he locked behind him. When he finished he rejoined the noisy crowd and was just about to go down the steps to the first floor balcony when he spotted Merline chatting to the barman. Nathaniel rushed downstairs taking two steps at a time, keeping his eyes, as best he could in the dark club, on Merline. He rounded the stairs and nudged his way through the crowds to Dela's table.
Nathaniel grabbed Dela's arms and pulled her to her feet shouting "Merline's here, we've gotta leave!"
Dela's angry face changed to fear. "Where?"
"Downstairs at the bar. Is there a back way out of here?
"Yeah, by the loos. Come on I'll show you." Dela grabbed his hand and pulled him to the front of the balcony and the stairs that led both up and down.

Dela scanned the bar, but Nathaniel nudged her and pointed to the foot of the stairs. Merline looked up and smiled. Her sunglasses covering the orange glow of her demonic pupils. Time stopped for a few seconds as the protagonists stared at each other.

Nathaniel snapped them out of it by pulling Dela up the stairs to the next balcony. Merline was after them in a shot, but a group of five lads, got in her way. She pushed past them to follow her prey.

Nathaniel and Dela had made it to the second storey and were already running for the emergency exit. They both skidded to a halt at the door. Nathaniel pushed the bar down and forward. The door opened half an inch but juddered to a halt because the door was secured with an iron chain and padlock. Nathaniel and Dela stared at each other in blind panic. If they lived through this Nathaniel would write a strong letter of complaint to the Health and Safety Executive.

"What'll we do now?" Dela screamed at Nathaniel at close range.

But Nathaniel wasn't looking at her, he was staring to the left of her at the figure slowly walking up to the crest of the stairs.

"Pray," was his glib reply.

Even though the place was packed with people and the music was deafening, all that faded into a blur for Nathaniel, Dela and the possessed Merline.

Merline reached the top of the stairs and with an unnaturally wide smile, she took off her sunglasses to reveal the burning pupils concealed behind them.

Nathaniel and Dela pressed themselves against the blocked fire exit as Merline advanced halfway to their frightened position.

"What about coins?" Dela shouted in desperation above the repressive cacophony of noise.

"No good, the body's still human!" Nathaniel shouted back, his eyes darting around him looking for a weapon to use against the advancing possessed human. Just then a poor unfortunate clubber wandered up to Merline looking for action and sexual attraction.

"Hey! Nice contacts beautiful, wanna dance?"

Merline stopped to examine her would-be suitor and his unstylish pulling gear.

"Not 'til hell freezes over, Mortal!" the possessed Merline replied, her right hand reaching out and grabbing the top of the young man's head.

"Hey! What you do….." but he didn't finish as the Merline thing lifted him up by the head and with ease threw the man over her head. The unfortunate young man flew over the second floor railing on to the dance floor, breaking his neck.

Nathaniel took the opportunity to grab an unwanted glass of lemonade from a nearby table and pushed Dela towards the left side of Merline and the toilet entrance.

Screams could now be heard form the dance floor below above the music, as the young man with the broken neck breakdanced as his body jerked the last spastic dance of death.

People started to panic and back away from the fiery-eyed woman. The Merline thing ignored all the pandemonium around her and kept her beady orange eyes on Dela and Nathaniel, who had managed to edge themselves around to her right side.

Only a fixed table and seats blocked their direct exit to the steps up to where the men's and women's toilets were situated. Yet they couldn't get round the table without getting close to Merline and near-certain death.

Nathaniel glanced back at the table and seats with a railing behind it separating the toilet area from the seating area. They could try climbing on the table and over the railings, but that would mean turning their backs on Merline and she would be on them in an instant.

Merline closed on them now, as bemused clubbers, even six-foot fifteen-stone men, were avoiding the crack-crazed bitch.

"You cannot avoid me!" the Merline-possessed creature cried, "I want my sacrifice and you, King's Paladin, are a bonus!"

Suddenly Nathaniel saw his chance as two huge bouncers in black bomber-jackets crested the top of the second floor stairs and made a bee-line for Merline. Grabbing Dela's arm with one hand and the pint of lemonade in the other, he rushed at Merline and threw the lemonade into her eyes.

The Merline thing staggered back screaming, its hands going to its steaming, molten eyes. The two bouncers grabbed Merline's arms and pinned the possessed woman's arms behind her back.

"Come on," Nathaniel pulled Dela past the bouncers and the waiting demon-thing and they pegged it down the stairs until they were on the dance floor again, pushing past the crowd around the broken-necked man and heading for the door.

Nathaniel took a quick look back as they exited the club and saw that the half-blinded Merline creature was still struggling with the two bouncers. The well-aimed glass of lemonade on her burning eyes had obviously had the desired effect, if only temporarily.

Nathaniel exited the doors and saw that Dela was already pushing her way to the front of a small panicky crowd in front of the cloakroom. Nathaniel retreated to the edge of the crowd, keeping watchful eyes on the doors of the club and Dela's progress at the front of the cloakroom crowd.

"I want my things now!" Dela screamed at the poor teenage girl behind the counter, her hands full of cloakroom receipts, her eyes slowly glazing over in panic. But everyone else was shouting and screaming and normally Dela would have had all her sympathy, but this was a matter of life and possibly, her death. Dela knew exactly where their things were, as she had worked the very same cloakroom four years ago. She glanced back at Nathaniel, who was staring worriedly at the entrance to the club itself.

*'I could get our things quicker myself* she thought, then her thoughts sunk in and she went into action mode. Dela vaulted the counter and ignoring the girl's wail of f-worded objections, ran into the cloakroom, located their stuff and scrambled back over the counter into Nathaniel's urgent, waiting arms.

There was no time for self-congratulation as Nathaniel pulled her towards the exit and out on to the dark, drizzling streets of London again. They were confronted by another crowd of people and an ambulance and crew treating someone on the pavement. Nathaniel and Dela had no time for morbid curiosity because that killed the cat. No, they ran, pulling on their coats as they did to keep out the chill night air and rain. They made it to the end of the building without signs of pursuit and Nathaniel hauled them to a stop at the entrance to a dark alleyway that ran down the side of the club.

"What's down here?" Nathaniel shouted, "Does it go anywhere?"

"Yes, if you follow it along to the left it eventually comes out by the shopping parade," Dela breathlessly replied.

"Come on then, beautiful," Nathaniel smiled in the lamplight and reached out his hand to her. Dela took his hand with a flush of love that spread like a bushfire from her head to her chest.

Nathaniel led her down the alleyway, which was lined with wheelie-bins and old pallets. It transversed the side of the club and came out into a wider road. Another alley blocked by two bollards lead off to the right, while a road went in the other direction. It was marked with double yellow lines and was used by the brewery lorries to deliver booze to the club. The road went on behind the clubs and neighbouring shops to a main road quite a distance ahead.

"That's where we want to go!" Dela pointed along the dark shadows to a well-concealed alleyway a quarter of the way down the road. "That'll lead us to the parade."

"Let's not dawdle, old girl," Nathaniel urged cheerfully and led the way towards the dark alleyway.

"Hey! Less of the old!" Dela replied.

Nathaniel chuckled, mainly in relief that they had somehow evaded Merline and certain death for a little while longer at least.

"Hey!" Dela grabbed his arm.

"You okay?" Nathaniel asked, taking her in his arms.

"Yeah. It's just I thought we wouldn't get out of that place alive, you know?" Dela's voice wavered a little for the first time since they had met.

"It's okay, it's okay. I love you. It's okay." Dela was shaking, so Nathaniel pulled her even closer and held her tight in the dark back street.

"Well, this is a sweet fucking Kodak moment!"

Dela and Nathaniel span in surprise as two shadowy figures emerged from the dark alleyway. The first tall figure ignited a lighter and lit a cigarette, the dull glow showing his features for a brief instant.

"Tee! What the fuck do you want?" Dela swore at the first cigarette-smoking figure.

Both stepped into the semi-light so Dela and Nathaniel could see the man who spoke was a six-foot plus black man. His companion was white, just as tall, but leaner.

"Now is that any way to greet an old friend?" Nathaniel could just about make out the smirk on the man's face.

"Don't kid yourself Tee, you ain't no-one's friend. You're just a user," Dela retaliated.

"Talking of friends, who's this cunt?" Tee's lanky companion asked, pointing a long finger at Nathaniel.

"Dela's latest trick I bet. Sucks dick like a porn queen doesn't she, mate?" Tee goaded with a thick chuckle.

"Look, I don't know who you are nor do I care, but Dela and I are in a bit of a hurry, so if you can step aside we'll be on our way." Nathaniel's words were strong and brave, but delivered with his Queen's English crisp accent made even Dela cringe a little.

"Consorting with the gentry now, eh, Dela?" Tee turned from talking to her to stare at Nathaniel. "I bet you pay megabucks to fuck her arse you rich tosser, something I used to get for free!"

"Dela, we don't have time for this. Who are these people?" Nathaniel for the fist time since she had met him sounded soulfully angry.

"That's Tee. His real name is Gabriel."

"Hey, shut the fuck up, bitch!" Tee-Gabriel spat, his companion just sniggered.

"Gabriel and I went out for a while, until he tried to get me hooked on smack so he could put me on a street corner somewhere and watch the cash roll in. I got wise, I'm my own woman and he's just a pathetic low life, small time drug-pusher and petty thief with an acorn dick."

"That's all I needed to know." Nathaniel swung round from looking at Dela and landed a punch square on Tee's nose, sending blood spraying everywhere.

"Go Nat!" Dela clapped her hands together in school playground glee as Tee was sent sprawling to the pavement.

Victory was short-lived as a signet ring punch to the side of Nathaniel's left cheek consigned him to the pavement also. Tall Dave moved to stand over Nathaniel, legs apart, smiling from the sweet punch. So Dela's scissors-kick to the bollocks was a bit of a surprise. Tall Dave crumpled like a soufflé taken out of the oven too early. Dela helped the bleeding Nathaniel to his feet, grabbed the bags and had time to kick Tee in the ribs before they disappeared down the dark alleyway to safety.

"Da fucker bloke ma dose," Tee spat blood on the wet pavement as he pressed two snotty tissues he found in his pocket to his broken nose.

Tall Dave exhaled loudly, not for the first time as he sat, back to the wall, on the wet pavement, his legs drawn up to his chest in agony.

"Your nose! You're worried about your fucking hooter? That whore of yours just kicked my plums up my fucking arse!" Dave shouted at his companion, even though it sent more waves of agony to his lower abdomen. Nathaniel and Dela had been gone at least ten minutes and the two drug-pushers were still recovering.

"Fuck off!" Tee replied, dabbing at his tender nose.

"I don't think I can anymore," and despite their harsh words and wounded states, they both laughed.

"Someone's coming," Tee whispered.

Tall Dave held his breath and grimaced as he pushed himself up against the alleyway.

Unseen female footsteps approached the alleyway and, like before, but slightly more hesitantly, they emerged from the shadows. A woman approached wearing sunglasses regardless of the time of night and the annoying cold drizzle.

"Stop right there, bitch!" Tee called out menacingly.

"Have you seen Dela Robinson or a man called Nathaniel Le Meuille?" the woman asked in a gruff voice.

"Hey! I know you, you're Dela's friend Merline!" Tee replied, recognising her despite the unnecessary sunglasses.

"Yes, have you seen her?"

"Yeah, you could say that," Tall Dave muttered.

"Yeah, and we're gonna fuck the shit outta her next time we see her! But as you're here we'll take it out on you first as foreplay 'til we catch her and her bloke!" Tee stated with evil intent.

"Then come and get it" Merline replied, pulling down and stepping out of her white g-string.

Tee and Dave exchanged bemused glances, this was turning into one weird night. They looked back at Merline, who had let her g-string fall to the wet pavement and pulled up her skirt, her hand reaching down to play between her legs.

"We haven't taken some of our own shit without remembering it have we?" Tall Dave asked, feeling nervous and not in the mood for sex.

"We only sell it; fuck, bitch you're asking for it," Tee shouted as he undid his zip and stalked towards her.

Merline smiled as he approached and as he pulled his semi-erect penis from his zip she fell to her knees to meet him.

"That's it girl, assume the position." Tee grabbed the back of Merline's head and thrust his cock into her open mouth.

"Suck my cock, bitch!" Tee sneered with delight, but in reality his helmet hardly tickled the back of her throat.

"Is she good?" Dave asked, rubbing his lower abdomen in a vain attempt to clear the pain.

"Yeah," Tee nodded, "but she's got a hot gob, must have been eating a Vindaloo before she came out!"

Tee laughed, Tall Dave laughed, Merline spat something onto the gravel and laughed. Tee froze in cold shock. Tall Dave coughed and Merline continued to laugh, Tee's bodily fluids dripping from her mouth.

Tee staggered back, Tall Dave swallowed down his own bile and Merline spat blood and laughed louder.

Tee looked down and screamed, while Tall Dave lost the fight in his throat with his Big Mac Meal and Merline rose to her feet.

Tee stared at the blood jetting from his groin as he continued screaming. Tall Dave couldn't hear the screams as he was doubled-up vomiting; Merline just laughed and stepped on Tee's bitten off penis as she closed in on him.

Tee's scream died in his throat, Tall Dave's throat was full of vomit, and Merline's finger nails held the shredded remains of Tee's throat.

Tall Dave was coughing and spitting bile as he looked over to see Tee's dead body come crashing down on to the wet pavement with a squelch. Dave tried to gasp for air as Merline approached where he was on his hands and knees in vomit. His stomach, chest and throat were wracked with pain and he could not summon the strength to rise as he saw Merline approach through his tear-clogged eyes. All he could do was crawl, the cold damp pavement sucking the heat out of his tensed fingers. He managed to get halfway into the alleyway when he noticed a pair of ladies' stilettos by the left hand side of his head.

Tall Dave's heart sank. He was a dead man and he would come to a 'bad end' just like his 'old dear' had prophesised years ago. He didn't want to look up at the killer queen, he didn't want to look death in the face.

Suddenly he didn't have much choice in the matter as Merline grabbed him by the hair and pulled him up onto his knees. She savagely jerked his head back so he faced her. The rain fell into his face, washing the tears from his eyes and vomit from his chin.

Merline's face loomed down at him, an evil grin on her countenance. Her face lowered to his level until they were only inches apart. Dave couldn't stand it any more and closed his eyes and waited for death.

"Keep up the good work," she hissed. She let go of his hair and Dave fell backwards against the slick alleyway wall. Dave crumpled to a panting heap as the woman who had murdered Tee just slipped away into the cover of the night.

Tall Dave lay panting on the wet pavement as the heavens opened and the rain pounded off everything. The hard rain stung his eyes, but Dave was glad, if he could feel pain he was still alive. Somehow he managed to push himself up and staggered off down the back road, trying not to glance at Tee's mutilated corpse.

"Now what?" Dela shouted over the sound of the thunderstorm that was drenching them as they walked briskly down the street by the parade of shops near her flat.

Nathaniel said nothing, but walked along in front with his head lowered, deep in thought. They couldn't stay here, in fact anywhere in London seemed dangerous.

"Hey!" Dela jumped in front of him and halted his train of thought and his movement. "What do we do now, where can we go to escape my possessed best friend, the Demon Lords of Hell and all their fucking minions?" Dela shouted at him. She was tired of running, tired of fighting and tired of being scared.

"I'm thinking, Dela." He laid one hand on her soggy shoulder and moved past her.

"Well, can you think a little faster, like before we both get killed?" she asked, walking beside him now.

"If you want to live, you must give me all the time and space I need, because if I make a hasty move …" he slammed his fist into his palm, "oblivion and eternal damnation follow!"

Dela breathed hard through her nose as the rain dripped off it. "Point taken," she nodded, "take all the time you need."

"Do you know where we can get a taxi this time of night?" he asked gravely.

"Yeah. By the station. Why? Where we going?"

"Not here, the demonic one has spies amongst the creatures of the night and their foul carrion." He took her arm. "Which way?"

"A couple of streets this way," Dela pointed across a zebra crossing.

"Let's go with all haste and I'll explain when I deem it safe. Come on."

Merline's glowing eyes watched as Dela and Nathaniel climbed into the only taxi outside the tube station. She ducked into a shop doorway as the taxi swung round and headed into the dark stormy London night.

The Merline/Ashmodaios, demon/human smiled an evil grin. Even though the pair had escaped again, the Demon Lord hadn't had so much fun for a hundred years. He would soon find their trail again, but as he was in this human form and had nothing else to do he decided to cause a little mischief while he could.

"I just wish it would cease raining, it stings the eyes." Merline laughed throatily and headed down the street, whistling a thirteenth century Greek melody.

"So, have you decided what our next move is yet?" Dela asked in the taxi. "No pressure," she added raising her hand, palms open to placate him.

"Well, we're heading for Trafalgar Square." Nathaniel sighed, "and then we're going to catch the night bus back to my house."

"The demon might figure that out," she whispered, "and set an ambush."

"I know, but I want to examine that disc on my computer and read through my ancestors' grimoire again."

"Eh?"

"The demon book," Nathaniel explained helpfully.

"Oh! Den what?"

"Well, we'll wait 'til first light before returning to the house and be as quick as possible." Nathaniel nodded towards the taxi driver, "I'll tell you more then."

"Okay, and I can finally get into some decent dry clothes."

"And have a fried breakfast in a little café I know." Nathaniel smiled at the thought of sizzling bacon. "They do the yummiest Baklava's there!"

"I have no idea what a Baklava is, but yummy sells it to me," Dela took his hand and they watched the world go by.

Merline walked down a few side streets, crossing black cats and walking on the cracks of the pavement for jollies.

"Ah, they don't make like this any more" he/she said to itself and it gazed across the road at a three hundred year old Catholic church.

Merline watched from behind a row of parked cars as a figure exited the vestry door and turned to lock the door after himself. It was the local priest locking up after a midnight mass, aching for his bed which even God couldn't keep him from.

"No, but a demon might," Merline whispered, reading the priest's mind.

Merline moved towards the priest who was trying to raise an umbrella against the pounding rain.

"Lead us not into temptation," Merline chuckled and quickened her pace to intercept the black clad man-of-the-cloth.

The taxi dropped them off on the northern side of Trafalgar Square and Nathaniel led Dela across the road into the square itself. A man was selling burgers and chips and with an agreeing nod they both made a bee-line for it.

Five minutes later they were munching their way through two greasy burgers with all the trimmings as they walked across the breadth of the square. The rain had slowed to a drizzle and they both could not remember eating a more fulfilling meal than the fat-filled burgers. By the time they had made it to their bus stop near Charing Cross station, they had wolfed down their burgers and wiped their greasy chops on their saturated sleeves.

In spite of the danger and their grim, predicament, they both looked at each other like naughty school children that had V-signed the teacher and got away with it unseen. Nathaniel checked the timetable, wiping rivulets of rain water from its glass to see that they had a quarter of an hour's wait until the bus was due to arrive.

"So," Nathaniel said, taking her in his arms for warmth, "Where shall we go on holiday when this is all over?"

"Somewhere hot." Dela frowned, "Will this ever be over?"

"Do horses run on courses? Now Crete is nice this time of year, hot sun, beaches and cheep beer."

"So's Antigua , hotter sun, better beaches, rum. A woman like me could go for a man who took her away to Antigua for a fortnight."

"I've always dreamt of going to Egypt, all those wonders to see, the Nile, the pyramids, the valley of the Kings."

"Yes, but you're missing one special ingredient, man, I'll be in Antigua." Dela laughed and Nathaniel crushed her to him in an attempt to playfully shut her up.

"Cairo," he continued.

"Antigua," she retorted.

"The Valley of the Kings."

"Rum."

"The Sphinx."

"Hot sticky nights with me."

"Antigua," he conceded.

"Antigua," Dela laughed, kissing his cold wet lips with a passion.

"Say it!"

"I can't!"

"Say it!" Merline hissed as she ground her pubic bone against his lower abdomen as she fucked the priest in the female dominant position.

"I'm a priest!" the sweaty forty year old Catholic abstinent Father pleaded.

"And I'm Mary, mother of Joseph, fucking say it and I'll suck the seed from your loins into my mouth," Merline smiled wickedly.

"But," the priest sweated, nearly on the brink of religious oblivion.

Merline lowered herself down and pressed her breasts against his pigeon chest, "Say it for me only, no one else will hear, not even God."

"I love Satan," the priest mumbled.

"I can't hear you," Merline chided, increasing her bouncing pace on the priest's penis.

"I love Satan," he said, "I love Satan," he shouted.

"Oh, you say the sweetest things," Merline chuckled and hoisted herself off the priest's penis just before it shot his load over his own tummy and chest.

"What! Where are you going?" the astounded priest asked, aghast at the mess she had left him in.

"I've heard all I needed to hear Priest," Merline smiled as he gathered his clothes.

"What I did, I deserve more," Father Shaw spluttered, "I gave you my soul."

"I know, and now I must be leaving, ta-ta." Merline pulled on her skirt and blouse and went to leave the priest's bedroom.

"But when will I see you again?"

"Very soon Father, very soon," and with a wild laugh she left the fallen priest and his shrivelled penis behind. Now back to the chase!

# CHAPTER 6

As dawn broke Nathaniel and Dela crept through the gate of Nathaniel's house and through the secluded garden to the back door.

Dela had a peek through the kitchen window and Nathaniel tried the back door; it was still locked. He pulled out his keys as Dela returned, shaking her head. She had seen nothing untoward in the kitchen.

Nathaniel gingerly unlocked the back door with a click. A shiver ran down his back, it was still quite cold in the garden, as the unseasonal winter sun did not touch the garden until lunchtime.

As they opened the door, they could see down the hall to the front door, where a pile of mail lay, all torn open. Opening the door wider they crept in. The house, apart from their footfalls, was entirely silent. They passed the arched entrance to the kitchen, a few kitchen implements lay on the floor, some of the drawers and cupboards were open. Nathaniel bent down and collected a meat cleaver for himself and handed a sharp carving knife to Dela.

They moved on into the hall. The living room and dining room doors were open, no sound emanated from either. A quick peek into each revealed no hidden dangers, only more signs of vandalism. They moved to the stairs, through a dusty clouded beam of sunlight shining through the small window in the front door. Nathaniel put his foot on the first step, resulting in a loud creak.

"Oh, sod this!" he muttered under his breath, then ran screaming up the stairs, brandishing the shining meat cleaver above his head.

Dela was left rooted to the spot at the foot of the stairs, her mouth agape and her breath gone. Dela inhaled at last as

Nathaniel's wild yells and foot thuds echoed around the house. Tightening her grip on the knife, she proceeded up the stairs at a fast trot after her deranged lover. Halfway up Dela saw and heard Nathaniel rush across the landing from the direction he had come, still screaming, still waving the cleaver like a tomahawk. When she hopped on to the landing she saw Nathaniel leaning up against the bathroom door frame, panting, the cleaver slack at his side.

"You okay?" Dela asked, concerned. Her eyes darted around the open doorways.

"Bit … knackered, … that's all," he wheezed, trying to catch his breath.

"Good," Dela said, and walked up to him. "What the fuck do you think you were doing, charging in like fucking Rambo? What if there had been a fucking demon hiding up here?" she shouted.

Nathaniel winced at her verbal attack. "Look, it's my house. I'm not going to creep around like some intruder. Anyway, the coast's clear."

"I understand that, but we're a fucking team, Nat," Dela's voice softened a little, "please tell me next time you're going to do something numb-fuckingly stupid."

"Okay, I promise," he nodded. "Now please stop shouting at me!"

"Is upstairs trashed as well?"

"If you mean ransacked, yes," Nathaniel answered, correcting her English.

Dela snorted at him, "and the book, is it safe?"

"The secret room remains concealed, so let's hope so," Nathaniel looked concerned. "Let's go and have a look, together."

"Better," she smiled and hand in hand they walked into his ruined study. A bottle of whisky protruded from the remains of

Nathaniel's computer terminal and the keyboard was snapped in half.

Nathaniel moved towards the wall and bent down and righted his leather-bound armchair which blocked the entrance to his hidden room. Nathaniel reached up to trigger the secret door mechanism, but found Dela's hand was already there, pushing the moose's left eye.

"Well remembered," Nathaniel complimented, and they both turned to watch the secret door swing in. Nathaniel pushed the door in further and entered his secret sanctuary with Dela close on his heels. To their relief, the book was still there, bathed in the blue glow of a single light bulb.

"Thank heavens it's still safe!" Nathaniel sighed in relief, moving into the small hidden room. Dela followed him, the lectern, the circle, the chest all there as before.

"So, we're taking the book outta here, is that wise? Ain't it protected by God or somefin here?"

"Yes, but if they set fire to the house a holy circle will be of no use. No, we must take it with us and protect it with our lives," Nathaniel replied in earnest.

"I was worried you were gonna say something like that, but will we be able to protect it from the Demon Lord?" Dela asked, sounding more like Nathaniel each hour she spent in his company.

"We must have righteous hearts Dela, and I have a little bit of a back-up plan," Nathaniel smiled and moved over to the chest.

"What's that then? You got a Uzi full of silver bullet in dere or somefin?" Dela mocked in her Caribbean tones.

"No, but you're on the right-ish road." Nathaniel opened the chest and began rooting through the things inside.

"Ah! Here we go!" Nathaniel pulled a long thin object wrapped in a green cloth from the chest and began to unwrap it.

"What's that in there? A shotgun?"

"No, it's the scabbard of Sir Garath Le Meuille, the first King's Paladin," Nathaniel replied with hushed reverence as he unwrapped the ancient artefact.

"Oh," Dela replied bemused, "wouldn't it be of more use with a sword or something in it?"

"Yes, it would, but the Paladin's Holy Sword was lost over fifty years ago," Nathaniel nodded, "But the scabbard has great protective powers and will radiate a protective holy aura around the book if kept at close proximity."

"I feel safer already," Dela whispered to her chest.

Nathaniel closed the chest and rose, dusting off the weathered leather scabbard.

"It looks a bit of a scabby scabbard, Nat," Dela said, not convinced it was of any use at all.

"And so it should!" Nathaniel replied sharply, "This scabbard was made in Bethlehem during the Crusades; it and the holy sword it once held was given to Sir Garath by King Richard the Lionheart himself."

"Nice story," Dela said, just for something to say, but Nathaniel seemed somewhere else and wasn't listening.

"The sword held monstrous power over the forces of darkness," Nathaniel continued, "the sword tip was blessed with holy water from the Holy Grail itself and such a weapon England has not seen since Excalibur returned to the lake." Nathaniel closed his eyes and could almost feel the heat of the battle outside the gates of Jerusalem, where the sword and Sir Garath won such renown.

"There on that holy soil did Garath Le Meuille save King Richard from deadly peril summoned from the netherworlds. There he was knighted and proclaimed King's Paladin and his humble sword blessed eternally." Nathaniel's head fell on to his chest and he was silent.

Dela stared at Nathaniel in awe, sensing now the blood of heroes surging through her saviour's veins. Countless generations of holy warriors, defending King and country against the threat of ancient evil. For the first time in many years Dela felt small and not in control of her own destiny.

"Touch it," Nathaniel said in a soft voice, offering up the scabbard to Dela.

"Why?"

"Trust me," he whispered intensely.

Dela shrugged, and grabbed the scabbard in between Nathaniel's two hands. At first she stared at Nathaniel, a bemused look on her face. Nathaniel just smiled reassuringly at her. Dela was about to speak and let go of the scabbard when she felt a vibration in the ancient artefact that started to flow pleasantly up her arm. Dela's mouth slowly dropped open as she could hear faint whispers emanating from all corners of the room. She stared again at Nathaniel in wonder now.

"Listen," he mouthed to her, and she did.

Closing her eyes in concentration, the scattered disjointed voices rose in volume. It seemed to her that the voices were saying or chanting in perfect rhyme, in some ancient language Dela did not understand. Dela suddenly realised that she wasn't frightened, but knew she should be. She opened her eyes and let go of the scabbard. The voices then faded slowly from her head, but a warm, safe glow remained deep inside her chest.

"Quick! Tell me what you heard or felt?" Nathaniel asked quickly.

Dela shook her head. "I dunno, I felt warm and safe and I heard the most beautiful voices."

"You heard the song of the Saints," Nathaniel stated, "that's fantastic!"

"It felt good, but what does it mean?"

"It means you have a righteous soul," Nathaniel explained.

"Eh?"

"Only the purest souls hear the song of the Saints. It means you're a good person, Dela. This scabbard and the sword it once held were blessed with the strength of God himself. The scabbard was made in the place of Jesus's birth, the sword was blessed with holy water from the cup of Christ." Nathaniel exhaled trying to get his point across.

"But what does it all mean? I'm a masseuse, not a nun!"

"You heard the song, you didn't come to me by luck, you were born to help me and share my quest. The fight against the forces of evil is on-going, millennia old, people don't just join the fight they are born to it. Destiny brought us together and together we will fight the Demon Lord and his minions, until they or we are vanquished!"

Dela wanted to laugh at him and tell him he was being ridiculous, but she could see the glint in his watery blue eyes and she had heard the song of the Saints.

"We better get a move on, eh? Merline or something else evil could turn up at any second," Dela said, deflecting the conversation away from what Nathaniel had just revealed to her. She wasn't special, she was plain old Dela who did topless massages, nearly got into heavy drugs, nearly got on the game. These were not the actions of a saint or crusader against evil, she was just an ordinary person, like millions of ordinary people all over the world.

"Okay, you're right," Nathaniel finally spoke. "Look, you stay here and I'll pop down to the shed to get a few things. I won't be long."

They left the room after Nathaniel had collected the grimoire from the pedestal. Nathaniel passed the scabbard and book to Dela as he closed and sealed the secret door again. Dela took both objects with trepidation, but she did not hear a song or feel no vibration this time.

Nathaniel saw her look and winked, "Don't worry, you only hear the song of the Saints once. Back in a sec."

Dela watched him race from the room and heard his footsteps thunder downstairs. Putting the book and scabbard reverently down on a chair together, Dela went over to the only window in the room. She peeked through the net curtains down on to the street below – no one was about. Across the way from the house stood an ancient, tall oak tree and in its branches sat a black bird of some kind. Dela was no twitcher. The bird (a rook) was staring straight at her, not looking anywhere but directly at her. Its beady eyes seemed to stare straight into her soul and a phrase that Nat had said earlier sprang to mind: "Demon Lord and his minions."

Dela shivered and blinked and the rook gave a squawk and flew away.

Dela was still looking out of the window when Nathaniel returned with a fishing tackle box, a catch net and a rod in a cover, fixed with ties.

"I think we should get our arses out of here as soon as possible," Dela said gravely, thinking of the Rook.

"You're right. Someone or something could return here at any time," Nathaniel nodded in agreement.

"What's with the fishing gear?"

"Aha!" Nathaniel cried aloud, his right index finger raised to the ceiling. "Just a little decoy. Somewhere to hide the scabbard and the book."

"Okay, but let's hurry. I don't feel safe here."

"The sad thing is, this is my home and I don't feel safe here either." Nathaniel frowned.

Dela walked slowly up to him and took him in her arms and they clung to each other for twenty or so seconds. They clung to each other because both their worlds had been turned upside down and nothing was solid, normal or real any more. Both their homes had been invaded and tainted by evil, they had nowhere to rest and nowhere safe to stay. They had to keep moving now and try and keep ahead of the Demon Lord that pursued them.

Fifteen minutes later with a change of pants and socks Nathaniel and Dela were sitting in Piggies Sandwich Bar. They had found their appetites and had both polished off two Fat-Boy Specials of sausage, eggs, beans, black puddings, fried bread, mushrooms, tomatoes, bacon and tea.

"You'se ready for your Baklava yet, Nathaniel?" Nickos asked from behind his counter.

"Give us five mins, eh, Nickos?" Nathaniel replied to the friendly café owner.

"Okey-dokey Boss," Nickos stated as he busied himself cutting up tomatoes.

"This one of your regular haunts then?" Dela asked, sipping at the top of her tea.

"Yeah. This and the Royal Oak down the road are my hiding places." Nathaniel wiped his bean sauce with the last of his fried bread and popped it into his mouth.

"Hiding from what?" Dela's voice lowered to a whisper, "demons?"

"No!" he chuckled, "Cordelia!"

"Nice," Dela smiled. "So now what, where do we go? We're homeless!"

"Up to Paddington Station to catch a train to Worcester," Nathaniel replied, wiping his mouth with a napkin.

"We're gonna check out that clinic, right?" Dela clicked her fingers and pointed at Nathaniel.

"Eventually, and we know Telal lived in Tewkesbury and my grandmother lives near Cheltenham, so we'll have somewhere to hide out too. Does that sound like a plan?"

"Yep."

"Nickos, we're ready for pudding," he said loudly to the man behind the counter.

"Okey-dokey" and Nickos brought two plates of Baklava for Dela and Nathaniel. "Enjoy my good friend, yes?" Nickos grabbed Nathaniel's shoulder with one hand.

"Efh-har-estoo" Nathaniel thanked him in Greek.

"No problem," Nickos beamed, "enjoy."

Dela and Nathaniel tucked in as the café owner watched over them.

"That's lovely." Dela beamed, licking her lips.

"I'm glad," Nickos said hand on heart. "You take care of this lovely woman, Nathaniel, she loves my cooking and isn't a fucking bitch like your old girlfriend, eh?"

Dela laughed out loud and Nathaniel looked down at his plate in embarrassment.

Just then a customer walked up to the counter to order and Nickos left to tend to him and save Nathaniel any further embarrassment.

Just after eleven they caught a slow train to Waterloo.

"What next, when we reach Waterloo?" Dela asked, as she stared out the window/door of the old slam-door train they were travelling in. The train slowed on its arrival at Vauxhall Station.

"Oh, we just need to get the Northern Line to Embankment, then the District Line goes straight to Paddington. Not a problem," said Nathaniel, smiling as today had gone completely to plan so far.

"I see a problem," Dela hissed, grabbing his arm in a pinching grip as she stared out the window and back down the platform.

Nathaniel, who had been facing forward, craned his neck and stared back out the grimy window to where Dela's eyes bulged. He just glimpsed Dela's demon-possessed friend Merline step up into the carriage right behind theirs.

"Let's move," Nathaniel urged, collecting their bags and fishing gear from the luggage rack.

They opened the connecting door between their carriage and the next and slammed the door behind them. They found themselves in a passage that led to the left hand side of the carriage past some First Class carriages. Only one carriage remained in front of them and Merline would be on them before they would reach Waterloo.

"Quick! In here!" Nathaniel opened the door of a toilet and pulled Dela inside. Dela locked the door behind them.

"What now?" Dela asked nervously.

Nathanial was pulling at the top of his shirt, lifting a chain and whistle that lay there.

"What're you doing with that?"

"Calling for reinforcements," Nathaniel stated as he put the long silver whistle to his lips and blew.

"Cerberus?" Dela asked.

Nathaniel nodded.

"Will he be here in time to help us?"

"I dunno, sshh!" Nathaniel blew on to his vertical forefinger, pressed to his lips.

The Merline/Demon Lord had got on to the right train; she sensed it. The King's Paladin and his whore were on the train somewhere. She moved along her carriage into an identical one ahead, moving along the central path between the seats.

She came to the last set of empty seats and sat down. The seat still felt warm and as she breathed in through her nose she could smell the scent of the good Paladin and tainted smell of his bitch's cunt. She closed her eyes and smiled, soon she would be smelling the sweet coppery funk of their blood.

Using her arms to lift her from the seat she pushed through the next brace of doors into an old First Class carriage. This smelt of disinfectant, the smallest trace of urine and the stench of new money. Merline moved along past the First Class carriage as a Eurostar train flashed past on her left through the cloudy windows.

Nathaniel slid back the cloth that covered the blessed scabbard and touched the holy relic to the door. They heard someone open a door and walk past, but no one tried to enter the "engaged" toilet. The window of the toilet was made of frosted glass and they did not know that they were entering Waterloo

Station until they heard the slow squeal of brakes and the light outside the small window grow darker.

"We're coming in to the platform, get ready to move." Nathaniel's hand went to the lock on the toilet door.

Nathaniel eased the bolt, painfully and slowly across and opened the door slightly. The driver of the train put the brakes to full and the train stopped on Platform Two.

Nathaniel heard someone approach and closed and locked the door again. They could hear the sound of doors being opened and people leaving the train. Nathaniel waited a couple of minutes for most of the passengers to alight, then opened the door again. The corridor was empty so he peeked his head out and looked from side to side, nothing. Grabbing the fishing gear and one of the bags, he left the toilet, with Dela similarly burdened and following close behind.

They came up to the first compartment which had both the connecting and outside door closed. Nathaniel ignored this one trying to find a compartment with both doors open so he would not have to make any noise or attract any unwanted attention his way. The next First Class carriage was ideal as both sets of doors were open.

Nathaniel held up his hand for Dela to wait and he crept forward and peeked quickly out of the carriage door. He saw her at once, but luckily Merline was looking the other way, watching a crowd of disappearing passengers.

"Get back," Nathaniel whisper-hissed, "she's waiting for us."

"Let's hide in the bog 'til she goes," Dela said as they bundled back into the corridor of the First Class carriage.

"No, she'll find us eventually and we would be trapped. No, we need another way off the train. We need a bit of parallel thinking," Nathaniel huffed, grabbing his jaw with his hand.

"What's that?"

"Thinking laterally." Nathaniel looked at Dela's blank face. "Sideways thinking," he added as explanation.

"Why don't we climb out of this train into that train beside us? Is that enough sidewards thinking for you, Nat?"

Nathaniel looked at Dela then looked at the train on the adjacent track on Platform Three in surprise. Then a huge smile covered his countenance. Nathaniel grabbed both sides of Dela's head and kissed her hard and fast on the lips.

"You're a genius!"

"Takes one to know one. Come on, how are we getting across?" Dela had the plan but not all the logistics worked out.

"Out the door." Nathaniel indicated the door next to him. "We push it open and open the door on the other side and scramble through somehow."

"What if the train pulls out?" Dela asked as he flung open the door.

"We fall," he responded. "Here, take the bags and scabbard, I'm going across."

Luckily for them the other train was almost empty, as it was due out of London at that time and hidden underneath the control room boxes above the platforms. Another lucky break was that the opposite door on the other train was nearly adjacent to theirs.

Nathaniel opened the door, holding on to it with his left hand. He stepped down on to the door's step and reached across for the handle of the other door.

Nathaniel, and Dela for that matter, drew in a sharp-intake of breath as his left foot slipped an inch and his whole body wobbled for a couple of seconds. Nathaniel regained his balance by grabbing hold of the opposite door knob to steady himself. Not wasting any time, he opened the door across the other open door and hauled himself into the empty carriage opposite.

"Quickly, throw the gear across," Nathaniel ordered as he went to clap his hands for urgency, but stopped himself because of the noise it would make.

Dela, with a glance to her right down the corridor, started by handing over the scabbard which Nathaniel easily grabbed and placed on to the seat next to him. He had to lean out for the fishing box, then stepped back as Dela threw their rucksacks over.

Finally, only Dela was left and Nathaniel stepped down and reached a hand across for her. A whistle blew somewhere next to Nathaniel's train on Platform Three. Dela took another nervous glance along the corridor and stepped down and reached for Nathaniel. He took her forearm and with a trusting glance into each other's eyes, he pulled her into his arms. They bundled themselves into the carriage and Dela sat down on to the seat and gathered their gear, as Nathaniel pulled the door shut, which, in turn, slammed the other door as well.

"We made it," Dela said from her seat.

"Don't count your chickens yet, my dear," Nathaniel warned as the whistle blew on Platform Three again.

Nathaniel sat down just as the train started to move off out of the station. Then the screaming started and for a second they thought it was the sound of the train's whistle, then cried out in terror as Merline's hands and face appeared at the open window of the train. All they could do was fall back on their seats as Merline's face, lips drawn back in a vicious snarl, reached for Dela.

Nathaniel scrambled on the floor for the scabbard, but as he grabbed for it the train lurched and it rolled from his grasp under the seat. Merline's fingers grabbed Dela's collar and pulled her towards her open mouth.

Forgetting the scabbard, Nathaniel lunged for the window in order to aid Dela. Merline let go of the door and Dela banged into the side of the carriage door, as the demon-possessed woman used her to stop her falling on to the track. With her now free hand she fended off Nathaniel with a light slap that sent him sprawling on to the seat, from which he overbalanced on to the floor.

Dela hung on to the luggage rack for dear life and Merline turned her face and spare hand towards her eyes.

A sudden shadow appeared beside Dela, with a roar and the vice-like grip of the demon was gone. The demon screamed, as Cerberus head-butted the possessed woman out of the window. Cerberus' bark was deafening as Merline slipped down and under the trains. The Demon Lord's eyes widened in terror a millisecond before the wheels of the trains ran across her neck, severing it from her body. At last Merline's soul was free, but hell's fire consumed her body and Ashmodaios' spirit fled back to Gehenna.

Dela sat down on her seat in shock and Nathaniel had just about sat up when Cerberus jumped on him and saturated his face with slimy licks.

"Cerberus!" Dela gasped in delight to see the big hell-hound.

"I'm glad to see you too mate, but get off me will you?" Nathaniel asked, ruffling the dog's fur in delight at seeing his companion again.

Luckily, there had been a change over in the control boxes and no passengers, except one six year old boy, had seen what had transpired.

The train chugged on to Clapham Junction where Dela, Nathaniel and Cerberus alighted and transferred on to a train to Victoria Station. There they squeezed on to a District Line tube to Paddington Station, their third main line London railway station of the day.

They grabbed some food at Burger King as they had half an hour until the next Cotswold Express to Worcester. They stood against a pillar as Cerberus chomped his way through three king-sized burgers and buns.

"So, we've managed to banish Ashmodaios again, at least for another three days, eh?" Dela said, sticking three chips into her mouth.

"Sssh, I've told you before, it's not good to mention his name in such a crowded place," Nathaniel harshly rebuked her.

"Nobody around here knows what's going on, lighten up Nat!"

"The minions of the underworld are everywhere, Dela," Nathaniel whispered, "and the weak-minded with corruptible souls can easily be swayed by the servants of the dark abyss."

"Now you're scaring me!"

"Good! Just because we've out-witted the Demon Lord so far, doesn't mean we can be complacent. Watch every shadow, check out every nocturnal noise, be vigilant against the ways of darkness, let your heart be your sword and your soul your shield against the minions of the underworld." Nathaniel's whispered tones trailed off and it seemed to Dela that he was somewhere else for a moment or two.

"That sounds like part of a speech or something, is it in your family's book?"

"No, it's something my father said to me a fortnight before he died."

Just then Cerberus barked and looked skywards towards the electronic timetables. Their train was now ready for boarding at Platform Five.

The train journey was a pleasant relief compared with their earlier journey. They found a pair of facing seats with a table in-between like a booth, near to the buffet car. Cerberus was somehow curled and crammed beneath the table and their feet.

Nathaniel let Dela sleep as he watched the landscape fly past, his eyes darting from the wet green-brown fields and woods to his sleeping companion. For the first time in days it seemed his thoughts were his own and they dwelt on the dark dangers that faced them. He had been in danger and had confrontations with dark forces before, but this was the ultimate end game. This was diabolical evil: Ashmodaios the Demon Lord of Hell, whom he had managed to banish by luck and a little knowledge twice from this plane of existence. One more time and the Demon Lord would be banished for three hundred and thirty-three years. Ashmodaios had been caught by surprise on their first encounter, and been unlucky on his second attempt in Merline's body. Nathaniel would make sure that there would not be a third time. Nathaniel felt the weight of generations of his ancestors on his shoulders, would he live up to their deeds? Would he be able to protect Dela and Cerberus, and stay alive himself to thwart the Demon Lord's plans? If he were to die, who would continue the battle? – "The Society" maybe?

Rummaging in his wallet, he found Mrs Dawson's card and noted the P.O. Box address on the reverse. Taking a pad from his holdall he began writing a letter as Cerberus and Dela slumbered on.

# CHAPTER 7

They arrived at Worchester Station at three o'clock. They walked from the station building into the car park and noticed that the sky was prematurely dark, full of rain clouds. They walked into town and booked into a B&B for the night. At five they headed into town and had a pizza and then a pint at a local pub.

The pub had a selection of tourist leaflets which Nathaniel almost entirely commandeered. He was leafing through one on the historic Warwick Castle, when Dela returned from the Ladies' toilet.

"Where's Cerberus?" Dela asked, sitting down in the old oak booth across the table from Nathaniel.

"Outside, answering the call of nature." In fact he had sent Cerberus out to post a letter for him.

"Oh," Dela shrugged, accepting his explanation, then snatched the handout from his grasp, "What's this all about?"

"This," Nathaniel started, snatching it back, "is a leaflet about the historic Warwick Castle." He smiled serenely back at her.

"Well, what has it got to do with us? Are we going there?" Dela leant forward and Nathaniel put the leaflet down and covered it protectively with his hands.

"No," Nathaniel shook his head, "Firstly, I was trying to uphold the façade that we are tourists and secondly, to see if any of these leaflets have useful maps of the local area."

"And do they?"

"No, we'll have to pick one up tomorrow when the shops open again."

"Or," Dela grinned wickedly, "we could go down to the petrol station at the end of this road and buy a local map there." Dela wrinkled her nose and looked smug.

"Or we could," Nathaniel pointed at her, "do that!"

"And buy some chocolate," Dela added.

"We've only just had pizza, you gannet!"

"I know, but I'm a woman. Women love chocolate, especially when they're stressed out, okay?"

"OK I get the chocolate thing," Nathaniel replied meekly.

Dela managed to laugh and so did Nathaniel nervously, as Cerberus trotted in from the garden door of the pub.

"Come on, let's get that map." Nathaniel rose grabbing his coat.

"And chocolate," Dela frowned.

"And chocolate," Nathaniel surrendered.

Cerberus had got bored and lay at the foot of the bed, asleep. While Nathaniel and Dela sat on the bed in Mrs Grimes' B&B looking at the map they had bought at the petrol station; Dela was finishing off a Bounty bar.

"Pershore isn't too far away, and we'll hire a car tomorrow and check this Fertility Clinic out and Doctor Geial." Nathaniel pointed at Pershore on the map as he spoke.

"I've got a great idea! Why don't we pose as an infertile couple and try and get in to see this Doctor Geial?" Dela suggested hopefully.

"It's too risky. I assume that this Doctor Geial has been warned that we may come and visit. No, we'll have to go into James Bond mode and try and sneak in for a look. Maybe the locals have heard rumours, or know something about the place."

"But why all the sneaking around? Why not a frontal attack?" Dela asked, getting bored with thinking before she acted, which wasn't her style at all.

"I don't want to alert the Demon Lord to our presence in this area. We must keep him off our backs for the next three days so we can devise a way of stopping him and his plan for invasion."

"Okay, you win. James Brown style it is." Dela relented, letting herself flop down onto the bed, lying next to Nathaniel.

"James 'who' style?" Nathaniel asked, picking up on her mistake.

"James Bond!"

"No, no, no. You said 'James Brown' style," Nathaniel lay down next to her, supporting his body on his right arm.

"I said 'James Bond' Nat, are you deaf?" Dela lay on her back, her blouse straining around the buttons of her chest area.

"No, you didn't!"

"I did!" Dela replied in a louder voice, poking at his ribs with one of her long fingers.

Nathaniel rolled on to her, arms either side of her head, groins pressed together. "No you did not, I distinctly heard you say 'James Brown'."

"Crap! Your ears must be full of shit, man! I said 'Bond'!" Dela said firmly, with the hint of a smile on her face.

"You're wrong!"

"Only an idiot would say 'James Brown'!"

"You said it, not me." Nathaniel smiled as he lowered himself towards her.

"You dare mate and I'll pull your bollocks off!" Dela moved one of her hands towards Nathaniel's tender bits. Nathaniel caught her wrist and pushed it to the bed.

" 'Brown'," Nathaniel said and pinned her other wrist to the bed.

"Bloody 'Bond'!" Dela hissed.

"Dela," Nathaniel smiled, lowering himself towards her pouting lips.

"What?"

"Take me to the Bridge."

Dela's face cracked up and in a flash they were kissing passionately. They slid into each other's arms and five minutes later they were having raw sex.

The day dawned cold, blue and icy and the grass made a crunch as Nathaniel and Dela crossed the grass verge to the privately owned car hire company. The place had just opened and a middle-aged man in a suit covered by a Barbour jacket was scraping the ice off a Ford Mondeo's window.

The man noticed them and stopped what he was doing. "Can I help you?"

"Yes. We would like to hire a car for the day please," Nathaniel asked, walking towards the salesman.

"Certainly. Any model in particular?" the man's gloved hand swung around slowly making their eyes follow and take in the frosty cars for hire.

"That Mondeo you're scraping off will do fine if that's okay," Nathaniel replied as he and Dela neared the man.

"No problem at all. If you'd follow me into my office I'll sort out the paperwork." The couple followed the smiling man into the nearly one-floor concrete structure. "Do you wish to pay by Visa or cash, Mister ..?"

"...Ford," Nathaniel lied quickly, wishing instantly he could have come up with a better alias, "and I'll be paying cash."

"Not a problem." The man opened his office door.

"A Ford in a Ford, eh?" the man smiled, "I bet you've heard that one before!"

"Not as often as you'd think," Nathaniel said in a quiet voice as they entered the office.

A quarter of an hour later and they were on their way to the clinic. Dela was driving, as Nathaniel had insisted, so she would have something to do this time. Nathaniel sat beside her in the passenger seat, the local maps unfolded on his lap.

"There's a wood marked on the map next to the clinic so park on the other side of that. If the map is correct we should be able to get close to the place using the wood as cover, if it's close enough."

"I heard some 'ifs' in that sentence of yours Nat," Dela stated as she slowed the car down at a T-junction.

"Well, we'll find out when we get there. If you drive past the gates first at normal speed, we'll see what is to be seen."

"Fine." Dela nodded, indicating and turning the car left.

"Do you want some music on?" Nathaniel asked after they had driven in silence for five minutes.

"As long as you don't put on any Britney Spears, I don't mind."

"Right," Nathaniel stopped, fidgeting with the CD in his pocket which he had bought with the map at the garage, and they travelled in silence for a further five minutes. On the back seat Cerberus whined softly to himself and put his paws over his eyes.

"That was it!" Nathaniel shouted as the hired car shot passed a turn-off, sign-posted with a simple sign saying 'Lords Private Clinic, No Entry and No-Through Road. For Patients and Staff Use Only.'

The road was easily missed as it was well-hidden in a large wood that they had been winging past on either side of their windows for the past five minutes.

"Do you want me to stop?"

"No, carry on, only slowly for a while, let's see what surrounds this clinic and the best way to get to it," Nathaniel replied, patting Dela's leg.

Nothing but trees were seen by Nathaniel and Dela on the same side as the turn-off for the next two minutes. Dela was about to turn the car around when the trees thinned away and farms, houses and then a small village appeared.

"There's a pub Dela, let's stop there and park in the car park." Nathaniel pointed at a pub with the sign-post of the 'Royal Oak'.

"Okey-dokey," Dela indicated and pulled into the car park which only had one green Land Rover parked in it.

"What now, Sherlock?" Dela asked as she pulled the handbrake and turned off the car's engine.

"It's too early for a pint and pork scratchings, so I suggest a brisk early morning walk, to whet our appetites."

"I knew you were going to say something stupid like that!" Dela said, shaking her head and opening her door.

In the back of the car, Cerberus woke with a wide, spittle-framed yawn.

Grabbing Dela's small rucksack with the book inside and the scabbard sticking out the top of it, they set off back along the road they had just driven down.

There was a small unkempt pathway on the left hand side of the road, which faded into a grass verge after a minute's walk. No cars went by as they crossed the road and entered the wood on the same side that they saw the clinic's entrance.

"We'd better go deeper into the woods so as to avoid being seen from the road Dela." Nathaniel waved at her to follow.

"And a better chance of us getting lost," she whispered.

"Did you say something?" Nathaniel asked, turning to face her.

"Nothing lover, except I want you to take me on a decent Caribbean holiday after all this crap has gone down." Dela put her gloved hands on her hips.

"That's a promise, and look on the bright side, even if we fail we could end up somewhere infinitely hotter," Nathaniel pointed downwards and turned and walked deeper into the icy roads.

Dela shook her head and followed him, "Bet you've seen the Blair Witch Project a hundred times, right? If I see any funny stick arrangements I'm getting my sexy bum outta here, understand?"

"Stop dawdling woman," Nathaniel said from ten feet ahead, Cerberus to his side.

"I'll give you dawdling!" Dela muttered under her breath as she followed him deeper into the secluded woods.

It took another ten minutes of trudging through the misty cold woods, keeping the road just in the corner of their left eyes to find the turn-off.

Still keeping their distance form the actual driveway, they followed it along and round until ahead they could see it widen before a tall iron double gate and an even taller and foreboding brick wall.

They crouched down behind a tall oak tree and Nathaniel pulled a pair of small binoculars from the rucksack. He put them to his eyes and studied the gate ahead. Two wizened gargoyles sat atop each side of the gates, on top of where they joined the walls. Even more worrying was a CCTV camera, mounted next to and trained on the gates and road.

"There's a camera on the gates," Nathaniel whispered without lowering his field glasses. The road inside the walls continued on, but the woods were replaced inside the clinic's compounds by rolling well-tended lawns of the plushest green.

"We'd better skirt the walls to see if there's a way over the walls or another way in." Nathaniel lowered his binoculars and passed them to Dela to have a look.

They kept at least twenty feet distance between them and the wall as they skirted the clinic's grounds. The wall was nine feet high all around and there was no sign of any other doors or ways into the place. CCTV cameras dotted the length of the wall forty feet apart.

"What'll we do now, James Bond? Jetpack over the wall or tunnel in like Steve McQueen?" Dela joked, staring at the ominous dark wall.

Nathaniel sneered at her, then looked up at the foliage above and around.

"I was thinking more of Tarzan myself," Nathaniel remarked, turning round to a tall Beech tree behind them.

"What!"

"Me Tarzan, you Jane!" Nathaniel chuckled and started climbing up the branches of the tree, the backpack over his shoulders.

"I don't believe this." Dela slapped her hands on her thighs and began climbing up after him. Cerberus looked up, sighed and lay down at the foot of the tree.

The tree was old and tall, with handily placed branches for climbing. Nathaniel stopped five feet above and overlooking the top of the wall and Dela sat on an opposite branch just below it. The clinic (cum Stately Home) sat amidst a well tended garden and front lawns. The place looked at least a couple of hundred years old and was obviously well kept and managed.

Dela and Nathaniel took turns with the binoculars keeping watch on the clinic, with little or no signs of life up until lunchtime. The occassional nurse, patient or gardener could be seen in the grounds, but nothing seemed untoward or sinister.

"My arse is killing me!" Dela exclaimed, shifting on her wet branch.

"So's mine," Nathaniel replied, not turning his eyes away from his clinic-trained binoculars.

"And wet." Dela moaned some more after getting no sympathy or response from her lover.

"Yeah, mine too," Nathaniel replied, agreeing with her.

"And I'm bored, cold and very, very fucking hungry." Dela growled a little louder in order to get a response.

Nathaniel put down his field glasses, "Are you trying to tell me something, Dela?"

"Derrrh!"

"Okay, look, nothing's happening here, so under duress I agree to a warming pub lunch at the place where we parked the car."

Dela was halfway down the tree before Nathaniel had finished his sentence. Nathaniel took one last look at the clinic, scratched his ear and then made his way down the tree after Dela.

As they walked back through the sodden woods Nathaniel remarked, "The pub is a good idea, we can quiz the publican or the customers about the clinic."

Dela stopped dead in her tracks. "Be honest, you're kinda enjoying this a little bit, aren't you?"

"Maybe a tad, but this is what I was born to do Dela, fight evil in all its guises," Nathaniel replied after a sheepish nod.

"But we could get spattered at any second. We're on the run and looking over our shoulders all the time. I know I'm a bit of a girl and like the odd thrill or two, but this game's a bit too scary for me." For the first time Dela's strong façade crumbled a little.

Nathaniel took her in his arms and looked down at her pretty face.

"I won't let any harm come to you, Dela and I'm glad in a way about this, because otherwise I would never have met and fallen in love with you."

Cerberus, twenty feet ahead of the couple, turned his head and sniffed. The woods had the faintest, oldest, familiar odour about them, one he couldn't place. The humans were kissing again, he wished they would hurry up because he was starving.

They made it back to the pub in time for lunch and as it was a slow weekday the proprietors were glad to accept Cerberus and his large food order. Dela got some stares from the local yokels, more out of curiosity than spite, she being only the third black person to drink there in thirty years.

Nathaniel chatted to the landlord as he ordered food and drinks for them all. Cerberus was having a pint of Bateman's draught in a bowl and a whole roast chicken to himself. Dela had a Southern Comfort and two rounds of bacon sandwiches and Nathaniel had a double Remy Martin and a huge steak and kidney pudding.

"What did you find out from the landlord?" Dela asked only after she had scoffed the last crumb of her sandwiches.

"The clinic's been there for five years. They bought the place from the local Lord. The Doctor sacked all the local staff and brought in all their own people from London. The staff have their own canteen and never mix with the locals." Nathaniel sipped at his drink as he ruffled Cerberus's head as he sat under the table lapping at his beer.

Also some of the local 'poachers'," Nathaniel whispered, "have seen things in the woods at night."

"What things?" Dela whispered.

"Strange lights, as well as hearing strange noises, plus the feeling of being followed. The locals stay clear of the place at night," Nathaniel retold to her.

"Anyone round here used the Fertility Clinic at all?"

"No. Only people with six K or more to spare are patients there and of course the locals are scared stiff of the place." Nathaniel took another swig of beer and thought some more.

"What we really need," he continued, "is to talk to one of the clinic's patients to find out if anything strange is going on there."

"And how do we do that if the locals don't go there. How would we find out who did?"

"We might be able to use the internet for local and country-wide news stories about the place."

"If we had a laptop or computer, which we don't, and," she whispered, "I can't see this village having a web-café, can you?" Dela sipped her drink and pushed a stray hair off her forehead.

"Then we'll have to use a bit of gumshoe-leather and pay a visit to the local paper or library." Nathaniel winked at her.

"And we're gonna do that now?" Dela asked, glad of the thought of getting away from the damp eerie woods for a while.

"No. First we keep tabs on the clinic for the rest of the afternoon at least."

"Oh great!" Dela sighed and even Cerberus whined from beneath the table.

"If that doesn't prove fruitful we will try the local rag and library on the morrow."

"I suppose you wanna go now, then?"

"That would be prudent," Nathaniel nodded in agreement.

"I don't want to be prudent, I just want a warm, comfortable, dry place to rest my ass." Dela complained as they rose to leave.

The rain had started up again by the time they left the pub. By the time they had got halfway through the woods to their vantage point, the rain was coming down in stair-rods. All three of them were soaked through by the time they reached the base of the tree they were using to watch the clinic in the morning.

Cerberus's fur clung to his body in soggy clumps and he sneezed twice in succession. Not for the first time since Nathaniel's ancestors had broken the silver chain that Hades had used to enslave Cerberus and keep him against his will as the Guardian of the Underworld, had he missed the warm eddies of the river Styxx. Cerberus could easily plane-shift at will back to his old searingly hot stomping ground, but he had been set free by a Le Meuille and he would keep his oath to serve them until there were no more Le Meuille's to serve. The weather on earth was lousy ten months out of twelve, but the food, the food was fantastic and varied with sweet, sour, hot and cold tastes and smells and he loved an after dinner brandy as a treat too. He saw his young master climb up the damp green tree and watched his bitch follow him up. Cerberus sighed and lay down on the wet ground under the tree; he hated all this inaction and just wanted to bite somebody's balls.

"This is nice, isn't it?" Nathaniel stated sarcastically as they returned to their morning perch. Except now the tree was soaking wet and the rain was pouring down.

"Nat, please, shut the fuck up!" Dela swore through pursed wet lips.

Cerberus on the ground snorted gleefully – he liked his master's new bitch as she had spirit.

The heavy rain slowed to a drizzle and finally ceased around three o'clock. Nathaniel and Dela hadn't even noticed the rain had stopped until a black van and dark blue stretch limo drove into the clinic's grounds and pulled up at the front doors.

"Dela," Nathaniel hissed, as he focussed his binoculars on the two vehicles. Dela looked up from her wet daydream of her and Denzel Washington naked on a Hawaiian beach.

The front doors opened and a tall, bald man in a forked beard and a white Doctor's coat, flanked by two burly male nurses, walked out to meet the vehicles. The door of the limo opened and a familiar figure emerged. Nathaniel focussed in on his face and recognised, from the Idiminu Building, that it was Telal.

"So the lift didn't get you, then?" Nathaniel whispered as he watched Telal embrace the Doctor. Then, as Nathaniel watched, Telal turned and it seemed, looked directly at him for a few seconds and smiled wickedly.

Nathaniel lowered his binoculars for a moment and blinked. By the time he had returned his field glasses to his eyes the back doors of the van were opened and the two nurses plus the black-suited van driver were pulling two trolleys out of the back. On the two trolleys were two women, heavily pregnant and apparently asleep or sedated. The two nurses pushed the women into the building with Telal and the Doctor following them. The cars then pulled away. The limo went round to the foreside of the building away from sight and the van drove out of the grounds.

Nathaniel lowered his binoculars and looked down at Dela.

"That looked bad." Dela spoke up to him.

"I fear that something heinous is transpiring in that house, and I'm not sure what we can do about it!"

"Are we going to try and break in ?" Dela asked.

Nathaniel stared at the house for a few seconds, "No, we tried that once in London, twice would be tempting fortune. No, we wait and watch, for the time being."

"Then I'm gonna climb down and find a quiet bush and take a piss." Dela started to descend the tree, taking care to cling to the wet branches.

"Don't go far Dela." Nathaniel looked down and warned.

"Only far enough to stop you or the mutt seeing me!"

Nathaniel's only reply was to raise his binoculars to his eyes again. Dela reached the bottom of the tree, picked up her handbag from the rucksack and stepped over the sleeping wet hound. A suitable bush with cover presented itself fifteen feet away and Dela trudged towards it hoping her travel tissues hadn't been soaked through.

Nathaniel looked around below and couldn't see Dela; a quick check of his watch told him that it was five to four and what passed for light in this weather was starting to fade. Nathaniel slung his binoculars over his neck and climbed down the tree as fast as his stiff limbs could muster.

Cerberus was already patrolling around the tree sniffing for Dela's scent by the time Nathaniel pulled on his wet and heavy backpack.

"Where is she?" he hissed at Cerberus, who was already following his nose towards a familiar scent emanating from behind a nearby bush. Cerberus trotted towards it and rounded it with Nathaniel ten paces behind. A female squeal of shock from behind the bush caused Nathaniel to break into a run. Cerberus bolted from behind the bush as Nathaniel skidded to a halt as he rounded it.

"Will you please fuck off!" Dela cried in embarrassment as Nathaniel found her squatting, knickers and jeans around her ankles, a large wad of tissues in her hand.

"Oh my God, sorry," Nathaniel wheeled round in total embarrassment, heat flushing his rain chilled cheeks.

Dela emerged flustered from behind the bush a minute later. "Don't say a fucking word!"

"Okay," Nathaniel raised his hands in supplication, "let's draw a line here and never talk about this again."

"Fine!" Dela pulled her handbag on to her shoulder.

"Good," Nathaniel stated. "We'd better go, it's getting gloomier by the second and I don't really want to be in these woods or anywhere near that clinic at night."

"I agree, let's go." Dela started off, following the also embarrassed Cerberus, with Nathaniel bringing up the rear.

Cerberus trotted in front trying not to sniff the recent odour that circulated in his nostrils. As he trotted along as dusk fell, another even more familiar smell faintly tickled his nostrils. His master was concerned about his bitch and frankly didn't have the nose for the job in hand. Cerberus padded ahead a little faster and took a long sniff of air. These smells appeared in picture form in his mind: Nathaniel, trees, wet, defecation, Dela and a faint odour of death.

Cerberus stopped stiff in his tracks, the smell of death, evil and ancient power was closing in and getting stronger. They were in trouble, and they weren't alone in the woods, something evil stalked them. Cerberus growled; a flicker of white caught the corner of his right eye, but was gone before he could fix his vision on it.

"You okay?" Nathaniel turned to face the on-coming Dela.

"Yeah." She gave a little embarrassed grin.

"Come here," he said and he pulled her close for a hug.

A smudge of white/grey caught from the edge of his vision. Dela felt Nathaniel go rigid in her arms and not in the usual sexy way.

"What's wrong?"

Another white spectre caused him to turn his head in the other direction, but it disappeared behind a tree before he could get a proper look at it.

"I think we're in trouble," he whispered in her ear, "follow me slowly." Nathaniel took her hand in his and they slowly walked towards Cerberus.

Another white apparition appeared ahead of them, closer this time, its form grotesquely human-shaped, but it merged into the trees and disappeared in a second.

"You ready, old friend?" Nathaniel asked Cerberus. Cerberus looked back and barked in agreement.

"When I say go, we are going to run like the fucking hordes of hell are after us," Nathaniel said slowly to Dela.

"What was that?" Dela asked, a white figure to her left caught her eye.

"A Sluagh, or in other words, the hordes of hell. Now GO!"

With that they ran with Cerberus ahead of them and Nathaniel pulling Dela by the hand. They ran as fast as the trees and bushes would allow. Many white spectres could now be seen; appearing in full vision now, behind, in front and to the sides of them as they avoided their pale evil countenances. On they ran through the wet darkening woods, with the pale and silent pursuers following after.

Suddenly, without warning, a pale Sluagh appeared from behind an oak tree, its arms raised for Nathaniel's throat. But Cerberus was jumping through the air before Nathaniel could react. He caught the evil spirit by the throat and both creatures disappeared behind a bush.

"Nat!" Dela screamed, as Nathaniel dragged her away from the bush, Cerberus and the Sluagh. "What about Cerberus?"

"He's an immortal spirit from the Underworld, we're the ones in trouble. Now run!"

They both ducked as one of the many pale avengers came at them from above. They staggered but regained their senses and footing to continue their flight. They ran along a sodden path, a row of nettle bushes, ignoring the wet mud that leaked into their shoes. They ran on trying to block out everything, not daring to look behind, as if that act of weakness would destroy them. Ahead stood two familiar old oaks, a few yards apart, which they recognised. The road wasn't far ahead now.

Dela was leading now and she was suddenly whipped round to a halt as Nathaniel was floored from behind by a Sluagh. Nathaniel let go of her hand as the ghostly white spirit with the deathly witch's face clawed its pale hands along Nathaniel's back.

"Run!" Nathaniel screamed.

For Dela time stood still. She could see Nathaniel sprawled in the mud, the evil Sluagh on his back, the damp woods and the two further Sluagh heading for her from behind the two ancient oaks. She did the only thing she could and ran. The road wasn't far ahead. She could flag down a car for help. Also the Sluagh were after her now and she didn't want to die like this: running away from the fallen man she loved.

The Sluagh on Nathaniel's back sent a paralysing chill deep into the King's Paladin's bones. The vile spirit grabbed at Nathaniel's backpack for purchase, with one ghostly taloned hand and grabbing the scabbard with the other. Nathaniel heard an ear-piercing scream that sounded like the shrill whistle of a kettle amplified to the tenth degree. Then there was nothing. The icy weight on his back had vanished and his ears rang a little. Nathaniel's body gave a shudder and he rolled over in the mud to find the pale hunter gone. He sat up and pulled his pack from his back and his eyes fixed on the scabbard. He undid one catch and freed it from the pack in his hands; it tremored like a vibrator.

Nathaniel stood up with a start. The woods were unearthly silent and he was alone, but more to the point, where was Dela?

Dela saw a long arching beam of light ahead in the descending darkness. It wasn't until then she realised how dark it really was now. To either side, like the evil spirits they were invoked to be, the laughing Sluagh pursued her.

A screaming Sluagh circled in front of her and the other closed in behind. It wasn't until she spun round that she saw she was trapped. The evil soul-stealers had manoeuvred her between two close trees and now with the Sluagh in front and behind she was done for!

"Nathaniel!" Dela screamed in desperation, half in fear of her life, half the fear of not seeing Nathaniel again.

Closer the Sluagh floated to Dela and she could see the witch-like countenance of the female spirits. They cackled with malice as they closed within feet of Dela. There were no cars going past now and the night was silent. Dela saw the claws of the Sluagh sisters close within inches of her and felt the bracing cold of their foul presence. Dela took a sharp intake of breath and closed her eyes for the last time.

A rustle in the bushes caused Nathaniel to skid to a muddy halt. Nathaniel raised his scabbard up in defence as Cerberus jumped from his hiding place.

"Good to see you Cerberus," Nathaniel said, rubbing the hound's head. "Have you seen Dela?"

Cerberus barked a negative.

"Can you track her?"

Cerberus answered by heading off at a trot, his nose pressed close to the ground following Dela's scent. Nathaniel followed Cerberus through the ever darkening woods, the feeling of fear rising more and more like an icy dagger in his spine.

Nathaniel could no longer see any sign of the Sluagh and that worried him more than when they were all around them. Cerberus could smell the scent of the female human easily – the funk of fear laced the wild path they followed through the woods.

Cerberus was moving faster than his master now; fully ten feet ahead. Nathaniel slowed his jogs and Cerberus bolted between two closely growing oak trees. Cerberus' nostrils flared in the semi-darkness as he tried to find where the Dela-scent continued from there.

Nathaniel reached Cerberus now and pushed past him to the other side of the oaks. Seeing nothing but dark trees he turned back to the hound.

"Where is she?"

Cerberus looked up briefly. Then anguish was now deep in his master's voice. There was a heavy scent of the Dela bitch here, plus the slightest tinge of urine. Yet there was something else also, apart from the hellish stench of the Sluagh. A scent that wafted down and into his nostrils for the barest snatch of a second.

"Cerberus, please! What's happened to Dela?"

Cerberus caught a stronger sniff from above and his eyes and head rose to the upper branches of the two oaks. Nathaniel's eyes followed Cerberus's and they both fixed on a dark object suspended from the trees at the same time.

"God. No!" Nathaniel exclaimed and sunk to his knees in the mud and began to cry. Cerberus looked at his pained master with empathy, then back to the object in the trees and howled a wailing cry of injustice.

A minute passed with Nathaniel kneeling with his hands covering his face. The dusk had descended into full-blown night now and Cerberus sensed other things abroad in the woods. Cerberus laid a paw onto Nathaniel's knee, trying to shake him from his despair and get him to safety. This was a side to Nathaniel he had rarely seen, in fact rarely seen in any King's Paladin over the last two centuries. Cerberus whined audibly and Nathaniel looked up, his face awash with tears.

"I know, old friend, it's time we weren't here."

Nathaniel jumped to his feet and began climbing the oak tree to retrieve Dela's bag that had lodged in the trees when the Sluagh had spirited her away. Nathaniel climbed twenty feet until he could reach her bag and as he grabbed it something in the woods caught his eye. The two oak trees were ancient and tall and on a slight hill so they towered over the surrounding trees. In the distance, just visible above the tree tops were two white figures flying over the woods towards the clinic's grounds. Between them they carried a darkish burden, until the dipped down below the tree lines. Nathaniel half climbed/half fell from the tree into the mud in front of Cerberus.

"They've got her, the Sluagh!" Nathaniel forced his tired body up. "Come on, there's still time to save her."

Nathaniel was running through the woods towards the gates of the clinic. Cerberus blinked, looked and ran after his master, Finally catching up with him after a minute; Cerebus was constantly amazed at the resources and inner strengths of humans. Cerberus led the way now. His eyes could see in the dark just as well, if not better, than in the cold light of day. You had to have good night vision after an eternity in hell.

Cerberus ran on, ahead of Nathaniel now through the pitch black woods. He heard a crack and skidded to a halt, turning around to see Nathaniel lying prone on the muddy ground. He bounded back and pulled the groggy human from his fallen position.

"I'm okay, let's carry on."

Nathaniel lent on the hound and rose gingerly to his feet and let himself be led by Cerberus slowly at first. Then they built up the pace and moved up to a slow run as the woods passed by on either side.

Finally they emerged from the woods by the gated entrance to the clinic. Two security lights shone down on the area from above. Nathaniel exhaled and coughed hard, his hands on his knees. When he looked up he saw the gates were opening. He pulled himself up to his full height and walked out of the woods on to the grass verge next to the road. He raised his hands to his eyes as the lights of three speeding vehicles shot out of the clinic's grounds.

The first was Telal's stretch limo, then the black van, but Nathaniel could do nothing as they sped past. The last vehicle was a silver Omega estate, but it was travelling slower than the other vehicles. As it neared Nathaniel saw the rear window glide down and a muzzle of an automatic weapon point out at him.

Nathaniel heard the machine pistol fire, saw the flash of its fire in the darkness. Then something hit him hard in the chest area and everything went dark and silent.

# CHAPTER 8

Nathaniel slowly became aware that he could feel hard, smooth stone under his face and body. His chest ached when he breathed and slowly his eyes adjusted to the darkness that enveloped him and tinges of flickering light became more apparent.

As his eyes adjusted further he realised that he wasn't in the cold wet woods any longer. The floor beneath him was smooth, cool alabaster, but the air around him was warm and his soaking clothes were bone dry. Nathaniel pushed himself up and although his chest and ribs ached, the bullets, he realised if they had struck him, would have done greater damage.

Sitting up, he found himself in a hot black-walled building, whose ceiling towered far above him. Behind him was a massive over-sized table of pure gold and next to it a simple bed of wood and straw, but made for a giant.

Apart from that the only other furniture was a vast opening in the opposite wall, the source of the red flickering light. Feeling like a doll in a real sized house, Nathaniel stood and made his way towards the vast fifty foot high entrance. As he walked he could feel the heat building up to such a great extent that it was if he were approaching a blazing fire. Just at the side wall of the opening, affixed to the wall was a lyre.

Nathaniel rounded the huge opening; red flickering light cast shadows on the lava-like rock beyond. Blinking through his tears because of the blistering heat, Nathaniel's mouth fell open and all the moisture inside him seemed to dry up.

Nathaniel wasn't in the woods any more, in fact he wasn't even on the same planet or plane. Next to the massive alabaster building was a set of gold double doors set into the black craggy rock; both the building and hundred foot high gates were on a ledge overlooking a vast red fiery larva sea that stretched as far as Nathaniel's watering eyes could see. Nathaniel glanced back at the building and saw a silver chain attached to the lava rock by a gold ring. It ended with a silver collar which was broken and seperated.

Nathaniel stood in awe of what he was seeing. The realisation started to creep into his mind. He knew now where he was and that could mean only one thing: the bullets from that car had hit him and he was dead. Because this was the entrance to Hades that Cerberus guarded, the fiery flow in front of him was the River Styxx.

Nathaniel moved forward slightly and to his right, behind Cerberus's black alabaster dwelling the ledge continued down a slope to a small jetty. There on the jetty stood Cerberus in all his majestic and gigantic three-headed glory, talking to a black-cloaked figure who stood on a barge next to the dock and ledge.

Nathaniel crept to the side of the black shiny building and peered round at the odd couple. Then, like an ancient ancestor who had been there before, he noticed that the figure in black's hands with which he was gesticulating, were just bones.

"Charon," Nathaniel whispered in shock, realizing he was staring at the boatman of the Underworld.

The dark-cloaked figure turned towards Nathaniel, but Nathaniel darted round the corner in shock as he saw that Charon had no lips, or skin, or hair to cover his skeletal white countenance. Nathaniel looked back to see that Cerberus and Charon were slowly walking towards him. He tried to swallow hard, but the heat left no moisture in his mouth and on jelly legs he walked to meet them.

"Welcome to my home," Cerberus spoke from the middle of his three heads.

"Am I dead?" Nathaniel asked, trying not to stare at Charon's skeletal face or "freak" at the fact that Cerberus was actually speaking English to him.

"No!" laughed Cerberus's left head long and loudly.

"I pulled you out of there a second before the bullets would have mown you down," his middle head answered.

"So I, we, can go back and save Dela?"

"We can; I can return us back and try and accomplish that." The right head spoke for the first time, its tone more serious.

"But we don't know where they've taken her." The middle head stated.

"Is there any way we can find out? Does anyone down here know Ashmodaios' plan?" Nathaniel rubbed his head; the heat was making him feel faint and nauseous.

"Do not speak that name aloud!" Charon's voice was shockingly chill and unearthly.

"Can you help?"

Cerberus's left head laughed wildly again, getting a stern look from his right head.

"There is someone you could summon," Charon said coldly, "the Seer of Knossos. I could bring him here."

"Where from?"

"From the Underworld, of course," replied Cerberus's serious head.

"Why would you do this for me?" Nathaniel asked, breathing hard to keep from being sick.

"For all eternity I ferry the dead from here to over the Styxx to their final destinations. I haven't brought anybody back from there for two thousand years." Charon turned and walked back towards the dock.

"Who is this Seer of Knossos?" Nathaniel asked Cerberus as he wiped the sweat from his brow, "and will he help us?"

"Come inside my abode and we can chat in comfort," Cerberus's middle head nodded. As they moved back towards the house, Cerberus' heads were smiling, frowning and talking all at the same time.

"The Seer of Knossos was an ancient wise man from Greece over a century and a half ago. He was favoured by the

Gods with the power of foretelling the future." The middle head explained as they entered Cerberus's cool dwelling.

"For a decade he foretold the future and helped a great many people," Cerberus's whimsical head added.

"But then by accident he saw the day and moment of his death," the serious head added. "Angered by his bleak future and feeling betrayed by the Gods his heart turned black. His advice was used to help himself to gain wealth and his hands that once aided, now laid themselves on the children of the local village." Cerberus lay down on his bed and Nathaniel approached it next to the three heads.

"He dabbled in the black arts, trying to use the death of young innocents to delay his shortened life. But the murders were in vain and on the day before he was due to die he took his own life and thus denied the Gods," his middle head continued.

"But they got their revenge, because every day for all eternity he has to relive the day of his death, whilst the spirits of the murdered children torment him," the humorous head laughed darkly.

"That is why he will help us; even an hour away from eternal damnation will be like a two week holiday in the Bahamas."

"And what then, my three-headed friend?" Nathaniel put one hand on Cerberus's paw.

"We go back and rescue Dela," the middle head replied.

"And stomp some demons to dust," the whimsical head added.

Nathaniel smiled thinly. "Then we'll have to try and stop As...." he paused, "his demonic plans for this earth."

"Where do you think she is then, Nathaniel? They were taking her away from the clinic," the serious head pondered.

"I'm not sure, maybe another place owned by the Idiminu Corporation. I know she could be anywhere, in any state."

Nathaniel bowed his head and as he tried to swallow the cricket-ball sized lump in his throat.

Cerberus and Nathaniel looked up and before them, in the entrance to Cerberus's abode, stood the figure of Charon, and a tall, old man with a robust grey/brown beard in ancient khaki robes.

Cerberus and Nathaniel rose to their feet/paws and walked over to where the two figures stood.

"Don't worry, he cannot cross the threshold or do you any physical harm," Charon advised.

"Listen carefully to his words, Nathaniel," Cerberus's left head whispered to him, "but be wary. He will try and find out things about you. Don't let him. He's wily and will use it against you."

"Understood," Nathaniel replied as they stopped a few yards away from the two figures.

"Who is he that stands before me that has the power to summon the dead from their eternal torment?" The old man looked up through his bushy eyebrows at Nathaniel.

"Just a man seeking answers," Nathaniel replied, choosing his words sparingly and carefully.

"Just a man. A living man at the gates of Hades itself commanding its gatekeeper and its ferryman, by Zeus's beard you have the nerve of a hero!" The old man's blue eyes glistened as he studied Nathaniel hard.

"Praise indeed from the renowned Seer of Knossos, but it is your skill and future-sight that I require," Nathaniel said, trying to praise the Seer.

"Ah! I wondered why I had been taken from my torment, to work!" the Seer laughed, "I vowed never to use my powers again."

"Ah, well, then Charon can take you straight back to Hell then." Nathaniel turned away from the Seer towards Cerberus.

"Don't insult my intelligence. You obviously need my powers and I obviously don't want to go back to my torment even if it were for but an hour only," the old Seer spat back.

"Good, now that I've got your full attention old chap, I will exchange a day here out of torment's way for the information I need," Nathaniel replied coolly.

"Sounds tempting, but what would you require of me first?"

"You will provide us with the whereabouts of a certain human woman held by demons back on Earth, for one day here in this house," Nathaniel stated.

"Do you understand that, tortured soul?" Cerberus's middle head barked.

The Seer looked slowly at all present and nodded slowly. "I agree."

"So how do we proceed?" Nathaniel asked, wringing his hands together.

"I need you to make a connection with the woman in mind. Do you have any items of clothing or personal things?" the Seer asked.

Nathaniel searched his clothes and could not find anything. "I don't have anything, but Cerberus could take me back to retrieve one of her backpacks."

"No, we cannot do that," Cerberus' serious head said.

"Why?" Nathaniel asked, turning towards his shaggy friend.

"My friend, we are in the outer plane of the seven hells. I've brought you here only as a last resort, otherwise you would have died. I've broken all the laws of the Underworld and repaid the debts owed to your ancient ancestor," his middle head stated.

"And now, if I pop you back, the demons of Ashmodaios would be on your back," his flighty head said.

"Yes," Charon spoke, "Ashmodaios has spies everywhere, his hoards could be upon us at any moment, we must do this now and return you to your pitiful human existence."

"So what do we do now?" Nathaniel exclaimed, anger rising in his throat.

"I can still help you," the Seer of Knossos said quietly.

"What!" Nathaniel exclaimed.

"I can still help you, but I must be able to touch you, take her image from your mind."

"No! It would be unwise to let this old trickster loose in your mind," Charon warned.

"I concur with Charon. The risks could be great. The Seer's mind could overpower your brain in an instant," Cerberus agreed with the ferryman of the dead.

"I understand," Nathaniel said, looking down. "But I have no choice!" Nathaniel pushed his hands through the invisible barrier and clasped the Seer's shocked hand. The Seer reciprocated and they were suddenly locked together, minds entwined, dead and living thoughts exchanged like a million emails simultaneously.

Nathaniel could vaguely hear Cerberus and Charon's exclamation of concern, but all that was peripheral to the deep blue eyes of the Seer. They seemed to grow and bedazzle Nathaniel so they took up the entire width of his vision. All he could see now was the watery blue pupils enlarged until Nathaniel's whole world was blue.

Nathaniel was suddenly aware that he wasn't in Cerberus's dwelling anymore; he stood on a sunny bleached hill. A circle of white pillars stood nearby; some sort of ancient temple, the columns were of Greek design. A little way in front of this stood the Seer of Knossos, a thin smile on his lips.

"Where the hell are we?" Nathaniel exclaimed, the sun hot on his head only cooled by the gentlest of breezes.

"Still in Hell my living friend, yet inside my mind, the place where I long to be, Knossos, Crete, at my temple, my oracle," the old man explained walking over to lower himself on to a stone bench next to the temple.

"Why did you bring me here?" Nathaniel asked, looking around. Everything felt so real.

"For my own reasons perhaps, and to help you also. This is where I channel my energy and seek the memories of the future," the Seer explained, his voice low, measured and without any emotion.

"So you'll help me then, see the future and tell me where Dela is being held?"

"I can do that and more. See your future if you so desire, but I have a price," the Seer smiled thinly, without any humour.

"Cerberus warned me of your tricks old man, but what could I, a mere mortal do to aid the dead, what could you possibly want?"

The Seer twisted on his bench to watch the pacing Nathaniel.

"What every tortured soul wants young hero, an escape from my torment!"

"You'll have your day of freedom. Now, tell me, where's Dela?" Nathaniel's face reddened as the frustration rose to his cheeks.

"Oh, I want more than that! I want my freedom. I want to return to the land of the living and be alive once more!" The Seer's eyes shone blue from underneath his bushy grey eyebrows.

"I haven't the power to grant such a thing even if I knew a way to do so!" Nathaniel exclaimed.

"Oh, there are always ways and means my young friend," the Seer cackled, "all I need is your word of honour that you will take me with you."

"But even if we took your soul back with us, your mortal body crumbled to dust when Homer was a lad," Nathaniel breathed in. Even the smells of Knossos were real to the King's Paladin. "Every body needs some body," Nathaniel half-joked.

"That, as you would say in your language, would be my problem. Just get my spirit back to the world of the living and I'll help you to find your woman." The Seer lent down and picked up some dusty soil, rubbing it between his hands.

"And you would promise not to come near or contact me or my kith and kin?" Nathaniel moved closer to the circle of pillars.

"It's a big world. I would return here in your time. It would be interesting to see the difference, eh?" the Seer smiled warmly, "you have my promise, young hero."

"Then you have my promise Seer," Nathaniel said sharply. "Now show me where Dela is!"

"Let us move into the circle, my young friend, and I and the oracle will show you what you desire." The Seer stood up and walked up two white steps into the circle of pillars itself; a single olive tree was the temple's only feature.

"Come." The Seer beckoned for Nathaniel to follow him into the oracle.

Nathaniel looked around; the surreal state he was in hit him for a brief moment. He was in Hell, with Cerberus, a skeleton dude and a dead Greek wizard whose mind he was now in, and in that mind he was in Greece.

"Oh well, in for a penny in for a pound." Nathaniel sucked in his cheeks, put his hands in his pockets and ambled slowly into the oracle.

"So, what do we do now?" Nathaniel asked, scratching his cheek, letting the whole situation just wash over him for the moment.

"The tree is life, the whole human race." The Seer nodded towards the tree. "Put your hands on to the tree."

Both men laid both palms on to the olive tree, and at once the air sizzled like a steaming, humid day with a storm brewing. Both men looked up into the boughs of the tree as a miniature electric storm localised only above the tree in the stone circle. Outside the blue summer's sky shone brightly and the world continued as normal. Dark storm clouds swirled like cyclones and lightning and thunder cracked loudly above their heads. Inside the maelstrom, in a blaze of eye-hurting electricity an image began to form.

"Do I do anything? Nathaniel shouted above the din.

"No need, the future will seek you out my friend." The Seer cackled with delight.

Nathaniel gasped; he could see Dela's unconscious form lying on a leather couch. Telal and another man were there, plus a blonde nurse and two heavies. The smaller bearded man was talking to Telal.

"Why did you bring her here? It could be dangerous, they might track her down and ruin the whole operation," the bearded, bespectacled man whined, wringing his hands together.

"You forget yourself, Doctor Geial, and whom you are speaking to." The half-demon Telal spat, but then his face calmed and he put his arm around the doctor with a friendly smile. "But come now, Doctor, your home is my home and Lance here has taken care of the King's Paladin." Telal nodded to one of the suited heavies in the corner of the room.

"So what have you brought this girl here for?" the Doctor asked with a cringe.

"The master wants her alive and unhurt until he arrives. She has escaped him more than once and I think he wants to teach her a lesson, a final lesson." Telal laughed and the scene faded away.

The scene cut quickly to a familiar house, but it was high summer and a sad looking Dela was talking to his grandmother. The scene cut again to the house on Manes Close. Mrs Dawson was there, but the future visions cut again. Nathaniel saw himself fighting some unknown, dark presence with a long gleaming sword. Then the storm faded away and the future visions ceased.

"Is that it?" Nathaniel exclaimed.

"Ah, the fickle fortune of fate! Yes, it is up to you to interpret your dreams." The Seer of Knossos cackled again.

"You bastard! What do they mean?" asked Nathaniel. His anger and frustration getting the better of him at last.

The Seer laughed louder whilst wheeling round, but the laughter died and caught in his throat.

There was laughter from outside the oracle's pillars and both Nathaniel and the Seer turned around quickly. Out from behind an outcrop of rocks children came, all dressed in pure white togas with gold string belts at their waists.

The children were whispering-singing some song in ancient Greek as they encircled the oracle, skipping and singing.

"No-oooo!" the Seer cried, sheer terror on his bearded countenance. His eyes flicked to every child, his head spinning this way and that.

"Your sins have sought you out Seer," Nathaniel stated, realising that these tormenting lost souls were the Seer's child victims. The Seer put his hands to his head and sank to his knees in despair.

"Mercy King's Paladin!" he cried, "we had a bargain!"

"Like the mercy you showed these innocent children?" Nathaniel spat. He turned his back on the Seer as the children moved past him into the circle to reclaim the Seer and resume his punishment for all eternity.

Suddenly the warm sun of Greece was replaced with the heat of Hell. He found himself standing by the dock next to Cerberus's home. The three-headed hound was next to him, and far out on the River Styx he could see Charon's boat as he ferried the Seer of Knossos back to his own private hell.

"Are you all right, my friend?" Cerberus's middle head asked, concerned, raising himself up and putting a paw on Nathaniel's shoulder.

Nathaniel blinked, staring at his canine companion then back at the boat disappearing into the steam rising from the River Styx.

"If I don't get Dela back, I'll never be all right again!" Nathaniel stared ahead, looking across the Styx, his eyes watering.

"I had to send the children in to save you. Did you have enough time?" Cerberus's stern head asked.

"I saw Dela in that Doctor Geial's house; she's alive until Asm…. 'til he arrives. We've got to get back to the woods my old friend and retrieve my bags and scabbard and we have to go now!"

"It's as good as done." Cerberus's three heads blinked as one and soon the heat of Hell faded into the darkened drizzle of a Gloucestershire dawn.

The dawn was cold, damp and the air was fresh with the smell of wet vegetation. Nathaniel shivered and looked around. Cerberus had returned to his one-headed earthly form. They had both returned to the place where Telal's henchman had tried to shoot him. His and Dela's soggy backpacks were still lying in the deep grass where he had dropped them. Both of them glanced at the closed gates of the clinic, rueing the day they had first seen them.

"Come on," Nathaniel shivered again and reached down to grab his and Dela's things. They returned to the confines of the woods as Nathaniel checked his bag, shocked to find the sword scabbard was still there.

They jogged as fast as their weary legs could carry them, realising that it had been ages since they had slept. It took them twenty minutes to reach the hire car, which was still in the pub car park. Cerberus sprang on to the back seats and Nathaniel eased himself in, the bottoms of his trousers soaked up to his knees. Nathaniel gazed at the empty passenger seat, a pang of uncertainty and sadness hit him hard.

Nathaniel swiftly shook his head and quickly started the car's engine, looked in his rear view mirror and reversed out of the pub car park. Nathaniel somehow managed to drive back to the B&B.

"Mr Robards!" The Rigsby look-a-like B&B owner chased Nathaniel up the stairs, "Mr Robards, I must talk to you!" The short balding owner grabbed Nathaniel's arm as they reached the landing.

"Are you talking to me?"

It was either the worn, withering stare he gave the man, or the dishevelled look and three-day stubble that made the owner release his grip and take a step back.

"What do you want? I've had a bad night!"

"Your room," the man squirmed, "it's not up to the standards I expect of my, erm, guests."

"What are you wittering on about man?" Nathaniel asked, tired and annoyed, trying to resist the urge to thump the man.

"Your room, sir!"

"My room." Nathaniel pointed at the door as he reached it, fishing the door key from his pocket.

"Could you, erm, leave it in less of a mess?" the man stepped back as Cerberus growled from Nathaniel's side.

Nathaniel frowned, then put his key in the lock and opened his room's door. The place had been turned over and was a total shambles. What stuff he and Dela had left behind had been opened, ripped, explored and thrown about the room.

"See?" said the man at the doorway.

"Leave us!" Nathaniel bent down to pick up some scattered chess pieces.

"But Mr Robards, I must …"

A loud, throaty growl finally sent the B&B owner running and Cerberus nudged the door shut with his head.

"Cerberus, old friend, I'm getting pretty pissed off with this." Nathaniel spat. "I think it's high time we started fighting back."

Cerberus barked back in total agreement.

Nathaniel washed, changed and took only the chess set and a change of Dela's clothes from the room. He didn't bother to tidy it up. He stopped at the car hire office and rented the car for the whole week, then filled up with petrol and food at the local garage.

He drove the car round the streets of Worchester on the look-out for a certain shop. The agents of Ashmodaios had learned of his and Dela's stay and the B&B and that worried him because they must have got the information from Dela. What worried him more was how much pressure, or dare he think, torture, they had done to her to surrender this information. Luckily for him and unluckily for them, he had locked the grimoire in the boot of his car after lunch the previous day. It was too big and heavy to lug around and this wasn't London so he had risked it. He never intended to be so long in getting back to it, via a trip to Hell. Worcester, unbelievably, didn't have what he needed, so he headed for Cheltenham, knowing every second he wasted could spell death, or worse, for Dela.

Nathaniel scratched the stubble on his chin and stared into the dim white glow of the computer terminal. Cerberus waited outside in the hire car, guarding both the grimoire and the scabbard while he sat in the Internet Café sipping a cup of coffee, searching the web for information.

He was just searching for rubbish really, 'til the person next to him finished and got up and left. Then, quick as a flash, Nathaniel logged into the secret Home Office website, using his personal password. A search for Doctor Geial, (not the most common of names) soon brought up a home address in

Tewkesbury. That was where Telal from the Idiminu Corporation had a home address also. The pieces were slowly slotting into place, and if this was a game of chess, he would be one of three white pieces looking across an incoming tide of black enemies.

Somehow he and Cerberus had to upset Ashmodaios' evil plans and halt the demon invasion. Yet that was something to cast to the back of his mind, he had to get Dela back alive or the earth wouldn't be a place worth saving. Nathaniel wrote the address on an envelope and paused only to email his boss to lie to him about a family bereavement, and request some more time off. Nathaniel exited the secured site, deleted the History options, paid his bill and rejoined Cerberus in the car.

"Payback time!" he stated, rubbing his companion's shaggy head.

Cerberus barked in agreement and Nathaniel drove off towards Tewkesbury as fast as the speed limit allowed.

Nathaniel just drove. He concentrated all his efforts on driving, looking in his mirrors, checking the road signs, making sure he was taking the fastest route to Doctor Geial's home address. He had no idea what he was going to do until he got there. He had no weapons, no allies (apart from Cerberus), no idea if Dela was still alive and no dramatic rescue plans either. Nathaniel just hoped that when he got to the house something would spring to mind.

Cerberus watched the King's Paladin closely. He was worried for Dela, but worried for his friend even more.

# CHAPTER 9

Doctor Geial's house lay back off a busy road outside the Newtown Industrial Estate. It had a semi-circle in and out driveway and had once been a farmhouse, but had long since been up-dated and added to. A high wooden fence and rows of tall poplar trees hid the house from prying eyes.

Dela was strapped and tied to a leather examination table which she found out when she had come to half an hour before. She was in a windowless room, with sparse hospital-like cleanliness. There was a large, five-bulbed light that hung down on an arm from the ceiling shining on her. A few chairs, glass cabinets with medical bottles and utensils adorned the room. There were two doors into the room, one behind her head and one in the right hand corner of the room.

A bearded man had popped in to check on her twenty minutes ago, but she had managed to feign unconsciousness while he briefly checked her over and left the examination room.

Dela was strapped in tight and her hands tied together under the leather couch. She had given up trying to break free after fifteen minutes of fruitless effort.

Dela was glad to be alive for the present after those demon-ghosts had got her, but where was she?

Where was Nathaniel? She hoped he was alive and safe from capture, otherwise she had no chance of ever getting out of this alive.

Upstairs Telal was in Geial's spare bedroom. He craved the job of painfully taking retribution on the girl who had thwarted his master for so long. He knew that she was for Ashmodaios's personal edification only and knew if he touched her his master would slay him in an instant. So he was taking out his unearthly sexual frustrations on Geial's blonde assistant's anus. The blood trickling down her legs caused him to thrust harder, and her to scream louder.

Outside Nathaniel drove past and saw that the black car was outside in the drive – the one the shots had come from last night. He drove on into town and found a supermarket car park to park in, stop and conjure up a plan of attack.

Nathaniel had the sword scabbard and the book as his only weapons, other than a wished for element of surprise. The scabbard may or may not affect Telal, but it would be useless against his human, gun-wielding henchmen.

Nathaniel reached over and grabbed his holdall from the back seat and pulled the ancient Grimoire from its protective plastic covering. Maybe the book of his ancestors would have helpful words or spells. He turned to a remembered chapter, written with an ink scratched quill. "How to thwart the servants of darkness." That might be a good place to start!

A man of retirement age, pushing a line of shopping trolleys past the front of Nathaniel's hire car jolted him back into the real world again. He looked up from the book to find the old geezer was staring at him. Nathaniel stared back wondering what the old man was glaring at. The old man in his brown uniform switched his gaze to an orange sign two cars away, FREE PARKING FOR CUSTOMERS, ONE HOUR ONLY.

Nathaniel put down his book and with a last glare, the old man pushed his trolley convoy towards the side of the supermarket. Nathaniel had finished reading anyway and a plan of action was formulating in his mind. Now he needed to go into the supermarket and buy a few ingredients for the receipt he needed.

The old trolley man watched the guy from the car enter the shop, then pulled a mobile phone from his pocket and pressed a special number.

"This is Hartley. I found him!"

Nathaniel headed straight for the herbs section of the supermarket. He knew he could easily get most of his required ingredients there. Other items he found at the foreign foods section. Nathaniel paid the bored blonde married lady in her early forties and carried his shopping back to his hire car. He noticed the old trolley man was pushing his chariots at the far corner of the supermarket car park, glowering at him from afar. Nathaniel quickly put his shopping in the foot space in front and below the passenger seat. Starting the car, he drove away as quickly as possible, heading back towards the Doctor's house.

As Nathaniel drove past the house once more he noted that there had not been any changes to its façade. Nathaniel parked the car in a nearby dirt track that led to a recreation field and a Scout hut. It was raining steadily so the football pitches and swings had been abandoned.

Nathaniel put his ancestors' book open on top of the dashboard and pulled a pestle and mortar from one of his two shopping bags. Following the instructions in his book, he began to grind the ingredients together. It took him fifteen minutes to grind them into a green/brown dust and Cerberus watched as he placed the dust into three glass bottles. Nathaniel spent another ten minutes chanting and vocalising the correct incantations over them, before placing stoppers in them. Trusting his luck again, after copying a few incantations onto some handy-sized folded pieces of paper, Nathaniel locked the book in the boot of the hire car.

Nathaniel and Cerberus left the car behind and made their way in the grey downpour towards where they thought Dr Geial's back garden was. Nathaniel took only his sword scabbard, three bottles and incantations as protection. Cerberus just brought himself.

The rain began to beat down harder on Cerberus's and Nathaniel's heads; even though it was only mid-day it seemed as dark as dusk. They walked purposefully through the downpour, hardly feeling the rain. It was a mere inconvenience as both their minds were focussed on one purpose: to rescue Dela at all costs.

A five foot high brick wall surrounded the perimeter of Geial's garden. Without stopping to think, Nathaniel leapt up and vaulted both his legs on to the wall, then rolled over the top of the wall and landed on his feet in some flower beds. With a bound Cerberus followed, but landed with a fluid motion, his head turning left and right quickly, aware of his surroundings at once.

Nathaniel walked out of the flower beds and from behind some bushes, with Cerberus behind him. A conservatory was only twenty feet away across a green lawn, not exactly a typical lair of demons. No faces or bodies could be seen at the windows of the large country house.

Nathaniel wasn't in the mood for stealth nor had a fear of death; he crossed the lawn and opened the conservatory door and walked in past the wicker furniture. Nathaniel opened a french window into a living room area. A surprised thug, bending over whilst looking through Geial's CD collection, stood up and turned around. Grabbing the phial from his pocket, Nathaniel threw it at the goon and spoke, "Aut vincere aut mori."

The glass exploded on the man's chest. The dust covered him; with Nathaniel's power words the henchman in the dark suit froze solid in his tracks. Only his startled and disbelieving eyes moved from side to side in fear. The thug had never felt so vulnerable, since his days of being bullied at school.

Nathaniel ignored the man and made for a door in the wall to the right of him. Outside the afternoon sky darkened considerably and thunder rumbled faintly over the Malvern

Hills. Cerberus growled a little warning to his master. "Aidentis fortunei juvat" (fortune favours the daring), Nathaniel replied in Latin. The door opened into a wide hallway, with many doors leading from it and a staircase in front and beside him.

Behind him, through an archway, was a large open-plan kitchen nearly the size of Dela's entire flat. A surprised henchman spun around and dropped the sandwich he was making. Both he and Nathaniel silently and frantically looked for his gun. It was on a work surface next to the sink where he had left it. Both he and Nathaniel found it with their eyes, then stared intently at each other's eyes for two seconds, which seemed an age. Then they both sprang into action, the man in the charcoal-grey suit for his pistol, and Nathaniel for his phial. Repeating the words he spoke in the other room, he tossed the phial across his body at the henchman, as the thug grabbed his gun and brought it to bear.

The glass phial shattered in the man's face, before he could fully pull the trigger. Nathaniel exhaled heavily, staring at the paralysed man, whose extended arm and pistol were pointing dead level with Nathaniel's face.

A flash of lightning from outside caused Nathaniel to snap back to the mission in hand. Outside darker clouds had rolled in and it seemed as gloomy as night. Nathaniel scanned the kitchen and seeing no-one else there or anything of importance he moved back and into the hall with Cerberus close behind.

Nathaniel gazed around at the front door, stairs, the busts, plants and waist-high Greek columns and the other doors on the ground floor. Both Cerberus and he stood quietly, trying to hear anything that would influence their next move. Only the beating of their hearts in their ears and the ticking of a grandfather clock could be heard.

Lightning and a loud peal of thunder echoed around the house, like it was trapped in some evil dimension. Time was ticking on the face of the grandfather clock, so Nathaniel knelt down beside his furry companion. Nathaniel tapped his chest and immediately pointed up the stairs. Then, pointing at Cerberus, he picked out the three remaining doors that led off from the hallway.

Cerberus nodded and put his paw briefly on Nathaniel's hand. Nathaniel grinned unconvincingly as a reply, then headed for the stairs. Cerberus watched Nathaniel begin his ascent then picked the door to the billiard room and pushed it open with his head.

Nathaniel gripped his scabbard in one hand, his last phial in the other and slowly went up the stairs. Every creak of the old wooden steps making him cringe inside, but he knew he had to press on and find Dela.

Cerberus's scan of the billiard/smoking room was quickly completed as the room was empty and looked as if it was rarely used. A long sniff told him Dela had never been in the room, so he left it and headed across the hall towards another closed door.

Nathaniel had reached the landing and was confronted by five closed doors. All were painted ivory and each held no clue as to what lay in the room beyond.

Nathaniel made sure the last phial was loose but safe in his pocket, gripped his scabbard and picked a door at random to go through. Gritting his teeth he grabbed the door handle and pushed the door inward, ready for what Hell could cast at him. Nathaniel found himself staring into a luxurious bathroom with black and white mosaic tiles and a huge sunken bath with separate shower, toilet and bidet.

Cerberus circled the library slowly. The dust in the room made his sensitive nose twitch and he was glad of only having one earthly head, not three. The room was still and cool; yet there seemed a warmth or mystic heat haze emanating from some of the books kept there. There was also the faintest sulphur funk of recent demon activity. Outside the storm raged on.

Nathaniel had checked out a computer room next to the bathroom; he would have liked more time to examine the PCs (two) and the discs and papers held there within but Dela was his prime objective. Nathaniel moved back across the landing passing the stairs to stand outside a smaller ivory painted door. Holding his breath, he turned the door knob and entered the room after the door had swung inwards. This looked very much like a spare bedroom, with bare polished floorboards and a single bed and wardrobes. The room was brownish, drab and out of place with the rest of the upstairs rooms. Net curtains hung from the windows and the room had a musty air as if it had not been used or even cleaned in a decade.

Nathaniel was starting to get anxious now. Lightning flashed through the bedroom window and a deafening clap of thunder broke over the house a few seconds later, making even him jump.

Nathaniel quickly vacated the dusty 1960s style room and moved on to the next door and kicked it open. This room was vastly different to the last drab one. It was bright with yellow and blue pastel colours, with a beige king-size four poster bed. It had white sheets and drapes on each post from the canopy above.

Nathaniel wasn't alone. On the bed lay a naked, blonde-haired woman. She was face down with her long hair covering her features. Nathaniel took two paces into the room and noticed small amounts of blood on the woman's legs that had dripped down to make a stain on the white bed sheets. Nathaniel edged closer to the bed, his eyes fixed on the motionless woman. He quickly darted around the room to make sure no demon, half-demon or henchman was lurking nearby. Seeing and sensing nothing untoward he lay the scabbard on the edge of the bed and reached out to feel the woman's wrist for a pulse; or at least warmth to indicate she wasn't dead.

Her wrist was warm and pulsed with blood, so he reached across her body and carefully grabbed her side and arm. With a deep breath he pulled her over so he could see her face and guess her state of health. She looked both attractive (in normal circumstances) and haggard. Deep dark rings lay under her bloodshot eyes; scratches marked her legs, torso and chest.

"Hey! Are you okay?" Nathaniel asked, feeling dumb as he spoke the words.

The woman awoke with a screech; her eyes flying open with a look of infinite madness in them and she flew at Nathaniel across the bed. The surprise and ferocity of the attack caused Nathaniel to jump backwards, lose his balance and with pin-wheeling arms fall back and down, his head thumping against a wardrobe door as he crashed on his back to the floor.

Shaking his bruised bonce, Nathanial managed to cry out "No! Wait!" before the crazed, naked lady leapt from the bed on top of him with a shrill cry. She landed half on top of him and as he managed to grab one wrist, another of her long nailed hands scratched at his eyes. Luckily she missed his left eye, but her nail left a nasty scratch on his cheek.

Nathaniel had fought vampires and demons before, but the honourable side of his nature found it difficult to cope with the crazed attack of this frightened, witless woman.

Nathaniel managed to pull one knee up and push the crazed nurse backwards, while he fumbled in his pocket for the last phial. She lunged at him again; this time Nathaniel managed to roll aside and she came crashing down on the floor beside him. Nathaniel slipped and scrambled from his knees to stand by the bed. He pulled the phial to throw and freeze the woman, but she was on him again. Launching herself at him as he began to throw, her hand connected with his wrist sending the phial flying on to the bed.

"Shite!" Nathaniel exclaimed, watching where it landed and not the wild swinging punch that knocked him to the floor.

Shaking his head, he rose to a half-crouching position, but the woman just kept on advancing, knocking Nathaniel's strong, six-foot plus frame sidewards into a dressing table, with a crash of glass as a mirror broke.

"Now that's seven years bad luck," Nathaniel shouted in pain. Grabbing for the nurse's shoulders he pushed and propelled her backwards, shoving her back on to the bed. With a crack the phial broke under her and Nathaniel whispered the "power" words that froze her tortured face in distorted rage.

"Poor thing," he said to himself as he rubbed at his bruises. Then he remembered the job in hand and collected his only weapon, the scabbard, and moved on to the last upstairs room. That was totally devoid of anything interesting. Cerberus barked quizzically from downstairs and Nathaniel rushed downstairs to join him.

Cerberus was waiting at the bottom of the stairs. He tilted his head and growled in his throat lightly.

Nathaniel rubbed his bruised chin.

"You really don't wanna know."

Cerberus nodded to behind the stairs and he padded off with Nathaniel following behind. Cerberus stopped at a wood panelled door under the stairs and sniffed. Nathaniel reached over his canine companion and pulled open the new door to reveal steps leading down into the darkness. Holding the scabbard tightly before him, Nathaniel descended into the darkness and Cerberus followed.

As Nathaniel felt down the wall his hand found a pull cord and gave it a tug and illumination appeared at the bottom of the steps. Nathaniel and Cerberus reached the bottom of the steps and the pair found themselves in a medium-sized wine cellar. Half-filled wine racks lined each wall, with a dirty table and chair in the centre of the room and a naked light bulb shining directly above it.

Nathaniel and Cerberus looked around the wine cellar walls and then checked the floor. The room was devoid of any doors, exits or trapdoors. Nathaniel sat down in the chair and ran his hand through his hair in despair. He stood up quickly, his mobile phone on his belt clipping painfully under the top edge of the table.

"Fuck it!" In a rage Nathaniel tore his phone from his belt and pulled back his arm to hurl it against the floor. But his rage sparked an idea and his intellect and wisdom gained control over his frustrated emotions.

Nathaniel brought the mobile up to his face and grimaced, then hit his phonebook button and thumbed his options 'til he came to Dela's number and dialled it. Nathaniel turned to Cerberus and put his forefinger to his lips, then tapped his left ear twice. Cerberus stopped dead in his tracks and cocked his supernatural ears to listen. On Nathaniel's phone, it showed that somewhere Dela's phone was ringing. Nathaniel just hoped it was still in her coat pocket. The companions held their respective breaths and listened.

Cerberus stiffened and moved closer to the racks of dusty wine bottles in the opposite wall to the entrance. Cerberus barked, then turned to look back at Nathaniel, his ears pricked upwards.

"What do you reckon? A secret door old friend?" Nathaniel examined the wine rack. He checked down each side and pulled, but the racks did not budge. He then moved around to examine the bottles. Nathaniel's eyes flicked from bottle to bottle, row to row, 'til he spotted something unusual.

One of the bottles seemed cleaner than the rest and had no covering of dust on it. Nathaniel grabbed the neck and lifted it up so he could pull the bottle out. But the bottle was attached to something at the back of the rack. There was a loud click and the rack moved two inches towards Nathaniel on its right axis.

Nathaniel grabbed the edge of the wine rack and pulled it towards him. A man-sized wood panelled passageway led onwards. Nathaniel turned to look at Cerberus, then entered. The small passage only lasted ten feet before an opening into a square anti-chamber with two wooden doors on each of the side walls. The other white painted wall contained a landscape picture and two large pot plants.

It looked to all intents and purposes like a doctor's waiting room. All it needed was leather chairs and old magazines. Tightening his grip on the scabbard, Nathaniel picked the right door and pushed it open.

On a black leather couch, roped, tied and taped down, was Dela. Nathaniel and Cerberus rushed into the doctor's secret examination room not concerned at all for their safety.

Dela's hazel eyes popped wide open as she stared in disbelief and joy at Nathaniel and Cerberus's arrival. Nathaniel grabbed at her bonds, pulling, tugging, ripping them free and Cerberus chewed off the straps that held her ankles. With her feet and hands free, Dela sat up and pulled the black electrical tape from her lips. Nathaniel kissed her urgently before she could draw a breath, let alone speak.

"Dela! I thought I'd lost you! You cannot imagine the lengths I went to to find you!" Nathaniel pulled back and blurted out, tears welling in his eyes.

"Tell me later. We have to get out of here!" Dela hopped gingerly off the black leather examination couch and pushed him towards the open door he had come through.

"Okay, but where's Telal and Geial?" he asked, leading her towards the way of escape.

"Right here, demon-slayer!" came a cruel guttural mocking voice from the now open sliding door to Doctor Geial's office.

Cerberus, Nathaniel and Dela all spun round in surprise, Cerberus with an evil growl in his throat. Telal stood in the doorway flanked by Doctor Geial and a henchman with an Uzi.

Cerberus was on them in a flash, but Telal stepped into the attack – a glowing red hand thrust down on to the hound's head.

"Epistrefo!" the half-demon commanded. A red glow surrounded Cerberus and then he vanished with a sulphurous flash.

"Cerberus!" Nathaniel cried, taking a step forward, the scabbard at head height.

"Stay, King's Paladin!" Telal sneered, "your pet is still a demon-hound and governed by the laws of Hell. He too can be banished back to Hades for three days, or didn't you know that?" The more that Telal sneered, the more the stretched skin around his mouth and cheeks seemed to ripple like fluid rather than human flesh.

"Hypage Satana!" Nathaniel extended his palm to Telal and tried to hold him back.

"Your knowledge of ancient Greek is impressive Mister Le Meuille, but altogether useless and out of place, rather like yourself."

Geial and the henchman advanced further into the room. Telal remained in front of them facing Nathaniel.

"Blanae Medecia Linguae!" [Falsehoods of a smooth tongue] Nathaniel replied, using Latin now.

"Smooth tongue, eh? But I speak the truth now. You are vanquished King's Paladin. Drop your scabbard and give in to the inevitable darkness." Telal chuckled, his eyes firmly fixed on the scabbard in question.

"Why? When I know only the scabbard protects me from you and you cannot touch it? Why would I throw away my only advantage?" Nathaniel countered the half-demon bravely, even though the situation seemed utterly bleak.

"Because even though you are partly correct, you seem to forget Lee here with the machine pistol will shoot you dead in a mille-second and then Doctor Geial will operate on your woman, opening up wide enough to endure my pleasure." Telal's eyes flickered red with belligerence.

Nathaniel glanced at the briefly rescued Dela, then returned his gaze to the half-demon. The King's Paladin's eyes stared deeply into the hellish pits of Telal's eyes. Slowly the grin faded from the half-demon's countenance, as the eyes of many generations of demon-slayers bore back at him through Nathaniel's eyes.

"Aut vincere aut mori" [To conquer or die] Nathaniel whispered in Latin, knowing this was the last throw of the dice and he was seconds from death.

Fates, gods, or just life intervened. Today was not Nathaniel Le Meuille's day to die. A familiar looking brown-skinned Chinese man suddenly appeared around the doorway, pistol outstretched before him. He and the henchman with the Uzi saw each other at the same instant. It was just a matter of which of the two could aim and fire quickly enough. The Uzi fired first, its deadly stream of bullets pounding into the door next to the rescuer's head. The man's pistol fired twice, as the Uzi rounds finally found their mark and slammed deep into his skull, shattering his forehead. Yet the intruder's first shot blew the henchman's Adam's apple wide apart, the second shot drilling into the ceiling. Both men collapsed to the floor dead, before even a drop of their blood had even fallen.

Telal and Geial stared at Dela and Nathaniel in disbelief at what had just happened. Telal was the first to react. He pushed Geial at the now approaching Nathaniel as he fled out the sliding door into Geial's office.

Nathaniel threw the Doctor to the floor as Telal slammed the sliding door shut and a man and woman appeared at the other doorway behind them.

Geial used the leather table to pull himself up. Grabbing a scalpel from a nearby table he launched himself at Nathaniel's back as the King's Paladin tried to slide open the door to the doctor's office.

A single shot rang out deafening everyone in the room. Nathaniel heard a smack behind him and blood, bones and brains hit the wall next to him. Nathaniel turned to see what remained of Doctor Geial's head and body clattered to the floor beside him.

Nathaniel turned to see Mrs Dawson and Mr Green standing next to Dela, who was holding her hands over her ears. Mrs Dawson stood dead still, a Sig-Sauer hand gun smoking in her outstretched hand.

Nathaniel nodded his thanks to Mrs Dawson and turned to pull the sliding door open. The door led to a small office with a desk, chair and shelves piled high with books, both ancient and medical. Jars filled one shelf containing disfigured and aborted babies and foetuses pickled for eternity in alcohol. Looking around the room, Nathaniel could see more disturbing sights and medical instruments; yet no Telal. A faint whiff of sulphur touched Nathaniel's nostrils; there were no doors or windows to aid the half-demon's escape.

Nathaniel turned round to face the door as Dela and Mrs Dawson entered the room. The bearded man was on his knees next to his dead colleague.

"Where did he go?" Dela asked, rubbing at her sore wrists.

"Spirited away!" Nathaniel exclaimed, slapping his arms up and down to his sides.

Dela nearly knocked the wind out of Nathaniel as she rushed into his arms and crushed her body against him. Nathaniel pulled her closer. His arms enveloped her body, holding her tight. He felt her hair against his cheek and his nose breathed the perfume of her body.

"Are you okay, Dela?" Nathaniel pulled away to stare into her hazel eyes. "Did they do anything to you?"

Mrs Dawson, feeling like a gooseberry in their tender reunion, left the study and returned to her own reality and her fallen comrade.

"I'm okay." She kissed him ardently. "Really, they didn't touch me. Too afraid, I think, saving me for the big demon boss, I guess."

Nathaniel held her face in his hands and kissed her softly.

"I'm so sorry I let you down."

"You didn't let me down, Nat. You came back for me against all the frigging odds. You know what they call that?"

"Love," he purred.

"No, stupidity." She half-smiled. "You could have got yourself killed and where would the world be without its demon-hunter general? But I thank you all the same." She snuggled her head into his shoulder and neck.

"Sorry to interrupt you, but we don't have much time," Mrs Dawson stated, returning to the sliding doorway. "How long before the sleeping henchmen upstairs start to come to?"

"You're right of course!" Nathaniel let go of Dela until only his arm was around her waist. "Erm, ten minutes maximum. I think you'd better call in the reinforcements to swamp this house and secure it, so we can search for clues and Telal."

"Nathaniel, we are the cavalry. Our nearest regional HQ is in Birmingham. We have to act now or get out of here." Mrs Dawson turned back to look at her dead colleague, a Society Investigator, with over twelve years experience, all gone.

Everything told him to get out of the house, but if they did the demons would return at nightfall to rid the place of vital clues to the whereabouts of Telal.

Nathaniel reached down to collect the dead henchman's machine pistol.

"Okay, we have to tie up the henchmen and one really nutty woman upstairs in one of the bedrooms."

"Okay, let's go. Mister Green, come with me."

They made for the door that exited the examination room.

"What about Mr George?" The other man asked as Mrs Dawson, Nathaniel and Dela trooped past.

"We have to attend to the living first I'm afraid, before we can attend to our fallen dead." Mrs Dawson patted Mr Green on the shoulder. "I'm sorry."

Nathaniel and Dela followed the two Society members past the corpses and into the secret passage that led back to the wine cellar. Back in Doctor Geial's study a pair of dead embryonic eyes watched everyone leave the room. A minute head turned and strained long alcohol-pickled muscles to watch them all disappear into the hall and secret passage. Then the foetal floating baby went limp and a green cloud detached itself from the body and began to fill the jar. The jar slowly began to rock to and fro on the shelf as it edged itself towards the lip of the shelf. In a second it went from tottering on the edge of the shelf to toppling towards a catastrophic meeting with the wood flooring.

"Wait!" Dela squealed such a shrill cry that would have made Michael Jackson proud.

"What is it Dela?" Nathaniel turned on the cellar stairs to see what she wanted. Mrs Dawson and Mr Green also stopped and turned at the top of the stairs.

"What about Cerberus?" Dela exclaimed, remembering the hound of Hell was gone.

Nathaniel flicked his head back to Mrs Dawson, "Go on," then returned his attention to Dela.

"It's okay," Nathaniel said, reaching out a hand to her.

Dela took his hand without hesitation and let herself be led up the shadowy stairs to the house proper.

Nathaniel finished tying up the first of his paralysed victims to a chair.

"So, you see, Telal did to Cerberus what we did to Ashmodaios."

"Wot? Banished him back to Hades, but for how long?" Dela asked, tying the heavy's feet together with a length of clothes line.

"Three days." Nathaniel sucked at his teeth. "We will be without my old family friend for three whole days."

"Will we survive that long without him?" Dela rubbed her hands on her hips and stood up to look Nathaniel straight in the eyes.

Nathaniel tapped his nose with his finger and winked at Dela, staring deep into her questioning eyes.

"What the hell is that supposed to mean?" Dela asked, getting agitated at Nathaniel.

"I'll let you know in three days," he smiled. It was great to have her back to tease again.

"And what if we wind up fucking dead before then, Nat?"

Nathaniel went to gaze out of the conservatory windows at the rain falling from the grey skies.

"Then you'll have the satisfaction of being right, for the rest of eternity."

"Aargh!" Dela spun round and punched the henchman in the lips. He had been eyeing her through half-closed lids for thirty seconds. The henchman's eyes closed again for another few minutes.

"Wait!" Dela cried, "You're telling me Cerberus and the Demon Lord only get banished from earth for three days each?"

"Yes."

"Doesn't that mean like he's as powerful as a Demon Lord?" Dela was thinking aloud, she had always seen Cerberus as Nat's Scooby Doo companion, not a powerful creature from Hell.

"Sort of, he's a one-of-a-kind Cerberus. A Demon Lord cannot kill him or enter his part of Hell. He is eternal, like his friend Charon, the boatman of the river Styx. Cerberus will guard the gates of Hell forever." Nathaniel moved to Dela and kissed her on the cheek. Nathaniel then patted her bum and went over to open the door which led into the hall. Pulling it open, he whispered, "Remind me never to piss you off again, okay?" and he went into the hall to see how the others were getting along.

Twenty minutes later all the living henchmen and the disturbed, now robed, nurse were tied to chairs in the living room.

"What do you have in mind now, King's Paladin?" Mrs Dawson asked as the rain still lashed down hard on the conservatory windows.

"I suggest that you and I head down into the Doctor's secret rooms and thoroughly search the place."

"But what" – Dela interjected.

"Dela," Nathaniel held his palm up to halt her in mid-flow, "you will stay here with Mr Green to keep an eye out and guard the prisoners."

"But Nath!"

"No But's Dela, it will be dark soon, we have to get the search over and secure our defences before the demons can walk abroad once more."

"Isn't there anything I can do?" Dela asked, softening her tone, knowing he was right.

Nathaniel flicked two fingers beckoning Mrs Dawson to follow and turned to open the door.

"Salt, my love. From the kitchen. To go across every window and door." Nathaniel opened the door, with Mrs Dawson in tow, without looking back.

Dela smiled. He had lousy taste in music, but he did have a certain old English stiff-upper-lip style.

Nathaniel and Mrs Dawson made their way down the steps to the cellar, while Mr Green guarded the prisoners and Dela headed for the kitchen.

Mrs Dawson pulled out her 9mm pistol; Nathaniel held his sword scabbard before him.

"Did you get through to your supervisor?" Nathaniel asked as they walked across the cellar floor to the entrance to the secret passage.

"I spoke to the Investigator General of the area himself. There's a spot of bother going on in Warwick. He cannot spare anyone until the morning." Mrs Dawson explained ruefully whilst they headed down the secret passageway.

"And what did your people in London say to that?" Nathaniel smiled and turned to her. "You seem the type of lady that doesn't take no for an answer."

"The Senior Investigator I report to sympathised, but even they could not send reinforcements 'til tomorrow morning." Mrs Dawson frowned, not making eye contact with the King's Paladin.

"So much for your Inner circle. Now you see why I work alone." Nathaniel gave a rye smile and entered the late Doctor Geial's examining room.

"Ah, but as you said, I'm not the type of lady to give up easily, so I contacted one of our sleeper members and he'll be here within the hour." Mrs Dawson beamed for the first time in a long time.

Nathaniel noticed how pretty her face now looked with a smile attached to it.

"Hope he gets here soon, because of the lousy weather we have about an hour and a half of daylight left, if you can call it that."

"Hope the sleeper knows what he's getting into. What is a sleeper member by the way?" Nathaniel asked, already knowing the answer.

Mrs Dawson was bending down opening a cupboard door and pulling out four surgical gowns.

"Sleeper's are our life blood. They are non-active members of the Society. They go about their daily lives, but have been touched or involved with the supernatural in the past. All are personally, physiologically investigated by us and are up-dated on unclassified or restricted worldwide information concerning the Society." Mrs Dawson unfolded one gown and laid it over the top half of Geial's corpse.

"So how many sleepers do you have Mrs Dawson?" Nathaniel took a gown from her and laid it over Geial's legs.

"Nearly five hundred worldwide if you really wanna know."

They both moved on to Mr George's corpse and with wrinkles of pain and anguish around her eyes, Mrs Dawson laid a gown over his bloodied face and torso.

"And do you have the authority to order a Sleeper member out of his daily life into a fight to the death with the hordes of Hell?"

Mrs Dawson laid the last gown on her friend's legs. "I deemed the situation was of the highest emergency and acted within that remit for this situation."

Nathaniel was aware that Mrs Dawson did not hold his gaze at all during the last question, but just stared at her fallen comrade.

"Did you know him a long time?" Nathaniel asked with a little more sensitivity, putting a hand on the High Investigator's shoulder.

"Nearly seven years. He was a good friend and a solid Society Investigator with ten years field experience." Mrs Dawson turned away from Mr George's corpse and looked up at Nathaniel mournfully.

"We better hurry and investigate Doctor Geial's study before your new man arrives. What's his name by the way?" Nathaniel moved off through the sliding door into the study cum office cum chamber of foetal horrors.

"James Warren-Gash," Mrs Dawson replied, following Nathaniel into the study.

"Hope he's better than his surname implies." Nathaniel swiftly crouched down with a crack of kneecaps. "Hello, this wasn't here before!"

"What is it?" Mrs Dawson asked on tip-toe trying to look over his broad shoulders.

"A broken medical jar and one of those freaky foetus on the floor." Nathaniel poked at the foetus and glass with a Parker pen he grabbed from the edge of the nearby desk.

"What the hell does that signify?" Mrs Dawson asked, thinking aloud.

Meanwhile one of the gowns laid across Mr George moved slightly and deliberately.

Meanwhile Dela was salting the windowsills in the kitchen whilst watching the light fade and the dark thunder clouds slowly inch towards the house. The rain had abated half an hour ago, but it would soon return and with it a four o'clock dusk.

After finishing with the windows, Dela salted the open doorway from the kitchen and made her way to the hall, turning on every light switch and lamp she could find. She didn't have time to meticulously work through each room, so she decided to open all the downstairs doors and salt the doorways only. If she had time and enough salt she would cover all the windows of each room too.

Mr Green shifted uneasily from foot to foot; one eye on the distant storm clouds approaching from over the dark trees of the garden, the other eye on the tied-up prisoners. One of the henchmen was awake, he had tried to struggle free at first, but the appearance of Mr Green's handgun an inch from his temple put him in more of a relaxed mood. The girl from upstairs was also awake and now had a small table cover in her mouth and wrapped round her head to stop her unrelenting screaming fits.

Mr Green was from a large Northern-Irish family and even though he had companions and allies with him around the house;

when he watched the dusk descend rapidly he'd never felt so alone in all his born days.

Mrs Dawson and Nathaniel continued to search the Doctor's secret study for clues, papers or evidence to the disappearance of Telal. Nathaniel and the Society High Investigator had pushed aside Geial's desk loudly and behind it was a small air conditioning grate measuring five inches by four inches.

"Maybe he did a vampire and in a cloud of mist disappeared up this vent," Mrs Dawson half joked.

"If you'd ever faced a Nosferatu you would have known that was a distinct possibility." The fierceness and venom in Nathaniel's voice startled her. She'd never seen him get so prickly about anything before. He was always so relaxed and well-balanced.

Mrs Dawson stepped back a bit, "Sorry, didn't mean to offend."

For the first time Nathaniel saw a gentler side to the Society Investigator. He looked at his shoes, then up at Mrs Dawson, a strange look crossed his face like a failed smile. Nathaniel stood up dwarfing her by over a foot, a dark and terrifying look on his normally handsome face. Nathaniel reached behind him and grabbed the scabbard tightly.

"Hey! What the hell are you playing at?" Mrs Dawson was shocked at the sudden change of events and Nathaniel's sudden mood swing. Mrs Dawson reached suddenly for the pistol, holstered in the back of her spine, but Nathaniel's reflexes were quicker and he grabbed her wrist with his free left hand.

Mrs Dawson looked up at the rage in the King's Paladin's eyes and felt fear. Nathaniel had seemed to grow in stature, taking on the role of an ancient demon-killing knight.

Like a dance, Nathaniel pulled her to him and turned around her at the same time. He brought up his scabbard and then whipped round exchanging places. Nathaniel brought the scabbard down as hard as he could on the advancing shambling corpse that was once Mr George's head.

Mrs Dawson stifled a scream as the ex-Mr George's head split in two with an explosion of blood and brain. A smell of deep sulphur assailed their nostrils and mouths and bile rose in their throats as they reeled backwards. A green vaporous cloud appeared from the tissue that had been the Society man's head.

Mrs Dawson's and Nathaniel's buttocks backed against the desk, the sword scabbard held loosely before him. A thin scream erupted from somewhere inside the zombified body or the green mist. They couldn't really tell which.

The green cloud shot suddenly to the floor where an abyss of heat and flame opened up as if from nowhere and the green cloud vanished into it. The flames and heat were gone and the hole to Hell snapped shut, without a trace of ever having been there.

Mr George's dead-again corpse fell backwards against the wall next to the door, hitting a plug socket and breaking it half off the wall. Mr George had died again, leaving a bloody red mess in his wake; this time he would remain still.

"Fucking hell!" Mrs Dawson exclaimed not believing her eyes.

"Incredible" Nathaniel whispered as he lent forward and prodded the floor where the hell hole had been with his scabbard.

"That banished his half-demon green soul to Hell for a while." Nathaniel agilely stepped through the late Mr George's brains and blood to examine the corpse close up.

"Careful!" Mrs Dawson had one hand to her white face, the other outstretched to the King's Paladin.

"It's okay, your former colleague is quite dead again." Nathaniel bent at the knees to examine the place where Mr George's head used to be.

"It's okay." Mrs Dawson felt sick, cold and distressed having just seen one of her closest colleagues' zombified head explode.

"Hello!" Nathaniel's long fingers moved into the gap behind the broken plug socket and pulled out a folded piece of yellow paper. "What's this I wonder?"

Mrs Dawson walked over the legs of the corpse into the examination room, past Doctor Geial's still motionless corpse and headed down the secret corridor to the cellar. She knew from her drinking days at university she had to get out of there or be violently sick.

Nathaniel covered up Mr George's corpse again and left the room, pulling the door across as he went. He gave Doctor Geial's corpse a prod with his sword scabbard from a safe distance. Satisfied that Geial was truly dead and troubling Cerberus in Hell, he left the examination room humming a Kylie Minogue tune.

Dela was salting a semi-circle around the front door of the house when a noise behind her caused her to spin round, an arc of salt from its plastic container following her.

It was Mrs Dawson coming up from the cellar looking slightly green around the gills.

"Hey, you okay, lady?" Dela asked. "Where's Nathaniel, is he okay?" Dela moved closer to the "Society" woman. Dela didn't trust her or like her, maybe because she seemed more Nathaniel's type than this Balham sister.

"He's fine, he'll be up in a minute." Mrs Dawson put her hands on her hips and took a deep breath.

"What's da matter, did something happen down there?" Dela's normally smooth lovely forehead wrinkled up like her grandmother's.

"You could say that," Mrs Dawson stated, straightening up, "We had a little unpleasant incident down there." Just as she finished there came a loud rap of the knocker on the front door.

Both women spun round, Mrs Dawson drawing her gun from its back holster, hidden by her blouse.

"Now we seem to have an incident up here also!" Dela quipped, but humour was the last thing on her mind.

Shutting the stench of death and old terrible memories behind, Nathaniel closed the examination room door behind him. In the picture-covered corridor-cum-waiting area he unfolded the yellowed paper in his hand. At first he thought the handwriting wasn't English. The letters curled so much that it seemed to come from a calligraphy lesson. It read:

*"They have taken my baby, I feel so empty. They are in league with the Devil. Please help. Anna Klose"*

"What the hell is this about and why was the paper so well hidden?" he wondered.

He turned the paper over in his hands for a while, then put it in his pocket and left the secret passage for the cellar. He so wanted to see Dela again and give her a kiss and a big hug.

Dela and Mrs Dawson seemed frozen where they stood, eyes glued to the front door. The knock came again on the brass ring on the heavy oak door. This time it seemed less loud and ominous, but still the two women didn't budge an inch.

The living room door opened and Mr Green with his unholstered gun appeared his head round the corner.

"What's going on? Was that the door?"

Both women involuntarily jumped a millimetre in their respective footwear, but at least it moved Mrs Dawson into action.

"Keep an eye on the prisoners, it could be a trap." Mrs Dawson waved her colleague back into the living room and walked towards the front door. When the Society Investigator had come level with Dela, she joined Mrs Dawson and they approached the door as one. They had come within two feet of the door when the knocker rapped again, twice.

"Hello, is anyone there?" came a young male voice, muffled by the thick oak door.

"Don't sound like a demon from Hell," Dela remarked to her white companion.

Before Mrs Dawson could do anything Dela stepped up and unbolted the door. Mrs Dawson raised her pistol in panic and aimed it dead centre of the door.

"Ready?" Dela whispered.

"No," Mrs Dawson explained, realising her gun's safety catch was on.

"Too late!" and Dela pulled the door inwards so it swung in to the left. A flash of lightning and then a peel of thunder chose that time to strike, as a tall thin figure was silhouetted against the dark dusk sky.

"Aargh!" cried the figure seeing Mrs Dawson and her gun: it quickly back-pedalled and went sprawling backwards over a push bike.

"Shit!" Mrs Dawson exclaimed.

"Fuck!" Dela jumped at the shock.

"Who the hell is that?" asked Nathaniel, coming up behind them.

Dela switched on the porch light and illuminated a young thin boy of about seventeen – tall, lanky with glasses and a mop of wet black hair plastered to his skull. He was trying to extricate himself from his bike as the three nervous demon-hunters approached him.

"Who are you?" Mrs Dawson asked, flicking her gun at the young lad to dramatic effect.

"James Warren-Gash. I'm – I'm your reinforcement, a Mrs Dawson sent for me," the teenager stammered nervously.

"We're screwed," Dela let out a whistle and turned around, looking for her salt bottle.

Mrs Dawson lowered her pistol in disbelief. Things were going from worse to fucking worse quickly.

Nathaniel reached down and grabbed James's hand. "Come on son, you better get inside, you're not safe out there."

James sat on a tall three-legged stool in the kitchen. Nathaniel had found a blanket to wrap round him and Dela had made him a strong sugary cup of tea. James, in his youthful naivety had expected a hero's welcome, or at least a thank you. He had got neither. Mrs Dawson, who had asked for his help, wanted to send him packing back into the near darkness and driving rain. The tall man argued with Mrs Dawson in the hall that he was here now and even though he wouldn't be any use they were stuck with him.

James felt wet, useless and miserable. He turned to look at the other attractive lady who had made his tea. James saw that she was looking at him suspiciously and he quickly looked down.

"So how come a kid your age is a member of this Ghostbusters' Society?" Dela asked, lounging against the washing machine.

"Me – er – my dad was an Investigator, he had a talent and it seems so do I, so I'm a Sleeper Member." James answered nervously, he always found talking to women hard work.

"Does your dad know you're here?"

"My dad disappeared on a trip to Romania two years ago, his body was never found; but he's dead." James sniffed, a raindrop dripped from the tip of his nose on to his jeans.

"I'm sorry man, but if no body was found how do you know he's dead?" Dela asked less harshly, moving closer to the boy.

"Because we share the same talent, we can talk with the dead." James let out a long sniff and wiped his wet face.

"You can talk to the dead," Dela repeated slowly, her forehead wrinkled in thought. "So how's Marvin Gaye then?"

"James, you can stay," Nathaniel stated, entering the kitchen as Mrs Dawson disappeared into the back room in a huff.

"You stick with Dela, okay?"

James nodded in silent agreement.

"We'd all better go into the back room for a while." Nathaniel beckoned to Dela and James to follow him. They all bundled into the room, James slightly worried that he could be tied up any moment like the henchman and Geial's nurse.

"James, sit." Nathaniel gently but firmly pushed James into a comfortable armchair. Mr Green was building up a nice log fire and Mrs Dawson was standing with her Sig-Sauer pistol drawn by the conservatory windows.

"Dela, I have to leave the house briefly."

"But…"

"No buts, the Grimoire is in the boot of the hire car, it must not fall into the enemy's hands for all our sakes."

Dela stared deep into her lover's eyes, knowing it would be useless to argue when his mind was made up.

"We're a team. I'll come with you," she pleaded.

"No. I go alone." Nathaniel kissed Dela hard on the lips before she could protest further; everyone's eyes, including Mrs Dawson's, were on them.

"Be quick, lover," Dela whispered, holding his face in her hands briefly, then let them drop.

Nathaniel smiled thinly and readied the scabbard in his hands, then turned and strode purposefully through the french doors.

"Where are you going?" Mrs Dawson asked, following him through the french doors and in to the conservatory.

"I left something priceless in my hire car. We need it and the enemy desires it destroyed. So I must go and retrieve it at all costs." Nathaniel unlocked the conservatory doors. Mrs Dawson put her hand on one handle to stop him.

"Leave it. It's nearly pitch black out there. The demons could be roaming the grounds already." Mrs Dawson found Nathaniel arrogant, reckless and also a brave ally.

"Then you best keep an eye open for them, okay?" Nathaniel clicked his tongue, winked, opened the french doors and slipped from the relative safety of the conservatory into the treacherous stormy night.

Mrs Dawson stood at the open doors, pistol poised, as Nathaniel pulled up his coat collar and disappeared into the dark folds of the night.

Mr Green and Dela moved into the conservatory to watch Nathaniel disappear behind the bushes at the end of the garden. Mr Green and Mrs Dawson then moved back into the living room. They hoped the light from the room would keep the demons at bay.

As soon as Nathaniel had disappeared behind the near darkness of the garden bushes his bravado started to plummet. His senses went on alert; he found the back wall of the garden and pulled himself up. He half-scaled one leg over the top of the wall, looking into the darkness for shadows or movement. Seeing no movement except the trees in the storm, he pulled himself over the wall and hoped the shadows all around him stayed where they were.

"See anything?" Mrs Dawson asked Dela from inside the house.

"No," Dela flinched as a flash of lightning illuminated the garden for the briefest of moments.

"James." Mrs Dawson walked towards the conservatory.

"Yes." James stood up from the sofa, but did not move any closer to the conservatory doors.

"Go into the kitchen and try and find any matches, candles or torches," Mrs Dawson ordered.

"Why?" he asked, moving towards the door to the hall.

"Just in case, James, okay?" she replied and returned to her vigil.

Nathaniel made it to the car without any mishaps – only his imagination to scare him. Holding the scabbard above his head he circled the car; nothing was hiding behind it. Pulling the keys from his pocket he opened the boot and pulled the rucksack that contained the Grimoire out. He pulled on the straps of the rucksack, switching the scabbard from hand to hand quickly.

He pulled the boot lid down slowly, expecting to see demons behind it, but found none. He closed the boot with a gentle click. The thunder rumbled after another flash of lightning. It was a good time to scan the area around him. None of the shadows in the dark seemed any worse than before, as night became day for an instant. He locked the boot for some reason, probably trying to keep the situation as normal as he could, even though this storm was making him feel uneasy. The rain had slowed slightly and he moved off back towards the garden and house.

Suddenly Nathaniel Le Meuille stopped dead in his tracks. "I've got a bloody car, der!" Nathaniel smacked his wet forehead with his palms and jogged back to the car and pulling off the rucksack and transferring it to his scabbard holding hand he opened the driver's door. Squinting through the now night darkness and rain, he scanned his surroundings and then jumped into the car.

He closed the door. No light had come on because he had removed it before he had raided the house. He central-locked all the doors and unlike any horror film, the car started first time and he turned on the headlights, then drove towards the gravel road that ran beside Doctor Geial's former house. Being inside the car was falsely comforting and the headlights he switched to full beam gave him a little extra confidence as he drove off.

James had worked as quickly as he could; he had been lucky to find one torch, a lighter, a large box of kitchen matches, a large box of white candles (four left) and strangely, a small box of small birthday cake candles (eight) in the larder. He had been walking out of the kitchen when he glanced out of the window as lightning illuminated the garden for a second. Petrified to the spot James had been sure he had seen a shadow creeping along the bushy border to the far left of the garden.

Why he hadn't thought of just driving the car before he had even left the house astonished him. Maybe he was only concentrating on just getting to the car, and the dangers inherent in that, rather than the return trip. He decided to drive right round to the front of the house. No use leaving the protection of the car. He drove past his incursion point, over the garden wall. He followed the road as it bent a little to the left and then slammed on the brakes. Ahead, on the gravel road appeared two lumbering demons, steam rising off them from the rain. They were straight ahead forty feet in front of the rental car, arms raised up against the glare of the headlights.

A hissing red demonic fist suddenly exploded through the passenger side window. Glass flew everywhere and Nathaniel felt a cold slash as a shard cut his cheek. A demonic face and arm appeared through the window, seeking the car's only occupant.

Nathaniel flung the gear stick into reverse and floored the accelerator pedal. The demon was there for a few seconds and then was left behind (or in front) as the car sped backwards. Trying to see where the demon fell occupied Nathaniel as the rental car slammed into the garden wall which he had scaled twice. The back window cracked all over but did not fall out and

Nathaniel's head gave the steering wheel a teeth-jarring head butt.

Nathaniel, for three long seconds, was out of it. He was awake, because he had a stabbing pain in his forehead and an ache in his teeth, but he did not know where he was or what was occurring. Only the sight of the rising demon a few feet away and his advancing friends (fiends) snapped him back to reality as lightning flashed everywhere in his dazzled eyes.

He tasted blood on his tongue from somewhere. He had to move; the nearest hell-fiend was only half a dozen feet away. Nathaniel turned and pushed himself through the gap in the front seats and found himself on his knees on the back seat.

Nathaniel looked back. The demon which had attacked the car was a yard away from his front bumper, and the brace of demons only ten feet behind him.

"THE BOOK!" his mind screamed and his torso jumped through the gap to grab the rucksack off the floor and the scabbard which he had totally forgotten. Grabbing them both in one hand and holding the side of the passenger seat with the other, he wildly threw himself and his prized possessions backwards.

The rucksack flew back behind him and punched a football-sized hole in the car windscreen, just as the first demon appeared: arms, shoulders and head through the glassless passenger window.

Nathaniel had no choice. He braced his feet on the back seat, closed his eyes, folded his arms over his head and dived at where he thought the hole in the back windscreen was. He hit the glass which exploded into the wet night and he rolled once on the boot of the car. He grabbed the scabbard and rucksack and pushed them over the wall, and with his pained body heaved himself over to land on top of them in a wet flowerbed.

He heard a howl of anger from the frustrated demons behind the wall as he groped in the mud and flowers for the bag and scabbard. He found the rucksack straight away but it took him five seconds to lay his hand on the scabbard. Every second seemed to last an hour; then with adrenaline pushing him on, he slipped and pushed himself into a half-upright position. Nathaniel resisted the urge to look behind and ran. Otherwise as he burst from behind the bushes, he might have seen the demon hop with ease over the wall behind him.

Mrs Dawson and Mr Green stood just outside the conservatory doors, an awning protecting them from the worst of the weather. Dela stood inside the conservatory, anxiously clutching her container of salt.

Just then they heard an almighty crash and saw the distant glow of soft light at the rear of the garden. A peel of thunder stopped them from hearing any more.

The inside door to the main room opened and James came running in eyes wide in panic. He ran past the prisoners and towards the conservatory doors as a dark figure appeared at the far end of the garden. Both pistols instantly trained on the dark figure as it ran closer towards the light emanating from the house.

"It's Nathaniel!" Dela screamed, as James pushed passed her and grabbed Mrs Dawson's gun arm and pulled it to the left.

"Over there, now!" James screamed in her ear.

A white creature with a horned head, a body of bones and tight skin had appeared from the left-hand flower beds and was flying (with white bat-like wings) towards the running Nathaniel. The storm above threw a bolt of lightning at a tree which exploded with a fiery crack at the end of the garden.

Mrs Dawson's pistol flared out in the darkness as she fired her entire clip in quick succession into the white-winged demon, while Mr Green's pistol also fired, but in a different direction down the garden at the red glowing abominations that came after Nathaniel.

Both the Society's members' bullets found their marks and each shot slowed the demons' advance for a second, but had no other effect.

"Dela get ready with the salt!" Mrs Dawson shouted loudly above the storm as she backed into the conservatory. Mr Green replaced his empty pistol clip and fired off another couple of well-aimed shots at the red demon chasing Nathaniel. The two shots, aimed at what Mr Green hoped were knee-caps, worked and the demon stumbled and fell.

Nathaniel was running on pure adrenaline as he sprinted for the conservatory doors. Rain and lightning stung his vision, thunder and gunshots exploded in his ears. He could see salvation and sanctuary before him, but he could also see in the corner of his right eye that the white demon was going to beat him to the outer conservatory doors.

Mr Green fired off one shot that bounced harmlessly off the bony-white demon's skull, then retreated inside the conservatory, shutting and bolting his door. Soon only one door was half open for Nathaniel. Mrs Dawson stood by that and Dela behind her, salt container at the ready.

The henchman, the insane nurse, Dela, Mrs Dawson, Mr Green and even James could see Nathaniel wasn't going to make it to the door in time.

Nathaniel was seven feet from the conservatory and the demon which was flying diagonally at him was only five feet away. He knew; his mind working at full speed, while the scene played out like it was a slow-motion Brian de Palma film, that he was seconds from death. When you are seconds from death you get desperate and when you're desperate you normally have only one last desperate roll of the dice. Nathaniel hoped the dice came up all ones and not six, six, six.

Nathaniel, with a last farewell prayer, threw his ancestor's sword scabbard at the white demon then ran with aching sides for the lone open conservatory door and comparative safety. The scabbard that had once held the sword of the King's Paladins, the bane of all demons, struck the bony-demon around the neck. An explosion of noiseless petrol-blue flame engulfed the spawn of Hell and vanished back to its plane of existence.

Nathaniel pelted through the door, crashed into a wicker chair and tumbled base over apex on to the conservatory floor. Mrs Dawson shut and bolted the glass door as Dela knelt and salted the entrance way to bar any demon intrusions for the foreseeable future.

The demon who had chased Nathaniel, its shiny glowing skin bright red in the dark, came to a total and unnatural halt outside the conservatory doors.

Dela suddenly rekindled her mother's unwavering faith in God and prayed that the demon would not come crashing through the thin glass which divided them and rip her pretty head off.

The demon's blood-red eyes stared at them through the glass doors: Dela half on the floor, Mrs Dawson and Mr Green next to the door, his prey on the floor and others in the room yonder.

"Everyone get back!" Mrs Dawson ordered in a hushed tone. She felt like she was in a circus stand-off with a lion.

Mrs Dawson and Mr Green retreated slowly, their pistols trained at the beast which gave them false comfort.

Dela scrambled back on her palms, soles and bottom, until she reached Nathaniel, who was sitting rubbing his ankle which he had bashed on the wicker chair. They hugged each other close in spite of the situation. "I'm back," he sighed, pulling the rucksack off his back.

"Don't you ever do anything so fucking reckless again, you hear me? We've only just hooked up again! Promise me you'll never leave me again!" Dela got up and then pulled him up after her. He limped a little on his tender ankle.

"I'll never leave you again Dela, I promise" and he let her help him hobble back into the living room through the french doors.

"James, light a couple of the candles. Quickly. We don't know how smart these demons are," Mrs Dawson ordered.

"Mr Green," Mrs Dawson continued, "take the salt and make sure the house is secure."

Dela threw her a look but didn't protest. It wasn't the time for her to get arsey and double checking her salting could save all their lives.

"So what are we dealing with here and how many?" Mrs Dawson asked Nathaniel.

"There's at least one more demon out there and we know Ashmodaios is serious this time," Nathaniel explained, "because it's raining."

"Of course! Yeah!" Dela exclaimed, getting his point, as if she were a demon expert.

"So?" asked Mrs Dawson, her arms out wide.

"These are no spirits or manes, these are proper demons from Hell's embrace. It's gonna take more than bullets and crucifixes to stop these guys. Nathaniel glanced back at the window, the red glowing thing was gone. Lightning illuminated the garden once more. It seemed devoid of any movement.

"We haven't much time, we need to prepare or we won't last the night." Nathaniel was deadly serious as the thunder above punctuated his words.

"So what do we need to do?" Mrs Dawson asked as she checked the number of bullets left in the clip of her pistol.

"Any rooms in the place with wooden floors?"

"The dining room has a wooden floor babes," Dela replied. She had been in all the rooms salting the windows.

"Then we have to move fast. Everyone to the dining room. We'll need to move the furniture about." Nathaniel patted James on the shoulder and moved for the door.

"What about these three?" Mrs Dawson pointed at the girl and the two tied up henchmen.

"Take the girl with us." Nathaniel paused to think for a moment. "Put them both in the little w.c. across the hall. I'm sure you and Mr Green can drag the chairs there."

Then Nathaniel was gone with Dela and James close behind. Mrs Dawson was left alone in the room with her three charges as lightning flashed outside again. The storm seemed no closer to abating and she suddenly felt very rattled indeed.

# CHAPTER 10

Luckily, apart from a huge table and chairs and a few cabinets, the dining room was sparsely furnished. Nathaniel, James and Dela dragged the table to one side of the room. Then while Nathaniel nipped off to the kitchen, Dela moved the chairs into the hall and James began dismantling the huge six-part table.

Nathaniel came back with some small metal Indian curry bowls and one glass mixing bowl, which he placed on the floor.

"I need one chair Dela, here." He pointed, "The cabinet must go also."

Dela obliged as Nathaniel opened his rucksack and pulled out his ancestors' grimoire and put it on the chair. He began to flick through it as he searched through his rucksack for a magic marker and some chalk with his other hand.

Nathaniel found the page he was after and began reading as chaos and movement carried on around him.

Mrs Dawson and Mr Green had dragged the two henchmen, still tied to their chairs, to a small lavatory near the stairs opposite the dining room. They managed to squeeze both of them in, facing each other. They checked their bonds were still secure and closed the door behind them.

The girl was silent now, probably so scared out of her mind that she might never find her way back to sanity. They untied her and easily led her to sit on a chair and left her staring into eternity in a cleared part of the dining room.

Nathaniel jumped up from his reading, ignoring everything around him and grabbed a sword from where it had been mounted on a wall. Finally the dining room was clear. Mr Green escorted James to the upstairs toilet because he had to go. Mrs Dawson stood in the hallway, pistol at the ready and Dela was re-salting the window ledge once more.

Nathaniel looked at a diagram etched with a quill hundreds of years ago. Then the King's Paladin began to draw a rough circle on the floor with chalk. Outside that circle he drew another roughly parallel, a foot's width apart. Nathaniel stood inside these circles and made changes, rubbed out and amended until they were both as near as round as he could manage. Nathaniel then took out a small black notebook and pencil and starting jotting down figures. Then he pulled a tape measure out and began measuring both circles and Dela watched as he went from the notebook to the grimoire.

Mr Green anxiously peered out of an upstairs window while James pee-ed nervously and quickly in the nearby bathroom. The storm still continued unabated. Mr Green scratched his nose; he'd never endured a storm that had lasted so long. The lightning and thunder seemed to be permanently above the house and that was downright unnatural.

Mr Green gripped his pistol harder as he saw a red shape briefly in the shadows of the garden. The bathroom door opened and James nervously came out.

"Come on lad, let's get you downstairs." Mr Green glanced out of the window again as he moved off, but the red figure had disappeared.

With everyone in the room now, Nathaniel continued to complete his protective circle with a thick black marker pen. The outer ring was now divided into thirteen separate chevrons. Each of the chevrons would have a symbol inside, seven already did having been painstakingly copied from his ancestral book. Bowls were placed on certain symbols around the circle. One contained Nathaniel's gold watch, another his silver lighter, a third a small bronze horse shoe from Dr Geial's living room, and the fourth was an iron nail pulled from a wall.

The circle was over five foot in diameter as it had to be spacious enough for six to sit comfortably inside it. James and the vacant nurse sat quietly on chairs in one corner of the room. Mr Green peeked through the front curtains of the living room, peering into the rain. Mrs Dawson stood in the hallway by the open door, keeping a vigil for the unexpected.

Dela walked over to her as Nathaniel tried to go as fast as he could to complete the protective magic circle.

"So what do you think about all this black magic stuff?" Mrs Dawson asked in a soft voice, her eyes flicking to Nathaniel.

"If you'd asked me a week ago," said Dela, "the only thing I ever prayed for was a lottery win and the only thing I had total faith in was my vibrator!" Dela's smile was beautiful and infectious, causing Mrs Dawson to grin back at her despite the situation they faced.

"I know, I'm in the Society and I've seen many supernatural things, but a pistol or a stake or a rational mind normally sorts them out."

"Tell you something," Dela stated, "me mother was a great believer in all things like this. I think she'd have liked Nathaniel, even though he's a little pastier than my normal fellas!"

"I know you have every faith in Nathaniel, but this makes me feel uneasy. It's like we are using some evil magic of the demons and I've never been so reliant on anyone else for my own life before." Mrs Dawson suddenly looked to Dela's eyes, like a normal thirty-something scared woman.

"I have total faith in Nat; we all have to if we are to ever make it out of this bloody house." Dela squeezed Mrs Dawson's hand, then walked back to watch Nathaniel's progress.

Mrs Dawson walked over to the fireplace. Two lighted candles burned slowly, even though the lights blazed throughout the whole house.

Nathaniel moved on to his next symbol. He still had three more to finish. He had to shut out all fears, including his surroundings and the other people in the room as he meticulously carried out his task.

Mrs Dawson moved to the window where Mr Green kept his vigil. "Anything?" she asked.

"Nothing but the rain," he replied. "Maybe – !" His words died on his lips the same instant as all the lights in the house flickered and went out. The nurse wailed in horror and the others choked a little with surprise. The two candles on the fireplace mantle were the only illumination in the room now. Torchlight appeared on the floor from Nathaniel. He made no other sound or movement, but continued working with his symbols.

Another torchlight appeared from the window from Mrs Dawson's hand. She and Mr Green rushed to the open door, scanning the hall for unwelcome guests.

"What are we gonna do?" James cried out, scared out of his young wits now.

"Nat?" Dela asked, moving over to comfort James and the crazed nurse.

"Not now, babe, bit busy," Nathaniel stated softly, continuing his work. "Try and stay calm old thing, got to concentrate."

Dela stared through the semi-darkness in disbelief at Nathaniel's calmness. "Stay calm! Fuck me, Nat, how can you stay so calm now?"

"Cos, my dear," Nathaniel paused to breathe, "if I don't finish this in time we are all dead, so if I can please get on."

If Nathaniel had been looking, he would have seen the scowl etched deep into Dela's face. Sensing Dela's brown eyes boring deep into the side of his head Nathaniel relented.

"Dela, get yourself, James and the woman into the circle; bring the cushions and bottles of water too."

Dela moved over to the now standing James.

"And Dela, be careful when you step into the circle, okay?"

Nathaniel moved on to the penultimate symbol as he tried to close his hearing off and ignore the world around him.

Mrs Dawson and Mr Green, on the other hand, were straining their eardrums to the maximum. Both stood just inside the hallway, both staring into the gloom, pistols at the ready. Mrs Dawson's torch beam went from door to door as an eerie silence filled the house. Thirty seconds passed and it seemed to the two Society members that it was like thirty minutes. Only Mr Green's slightly harder nasal breathing could be heard as they waited nervously.

From upstairs, somewhere in the dark, a floorboard creaked. Both Society members spun their pistols and the torch beam was aimed up the stairs. Five seconds of breath-holding silence passed, then from upstairs another floorboard creaked followed a second later by a heavy footfall. Another heavy echo-ey footstep (foot-thud more like) was heard above them upstairs, but getting louder, getting closer. The Society duo exchanged a quick one second look of anxiety, then all their strained senses returned to their stair vigil.

In the dining room Nathaniel was finishing off the penultimate ward of protection (with the marker pen). He could not hasten as any incorrect copying from the book could render the circle useless.

The footfalls deep and heavy, like a Sumo wrestler wearing iron-clad slippers, grew louder and closer. Something was in the black shadows that lay heavy on the landing; two smudged pastel red glows of light could be seen.

Into the beam of Mrs Dawson's torchlight it stepped – a seven foot, red fiery skinned demon from hell's furnace. Black ebony horns lanced from its massive cranium and two sets of arms, with jet black razor sharp nails, moved to the top of the stairs. It did not need to embrace the dark shadows any longer, it was majestic, powerful, without fear and full of the malice and torture of a million souls. It roared at the frail man and woman cowering at the bottom of the stairs and planted a huge cloven foot on the top step.

Inside the circle the nurse whimpered and buried her head into James's shoulder. Any other time this would have made him cum in his pants, but the demon's roar had turned his bones to chalk.

Nathaniel moved on to the last empty chevron and re-consulted his ancestors' book before he started the last glyph. Dela looked around the room anxiously. She was exhausted and felt like she had neither the energy levels or strength of will to see this through until dawn.

Another step down form the demon forced the trembling Society Investigators into action. Shots rang out, one-two, one-two from their pistols. The bullets found their mark and the demon stopped and swayed in its step for a second, then descended another stair. The pistols rang out again, both head shots making the foul beast of Gehenna recoil briefly in pain.

"Go for the eyes!" Mrs Dawson cried out in desperation. Both pistols fired again, one grazing the demon's horns, the other burying itself deep into one of its lava-pit pupils. The demon howled from deep inside its chest, its hands moving up to its wound. This managed to delay the swaying demon for a couple of seconds, then it was descending the stairs again.

The demon smiled, its fangs showed through the smoky torch-beam as it headed for the Society duo, clawed hands reaching forward. Mr Green fired again, hitting its chest and left arm. The foul thing hardly recoiled at all. The next shot was a surprised click.

"Re-load!" Mrs Dawson ordered.

"No time, let's go!"

Mrs Dawson fired two parting shots into the demon's head as Mr Green pulled at her arm. The demon paused as the two ran back into the dining room. Mr Green slammed the door behind them and then jumped into the large circle on the wooden floor. Each fumbled for new ammo clips as the door to the dining room was pushed to the floor off its hinges.

Its red body was framed by the pale light in the room. Mrs Dawson and Mr Green were not in any way near to re-loading their guns; James and the nurse closed their eyes and held each other tight, while Dela stared at Nathaniel.

The demon roared and stepped warily into the room, where it met unusual resistance. A black marker pen flew across the room and bounced off the end of its nose. The demon was taken aback for a second, then charged at the standing Nathaniel le Meuille.

"Barra kako daimon!" Nathaniel cried aloud and all around him the symbols in the chevrons glowed with an eerie ethereal light. The demon struck the boundaries of the circle and suddenly recoiled in shock, pain and terror.

"Begone wicked demon!" Nathaniel cried aloud in English this time. With an almighty roar the demon fled the room.

Everyone in the circle stared at Nathaniel in awe. Everyone except Dela. The glow of the symbols and the chevrons dulled 'til only faint lines could be seen, then nothing. A heavy silence filled the dining room. Mrs Dawson and Mr Green watched as Nathaniel turned to face them.

"You all better prepare yourselves." Nathaniel spoke slowly and with grim intent, "for the longest night of your lives."

"But, but the demon's gone," James stuttered.

"And he'll be back," Nathaniel stated without emotion as he reached down to collect his torch from the floor. Nathaniel checked his symbols carefully, one by one, going round the circle.

Mrs Dawson and Mr Green started to reload their pistols. They were trained for proactive supernatural investigations.

Dela stood close to Nathaniel grabbing his arm to get his attention "What now clever clogs?"

"We wait and prepare for what hell has to throw at us." Nathaniel held Dela in his arms and kissed her cheek. "Just don't trust anything you see or hear outside this circle for the next five hours."

Somewhere in the house (it sounded like the landing) a grandfather clock struck two o'clock. Nothing had been seen of the demon for the last half-hour. Sounds had been heard around the house, but whether it was the demon or tortured spirits of the past, they could not tell.

Mr Green was standing watch, trying to stamp a bout of pins and needles from his left foot. Mrs Dawson was sitting cross-legged, her head slumped on her chest, pistol in her hands resting between her legs. She occasionally fought the sleep that had overtaken her, but it was too strong even in these circumstances. James and the nurse were each curled up together in a spoon-like foetal position, heads propped on cushions.

Nathaniel was alert and awake. Dela was lying on his legs, awake because she had slept too long without him recently.

Nathaniel tried to think of what the hell fiends would do next; the more he thought, the more things he came up with to worry him. The attacks they could rain down on them could be legion and whether he could save all the people in the circle frightened him immensely. The silence was unnerving, even to him. He was glad James and the nurse were asleep.

"Nathaniel." A woman's cool cultured and crisp voice woke Nathaniel's mind like it called to him from a dream. Nathaniel looked up and there, standing in the doorway, dressed in a flowing white dress, was his sister.

Mr Green had bent down to wake his superior, but Nathaniel had turned and stopped him with a shake of his open hand. Dela opened her resting eyes and jumped to her knees.

"Who's that?" Dela hissed.

"A phantom Dela. Pay it no attention, the circle will protect us." Nathaniel said resolutely.

"How can you tell?" Mr Green whispered above him, pistol in hand, but not pointing at the figure.

"Don't you recognise me, Nathaniel?" The woman with long flowing brown hair glided into the room closer to the circle.

"Because that is my sister and because hell-demons have a poor sense of Earth geography they fail to realise that she lives in the United Stated now," Nathaniel explained.

"So what is it, if it ain't your sister?" Dela asked.

"A phantom, placed before us by the powers of darkness. Or the demon in disguise, wishing us to see this image."

"Won't you come and hug your sister, Nathaniel?" the vision in white asked in a sugary voice.

"Of course Eleanor, come closer inside the circle and I'll give you a big hug." Nathaniel tempted her back, knowing his real sister would have nothing to fear from the circle. The vision made no attempt to come closer to the circle.

"I'm bored, Eleanor," Nathaniel sighed and pulled a ten pence piece from his trouser pocket and whizzed it at the woman/sister/demon. The Eleanor figure parried the coin away with its left hand, which turned magna red for an instant and the Eleanor phantom cried out in pain and ran from the room.

"One-nil to the circle boys," stated Mr Green triumphantly.

"What was that?" Mrs Dawson asked awakened by the talking.

"Just the other side testing our perimeter," Nathaniel explained. "Nothing to worry about yet."

"What will they try next do you reckon, Nat?" Dela asked, reaching up to grab his left hand and attention.

"It could come in any form; knowing them all could be more frightening than ignorance, my love." Nathaniel stared at the doorway, then down at Dela, a thin forced smile on his lips.

Half an hour passed without noise or movement from outside the circle. James and the nurse were asleep, though having fretful night terrors. Mr Green sat resting while Mrs

Dawson stood and kept watch. Nathaniel cuddled Dela to his chest, both were awake and alert, just catching what could be their last moments of comfort together.

Mrs Dawson sniffed. A bad odour was faintly catching her nostril's attention. A loud crack, like a log on an open fire, really caught her attention. Nathaniel stiffened at the noise, another wooden crack followed it and then a crunch. It seemed to becoming from the floorboards inside the dining room. To the left of Dela's sitting position a floor board flew up as if hit by a hammer form underneath. A red glow streamed through the broken wood, which was three feet outside the protective circle.

"Quickly Dela! Get everyone awake and alert for danger."

Dela set about doing Nathaniel's bidding.

Another crack and a floorboard exploded in two pieces to the right of Mr Green who rose with a start, pistol ready. A red hand like a child's but with vicious pointed black nails rose from the red maw. Cracks were heard and floorboards broke in a circle around the sphere of protection now.

Nathaniel knelt, watching a ring of fire slowly take shape around the circle. Mrs Dawson and Mr Green stood in awe at the terror unfolding around them. Dela woke James with a start and he cried out in shock, which woke the poor nurse beside him who just screamed in terror.

And so they came: small impish creatures of fiery red, the size of three year old children with two thin arms, legs, head and bodies. But here the similarities ended. These devilish imps with skins as red as blood; with freakish rounded heads, pot bellies and thin limbs clawed their way out of the pits of hell into the dining room. Some carried single headed spears or tridents, all had big black eyes and lipless mouths, packed with razor sharp teeth.

The scene vaguely reminded Nathaniel of his favourite film "Jason and the Argonauts" when the hydra's skeletal warriors pulled themselves out of the ground.

This was no film, this was now and out of Hell's heart crawled fifteen demon imps, and they were not there to revel in the flames from which they came. They soon turned their attention to the humans huddled before them.

Nathaniel jumped to his feet and flung his arms wide, before the imps could reach them.

"Barra kako theos, barra kako daimon, barra daiman. pneuma ar, pneuma ub, barra demon abus!" Nathaniel shouted and a blast of yellow light surged up from the chevrons and mystic symbols of the protective circle around them.

"Be gone wicked god, be gone wicked demon, be gone demon, spirit of the sphere, spirit of the circle. Be gone demon to the abyss!" Nathaniel repeated in English for good measure.

One of the devilish imps screamed like some tribal pygmy warrior and charged the circle. Its clawed hands, toes and long nose vaporised in a flash of blue smoke, as it come into contact with the barrier. The creature now mewed in agony as it staggered back from the circle of protection, staring mournfully at its mutilated arms. It turned to its nearest compatriot for help, which approached with apparent sympathy. Then the healthy imp pulled a long knife from behind its back and in an instant chopped off its injured fellow's nose-less head.

The nurse struggled in James's embrace and screamed bloody murder; the others, apart from Nathaniel, looked on in amazement.

"Least we know the circle is protecting us," Nathaniel stated.

Everyone flinched back a pace as the imp's head was tossed at the humans in the circle. The head vanished with a blue flame as it hit the invisible sphere and everyone took an involuntary step backwards.

The imps screamed and stamped all around them, making a constant cacophony, that assaulted the nerves of everyone in the circle. Dela put her hands over her ears; if she hadn't been as scared as she was, she would have got bored with the harmless-looking imps' antics. Yet it was as Nathaniel had told her before, "Never judge a book by its cover" and "Never underestimate a demon, whatever its size or comic appearance."

"Why don't you just fuck off!" jeered Mr Green and pointed his pistol at the nearest imp and fired. Its head exploded like a blood orange and its fragile little body fell over in a most satisfying manner.

"Save your bullets Mr Green," Nathaniel warned. "You may need them for more fearsome foe before this night has ended."

Mr Green looked at his superior questioningly. "Good work, but better conserve the old ammo, eh?" Mrs Dawson said diplomatically.

"Okay," he nodded, "but it was worth the bullet," he added softly.

A sudden rising scream shook everyone inside the protective circle. Everyone turned to see the nurse (from whom the scream had been emitted) being dragged kicking and screaming, legs first, out of the circle.

When the imp had attacked the sphere everyone had involuntarily stepped, slightly, backwards. The nurse, who had been sitting on her knees in James's embrace, had unfortunately put her left foot and ankle out of the circle. Five imps had grabbed her and had pulled lower half out of the protective circle. James had grabbed her right arm and had his right hand under her left armpit trying to pull her back in.

The nurse was, to her credit, struggling and screaming for all her worth. Seven imps pulled at the woman, pulling her almost out of the circle and James's arms with it. Dela grabbed James around the waist to steady him. Mr Green carefully aimed and blew the head off one of the pulling imps, but he struggled to find a second target for fear of hitting the nurse's legs.

It was all over in seconds as an imp skipped up along the nurse's back; it speared the nurse in the right arm and then James in his left arm in quick succession. Both let go in pain. Dela pulled James back into the protective circle as he clutched his wound. The poor nurse was pulled screaming down under the open floorboards with all the imps following.

They heard one last pitiful wail of despair and she was gone. The imps, squealing with ghoulish delight, followed, except one that Mr Green blasted into red puke in anger. The red glow disappeared and tiny hands pulled and pushed the floorboards back to the state they were before the attack.

Everyone stood or sat in utter, silent, shock. The nurse had gone in seconds, like she had never existed and the room lay silent as a tomb.

"Feck!" stated Mr Green, his pistol circling the floor in disbelief.

"Argh," said James, and he began to blub like a baby. Dela reacted first, pulling off a cushion cover and wrapping it tightly around James's wound, tending to it as best she could.

Nathaniel sprang into action, examining the part of the circle where the nurse was pulled across, checking for damage to the circle's power and integrity.

Mrs Dawson slumped down hard on her arse, the slight pain welcome because it meant she was still alive.

"We didn't even know her name," Mrs Dawson said to herself.

"Roxanne," James whispered, then sniffed loudly. "Her name was Roxanne." On saying her name for a second time he burst into more tears.

"Is it all that you expected?" Nathaniel asked Mrs Dawson, half a (silent) hour after the nurse had been snatched from them.

"What, do you mean, this?" she asked, shrugging her shoulders.

"No, living in fear for your life. This isn't misty photos, or things that go bump in the night, or a poltergeist. This is the real battle of good and evil, light and dark, deadly serious, not some amateur ghost-buster's club."

Nathaniel spoke with a passion and black edge that Dela had not heard before. Standing before her in the semi-darkness was the King's Paladin and only now did she realise what that job and his life entailed. This was no nine-to-five job or hobby, this was something he was born to be or cursed to be.

"That's why the Society needs you," Mr Green said. "You're in the field experience."

"Hmm," Nathaniel snorted. "After this Dela and I are retiring to the Caribbean."

Dela looked up at Nathaniel with love in her eyes and smiled in spite of the situation. Nathaniel saw her smile and even though his stern face did not budge an inch, he winked at her.

"What was that?" James exclaimed loudly, pointing to the door. It was the first words he had spoken in an hour, since the nurse had been snatched from them.

Everyone was sitting in the circle, lost deep in their own mortal thoughts. They all turned to face the doorway as James stood up. A red glow could be seen walking along the hall. The demon was abroad again. Somewhere in the hall a door was opened and two different muffled screams could be heard.

"Geial's men," Mrs Dawson hissed.

The screams grew louder and panicky and a struggle could be heard, then deathly silence.

"That's the end of those fellows then!" Mr Green stated.

Nathaniel said nothing. He had his eyes closed and was deep in thought.

Dela, on the other hand, was getting cabin (protective circle) fever. She wasn't used to sitting around and twiddling her thumbs and all that stiff-upper-lip stuff. She wanted to scream and shout and kick arse. That was her way. But she was way out of her depth at the moment. She just had to trust Nathaniel (the man she loved) to save her, indeed save them all, from damnation.

Then she and the others heard footfalls in the hall getting louder, coming towards the door. In, without announcement, walked Geial's men, or their bodies at least. Their eyes were a mass of broken red blood vessels and their minds were obviously somewhere else.

The two Society members drew their side arms. Each one picking a different target. One man stumbled to the far corner of the room and knelt down, his head on his chest like he was performing an unholy prayer. The other man walked up to the circle and stopped only inches from its borders. Mr Green raised his weapon and pointed at the man's head.

"No!" shouted Nathaniel, "don't be tempted to shoot, the circle will protect us!" Nathaniel put his hand on Mr Green's arm, who turned and frowned at him, but let his arm be lowered slightly.

Then with the funk of fiery sulphur, the bright red demon strode into the room. A wicked, cruel smile cut across his face as he looked at the nervous inhabitants inside the circle. The demon strode over to the kneeling man and stood before him laughing wildly. Without a hint of hesitation, worry or remorse the red demon plunged its black nailed fingers into the eyes, nostrils and mouth of the poor henchman. Blood jetted from the unfortunate man's eyes and nose and screams escaped from his mouth.

Dela, James and even Mrs Dawson turned their heads in disgust. The demon laughed aloud and pulled the man's head off his shoulders, leaving a stub of bone and jetting blood shooting into the air.

Mrs Dawson, who had looked round, turned her head again, her face turning pale green. Mr Green couldn't believe his eyes, but managed to keep looking as he swallowed a large lump of bile back down his throat. Nathaniel breathed hard through his nose and tried to remain calm. He had seen much worse.

The demon easily lifted the man up, held him by the waist and whistling some unearthly tune, started to make a circle of blood. Round and round the demon spun making a circle with the henchman's bodily fluids. Worse was to come as the blood waned – the demon began to squeeze and crush the poor man to get more blood from its victim.

The demon then threw the head at the circle, which missed them by inches, but still splattered the occupants with blood. The body, finally squeezed of blood, was tossed casually into a corner. The demon then spread its hands in the air and began to chant in an evil tongue, unknown to even Nathaniel. Cruel were its words, barked from its odious maw, yet everyone watched in unnatural fascination.

Blue flames began to jump and bounce inside the circle – the flames flicked to yellow then red as the demon's dark words of invocation continued. Nathaniel could see small fire elementals dancing in a grotesque mockery of a children's nursery rhyme in the flames. They would seem like bobbing bits of the fire to everyone else, but the King's Paladin could see their dance.

The demon cried a word aloud, one which Nathaniel knew and sent the blood pumping round his heart, icy. The red demon stepped away from the fire and the henchman retreated from the circle's edge to the doorway. A fiery flame and stench of sulphurous yellow smoke filled that side of the room.

When the smoke dissipated a figure now stood in the circle of blood. Dela buried her head in her hands with cold fear, and beads of cold sweat ran down Nathaniel's forehead. For there in the invoking circle, in his human guise, stood Ashmodaios, the Demon Lord. The Arch-Duke of Hell, stepped out of the circle, adjusted his expensive-looking black suit and walked over to the protective circle.

"Mr Le Meuille, we meet again, and Miss. Robinson, how very fortunate I am." The tall, tanned demon in the form of a bearded middle-eastern man intoned. "And you have guests also, three of those Society amateurs. My, the company you keep, Nathaniel!" Ashmodaios moved within inches of the circle.

"Nice to see you up and about on Earth again, Ashmodaios. Has it been three days already?" Nathaniel replied with all the coolness and bluster he could manage.

"Even you, King's Paladin from the ancient line of demon hunters and witch burners can't keep a good man down." Ashmodaios emphasised the "good man down" part of his words by pointing to the floorboards.

"Good man?" Nathaniel asked glibly.

"You and I, Nathaniel," Ashmodaios tuned around and walked three steps away, "are a dying breed from a time that doesn't exist any more." Ashmodaios smiled; Mrs Dawson noticed the size of the Demon Lord's incisors. "How many men are left in the western world who can invoke such a powerful sphere of protection? Not many I'd wager, less than the fingers on both my hands," Ashmodaios showed Nathaniel his palms. His nails looked sharp and black.

"I'm wondering why you are here?" Nathaniel asked, cocking his head to one side and crossing his arms.

"To kill you all, of course!" Ashmodaios smiled, his gentle tones not changing.

"Why you, a Demon Lord, the Arch-Duke of Hades, here with…" Nathaniel looked at his watch, "…one hour to go before dawn?"

"Come now Nathaniel, don't belittle yourself. You're a big player, a big nuisance, a big kill." Ashmodaios moved closer to the circle once more.

"No, Ashmodaios. The reason is you're scared. The big boss has sent you back to Earth with your forked tail between your legs because you failed. You let a human defeat you. Even for three days that must come as an embarrassment in Lucifer's court!"

Ashmodaios's eyes turned from brown to blood red in seconds, an eternity of wrath boiled like molten lava behind those demonic irises. Ashmodaios moved closer as if to grab Nathaniel.

"Barra kako theos, barra kak daimon, barra daimon, pneuma an, pnuema ub, barra daimon abus!" Nathaniel shouted out the words of protective power and shuffled back a step. Once again warm yellow light like a winter's dawn surged up and around the people in the protective circle.

Ashmodaios recoiled a step from the glow, his enraged eyes still trained on Nathaniel.

"That's why you're here, to try and breach the circle! Well, you're out of luck, demon!" Nathaniel did something no living human had done in a century: laughed at a Demon Lord.

"You seem to forget yourself mortal," Ashmodaios spat trying to regain some composure, "I am eternal and one day soon, hopefully at my hands, you will die."

"What, when the invasion comes, Ashmodaios? 'Cos we know all about your little plans, sonny-Jim." Nathaniel stood proud and erect like one of his ancestors, yet without the armour.

"Oh, I'll get you and your little helpers before then Mr Le Meuille, I promise." The Demon Lord strode towards his invoking circle again.

"Still got to fit in our little game Arch-Duke," Nathaniel moved an imaginary chess piece in the air.

"So it has been requested, so it will be done as it is written in the scriptures." Ashmodaios stepped into the now flaming circle. "I look forward to our next meeting and your next move," Ashmodaios saluted.

"As do I," Nathaniel replied as fire enveloped the Demon Lord and he was gone.

The remaining last demon snarled something at the last henchman, then he too stepped into the circle of flame and vanished in a cloud of yellow smoke.

The henchman turned and walked briskly out of the once ornate and swish dining room. Mr Green lowered his gun to the floor and exhaled loudly, in a relieved and exaggerated manner.

"Is it over Nathaniel?" Dela asked from her sitting position next to Mrs Dawson.

"For the time being, yes," Nathaniel stated, "but don't rest on your laurels yet."

Nathaniel turned and faced the others.

"Well, my hands have gone numb from sitting here." Dela's bright brown eyes suddenly stretched in their sockets. "Nat! Look out!"

The henchman who had caused Dela's screamed warning had returned to the room and was bringing an automatic weapon to bear on the King's Paladin's back.

A shot rang out and Nathaniel squeezed his eyes shut, waiting for the painful impact. It never came.

What did happen was the henchman's left knee exploded, scattering blood and bone in all directions and the shocked man tumbling forward on to the wooden floorboards. Putting his arms out before him to stop his fall caused his machine gun to be released and skid across the floor into the circle, where Nathaniel put his shoe on it to stop it dead. The impact on his shattered knee as he fell caused the six foot, fourteen stone man to pass out in pain.

"For God's sake, leave us alone!" James wailed at the top of his lungs, then collapsed into a foetal position in a flood of tears.

Nathaniel looked down at Mrs Dawson whose pistol held arm was still pointing past his left leg. The smell of the fired weapon wafted up into Nathaniel's nostrils and he coughed. He was alive and very glad that he was able to smell and cough.

Dela hugged Nathaniel, whispered a thanks to Mrs Dawson and then bent down to comfort James. Not because she wanted to, or that she was any good at helping the distressed, but because of the fact that no one else would.

Mrs Dawson stared through blood-shot eyes at the man she had just shot. Blood gushed from his shattered knee on to the wooden floor. Human blood, not vampire or werewolf, or even demonic blood, but a foolish human's blood.

"Nice shot." Nathaniel looked down at his saviour and smiled, "Much appreciated."

Mrs Dawson, who was usually never short for words, ideas or plans, just lowered her gun and closed her pretty green eyes. She had nothing left to give and prayed for an end to this accursed night.

Her prayers were answered, but not for another forty minutes, when a dull dawn started to register in the distant sky. The house was silent; the storm had ended, but no-one could tell you when it had dissipated. The clouds were white and thick, yet the new day was more welcome than Christmas Day!

They had survived for another dawn at least. Nathaniel was first to step out of the protective circle; he went over and used a cushion cover to bandage the unconscious henchman's leg and Mr Green followed, his pistol in his hand for Dutch courage. Then Mrs Dawson emerged and she immediately went to look out of the window. Dela left James sleeping in the circle on a cushion and went and kissed Nathaniel long and hard on the lips.

"What a night!" Dela mused, "I'm so knackered."

Nathaniel held her at arms length, "If you're tired you must be alive, if you're alive, you live to sleep another day."

Dela gave him a puzzled grin, "I'm never gonna suss you out am I?"

"I dunno," he grinned, "ask me again after our tenth wedding anniversary." Nathaniel kissed Dela on the forehead and left her bemused in the middle of the room as he went into the hall.

Mr Green was tying the henchman's wrists together with a servant's bell cord he had pulled down from the wall. Dela looked around at her various companions as they busied themselves in the post-traumatic dawn. The sight of the other henchman's cadaver sent bile to her throat so she decided to follow Nathaniel out of the room.

She found him in the kitchen filling a bucket of cold water as he pulled a large white tablecloth from one bottom drawer.

"Can I help?" Dela asked from the doorway.

"Can you grab that bucket?"

Dela turned off the cold tap just before the bucket started to overflow. "What now hun?"

"Follow me, Miss. Robinson." He winked and left the kitchen, the large tablecloth in his hands.

Dela struggled after him as the bucket was burdensome. She followed Nathaniel back into the dining room.

Nathaniel unfolded the tablecloth and flapped it before his face before laying it over the headless cadaver in the corner. Then, taking the bucket from Dela, he sloshed it across the floor, washing away the red demon's bloody invoking circle.

"What now, babes?" Dela asked, yawning halfway through.

"Like you, I'm dead on my feet, Dela," Nathaniel yawned, catching it from her, "but we need somewhere safe, so we can sleep and re-group."

"Any ideas?" she asked, "Are we in with this Society lot now, Nat?"

"They have their uses, but even with all their resources and experience, they can't keep us safe from Ashmodaios."

"Don't tell me," Dela smirked, "you have a plan!"

"Why's that funny, Dela?"

" 'Cos you always have a plan, my knight in shining armour." She kissed him on the cheek.

"Only a last resort really, but we are down to last resorts now, babes." He gave her bum a quick squeeze. "Grab the book and our bags. I'll have a word with Mrs Dawson and then we'll be off."

"Okay, you're the boss. Well, for the moment at least babes."

Nathaniel rubbed his tired eyes then walked slowly over to the windows to talk to the Society lady.

"It's time we were going," Nathaniel stated as he came and stood next to Mrs Dawson.

"And we will, once the Society sends some cars and reinforcements," Mrs Dawson said with tired relief in her voice.

"No, you don't understand," Nathaniel corrected her. "Dela and I are leaving now."

"What!" Mrs Dawson exclaimed, the fire returning to her bloodshot eyes.

"Look, thanks for your help last night in saving Dela," Nathaniel started, "but now we have to go and get to safety during the hours of daylight."

"Look, Nathaniel, we are all in this together now, you need us," she pleaded, "and we need you!"

Nathaniel turned his back on Mrs Dawson and walked across the room while Dela stood next to the circle with their stuff.

"You're leaving?" asked James, who had just woken up.

"Yes," Dela replied for Nathaniel. "You take care of yourself, babes."

Mr Green watched on silently as Dela and Nathaniel headed for the hall.

"What the fuck are we supposed to do now, King's Paladin?" Mrs Dawson screamed after them at the top of her lungs.

Nathaniel stood at the doorway and half turned. "Do what the Society does best: learn, analyse, tell its network and try to halt Ashmodaios' demon invasion."

"And what about you two?" Mrs Dawson flapped her arms against her sides in frustration.

"Dela and I will do what we did from the beginning of the ghastly affair; try to stay alive." Then they were gone into the hall and made their way towards the conservatory and rear of the house.

"What are we gonna do now, hun?" Dela asked as they walked out of the french windows and on to the sodden grass of the garden.

"Get to the car," Nathaniel replied.

"And after that?" Dela asked.

"Grab the rest of our possessions," Nathaniel replied, again moving across the lawn to collect the wet scabbard.

"And then what?"

"Get as far away from here as is humanly possible before it gets dark again," Nathaniel explained, examining the scabbard for damage.

"And where are we going?" Dela asked, knowing how Mrs Dawson had felt earlier.

"Somewhere safe." Nathaniel reached the back garden wall and put his hands together so he could boost Dela on to the top of the wall.

"You're not gonna frigging tell me are you?" Dela said, putting her shoe into his interlocked fingers.

"Up we go," was his only reply.

Dela gave up as she scaled the wall. He had saved her life – no - soul, twice so she could cut him some slack now.

They both scrambled down the wall on to the bonnet of the wrecked hire car.

"Guess we're hitch-hiking eh, Nat?"

Nathaniel only smiled and opened the boot of the car to collect the last of their gear.

"Least it's stopped raining," she added as they began to trudge hand in hand down the lane that ran next to the house.

# CHAPTER 11

The drained pair, unable to get a lift because of their unkempt and bedraggled appearance, yomped for an hour and a half, until they reached Tewkesbury. Nathaniel shelled out for two sets of fresh clothes for each of them and a large rucksack to carry them and other possessions in.

They went to the local swimming baths, not to swim but to shower and wash their bodies and hair, with the anonymity of not being asked their names or having to book into a hotel or B&B.

Feeling slightly refreshed, but with sore feet and bloodshot eyes, they popped into McDonalds and tucked away two large burger meals each.

"What now, then?" Dela asked, stuffing a chip into her mouth.

"We finish our meals then get moving." Nathaniel dabbed his salty lips with a paper napkin.

"It's eleven thirty," Dela pressed, "it's a bright day, but it's still gonna be dark before five o'clock."

"I know." He put down his napkin and stared into Dela's lovely hazel eyes. "Taxi to the station, get train tickets for two stops past our destination, then a little walk."

"Don't like the sound of the little walk bit," Dela said with a mouthful of burger.

"Come on, eat up, we're going." Nathaniel stood and began clearing up around Dela.

"I miss Cerberus; he's a far better conversationalist than you." Dela wined in her usual jokey way.

"Well, if you live another three days you can tell him that in person." Nathaniel flashed her a quick grin and kissed the top of her apple-blossom smelling hair.

An uneventful taxi ride and a twenty minute wait for their correct train seemed to take hours to Nathaniel. It was still only lunch time really, but he knew darkness was only three hours away and would come swiftly. He didn't want to get caught out in the open after dark. Even less so now Cerberus had been banished back to his home for three long days and nights.

Nathaniel looked down lovingly at Dela, who had fallen quickly asleep on is shoulder one stop into their train ride. He needed Cerberus's powers and strength and he missed his big smelly companion like mad.

A squeal of brakes and a sudden jolt brought both Nathaniel and Dela out of their fatigued naps. They exchanged scared glances. They had both nodded off to sleep; Nathaniel two stops after Dela on the forty minute train ride.

Nathaniel cursed himself and looked at his watch, three o'clock only an hour and forty-five minutes to sunset.

"Where the hell are we?" Dela hissed in a confused whisper.

"Dunno," Nathaniel replied anxiously, but according to the train timetable they would have reached their stop fifteen minutes ago.

"Excuse me," Nathaniel said to a lady in a seat across the aisle from Dela and himself, "what is the next station?"

"Filton Lane," smiled the blonde lady in her late twenties. "Should be there in about five minutes," she beamed.

"Thank you," he replied, then turned to Dela, "we missed our stop by two stations."

"Then we'll have to change at Filton and catch a train back as-quickly-as-possible, babes," she replied, rubbing his arm for comfort.

"Or maybe get a taxi from Filton Lane all the way to our destination." Nathaniel tried to put great reassurance into his smile, but knew it was only half-hearted.

The next station did not appear for another ten minutes. By then Dela and Nathaniel were waiting anxiously by the electric door of the train, desperate to alight. Nathaniel pounded at the open button for the entire length of the platform as they glided to a halt.

They dashed out of the station to see a taxi disappear out of the station courtyard.

"What now?" Dela asked.

"Dela pop inside and see when the next train back arrives, and I'll keep an eye out here for another taxi."

Dela hurried off without a word as Nathaniel peered up and down outside. Dela ran back three minutes later, puffing hard, "Train…in three…minutes."

Nathaniel scanned the horizon for taxis, but there were none in sight.

"Come on then," he said taking her hand and dragging her towards the steps to take them up and over to platform three.

Dela frowned as she rushed over the tracks for the third time in four minutes. Seven minutes later they were on the train heading back two stops and fifteen minutes later they were back where they should have been in the first place.

Nathaniel glanced at his watch – they had barely fifty minutes till dusk, this was going to be tight. Another ten minute wait for a taxi did nothing to ease the tension. They started off to the address Nathaniel gave to the silent or grumpy taxi driver. Nathaniel glanced at his watch, then saw Dela's worried face and took her head in his hands to reassure her.

"How long will our trip take?" Dela asked.

"Too long!"

Half an hour had passed and the sun had sunk behind a hill and dusk was approaching. They had left the towns and villages way behind. They were far into the countryside and Dela had never been anywhere so green and remote. Fields and dark woods flashed past the taxi as it sped past what looked like a village. All the houses, shops and pubs were boarded up, burnt out or half collapsed.

"Where's this place?" Dela asked, staring out at the dark empty façade of a once living village.

"Where I was born," Nathaniel replied simply.

"And this is where you get out!" Exclaimed the boorish taxi driver, bringing his car to a sudden halt.

"But you aren't even at the top of the hill yet!" Nathaniel exclaimed.

"And nor will I," the driver retorted without looking back.

"Hey mate," Dela raised her voice, "we have money so fuckin' do your job."

"I'm not your mate and I'll go no further than this accursed place." The driver squeezed his wheel harder.

"What if I pay you double?" Nathaniel asked, putting a steadying hand on Dela.

"Get out of my car," roared the man.

"Why didn't you say when you took our frigging fare?" Dela exclaimed, pushing Nathaniel's hand aside.

"Get out!"

Nathaniel looked at the failing light. This wasn't getting them anywhere. He pulled a twenty pound note from his pocket and threw it at the man's face.

"Dela, we're out of time, leave this cowards to his fears." Nathaniel pushed open the door and pulled Dela out after him.

"Hey what the fuck Nat," Dela howled, "what we gonna do now?"

Nathaniel grabbed their things and slammed the door shut. Then watched the taxi do a U-turn and speed off towards town.

"We haven't much time; we'll have to yomp, my love."

Nathaniel pulled on his rucksack and picked up Dela's for her.

"Wait a fucking minute, Nat; this is like some old Hammer horror movie here. Why's this village deserted, why did that backwater retard not wanna go further, where are we going, and why the fucking hell does this always happen to me?" Dela screamed aloud to the darkening desolate village.

"Well, we'll have to discuss this on the way. We've got to move now before it's too late, or we won't be talking; well, only in Heaven." Nathaniel shoved Dela's backpack into her surprised hands and began to march up the incline of the road, through the deserted valley.

"Nat!" Dela roared, but after he didn't turn around or stop, Dela struggled into her rucksack.

Nathaniel didn't have to explain anything, because Dela had copped a major strop and was giving him the silent treatment. They had left the deserted village behind them and daylight also.

The road was long, steep and winding and both Dela and Nathaniel's calves were soon burning. There were no street lamps, no passing cars, no birds, no noise. It was dark, cold and desolate. Nathaniel's eyes peered into the black hedgerows and walls that lined their route, fearing any movement or noise.

"So!" Dela paused, her voice startled her in the silence, "where are we heading?"

"To the old Le Meuille Manor ground. Well, what's left of it," Nathaniel replied.

"Why, what happened to it?"

"It burnt down ninety years ago. So did the old Norman abbey on our grounds and that started the decline of the village below. Which finally died fifteen years ago, when the pub closed and the last household moved out."

"So where the hell are we going?"

"The old rectory which sits apart from the house and abbey and was the only place the fire didn't touch. It sits on holy ground so it's the safest place I can think of. We can go there and rest and not have to worry about watching our backs for a while."

"How long will it take to get there?"

"Too long, I fear," Nathaniel whispered.

A long, strained howl echoed from somewhere lower down the hill. Both felt their blood freeze in their veins and found themselves holding their breath.

"I assume that wasn't Cerberus back early," Dela said nervously.

"No," Nathaniel replied, gawping back down the dark road that they had just traversed. "Can you manage a little jog?"

Another howl echoed around the hillside, from another part of the hill.

"I think I could manage a sprint now," Dela ventured.

"Ok, let's go." Nathaniel grabbed Dela's hand and they began to run up the road.

A howl behind brought them to a scared halt and then another howl replied to the first across the hedgerows to the left of them.

"Dela," Nathaniel whispered, "get the scabbard out of my backpack for me, quickly now."

Dela fumbled with straps and rummaged in the backpack for the scabbard. Dela's hand finally found the scabbard, when the dual howls echoed nearer than ever.

Dela hastily pulled the scabbard free and handed it to Nathaniel. "What now?"

"A short-cut I think, come on." He grabbed Dela's hand once more and pulled her towards a five bar gate that parted the hedgerow.

They were halfway across a sodden grass field when they heard the feared sound of paws following behind them.

"We need to make it to that ditch Dela," Nathaniel shouted. Turning around he could see two dark shapes following, eyes burning red in the gloom.

"Dela run," Nathaniel screamed, falling behind her a couple of steps.

The sets of eyes separated, ran twenty feet apart, whilst moving nearer, try to get parallel so as to be ready to strike.

They were within twenty feet of the ditch, which was bordered by a hedgerow, when their luck failed. Dela's foot foundered in a rabbit hole and she fell badly. The red eyes, two pairs, narrowed onto the fallen woman and angled in for the kill.

All Nathaniel could do was stand over Dela's prone body, the scabbard held in both hands at shoulder height. Dela scrambled up into a sitting position as the right hand hellhound attacked first. Nathaniel got in a good strike with the scabbard around the hound's black furred head. It howled and fell back, but he didn't have enough time to defend himself against the second hellhound.

Nathaniel managed to turn sideways as the hound hit him, but luckily its gaping maw fixed upon the lower part of his rucksack.

The impact knocked him forward sprawling over Dela's body and as she looked up they clashed heads. They fell backwards, the hellhound's claws ripping at the backpack. Dazed, Nathaniel dropped the scabbard and fell heavily on Dela, trapping her under him. Dela's hand stretched out for the fallen scabbard, as the hound bit and tore at the backpack.

"Shit," Dela cried, her fingers inched short of reaching the scabbard. She was scared; death was only moment away for both of them.

Suddenly the hound let out a squealing howl and jumped off Nathaniel's back, its feet burning from touching the Paladin's ancient grimoire.

"Nat, come on, move your arse!" Dela screamed at her groggy lover, pulling at his coat.

"Okay," Nathaniel grabbed the fallen scabbard and they began to crawl painfully towards the ditch.

Dela and Nathaniel felt the cold wet mud squelch under their knees and hands as they pulled themselves towards the ditch and hedgerow. Any second expecting the snap of hot jaws on their exposed necks.

Then they heard the dreaded sound of attacking padded paws.

"Go Dela!" Nathaniel stopped and turned on his side, his scabbard ready to hit out.

"Nat, no!" Dela screamed. She also stopped dead, turning her head to peer back into the darkness. Then the night went a little crazy, or crazier. Dela screamed, a dark hound shape appeared over the prone King's Paladin; then the night exploded and a part of the dark shape flew off before it fell upon Nathaniel, winding him.

Another explosion tore into the dark night, followed by a bloodcurdling howl, followed by silence. Nathaniel was stuck; and in pain – out of breath and totally bemused.

Dela crawled over to him and pushed the dead, bleeding hound off him.

"What the hell is going on, Nat?" Dela shouted, pulling him into a kneeling position.

Nathaniel rubbed at his groggy eyes, "Nana."

"Eh?" Dela replied.

Nathaniel pointed behind Dela to where a figure advanced with a shotgun.

Dela turned to see an elderly lady, in a Barbar jacket, wellies and a floral frock carrying a double-barrelled shotgun.

A flashlight flashed suddenly into their bloodshot eyes. "Who are you bloody foolish fellows, and what are you doing here after dark?"

Nathaniel shook his groggy head, then looked up into the torch's beam. "Evening, Nana!"

"Bubs, is that you?" Nana squawked.

"It's me, Nana," Nathaniel sat up on his knees, "how are you?"

"You would bloody know if you ever bothered to visit or phone," she rebuked him. "I even have an email address now."

"Sorry, Nana, been busy," Nathaniel pulled Dela to a sitting position.

"Just like your bloody father, he was always out and about saving the world. He never visited me either. Who's this then?"

"Nana, this is Dela; we need your help." Nathaniel explained.

"Well, who the dickens are you girl, where's that skinny, nasally girl you were engaged to?" Nana looked from one prone figure to the other, cross-examining like an SS interrogator.

"We broke up Nana," Nathaniel explained. "Now can we get indoors, it's not safe out here."

"Hmm, you youngsters today, no stamina." Nana turned around. "Come on Bubs and your lady friend."

Nathaniel and Dela pulled each other into a standing position, picked up their gear and followed Nana and the retreating torchlight.

"Nat, is she always like that?" Dela asked.

"No, we caught her in a good mood tonight."

Dela smiled, then from his tone realised that Nathaniel wasn't kidding.

Finally they were safe, sat in the rectory's parlour room in front of a roaring open real fire. Nathaniel and Dela sat in high-backed leather chairs either side of the fire, as Nana pottered about in the kitchen next door.

"Heard from your sister lately, Bubs?" Nana asked from the entrance to the kitchen, she held two steaming mugs in each hand.

"Had an email a couple of months ago. She seems to be enjoying her stay in the states."

"Hmm, your sister could enjoy herself in a nunnery," Nana pushed one mug towards Dela, "Take it, it's hot girl."

Dela bit her tongue and grabbed the scalding mug of Bovril from Nat's grandmother. She shot a glare at Nathaniel, who just raised his eyebrows in response.

"Thank you, Nana," Nathaniel took his mug, then stared at the fire.

"Least someone's got some manners," Nana said, moving back towards the kitchen to get her Darjeeling.

"Nat," Dela hissed at him, not impressed at all at his elderly relative's coldness towards her.

"She likes you," he whispered, nodding his head and smiling.

Dela scowled and mouthed a very rude expletive.

"She saved our lives," he added.

"So what trouble have you got yourself into now?" Nana asked, returning to the parlour.

"Me, Nana, in trouble? Perish the thought!" Nathaniel joked.

"Hellhounds in my back field, you and this girl seeking sanctuary at the Rectory. Where's that god-awful bloody dog Cerberus. He's normally hanging around, stinking up the place?"

"We have a slight demon problem, Nana, nothing to worry about," Nathaniel started.

"Really," Nana sat behind them, a cup and saucer on her lap.

"We just need a safe place to stay for a while. Cerberus had to pop home for a bit. I'll explain more later," Nathaniel explained vaguely.

"Well, we will talk more in the morning; first I'll fix your dinner. Then I'll sort out the spare room for your lady friend; you'll sleep in your usual room Bubs," Nana stated.

"Spare room? I thought Dela could sleep with me tonight Nana." Nathaniel looked from Dela's stern face to Nana's equally stern face.

"Well, you thought wrong young man, this is my house and you need my help," Nana replied, then sipped her tea.

"But Nana-"

"No buts Nathaniel, you're welcome to find somewhere else to stay if you like." Nana picked up a digestive and nibbled on it.

Nana had retired to bed at ten o'clock, with a warning about bed-hopping shenanigans. Nathaniel sat on the seat next to the fire, with Dela on his lap snuggling up to him.

"This is nice," Dela stated nuzzling his neck, "we are safe here, aren't we, Nat?"

"This is the safest place in England, for us at the moment." Nathaniel kissed Dela's cheek. "This is an old rectory built on holy ground. He cannot get us here."

They hugged closer, the orange glow of the fire illuminating the darkened room.

"So lover, what's the plan?" Dela asked, looking deep into his eyes.

"First a good night's sleep; so probably a good idea that we're in separate rooms tonight, eh?" Nathaniel grinned.

"Mmm, you're probably right, I'm knackered." Dela stifled a yawn. "Can't remember the last good night's sleep we've had."

"Then we have to wait for Cerberus to return, get our energy back and come up with a plan," Nathaniel mused.

"What are we gonna do 'til then?" Dela bent her head back and yawned loudly.

"Sleep," Nathaniel tittered, "rest, eat. I'll show you around the estate."

"What you got council houses up this hill too?" Dela asked in a dreamy voice.

"No, silly; the grounds, the old abbey, the house." Nathaniel explained, twirling his hands in delight.

"Mmm, nice," Dela exhaled, nuzzling closer to Nathaniel and sleep.

"Right, let's get you to bed young lady." Nathaniel held Dela and pulled themselves out of the chair, "and myself too."

Now down in the deserted village of Leon's Hill, where the shadows reigned, dark figures moved inside the boarded-up pub.

Dawn appeared cold, misty, yet bright and Dela and Nathaniel slept in 'til late and Nana let them. She was up at seven, when outside to feed the chickens and geese, tend to her two horses and give scraps to the goat. She collected the eggs and set about breakfast. She wouldn't admit it, but it felt good to have company at the rectory again. She was also concerned: matters were usually pretty dire to send the King's Paladin back to the family home for safety. She worried for Nathaniel because she not only married a King's Paladin, but had also given birth to two.

The time was coming when she might have to become proactive again. She had been a widow for too long and lost both of her sons and she was damned if she was going to lose her last grandson.

"Morning, Mrs Le Meuille." Nana looked up and saw Kane Ferguson in his usual worn green cap, double pullovers of green and brown, brown cords and wellies. He had his spade in his hand, a cocked grin with his perpetual roll-up hanging loosely from his lower lip.

"Morning, Kane, you bring that bacon and black pudding I rang you about?" Nana moved closer, a basket on her arm.

"Yes, Eliza." Kane's seventy five year old eyes shined blue and icy.

"Less of that, you old goat," she chastised, "I have company at the Rectory."

"Company, you say?" Kane mused. "Must be Master Nathaniel if you wanted black pudding."

"You've been working here too long Kane, you know all our secrets," Nana managed to break into a grin.

Kane Ferguson shambled up and kissed her softly on the cheek. "No one else would put up with you."

He placed the bags of food into her basket and wandered off towards the sheds whistling to himself.

Nana watched him go, pursing her lips, and then went inside to cook her guests a hearty country breakfast.

"Fred Penswick's homemade farm black pudding, now I really am home," Nathaniel enthused, between shovelling his breakfast into his mouth.

Nana looked on with pleasure as he wolfed it all down and Dela looked on with mild disgust.

"You not eating your black pudding, Dela?"

"No," Dela looked queasy, "be my guest."

Nathaniel stabbed his fork into Dela's black pudding and soon began carving and eating it.

"So, young man, even though I'm glad of your company, why are you here?" Nana asked bluntly.

"We've had a little demon trouble," Nathaniel answered in between chews and swallows.

"You're a King's Paladin; it takes more than a little demon trouble to send you scurrying home." Nana pursed her lips and pursued her questioning.

"Well, a Demon Lord and his horde if you want to be exact Nana," Nathaniel stopped chewing, but kept his eyes fixed on his plate.

Nana felt dizzy, so sat down on the chair next to her grandson, "Who?"

Nathaniel looked into her eye, chewing his bottom lip. "Ashmodaios," he whispered.

Nana's face went ashen. "Oh Lord, not that accursed name again, will our family ever be rid of that fiend?"

"You've heard of him before, Mrs Le Meuille?" Dela asked, eating a nicely fried tomato half.

Nana scowled at Dela, sending an uncomfortable shiver down her spine.

"Don't interrupt girl, this is serious." Nana pulled back her chair and made for the back door. She had tears in her eyes as she fled into the back garden.

"What did I say, for fuck's sake?" Dela ejaculated.

Nathaniel grabbed Dela's hand and squeezed it. "It's not you, it's Ashmodaios, he killed my grandfather, Nana's husband."

"Oh, God, she's gonna love me even more now eh, why didn't you tell me?"

"Yeah, I should have, but when? We haven't had much time to talk lately." Nathaniel rubbed the back of her hand.

"Will this ever be over, Nat?" Dela asked earnestly, her face softening.

"One way or the other, but trying to find a way to stop the invasion; stop Ashmodaios chasing us and us having a happy ending is the hard bit." Nathaniel sucked his teeth, thinking to himself.

"So what's the happy ending, then?" Dela smirked.

"You, me, three weeks in the Caribbean; big ring; lots of sex; babies; booze; what you think?"

"All in three weeks, eh? We will be busy!" Dela chuckled.

"Just gotta come up with a plan now, eh: to get us from A to D."

"Any luck, den honey?"

"Not yet," Nathaniel jumped up. "Let's go for a walk around the grounds, see if I can get ancestral intervention."

"So what did you think of the old house, then?"

Dela glanced back at the rubble that had once been the Le Meuille's fifteen bedroom ancestral manor house.

"Bit basic, could do with a TV makeover show coming round for a few years," Dela joked.

Nathaniel held Dela close to him. The morning was cold, grey, but dry.

"Anything left of the old place, then?"

"Only the cellars," Nathaniel replied, "and nobody wants to go down there anymore."

"So, what's next on the mystery tour?" Dela asked flippantly.

"The copse, the crypts and the world famous chickens and goats." Nathaniel held her close and kissed her cold cheek.

"Chickens and goats? Sounds like Antigua." Dela laughed and it seemed to travel for miles across the hill.

When they exited the copse Nathaniel led her to the crypts which were down a small gulley which was ringed by a stone wall. An iron gate, usually padlocked, led the way into the crypts. The crypts themselves were dug into the hillside and two huge stone doors barred the entrance. Two steel rings were used to open the doors – one door was wide open.

Nathaniel stopped Dela in her tracks; both sets of gates were open. Nathaniel pulled Dela back to the safety of the copse and hid just inside the shady trees.

As they watched Nana and Kane Ferguson come out of the crypts, carrying a torch and small stone casket.

Kane carried the casket to a wheelbarrow, which was hidden from view behind the crypts. Dela and Nathaniel watched as the two elderly tomb raiders headed off towards the Rectory.

"What do you think they were up to?" Dela whispered whilst standing up.

"I wish I knew." Nathaniel frowned and stood up and dusted off his knees.

"What's down there that's so interesting?"

"The tombs and sarcophaguses of the first King's Paladins: the graves are over there of the later King's Paladins." Nathaniel pointed to a hedged green field, just past the crypts.

"So what do you think was in that heavy box? Have you seen it before?" Dela fired off the questions as she left the shade of the trees.

"No," Nathaniel answered two questions at once and left Dela behind as he strode off towards the crypts' entrance.

"Hey, wait for me." Dela followed in Nathaniel's wake.

A search of the crypts provided nothing of interest. Wherever the stone casket had come from was still secret.

"What now, honey?" Dela asked as they left the crypts.

"Suppose I'll have to have a quiet word with Nana." Nathaniel pursed his lips and sucked his tongue.

Dela and Nathaniel made their way back towards the Rectory.

Nathaniel and Dela saw Kane Ferguson in the yard and they waved at him. Nathaniel noticed that Kane was holding a hammer in his other hand as he waved back.

They both entered the kitchen. Nana was there, peeling potatoes in the large white Belfast sink.

"Think I'll take a bath if that's okay." Dela spoke loudly, giving Nathaniel a pat on the behind for luck.

Nana raised her eyebrows, but managed to keep any verbal retorts to a "Hmm."

Dela swallowed her usual catty retorts and headed off upstairs to the bathroom for a long soak.

Nathaniel watched her go. He had faced many perils in his vocation: vampires, demons, devils and ghosts, but he felt very lonely and nervous now.

"Nana," Nathaniel ventured, moving over to the sink.

"Yes, Bubs." Nana seemed as normal as any other time. "Would you like roast lamb for dinner?"

"Yeah, fine Nana." Nathaniel leant back against the sink and looked intently at his grandmother.

"Do you have something to tell me, Nana?"

She retorted in her usual manner.

"Let's say, what are you and Kane Ferguson up to?"

Nana lost her grip on her potato and it dropped into the bowl of water with a splash.

"What do you mean, Nathaniel?"

"Come on Nana, what are you up to?"

Nana's cheeks flushed and she stared down at her bowl. "Even a woman of my age can get lonely Nathaniel. It's not like my family ever visits me. It's nothing crude or to be ashamed of. I still miss your grandfather, but he's been gone twenty-nine years and Kane has never married."

"What are you on about Nana?" Nathaniel asked bemused.

"About my relationship with Kane," she barked back. "I don't want to die a lonely old widow."

"Eh," Nathaniel choked, "you're shacking up with Kane?"

"Yes, Nathaniel, what else were you on about?"

"The stone box – I saw you and Kane bring out of the crypts," Nathaniel stated.

Nana's mouth formed an O-shape and she picked up her potato again.

"Drop the spud Nana; now tell me what the hell is going on?" Nathaniel moved closer to the sink to stare at Nana's left ear.

Nana's head didn't move an inch and the only noise was of Nana exhaling loudly through her nose.

"I swore I'd never watch another Le Meuille man die in the name of all that is unholy." Nana was trembling as she turned her head to face her grandson. "But if I don't help you I fear you will die anyway. This foe is too powerful for you to vanquish alone, so you need help."

"What help?" Nathaniel put his hand on her arm.

"From what you have told me the world is in peril, a Demon Lord is after your blood and you have to stop him and you haven't got a plan of action have you?"

"No, not really." He shook his head. "That's why I came here to think, to rest, to devise a plan."

"And have you?"

"No, nothing that guarantees Dela and I surviving the encounter."

"Then I have no choice. Help me move the kitchen table." Nana moved to the head of the table and Nathaniel moved to the other end.

"Drag it towards the sink, Bubs." Together they lifted the heavy mahogany table out of the way.

Nana bent down with the agility of a woman half her age and pushed one corner of the stone flooring which swivelled up to reveal a brass, hand-sized pull ring.

"Would you mind doing the honours, Nathaniel?" Nana pointed at the ring.

Nathaniel gingerly leant forward, grabbed the ring and pulled up a four by three foot section of the floor. In the dark cavity was the stone chest that he and Dela saw Nana and Kane remove from the family crypt.

Nathaniel knelt down and heaved the stone casket from its second hiding place of the day.

"Put it on the table please, Bubs." Nathaniel with arms straining, plonked the casket on the solid farmhouse kitchen table. Nana went to the larder and knelt to pick up a hammer and chisel.

The casket's lid was held in place by two circles of lead that linked through eyelets in the lid and bottom. Nana's chisel was placed on the lead and hammered off with four stout hits.

Nathaniel looked on, impressed at his Nana's constitution and strength at her age. He moved forward and helped his grandmother to remove the thick lead bonds. Nana swiftly lifted the stone lid before Nathaniel could offer.

Inside was an oilskin, which Nana lifted from the casket and set on the table to unwrap it. Nathaniel leant closer, intrigued, but unsurprised at the latest turn of events. Any other family and this would be a shocking, unusual occurrence, but in the Le Meuille family it was run of the mill.

Nana finally pulled open the last flap to reveal an ancient-looking large iron key.

"What is it for?"

"It opens a crypt in the village graveyard," Nana explained.

"Which crypt?" Nathaniel asked, interrupting her.

"The Ferguson crypt, set under the old burnt out church. You must use the key to open it up and find Rory Ferguson's stone coffin. Open it up and inside you'll find the sword," Nana explained simply.

"Sword," Nathaniel whispered, "no it can't be, not THE SWORD!"

"Yes," Nana nodded, "I hid it forty years ago."

"You, Nana, but why?" Nathaniel exclaimed, "I thought it had been taken when Grandfather died, by the enemy."

"So everyone thought," Nana nodded, chewing her cheek. "Only Kane and I knew the truth."

"But why hide the King's Paladin's greatest weapon? Dad could have really used it and me too." Nathaniel walked up and down the kitchen in shock and anger.

"And that was my reason. I had just lost my beloved Arthur and I didn't want to lose my sons too. I thought if I hid the sword, then the King's Paladin myth would die; without the sword your father would be a doctor or road sweeper." Nana sat down with a bump. "Any job that had more life expectancy than a protector against demons, devils and the undead."

Nana looked up at her grandson, "But it didn't work, Cerberus came back three years after Arthur died and your father found the sheath and the Grimoire and the line of the King's Paladin continued."

"Why didn't you retrieve the sword for my father, then?" Nathaniel crouched down on his haunches and took his grandmother's hand, which seemed frail and trembling compared to a few minutes ago.

"Your father didn't need it," Nana explained. "He had Cerberus, but because he didn't have the sword he used the book. He poured over it every night, delved its every secret and became powerful in its arts."

"More than I, I've always been a lax student." Nathaniel admitted.

"You're more like your grandfather Nathaniel, a warrior type, your father was a bookworm and he used it well, God bless his soul. When Arthur died it hit him so hard, he was only twelve. He retreated into himself a bit, read volumes of books, sometimes one a week." Nana sighed, "It served him well, research was key to his attacks and he was lucky too, he faced many vile perils: vampires, devils, werewolves and more, but never an arch-demon."

Nana smiled and kissed Nathaniel's forehead, "You're a great King's Paladin, could be a better grandson, but you need the sword now. The world is in peril if this demonic invasion succeeds. Only the Paladin's sword can stop that now."

"Thank you, Nana." Nathaniel hugged her, then went upstairs with the key in his hand to tell Dela.

"I just hope it will help," Nana whispered to the empty kitchen.

The next morning Nathaniel and Dela were ready, breakfasted and waiting to leave the rectory at nine am. Kane was going to drive them down to St. Cuthbert's ruins in the desolate village.

To Dela's surprise, Nana kissed them both and wished them good luck. "You be careful in the village, fell things inhabit its bricks and mortar now."

"We will, Nana." Nathaniel hugged her, then he and Dela walked into the cold damp morning. Kane pulled up two minutes later in his Landrover.

A slight mist hung in the air of the hill as they made their way out of the estate. They went down the country lane that led the way back down to the village. As they stared out the window and through the hedgerows, they could see a circle of fog shielding the village below from sight. The clouds above were grey and black and it felt like the bleak-mid-winter to Nathaniel.

As they descended the fog rose up to meet them until visibility was only twenty feet or so. Dela liked foggy London days usually because, like snow, they were rare now. She did not like this fog and assumed it was unnaturally formed and not forecast by any meteorologist.

Dela saw a sign up ahead for the once picturesque village, or it would have been if it weren't shrouded in fog and deserted.

"Stop the car here, Kane," Nathaniel said a minute later. They were in the village; its buildings faded ghostly forms in the mist. A small overgrown circular green was ahead. The road circled the green with its remembrance cross visible at its centre. The road continued on to a junction, where another road turned off to the right and up a slight incline.

"The church crypt is down that road about four hundred yards. Kane, I want you to take the Landrover back up the road 'til you find a place to park, where the fog clears a little. Wait for us two hours only. If it we're not back then, we won't be coming back, okay?"

"Mrs Le Meuille says I am to stick with you and protect you," Kane replied without much tonal variation.

"Kane, she is in need of your protection more. If anything happens to us I want you to look after her to the very end," Nathaniel replied, "now, let's get going and Kane, you get yourself to a safe distance, okay?"

Kane nodded. He wasn't a coward, but the fog and this village made the hairs on his nose stand on end.

Nathaniel and Dela felt the cold and wet seep into their shoes as they moved onto the green.

The watched as Kane swung the Landrover roughly into reverse, back up and around the green, then shoot up into the fog, its taillight the last thing to fade away.

"Come on, my little dove, foul work awaits us," Nathaniel chirped gingerly, sounding more like his old self again.

"Okay, big boy, let's go," Dela replied, reaching out to hold his now extended hand. Dela could see the old glint back in his eyes, now they had a secret powerful weapon, Nathaniel would come up with a plan and, more importantly than that, they had hope again. Not enough to give her back all her old confidence, but Dela knew a little hope to Nathaniel was like a 100% sure fire plan to any other normal person.

The green and the war memorial cross faded into the swirling mist as they moved up the incline of the hill towards the ruins of St. Cuthbert's church. They kept to the left of the road, where it met the verge, so as to keep their bearings. A holly hedge ran parallel with them on the left, three yards in front of the grassy verge. The only other things Dela could make out were vague outlines of dark leafless trees on either side of the road. The graves on the right hand side that still had living relatives had been exhumed and reburied in a new cemetery in town. The others that still stood on the left hand side remained, the ancient dead in a dead village.

"The crypt is this way." Nathaniel's words seemed very loud to him in this silent world they temporarily inhabited.

Dela gave a thin smile and let herself be led to the only remaining walls of the church.

All the while, red, fog-penetrating eyes observed them from the top window of a nearby cottage.

"So what are we looking for now?" Dela asked, flashing her torch from the wet floor to the ceiling. Steps adjacent to the standing remains of the church had led them down to the Ferguson's crypt. Lucky for them it was relatively untouched by the damage above.

A robust and ancient-looking iron gate faced them now and Nathaniel pulled out the key. He used both hands and all his strength to unlock the gate to the inner crypt and rows of Ferguson tombs and sarcophaguses.

A combined shoulder barge from Nathaniel and a hard kick from Dela set the iron gate shuddering inwards. They managed to get it halfway open and squeezed through easily enough.

The inner crypt was darker and danker than being in the fog. Tombs and stone caskets lined the length and breadth of the stone corridor. This led into a small chamber, four coffins wide and one coffin's length deep. Unlike the horror films Dela had seen, they found Rory Ferguson's tomb straight away (it was directly in front of them at eye level).

Dela had been expecting Indiana Jones-style pits and traps, or secret doors or mind-boggling puzzles. There were none, only an ancient locked iron gate and a huge stone sarcophagus. The tomb of Rory Ferguson was set in a recess in the wall, so there was a great amount of space for them to manoeuvre the lid off the tomb.

Motioning with his torch, Nathaniel directed Dela to help him slide the top end of the tomb lid towards the alcove.

"Ready?" Nathaniel enquired, his hand and body tensed to push. "Go!" They pushed with all their combined might and managed to push the lid two inches towards the alcove wall. Another, then another two heaves left an appropriate gap for them to see inside.

Nathaniel and Dela's torches gazed inside, but not much of old Rory Ferguson remained. Mainly dust and a few stubborn bones, plus an old ring, yet on either side of his remains lay not one, but two long swords.

"There's two swords, Nath!" Dela exclaimed.

"Nana," Nathaniel sniffed, "always up to some little game."

The swords were very different to each other. The one on the right of Rory was gold plated, with a gold pommel, encrusted with rubies, emeralds and topaz. It had silver runes etched along the length of its blade; it was simply exquisite and worth a great amount of money.

The other sword was chalk to the golden one's stilton cheese. It was made of steel and was dirty and rent in places. It also had a steel pommel and its grip was wrapped in ageworn leather strips.

"Which is the King's Paladin sword then, honey?"

"The…" Nathaniel stopped as a new line of thought shot through his brain like lightning. "…Not sure." His hand went to his mouth and he coughed, "So we'll take both." Nathaniel reached into the tomb gingerly and took out the swords slowly and carefully, one-by-one. Taking a blanket from his holdall he wrapped the bundle around with two tight loops of duct tape, so he could carry it securely.

"You're not gonna take a peek in your book to see which is the right one, then?" Dela asked kneeling down next to him. Even in the darkest hour, he still got a thrill when she was close to him.

"A bit later. Let's get out of Dodge city first, eh?" He finished wrapping, picked up his pack then stood.

"Dodgy city more like," Dela joked, "or village of the damned."

"Okay, enough of the film noir rhetorical, babe, time to move your sexy arse." Nathaniel patted Dela's rump for good measure.

"Dis girl don't need telling twice, if you know what I mean."

Nathaniel closed the tomb lid as best he could then they retraced their steps to the iron gate. Dela banged it shut after her as Nathaniel retrieved the key once more and locked the Ferguson gate again.

The noise of the gate seemed so loud to both their ears, making them realise how silent the fog-shrouded village really was.

"That wasn't too bad," Dela spoke softly.

"No," Nathaniel replied, walking up the crypt's stone steps, "worrying, isn't it."

They were back outside now in the cold enveloping mist, dodging rubble and fallen headstones as they made for the lych-gate again.

Dela stopped dead in her Nikes and put her right arm across Nathaniel's abdomen to halt his progress also.

"There's someone there," she whispered.

"Where?"

"In the fog past the hedge," Dela pointed, "and another one, look!"

Familiar dread crept into the soles of Nathaniel's shoes and spread rapidly up his body to his head.

Outside the hedged boundaries of the church, two, no three, fog-shrouded figures could be seen. Dela and Nathaniel whirled around; other faint human shapes could be made out blocking their exit from the churchyard.

"I think we spoke too soon about getting off easy this time," Dela said, straining to look through the fog.

"Come on, let's get closer for a better look." Nathaniel urged her forward.

"Closer?" Dela questioned.

"Hopefully the consecrated ground will protect us and if it doesn't we better find out, eh?" Nathaniel trotted forward holding the blanket bundle of swords; Dela looked behind her at the mist-shrouded ruins of St. Cuthbert's, then followed him.

Nathaniel halted his reconnoitre eight yards from the lych-gate and hedge boundary. Numerous dark human forms were now half visible in the fog. Twenty or so he reckoned, even that close no features or what they were wearing could be clearly seen.

"Hello, can I help you?" Nathaniel shouted loudly at the three nearest dark forms.

Dela jumped, the shadows passed the hedge and Nathaniel remained perfectly still.

"What now, invite them round for tea?" Dela quipped, wondering how he ever survived without her.

"Plan B." Nathaniel suddenly crouched down, picked up half a brick and heaved it at the nearest shadow. It hit the dark figure high on the chest with a thud, causing the figure to fall backward and be quickly devoured by the fog.

Nathaniel and Dela looked at each other mirroring each other's shocked expressions; neither of them had expected that to work.

The figure was quickly replaced by another shadow.

"What now, Einstein?"

"Plan B and a half," Nathaniel replied bemused, as he himself had expected the half brick to go sailing through the shadowy figure.

"And what's that when it's at home, Hun?"

"Grab as many bricks and large stones as we can fit and carry in the backpack, then we pick a place where we can get through or over the hedge and peg it back towards the road and waiting Landrover," Nathaniel enlightened her, and looked at the church boundaries to see where the best escape route would be.

"Is that it?"

"You want more or have a better idea?"

"No." Dela mentally scratched her head, "It sounds kinda basic for you, something I would come up with."

"Then you must be having a positive effect on me Dela. Your directness is rubbing off on me." Nathaniel explained. "So what's the quickest point from here to the car, A to B, as the crow flies?"

"In a straight line," Dela ventured in a soft, unsure voice.

"Barring houses, ruins, worm-holes and E-space, you are correct. Now let's get some ammunition, eh babes?"

They watched the shadows in the fog as they collected large stones and bricks as ammunition. None of the figures made any attempt to enter the graveyard.

Nathaniel bore the heavy backpack and had two half-bricks in each hand. Dela had a large stone in her coat pocket and carried the wrapped up swords.

"Hey, why can't we use the sword, swords?" Dela heaved the bundle into a better holding position against her chest.

"My dear, that would be like using a stick of dynamite to crack an egg. No, we need to hold back with the sword to the last, finally we have a secret weapon the enemy thinks is lost," he whispered in reply.

To Dela it seemed that Nathaniel aged twenty years as he spoke and truly looked like a King's Paladin.

"Okay, now what?" she ventured sheepishly.

"Now we peg it." Nathaniel began to run to the left-hand corner of the graveyard, "Run!"

Dela followed a few shocked steps behind, this was more like her 'Nath'.

A stone wall rather than a hedge came into view as they raced along the exhumed part of the graveyard. Behind the scalable five foot wall, was a seven foot wooden fence and a house came into view.

Behind them the shadows began to move in the encompassing fog.

Nathaniel helped Dela clamber up the wall and followed a little after, hindered by the bulk of stone in his backpack. They looked over the fence into a small back garden, which was more like a courtyard with a few overgrown or dead plant pots. Seeing nothing too sinister, they straddled the rickety fence and slid over, landing in a sparse raised flower bed.

The house had an L-shape extended on the left where the old outhouse had been added to and connected to the house to add living space. They moved up alongside the extension where an alleyway could be seen along and under the terraced cottage. Nathaniel and Dela made their way towards it.

They reached the alley without being accosted and ran its dark echoing length 'til they came out into a small cottage's front garden. Over the wild lavender hedge stood a dark shadowy human shape, waiting for them.

Nathaniel flung one half-brick he held on the run which missed by a country mile, the next he shifted from left to right hand. This piece of old church hit the shape on the head and it fell into the fog. Dela handed Nathaniel two more rocks as he kicked down a time-ravaged fence to aid their escape.

Dela let fly at a previously unseen shadow, hitting it where she hoped a nose would be and down it fell into the sea of fog.

Ahead and to the left was an old pond and fields. They made their way towards its entrance, which kept them in a straight line retreat back to the Landrover. Twenty or more shadows loomed up to block their way. Dela glanced behind and saw that eight more figures had appeared there to stop their retreat.

Their only escape was down the lane now, slightly away from their route, but better than capture. A well aimed half-brick took care of a shadow who had got too close to Nathaniel's left side. Down the lane they ran until they came to a T-junction back onto the main street of the village. Left was where they needed to go, but both were stopped dead in their tracks as thirty or so shadows blocked their escape out of the village. Twenty or more shadows advanced down the lane, blocking their retreat and another twenty emerged from the fog twenty yards to their right, trapping them.

Dela and Nathaniel threw everything at the thirty or so shadows, blocking their way out of the village.

It was a good effort but even if all their missiles had found their mark, there still would have been too many shadows left to escape past. The pair backed up as the shadowy figures shuffled slowly towards them through the fog.

They were on the pavement now, a street lamp next to them, with no light, making it useless. Nathaniel pulled out his torch, determined to see the foes that had them trapped in a slowly closing semi-circle.

The beam flicked up in the eerie light, the fog making its beam appear to be a light sabre. The face it found was human, or once had been living, now it was ashen grey with lifeless eyes that held behind them no independent thought.

Nathaniel wondered what had happened to the villagers he had once known; now he knew what befell those who had not sold up and left. No spell or charms could halt these undead and they were getting closer.

A creak of a sign above their heads told them that they had backed up to the front façade of the village pub.

"Let's try and get in here," Dela shouted at Nathaniel as the village horde closed in. Nathaniel followed Dela to the doors. He needed time to think and this would be as good a refuge as any. Nathaniel was trying to keep an eye on the closing mob and pull a hammer from his backpack, whilst balancing his torch under his armpit.

To his surprise, Dela pushed the door inwards – it was open, that worried him more, it smelt like a trap to him. Dela went inside quickly as the shuffling horde had reached the pavement. Nathaniel had no choice and plunged into the dark interior of the public house, fumbling for his torch once more.

Inside the dark cosy confines, Dela was sweeping her torch back and forth, but the only shadows were those of the bar, table, chairs and old cigarette machines. Knowing he had no time and little choice, Nathaniel locked the doors behind him.

Luckily, the pub was old and its windows small with diamond-patterned, lead-rimmed glass. The bar area was relatively small, with doors leading off it to the Saloon bar, toilets and the upstairs of the place.

"Dela, make sure the Saloon bar's entrance is secure," Nathaniel barked and she set off like Kelly Holmes to make sure.

Nathaniel secured the top and bottom bolts of the doors he had come through and pulled the cigarette machine across them for good measure. He made his way behind the bar area next, hoping Dela had not run into any trouble. There was a backdoor, which was already locked and bolted and by the look of it hadn't been opened in some time. The upstairs would have to wait for now, as he exited through a passage with the Men's and Ladies' toilets on either side, leading him into the Saloon bar and Dela's arms.

"Fuck!"

"Fuck!"

Both exclaimed the same expletive as their sphincters dilated quickly, each fumbling about in each other's embrace before they both realised they weren't being attacked.

"Shit!"

"Shit!"

Both exclaimed again, their heart rates lowering as they took a step back from each other.

"That was fun," Nathaniel finally stated, "Now is this place nice and locked up?"

"Yeah, even wedged a stool into the door handles," Dela replied with an exhalation. "What now, Nath?"

"You hold the fort down here, while I check on upstairs," Nathaniel spoke fast so Dela could not interject. "See if you can find some spirits for Molotov cocktails, okay?"

"Okay, babe," Dela said to Nathaniel's back and then the door marked toilets swung back leaving her alone. It was dark and shadowy with the sounds of shuffling feet outside, but it had one good thing in its favour – no fog.

Nathaniel searched the top flat part of the pub at full speed. He had no time to spare and lucky for him the sparsely furnished bedroom, living room, kitchen and bathroom held no terrors for him.

He found no clues, no bodies and nothing that could be a useful weapon. What it did have was windows and a look outside revealed something very interesting. The shadowy mob had encircled the George and the Dragon public house, but were making no attempt to gain access to the place. A check of all the windows around the pub showed the same foggy scene. A ring of undead, not attacking and not retreating: some other external force was keeping them here.

"Their keeping us prisoner here 'til the big guns arrive," Nathaniel explained to Dela as they sat in the lounge bar, sipping some gin Dela had scavenged.

"Dare I ask who the big guns are?"

"*Arch*-Demons, I'm afraid." Nathaniel over-emphasised the first word in his sentence.

"Thought so." Dela necked the last of her gin, which was one of only four bottles she found in a cupboard under the stairs: the pub was now dry.

"So what now, get drunk? Hide in a circle in the floor? Or get out the old…" Dela made slashing and whooshing noises like she was something out of Highlander.

"We prepare." Nathaniel's curt and open reply made Dela sigh inwardly.

"Here we go again," she whispered to the Gordon's bottle and poured herself another drink.

Meanwhile Nathaniel busied himself by moving all the furniture back against the walls and seats. Dela licked her wisdom teeth with her tongue, waiting as Nathaniel placed a small round table in the centre of the lounge bar. He placed only one chair on either opposite side of the table then got a box out from his backpack.

He brought out the chess-set it seemed that he had bought a lifetime ago.

"Chess?" Dela asked.

"Chess, Dela. An ancient game played throughout the eons and if who I think is coming, it will hopefully save our skins for another few days."

Nathaniel carefully set out the board, white facing his black to the empty chair.

"So what next? Darts with Buddha? International pro-celebrity tiddly-winks with the Devil?" Dela joked from behind the bar.

"Sounds like fun, Miss. Robinson," spoke a rich familiar voice from the open Saloon door. "Or Russian roulette with me and a fully loaded pistol," mocked Ashmodaios, stroking his goatee beard.

Dela screamed and even Nathaniel, who had been expecting this, jumped.

The Arch-Demon strode jauntily into the room, "So who wants to suffer infernal agony and suffering first?"

"You, you bastard!" Dela retorted bravely, her foot pushing the blanket bundle of swords further under the bar.

"Ladies first, I think." Ashmodaios licked his forked tongue salaciously.

"No, demon, the board is set and we must play!" Nathaniel shouted with more authority than he or anyone who knew him could imagine.

"So it is written, so it shall be King's Paladin." The Arch-Demon strode towards his chair, "But it's only delaying the inevitable."

As Nathaniel finished setting the last piece, Ashmodaios sat down opposite him and grinned.

"Better get your whore to bring us some wine then, or do I have to cross her syphilitic hands with silver first?" Ashmodaios chuckled as he removed his long leather coat and dropped it to the dirty floor.

"Fuck you, cunt!" Dela spat with hatred.

"No, that is your game Dela Robinson, mine is chess." Ashmodaios stroked his beard and surveyed the board, "Shall I be black then?"

"Dela, please," Nathaniel pleaded calmly, "keep calm and bring us two glasses of wine."

"Why?"

"Because that is what must be done if you want any chance of seeing another day," Nathaniel sternly replied, looking at her across the room. She knew he meant business.

"Okay," she replied and searched the bar for two glasses to go with a bottle of red Chianti that Nathaniel had discovered in the cellar earlier.

"Shall we cast the battle figures across the chequered board my young opponent?"

"We shall, and the winner gets full immunity from attack from the enemy or his allies for a full day and a full night after the conclusion of the game," Nathaniel stated, staring into the demon's red eyes.

"Agreed. Ah the wine, most serville of you girl." Ashmodaios smiled and took a sip from his glass that Dela had finally laid on the table. Nathaniel sipped his also and squeezed Dela's hand as she went back to her position behind the bar.

"Do you know this is the first time in a hundred and eleven years that I've played this game of life and death? The internet era is dirty, sordid and fun, but it's far too easy to corrupt souls in this age."

"My move I think." And Nathaniel moved one of his centre pawns two squares forward. He had had enough of the demon's prattling and wanted to get started before he lost his nerve.

"I'm so excited I could fire bomb a city and then violate the corpses of every child myself, personally." The Arch-Demon glanced at Dela and then winked, his hand raised as he tilted his long forefinger towards the board. In response, one of his black pawns on the far right of the board moved forward two spaces.

Nathaniel tried to block out everything but the board. He knew the Demon Lord's plan was to upset him into an error. He would have to use all his mental ability to last the first few vital moves of the game, within a game.

"Ever smelt or felt a ten year old girl's sphincter hiss as your burning member rapes her as she cries for her mother, King's Paladin?" the demon asked as Nathaniel's hand lowered over his pieces, then made one decisive move of a pawn one square advanced against the black pieces.

"No, can't say that I have," Nathaniel replied coolly, with a steady voice.

"Sick fuck," Dela whispered to herself as she helplessly watched on, sipping her gin.

"This reminds me of a game I had with Marcus Licinius Crassus in 64 B.C., just the same start, always gave fabulous orgies did old Crassus." Ashmodaios chatted away to himself, trying to unsettle Nathaniel.

His fingers pointed, bent and extended and another pawn moved into battle."So what's the weather going to be tomorrow then demon, foggy perhaps?" Nathaniel retorted with his own inane banter.

"You English and your weather, such a fixation. Fog has its uses, but when we rule Earth it will be clear sunny skies every day, so everyone can see clearly what horrors we will bestow upon all mankind." Ashmodaios sipped his wine as Nathaniel eyed up his next chess move.

Dela sat on her stool behind the bar, with her face in her hands, elbows resting on the bar. She shook her head suddenly and blinked realising that she had been briefly asleep.

Her watch told her it was two o'clock in the morning, but with the fog outside it could have been any time. The King's Paladin and Arch-Demon Lord had been playing for two hours now and slowly the board was losing its pieces. Dela didn't know chess from backgammon or other such posh upper crust games. She hoped Nathaniel was doing well, but she didn't have a clue if he was.

Nathaniel's Queen swept up the board three spaces and took one of Ashmodaios' knights.

"Tempting," Ashmodaios said, "Demons love temptation." The long-nailed finger of the Demon-Lord pointed again and his queen was sent five squares forward to take the white Queen.

"Check!" The demon clicked his tongue as he said it with a sly smile.

Nathaniel showed no emotion, but Dela looked on in shock, losing the queen and the word "check" filled her brain with fear.

Nathaniel sighed and brought his remaining Bishop down from an attacking position to take the demon's black Queen.

Nathaniel smiled inwardly as the Arch-Demon's eyes blazed with rage. Both spoke not a word now, so different to the earlier boasts.

The demon's Rook, which had been behind the Queen before its ill fate, moved down swiftly to take Nathaniel's last Bishop.

The demon made a guttural sound deep in his throat, "check."

Nathaniel swiftly moved his exposed King behind a Pawn and to safety, a white Rook defended it along the bottom line of his board from another swift attack from the demon.

"You won't win, Nathaniel," the demon hissed.

*'Who says I'm playing to win?'* Nathaniel thought to himself.

Two more hours of play deadened Dela's mind; she kept herself awake by refilling both the chess players' glasses again. The bottle was now empty and so was much of the chessboard.

Each player had only five pieces left and the demon was perplexed. It still hadn't entered his twisted demonic mind that Nathaniel had never played to win. That's why his tactics couldn't bring about victory and both players had haemorrhaged the best of their attacking pieces.

Time was ticking on 'til dawn and he was still here playing chess with a mortal man. He had places to be, invasion plans to execute, souls to extinguish.

"If I win this game do you fancy best of three, or do you have somewhere to go?" Nathaniel asked, retreating from the demon's latest attack.

"If I can't spare time with old friends before their world is conquered, when can I?" The Demon Lord smiled in return.

"You're too kind Ashmodaios, but I can spare the time, can you?"

"Enough to finish you off King's Paladin, check." The demon moved his knight into an attack on Nathaniel's King.

Nathaniel swiftly swept his rook across the board and took the Knight. The demon grimaced and swiftly reprised with a Pawn to take the white Rook. Now they were left with a King and three Pawns each. All three Pawns were now blocked by the opposite coloured Pawns and only the Kings could roam uselessly about the board.

"Stalemate I think, unless you want to concede?"

"No," the demon spat back, his evil red eyes surveying the board. The human had tricked him into wasting the night away. The Demon Lord stood, his chair and the chess board and pieces instantly combusting into yellow flames.

"You did not win human, only delayed your death by a few hours." Ashmodaios rose into a large, red skinned figure, his clothes melting in the flames coming from his body.

"I hate bad losers." Nathaniel sat watching the angry demon calmly, "Or bad stalematers, even."

"Why should I not tear off your head right now? Who would judge me?" The demon raged.

Dela looked at the beast from Hades towering over her man and quivered with fear and anger.

Nathaniel just pointed up, then down and smiled, "Oh, and our independent adjudicator, of course."

Nathaniel pointed towards the Saloon bar, as a familiar three-headed hound smashed the door from its hinges and leapt into the room.

"Cerberus!" Dela shouted with uncontrolled joy, clapping her hands in relief.

"Well, not that independent, but he'll do, eh?" Nathaniel winked at his old friend's timely return.

"Now piss of back to your own plane and take your rabble with you!" Nathaniel spat.

The demon laughed. "Such petty victories and delaying tactics will not change the outcome of war and my victory."

"We'll see," Nathaniel replied standing up to the demon at last.

"So be it," The demon replied, thinking. "The game was tied so pass onto the decider. If games fail, each must face each other in combat mano el mano."

"I know, so be it." Nathaniel stood defiant against the fiery Demon Lord and Duke of Hades.

"Three times three, the number shall be, weapon, place and time, choose which one shall be mine." The demon chanted the ancient rhyme from an age old Minoan text.

"In three days' time, around midnight," Nathaniel stated firmly.

"You, Dela Robinson, choose a weapon." The demon pointed at her, matter of factly.

"Swords," was Dela's quivering reply. It was the first thing that came out of her tired mind, on the tip of her toe so to speak. Had she done the right thing? God, Nath had never briefed her on this.

"Oh, good choice, Miss. Robinson, just let's me decide the place." The demon mused, calmer and in control again. "I know, how about my alabaster palace in the fiery planes of hell? I'll even send transport. Shame I'll miss the invasion of your world, but I think you chose that day on purpose, eh King's Paladin?" The demon lord waved a finger at Nathaniel. "And swords, Miss. Robinson, a very noble and gallant way to watch your lover die. I assume these two will be your second and standard bearer as allowed." The demon flicked his hand in Dela's and Cerberus's vague direction.

"If you guarantee their safe passage after the combat, then they will be," Nathaniel retorted.

"By the book." With that he was gone, in a fiery green cloud of smoke, with flames licking around the floor where he stood.

"You did it," Dela exclaimed, delighted, "now what did you do?"

"Bought us some more time," Nathaniel explained to her. "Cerberus, old pal!" Nathaniel shouted, running into the hellhound's raised paws. The beast had returned to his normal one headed form. They nuzzled and wrestled for a few minutes and Dela slowly approached.

She bent down, put her arms around his furry neck and hugged him tight.

"Can't get better than a pack of three," Dela stated and they all began laughing with relief.

Outside the fog was lifting like the night and the undead inhabitants of the village shuffled back to their not so final resting places. The reformed trio now left the confines of the cold village pub and headed up the road towards the Rectory.

They had not gone more than fifteen minutes up the road when they heard the sound of an approaching car from around the bend.

They only had time to step off the road into a wet, wild verge, when Kane Ferguson's Landrover came speeding around the corner. The Landrover pulled up a few yards past them and Nathaniel noticed that Nana was in the passenger seat with a shotgun.

Nathaniel heaved up his bundle of swords and the others walked over to where the Landrover idled loudly.

"Bubs, you're okay!" Nana opened her door to get out and hug him, "We feared the worst."

"I waited for hours Master Nathaniel, then headed back to get your gran," Kane explained, "I hope I did the right thing."

"Excellent work, Kane," Nathaniel replied, pulling open the boot for Cerberus to jump in. "We picked up an old friend in town and what we came shopping for."

"Still got him I see," Nana asked not too kindly.

"We have each other and Dela also," Nathaniel pointed out as they all clambered into the Landrover.

"Then home, Kane, please," ordered Nana briskly. When they were all aboard and doors pulled shut, Kane did a three (more like five) point turn and headed off back up the hill and to comparative safety.

# CHAPTER 12

"Good idea to have a dummy sword Nana, to foil the tomb robbers, eh?" Nathaniel said to his grandmother, upstairs in the rectory as she changed the spare sheets.

"I didn't just come down in the last shower you know, young man." Nana folded and patted and turned the sheets as she spoke.

"I have three more days to come up with a plan, until I have to face him again." Nathaniel picked up the dirty sheets from the floor to put in the linen basket for his grandmother.

"So you got any idea on how to stop him?"

"Yes, I do," Nathaniel nodded. "Can I use the telephone in your bedroom, Nana?"

"Of course you can," Nana replied, taking the dirty linen from his hands. "A secret, is it.?"

"Yes," was his only reply. So like his father and grandfather before him. Eliza Le Meuille hoped he would not be joining them in Heaven shortly.

"I need your help," Nathaniel spoke down the phone, "and you need mine."

"I realise that," he replied.

"You know where. That's good because I've come up with a plan to stop them." Nathaniel looked around his Nana's empty frilly bedroom nervously.

"I need to meet you face to face."

"Okay, now let me tell you where and when…"

Dela meanwhile was catching up on sleep in her room. Kane was in the potting shed scrubbing old plant pots with a soapy wire brush. Nana was in the utility room filling the washing machine with the bed sheets and pillow cases. Cerberus was enjoying his first batch of fresh air for three days and snacking on the odd fox or badger he found. He padded around the perimeter of the estate, especially the ruins of the Le Meuille Mansion house.

When he had finished his phone call Nathaniel popped his head into the bedroom where Dela slept. She was snoring slightly. He smiled and left her to it.

Next he went downstairs and slipped out the front door to avoid Nana. He crept round the side of the house, crouched low behind the hedges and found Kane in the potting shed alone. The shed was behind some other outbuildings: sheds, the old stables, and was unseen from the kitchen or utility room windows.

"Kane, can I have a quiet word with you?" Nathaniel asked politely as he entered the dirty old potting shed.

"What can I do for you, Master Nathaniel?" Kane asked, putting down his pot and brush.

"I need to ask you for a favour, and I need you to keep it a secret from the ladies of the house."

Kane scratched his strawberry-shaped nose and nodded. "Go on, but I don't like deceiving your grandmother."

"Nor do I, or Dela, but it's better this way, trust me."

"What are you after?"

"Early tomorrow morning, say about half five, I need to borrow your Landrover for a couple of hours."

"You're not going back to the village are you?"

"Not on your nelly, Kane. I just have an errand to run alone," Nathaniel explained. "And it has to be a secret, okay?"

"Yes, I understand; I'll leave the keys in the ignition and the doors unlocked for you tonight." Kane nodded, and was his way.

"Good man, I knew I could rely on you, thank you." Nathaniel shook the old man's dirty hands and nodded. "I approve, you know." Nathaniel winked and left the old retainer to his pots and thoughts.

Nathaniel was up early as planned, leaving Dela, Nana and Kane asleep in the Rectory. The kitchen clock said five thirty-one as he left the house, an apple in his left hand.

Kane had been true to his word and left the keys in the Landrover. Nathaniel bit into his apple and opened the driver's side door.

Cerberus padded out the kitchen door after him, wondering what was going on.

"You go back in old friend and get warm. I have an errand to run in Cheltenham, okay?" Nathaniel clambered into the Landrover.

Cerberus looked at him, worried about his companion's safety.

"I need you here old friend, to look after Dela and Nana," Nathaniel explained. "I'll be back before lunch time, you old worry-wart." Nathaniel pulled the driver's door shut before Cerberus's mournful eyes pleaded with him to stay again.

Nathaniel put the apple into his teeth and held it there. He started up the Landrover and sped off towards the gate.

Cerberus watched him go, then slowly padded inside again. He hoped Nathaniel was doing the right thing.

Nathaniel took the back road down the hill that added twenty minutes to his journey, but more importantly it bypassed the village by some way.

He still managed to be in Cheltenham in forty-five minutes, which was pretty good going. He parked in Tesco's parking lot with time to spare for his secret rendezvous.

He turned off the engine and waited. The DJ on the radio was annoying him so he clicked that off as well. Silence suited the situation, so he could be aware of any approaching vehicles.

In the end, he had only to wait three minutes before a dark blue Vauxhall Zafira people-carrier pulled up in the parking bay but one to his right.

The vehicle had three occupants, two male, one female. Only the woman got out of one of the back seats.

Nathaniel opened his door also and jumped down onto the concrete parking lot.

"Nathaniel," said the woman, "this is a most unexpected pleasure."

"Good to see you again, Mrs Dawson; we have a lot to discuss." Nathaniel motioned to the open doorway of his Landrover.

"I was surprised to hear from you again!"

"Not as surprised as me, believe me," Nathaniel replied, escorting her as to open the passenger door for her.

"So why did you get in touch again, Nathaniel?" Mrs Dawson asked from the warm confines of the Landrover's passenger seat.

"I need your help!"

Nathaniel had managed the impossible: he was back to the Rectory by seven minutes past eight. Neither Dela or his Nana was up yet. Kane had given his grandmother tea in bed and she had yielded to his red-cheeked charms.

Kane had just returned to the kitchen from upstairs and Nathaniel walked in from the yard.

"Business go as planned Master Nathaniel?" Kane asked, his emotions held in check as usual. The Ferguson family had served the Le Meuille family for generations. They had seen the glory days of the King's Paladins, now Kane, the last Ferguson, was witnessing the waning of those years.

"Yes, thank you, Kane," Nathaniel nodded, handing back the car keys.

"Good," Kane replied.

"Thanks for letting me borrow the Landrover."

"Don't mention it," Kane stated quietly and went about washing up the breakfast things.

The conversation ended there. Nathaniel wanted to thank him for looking after his grandmother and say that he approved of their relationship. As with many men he was afraid to say those words and Kane would have been embarrassed to hear them. Nathaniel stood in an embarrassed silence for a few seconds; thrust his hands deep into his pockets, sucked his lip and headed off towards the stairs.

The gloomy morning barely showed through the drawn bedroom curtains. Opening the door had not woken the beautiful slumbering form of Dela Robinson.

He closed the door silently as he watched her chest rise and fall in the semi-dark. He slipped off his shoes and went round the bed to lie down beside her.

She stirred and turned towards him, her eyes flickering open. She gave a long, whole-body stretch and said, "Morning, Baby."

Nathaniel bent down and kissed her dry lips, his hand caressing her cheek.

"Mmm, that's nice," she purred, her eyes adjusting to the gloom, "you're dressed!"

"Not for long!" He started to unbutton his shirt and kissed her long and hard.

"What's come over you, honey? Is it the country air?" Dela asked, helping him with his jeans button and zip.

"Just making the most of the time we have left," he answered, pulling up her night time t-shirt so he could suck her exposed, erect nipples.

"Hey, I don't want any of that negative talk Nath," Dela chastised him gently, her hands tugging his jeans down.

"I don't want to talk at all hun," he lowered himself down on her and parted her lips with his tongue. He pulled the cover over him and they did not surface again for another two hours.

Mrs Dawson picked up her mobile and answered it on the second ring.

"Dawson here!" She answered promptly.

"This is Hawk," a male voice said coldly and simply, "we have them."

"Where?"

"An old Idiminu Corporation warehouse in Feltham, Middlesex – they arrived last night. One of our sleepers was staking the place out," Hawk explained, a touch of excitement creeping into his voice.

"Is it all the half-demons from the fertility clinic, do you reckon?"

"There were two cars, a black van and a large container lorry, so I hope so," Mr Hawk replied.

"And the Council of Seven?" Mrs Dawson's question was laced with trepidation.

"They have given you command of five active cells and given temporary Senior Investigator status 'til this crisis has ended. Welcome to the fifth Circle, Jane."

"Thank you," she said, her eyes wide in shock, "I'll be back at ranch in three hours, to brief the High Council myself."

"I'll let them know: this is your big chance Jane, don't fuck it up," Mr Hawk replied.

"Big chance Hawk!" She shook her head even though he couldn't see it. "If I mess this up we're all fucked."

"True."

"Catch you later."

"Bye."

Mrs Dawson closed her phone and stared down at it. A world's weight of responsibility pushed down on her demure shoulders. With this and the task the King's Paladin had set her, she'd dare not fail, for the world's sake. Her people-carrier sped on towards London; as in Nathaniel's and Ashmodaios' chess game the final pieces were moving into place. She just hoped she really did have the guts and brains to match the responsibilities being heaped upon her.

The next day dawned sunny and as frozen-fresh as a bag of Iceland peas. Everyone at the Rectory sat down and broke bread and boiled eggs together. They had each decided that today would be a normal day, with no mention of the perils that lay ahead.

The sun had taken the frosty head off the grass by ten am, so Nathaniel, Dela and Cerberus went for a stroll together around the grounds.

Cerberus trailed behind the couple as they walked with arms around each other's waists; he wanted to be with Nathaniel too, but gave them personal space. They didn't speak a good deal. Nathaniel would point things out, such as where he used to play with his brother during summer holidays or elaborate on the history of the manor or old abbey.

They came out of the copse where they had spied on Nana and Kane, walking fast through the crypts this time to a neat green hedge. The large rectangle boxed in with hedges was where the most recent graves and tombs of the Le Meuille family were.

Cerberus nodded respectfully and set off back to the copse to relieve himself, a mortal trait he enjoyed enormously. There was not lavatory or litter tray in his hellish abode (or need for it), nor food as he was immortal.

Nathaniel took Dela's hand and led her to three less weather-eroded gravestones, two crossed and one oblong. They all had two things in common, the same surname and same date of death.

"Your parents and your brother," Dela said, gripping his arm tightly as she put her head on his shoulder. "I'm so sorry, Nathaniel."

"It's okay, it was a long time ago. At least you've met most of my family now." Nathaniel stared at the graves like his eyes could penetrate into the earth to see them again.

Dela stared also, but different thought came to mind. She hoped to God that there would not be another fresh grave cut into the lush green grass soon.

Mrs Dawson sat in the cold warehouse office and watched the bank of four monitors before her. Their sleeper agent or first circle member of the Society owned the industrial estate where the Idiminu Corporation had their safe warehouse. It had been rented to a dummy company called Phelps International PLC. A swift check by the owner at Companies House, a standard check he always did for companies renting on his sites, had revealed Idiminu as the parent company. Five years before this meant nothing to him, but when the 'Society' had contacted its members worldwide to be on the lookout for Idiminu, it meant everything.

He, Julian Barrington, was a millionaire and had been a 'Society' sleeper for fifteen years. Money or class was no way to progression in the 'Society'. There were no black balls, no meetings and very little contact over the years. Julian doubted now he was fifty-three that he'd ever move up from his first circle rank.

Two days ago he'd been watching the Idiminu premises as ordered and come up trumps big-time. The information he had reported in (the arrival of the vehicles to the Idiminu warehouse) brought a swift response.

Now he stood in one of his newer warehouses over the other side of the estate. Three active cells led by an extremely active brunette woman in her late thirties were calling the shots. Ten 'Society' members plus himself were in the warehouse keeping tabs on the Idiminu warehouse from CCTV cameras around that area of the industrial Park.

The members were of all ages and size, shape, colour and creed. Julian Barrington sat humbly in a corner and gave all the assistance he could when asked.

Mrs Dawson stared at the monitors, no movement yet. The car had come and gone and the cell she set to watch the house on Manes Close reported that was its destination each time. Her remaining cell was in Cheltenham, just in case the King's Paladin required help again. It was a risk to have them there, so far away from her, but risk was all part of the game.

Deep beneath the cellars of the British Museum in an ancient and large-ceilinged room sat seven figures. The décor was late Victorian, the seats they sat upon were Chippendales and the table was huge, ornately inlaid and oval in shape.

The room was also oval shaped, with ten foot high oaken doors at each peak. Portraits of past members lined each wall between the lamps that illuminated the room.

"So how do you think she is doing?" Asked an older grey-haired man, whose day job was as a world-renowned film actor.

"She seems to have everything covered," answered an attractive woman in her late twenties, who had a slight American accent.

"Could we do anything more to help?" asked a lady in her late fifties, her Minister of State tones breaking through.

"I think we can," replied another seated man, only in his mid-twenties, with golden blond hair. He looked across the table to a half bald man in his late fifties, who was sitting with excellent posture in his chair.

"I'm sure I can arrange a little help from the heavens," smiled the Air-Vice Marshall thinly.

"Then do it, Wings," came an ancient, weak and muffled voice from the chair of the High Councillor of the Inner Circle.

All heads turned towards the High Councillor's chair and each put their right closed fist on the table to demonstrate their agreement.

In the warehouse rented by the Idiminu Corporation twelve men stood in line, their backs to a large Arctic trailer. Outside in the dark of night the CCTV cameras kept watch and so did Mrs Dawson and her society cells.

Two figures stood facing the tall, well built men.

"Are they ready to defend the breach?" Asked the fork-tongued voice of Ashmodaios.

"Yes, my Demonic Lordship," said the man of Japanese appearance, bowing.

"I will miss the start of the invasion Telal, so I will leave you to marshal our forces." Ashmodaios walked towards the first hybrid man and looked him up and down.

"I will not fail you father," Telal bowed his head.

"I'll bring you back the head of the King's Paladin as a victory prize, Telal." Ashmodaios laughed curtly. "And his whore too, it would be poetic victory if you would impregnate her with my grandsire."

They both laughed long and hard at this as Ashmodaios inspected his half-demon soldiers.

The day before the invasion dawned, or tried to the black and grey rain-filled clouds made sure the morning was as dark as any night. In the Rectory kitchen Nana had been forced to turn the light on as it had become so gloomy.

Kane entered through the kitchen door with rain, leaves and wind following him.

"Looks like a storm's coming girl," he prophesied sliding off his soaked cap, Barbour and his wellingtons.

Nana looked out at the rain and sighed, despair in her old heart. Only yesterday it seemed bright, sunny and her heart was contented with a trace of hope and the greatest feeling one sometimes feels of just being alive. Now the dark had descended and the storm clouds had arrived on the horizon, and fear filled her soul.

"Tea, Eliza?" Kane asked as he walked over to stand next to her, sensing her sadness.

"A hug would be better, you old ruffian," she looked up at him with her watery, sad, grey eyes.

Kane took her in his large arms and pulled her to his chest and they held each other as the storm moved ever closer.

Dela and Nathaniel lay naked together in bed after their fifth love making session since yesterday. It was sometimes rough, animalistic but needy, sometimes slow, caring and deliberate, but always with high emotion fuelled with love.

Dela knew whatever the outcome, wherever she ended up, alone or with Nathaniel, her life had changed. She could not go back to being the old Dela Robinson anymore. She would miss some things, true, but she had gained so much more, mutual never-ending love.

"What's going to happen tomorrow night?" Dela asked vaguely as she rested her head on his chest.

"One way or the other it will be the end," he replied honestly and emotionlessly.

"That's not very reassuring, Nath," Dela leant up, propping herself on her elbow to look at him.

"It's the truth though, Hun. The demonic invasion plans, the half-demons, my duel with Ashmodaios; there are many variables that could affect the eventual outcome of the endeavour," Nathaniel explained as only Nathaniel could.

"Eh? Speak English!"

"I thought I had," he smiled thinly.

"I mean thicko Dela Robinson GCSE English, babe," she said, exasperated at his long way of explaining things.

"Okay," he submitted, "a shit load of things are going to happen at once, if anything goes the slightest bit off plan, I, you and the rest of the planet Earth will be fucked!"

"Better," she nodded, her hair falling onto his chest, "I got that, didn't like it one iddy bit, but I understand now."

Nathaniel looked at her, watching the cogs whirl around, thoughts pulsing around her brain for ten seconds or more.

She looked up into his eyes, even though the poor light from the window made it difficult for Dela so see his eyes clearly. "Can you beat him, Ashmodaios, in the duel?"

Nathaniel sighed through his nostrils, then lay back into the pillows staring at the shadowy ceiling. Then he smiled as though something funny had suddenly occurred to him. "We only have a hope in Hell's chance," and he followed it with a little chuckle.

Dela punched him on the shoulder. "It ain't funny, Nath."

"I know Dela," Nathaniel lightly grabbed the back of her head and pulled her onto his lips for a passionate exchange of kisses.

When they parted he said, "All we can do is do what we have done since we've met, keep on fighting, together!"

"That's good enough for dis girl," and Dela leant forward to kiss him this time.

Mrs Dawson yawned and rubbed the sleep from her eyes as she lay in the camp bed. She had only offered herself four hour's sleep and her body craved more. She sat up and made her eyes open, time enough for sleep one way or the other, this time two days hence.

Her bedroom was one of the empty warehouse offices, which only had a desk and a four drawer filing cabinet for décor. She dressed quickly and then had ten minutes to refresh herself in the warehouse ladies' before rejoining the fight.

To her relief nothing to report had happened during her sleep – no people, vehicles or demons had come or gone at the

Idiminu warehouse. Nothing had happened at Manes Close or Cheltenham either.

"All quiet on the Western front," Goldenboy remarked, "in fact, all quiet on all fronts." Mr Goldenboy was with one of the new cells under her command, a third circle Investigator, whose day job was a CCTV engineer at the UK's biggest security firm.

"The quiet before the storm, eh?" Mrs Dawson replied. Goldenboy, aged twenty-eight, was permanently happy and had a rare talent as it rubbed off on those around him. His hair was naturally golden, he was over six foot and Mrs Dawson was sure that the girls must all fall at his feet.

"Darkest hour is before the dawn," added Sparky, another of Goldenboy's cell and a computer and electrical wizard.

"Okay, getting boring now," Mrs Dawson, ten years or more their senior, brought them back to the job at hand. "Invasion day T-minus one!"

The storm finally offloaded over the Rectory at lunchtime. It took Nana and Kane back to their Blitz days. Dela and Nathaniel watched the lightning, thunder and hail show from an upstairs landing window. They could see the lightning illuminate over three counties from atop Leon's Hill. They huddled together, watching the storm and trying to ignore the thoughts that entered into each of their minds.

Ashmodaios stood in his black alabaster palace in the deepest regions of Hell. Inside its football stadium-sized courtyard, Colb, the storm demon, Ashmodaios' lieutenant, inspected his troops for the invasion. A legion of the foulest demons Hell could find, ready to devour the living. His job was vital to the operations, to keep the storms and darkness covering England to continue. His half-demon had started the darkness, but his powers were limited. The legions at his command could only march in the darkness that his storms would provide. That's only why Telal and the other half-demons opening the bridgehead and keeping it secure were vital.

Above him, back from one of his temporary Earth visits, Ashmodaios sat upon his ruby-covered throne. A huge smile fixed on his red lips as he sharpened the scimitar that lay across his legs.

Everyone involved slept fitfully that night – Invasion's Eve. The dawn did not arrive, the night just got less umbra as the clocks clicked past seven o'clock. No birds sang in the leafless trees, no cocks crowed in the backyard. The last day of the world dawned, in silence, yet only a few recognised these portents of Armageddon.

Nathaniel awoke with a start at one minute and thirteen seconds past seven. The images of his nightmare already lost to REM sleep. He reached for his wrist watch as he fought to control his breathing, he illuminated the dials and saw it was still early.

Somehow Dela was asleep, snoring softly, so he took a deep breath and lay down beside her, his front to her back. She, awake or asleep, grabbed his hand and pulled it over her chest. Nathaniel snuggled into her closer for possibly the last time ever and held her tight until he drifted off again.

Mrs Dawson's eyes flicked open in shock – where was she?

Then she remembered as her eyes made out the gloom of the warehouse office. Things slowly came back to her; it was the eve of destruction that she must help to stop.

She shifted in her cot bed as something felt different, there was an extra deadweight in the temporary bed with her. Her eyes darted left to see Mr Goldenboy's blond locks next to her. She remembered inviting him to bed late last night, for if the world was going to end she hadn't wanted to spend her last night alone.

Then she started to cry, silently the tears gushed from her eyes for her late husband and lost family.

"I'm sorry, Mark," she mouthed to the ceiling, then dried her eyes and kicked Goldenboy out of the bed.

Telal had looked out of his office warehouse window and smiled. Tomorrow he could shed his human skin and side forever and take his place at his father's side as ruler of a dominated Earth.

The day, dark and wet, dragged on not knowing what fate would befall it tomorrow. Some hoped the day would go slowly, other fast and others weren't sure either way and wished it was tomorrow and everything had been resolved.

Nathaniel wasn't sure which he felt; he wanted to spend more time with Dela, but he wanted the duel with Ashmodaios to be over. Yet he didn't want his possible last day on Earth to be so dark and depressing. He wanted to spend time with Dela in the Caribbean sun, lying by a pool or swimming in a topaz sea, not in a wet, stormy, dark winter's day, with the end of the Earth nigh.

Nana had decided to treat them all to a huge holiday-type roast capon with roast potatoes, stuffing and three veg. Not that anyone felt festive, but they ate as much as they could manage. The apple pie and homemade vanilla custard nearly finished poor Dela off. She rubbed her full belly, which felt like she had put on a stone in one lunchtime. She called this the Armageddon diet – eat anything you like today because tomorrow it won't matter.

"Movement!" Mr Green shouted across the warehouse.

Mrs Dawson, Mr Goldenboy and the rest of the Society Cell members ran over to the computer monitors.

"What we got, Sparky?" Goldenboy asked, leaning over his shoulder.

"The shutter's gone up and one vehicle is emerging." Sparky tapped at the computer keys.

"Kenny, get the car ready!" Mrs Dawson ordered to the new member of her cell, who ran off to start the car up.

"Do we go after them?" Mr Goldenboy asked excitedly.

"Depends on how many cars leave," Mrs Dawson answered him, her eyes fixed on the black and white monitor.

"The shutters are coming down, looks like only one car leaving." Julian Barrington spoke what they could all see, from his position standing behind Mrs Dawson.

"Right, Mr Green with me, we're going to follow that car; Mr Goldenboy you're in charge. Phone me every fifteen minutes with updates, okay?" She began to head for the end of the huge warehouse where the 'Society' vehicles were parked.

"Okay, and take care, okay, Mrs Dawson?" Goldenboy called after her.

She wanted to chastise him for his last remark, but couldn't think of anything to say that wouldn't sound unprofessional. So she let the words go and ran with Mr Green to the waiting black Lexus.

They made the car they were after at the roundabout, just outside the road leading to the industrial estate. The red Toyota they were following turned left away from London and towards the thirty minute drive to Manes Close.

"Is all the equipment stowed in the boot?" Mrs Dawson asked Mr Green.

He looked back at her from the passenger seat. "All the items you requested are on board."

"Do you think we need back up?" Asked Mr Kenny, the new member, replacing the late Mr George.

"With the cell already in place we should be okay, thank you, Mr Kenny." Mrs Dawson replied tartly. She had three men in Cheltenham, seven at the warehouse and when they arrived, six at Manes Close. The Society only had eight hundred and ninety members worldwide. Half of them were non-active sleeper members like Julian Barrington. She had control of five cells out of fifty-six worldwide, she hoped the High Council had given her enough men.

"Is everything ready?" Mr Wings spoke down a telephone in the Communications Room of the Society's headquarters.
"Ready, sir." Came the curt, military reply.
"Then proceed with Operation Harris immediately."
"Yes, Air-Vice Marshall." The line went dead.
"Mr Phones, send a message to our cells in the warehouse to keep inside and not leave under any circumstance, unless the targets move out, understand?"
"Yes, Mr Wings."
"Good man," and the balding RAF man left the room, he had to be back at the MOD by four pm.

"Mr Goldenboy," Mr Sparks whispered, "a priority message from HQ, code A, from the Inner Circle itself, for your eyes only."
"Code A, that means I can't even tell Mrs Dawson. Give it here, Glen." Mr Goldenboy's smile dropped and his eyes read the brief message.
He looked at his watch, a quarter to four. "Sparky, get everyone inside the warehouse, all watching the monitors."

In a road behind a set of local shops sat a Lexus and a Vauxhall Zafira. Manes Close was only a minute's drive away. Mrs Dawson sat now in the Zafira watching a portable monitor on her lap that showed a picture of 3 Manes Close where the invasion was set to take place. A Society member/ BT engineer had hidden the spy camera on a telephone pole in Manes Close over a week ago. The red Toyota was parked outside number 3 and the container lorry which had been there for two days sat outside numbers seven and nine.

Mrs Dawson looked at her slim gold watch her husband had given her on her twenty-fourth birthday – it said ten to four.

Up above London the electrical storm raged. Dark clouds covered the heavens and rain pelted down like the world was weeping. Lightning flashed, followed by heart-stopping thunder. In this maelstrom flew two Tornados from their base in Norfolk.

From a telephone box in Dudley, a man dialled the first of two numbers from memory. One was to the anti-terrorist unit of Scotland Yard and the other was to the duty officer inside Number 10 Downing Street's press office. Each would get the same message: that terrorists had planted two bombs in Greater London that would detonate at four pm today. The man, a society sleeper member, then went back to his patrol car and headed off into town.

Inside the control tower of the Norfolk RAF base everything was normal. Only four planes were in the air, two on their way to Scotland and two on a special training mission. There was a problem downstairs – the secondary backup power supply controlled by the computers had mysteriously packed up.

Not a major headache for the duty Flight Lieutenant, the computer bods were looking into it. It did become a major problem at 15.57 hours, they had a power failure. A switch had been accidentally turned off at the local power station and would not be noticed for ten minutes.

Meanwhile at the base all communications, satellite navigation systems and radios were dead. Only batteries powered the emergency lighting.

"Oh bollocks," stated the duty Flight Lieutenant.

At 15.59, the two Tornados released four guided missiles each and peeled off to return to base.

The missiles stammered into their targets with deadly effect, bringing death and destruction with them.

The Society members stationed in the warehouse on the other corner of the Industrial Estate did not know what the hell was happening. A blinding flash illuminated their monitors; darkness became day outside, then with a mighty boom the warehouse shook and glass windows fractured. Instinct set in and all members dived to the ground.
Luckily, they had more wall than windows next to them or they would have been cut into ribbons. The roar diminished and the dark returned, yet with an orange glow out of the remaining south easterly windows. The Society members slowly rose from the floor with only minor cuts and bruises, to find all the monitors hissed grey, black and white with interference. A swift few taps on the laptop keyboard established was no signal to be received.
Mr Goldenboy, Julian Barrington and the others staggered to a window to see what had happened. Barrington's jaw dropped, half of his industrial estate was aflame. They could see from over the next building, flames rose seventy feet into the air where the Idiminu Corporation warehouse had been. Now if they could see it, all that remained was a huge crater and one wall.

Across London metal, brick, glass, chairs, discs and bits of corpses rained down onto the street below. Four explosions that had merged into one cataclysmic attack that had destroyed three floors of the Idiminu Corporation building. Half of the top floor had collapsed like a deck of cards, the other half was engulfed in flame and smoke.

Over three-quarters of the building's occupants died, some because of the explosions, some through the fire, many by smoke inhalation. No half-demons survived the attack. Three hundred and fifteen people would be dead in the next hour, inside the building and on the streets below and the pub opposite. All three half-demons inside were destroyed with their employees, one to every hundred lives.

Fifteen minutes after the attacks, Kane Ferguson ran into the kitchen from outside, where Dela, Nana, Nathaniel and Cerberus had been sitting quietly.

"Quickly, into the living room," he ordered breathlessly. He disappeared into the hall which led to the living room. They all looked at each other and then bundled after him as quickly as their respective legs would carry them.

Kane was bending over and turning on the television as they entered. BBC One slowly flicked on.

"Kane, what is the matter, dear?" Asked Nana, concerned at his behaviour.

"Just watch," was his only reply.

A BBC newsflash was showing and not the scheduled 'Wildlife on One'.

"Just to repeat," read the stern newsreader, "two explosions have happened at four pm today across London. A warehouse in Feltham, Middlesex and an office block in Docklands belonging to the Idiminu Corporation have been torn apart by massive explosions. It is too early to tell yet if this is the work of a terrorist organisation…"

"Fuck me!" Dela exclaimed.

Nana looked at her, but said nothing.

Nathaniel thought he knew who had done this, but was surprised by the ferocity of the Society's tactics. He had severely underestimated their resolve, power and resources. He hoped that Mrs Dawson would aid him so precisely also, but said nothing.

"What do we do now, Bubs?" Nana asked her grandson.

"We wait," he replied and turned and headed off to the W.C.

"What did you see?" Mr Goldenboy asked a breathless Mr Barrington as he entered the warehouse again.

"There's nothing left of the warehouse, it's been totally blown up," the man who owned the industrial estate spoke in one long, shocked tone.

"The firemen will be here any minute, Mr Goldenboy, we have to evacuate," ventured Mr Sparks from the shattered window.

"Okay, let's roll, we are getting out of here before the cops show up," he ordered. "Barrington, go outside and talk to the emergency services, delay them."

Barrington nodded and shuffled off towards the door, overwrought and in shock.

"Sparky, get me a phone, mine's busted. I've gotta brief Mrs Dawson, pronto."

Mrs Dawson already knew. They had heard on the car radio as they monitored Manes Close. She had been trying to contact anyone on the High Council without any success, and she wanted answers immediately.

She tried to contact her people at the warehouse, but communications were down. She could only sit and steam quietly, until the phone suddenly rang.

At the Rectory everyone was still inside the living room, watching the real life drama of the attacks unfold. Programmes had been cancelled and experts called in and pictures of the destruction flicked across the bottom of the screen. A sudden thud on the front door woke them from the news.

"Everyone stay where you are," Nathaniel spoke, raising an open palm to all present. "Come on Cerberus, let's have a look." Nathaniel turned to Dela to mouth 'stay here'. She, like everyone else in the room, had jumped to her feet at the noise. She nodded, rather than raise her usual fuss, it wasn't the time for arguments.

Nathaniel, with Cerberus at his side, made for the front door. Neither Nathaniel's nor Cerberus's keen ears had heard any other noise since the initial thud and they hoped this was a good sign.

They reached the front door and Nathaniel peered through the spy hole, but could see nothing but darkness and the usual hedges.

Dela meanwhile had crept after them and peered down the hallway to look at what could possibly be at the door.

"Ready?" Nathaniel glanced at Cerberus and his companion from Hades growled softly back in the affirmative. Nathaniel held open the bolts, then pulled the front door inwards quickly towards him. Cerberus sprang out into the wet bleak night to confront whatever had made the noise.

There was nobody there, but embedded into the top of the door was a black arrow with a piece of parchment tied to the shaft with a red ribbon.

Cerberus did a little reconnoitre of the front cottage garden, while Nathaniel with a little effort and rocking pulled the arrow from the door.

Dela came up the hall with Nana and Kane in tow, while Nathaniel pulled the ribbon and carefully untied the parchment.

Cerberus returned, shaking his shaggy head, an indication that there was nobody in the vicinity. Nathaniel moved aside to let him re-enter the Rectory and closed the door behind him. Nana switched on the hall light so that everybody could see.

Nathaniel unravelled it and everyone crowded around to look:

*Dear King's Paladin +2 guests.*
*Your carriage awaits!*
*Be at the Mansion by seven o'clock.*
*Dinner will be at seven-thirty sharp.*
*Followed by our duel at eleven-thirty and invasion of your Sceptred Isle at Midnight.*
*Which you may have to miss, on account of your being deceased.*

*Yours in anticipation.*

*Ashmodaios*
*(High Demon Lord of Hell, soon to be ruler of Earth.)*

"What's the time now?" Dela asked looking around for a clock.

"Twenty to seven," Kane replied, looking at his wrist watch.

"Kane, take these outside somewhere and burn them, then bury their ashes," Nathaniel asked, handing the old man the arrow, parchment and ribbon.

"Yes, King's Paladin," Kane replied and took the dark objects away to destroy them.

Nathaniel raised an eyebrow at the 'King's Paladin' bit, instead of 'Master Nathaniel'. Kane, as Dela would have put it, was trying to 'big him up'.

"Twenty minutes isn't long," Nana moaned, "Can't you just stay here? Safe in the Rectory."

Nathaniel reached out his arms and tenderly held his grandmother's shoulders, "I wish I could stay Nana."

"So do I," added Dela.

"But I'm a King's Paladin and I've given my word. I must face Ashmodaios and stop his invasion." Nathaniel seemed to have matured another ten years in the last few hours.

"I've left the tome of the Ancients on your bed, Nana," he smiled, "I'll claim it back later, okay?"

"Okay, Nathaniel." Nana's hard countenance crumbled and tears glistened in her eyes. "I'll keep it safe, Bubs."

"Dela," Nathaniel asked, "can you go upstairs and get my sword and scabbard? Better wrap it in a blanket so the demons can't spot it so easily."

"No probs," and Dela bounded off upstairs to get it.

"I love you, Nana, you've always been here for me when I've needed you. Can you be here for Dela also, if anything were to happen to me?"

"I love you too, Bubs, and yes I'll look after her, because I see that you love that feisty girl too," Nana replied, burying herself into his hard chest.

Nana scratched the top of Cerberus's head. "Take care of him, Cerberus." Cerberus looked up and saw fear and pain in her mortal eyes. He had known her all of her adult life and those words were the nicest he'd ever heard her say to him. He just stared at her in pity, one of his earthly barks did not seem appropriate.

Dela came bounding down the stairs, a long thin bundle of blankets in her arms. "What now, Hun?" Dela asked as she reached the last step.

"We say our farewells and head off to catch our ride, I suppose." Nathaniel didn't want to leave the Rectory's safe, warm and bright confines to brave the elements and take a trip to Hell, and, he hoped, back!

Mrs Dawson watched the rain pelt against the windows of the people carrier, like a torrent of tiny nails stabbing at the vehicle. Mr Goldenboy and the rest of the Society cells from the warehouse had now joined them.

Only Barrington, the sleeper member and owner of the industrial estate, had remained to make doubly sure that nothing demonic had escaped the blasts.

"So when are we going in?" Asked Mr Green, interrupting the noise of the rain on the windows.

"The nearer to midnight the better. At the moment they are awaiting an attack, hopefully at midnight they will be concentrating on the portal," she explained.

"Do we have enough men?" Asked Mr Kenny from the driver's seat.

"Twelve to attack just before twelve," she almost said to herself. "We have to go in hard and fast, no stopping for the injured, just get me in sight of that portal and let me handle the rest."

# CHAPTER 13

The Rectory was now a smudge of light behind them through the hedgerow, trees and battering rain.

Cerberus lead the way, his coat matted to his flanks, ready for anything. Dela followed with her coat on and hood pulled over her hair. Nathaniel came last, carrying the bundle under his arm. He hated the rain, but was sure the fires of Hell would soon dry his clothes out.

They trotted through a copse of trees to the ruins of the Le Meuille mansion. A hundred years before the gardens had been magnificent, as had the mansion with its Greek entrance columns and fine rooms.

Now it lay in ruins. The Le Meuille money kept the Rectory and Nathaniel's town house in the red and viable, but could not stretch to the millions it would cost to restore the mansion to any respectable state. The sweeping driveway was still there, weed-choked, but a reminder of another age where carriages would sweep up to the entrance for balls and parties.

The three very different, but very sodden man, woman and hound from Hell stopped where the entrance columns once stood erect and proud. Nathaniel pushed back his coat sleeve and illuminated his watch, it was about a minute and half to seven o'clock. The three rain-drenched figures huddled closer for warmth and awaited their fate.

A thunder crack broke right above them, making even Cerberus jump a little. A few seconds later lightning struck the driveway and the earth cracked asunder. Out of the crack leapt red and orange flames and with them a black opulent carriage pulled by four Knightmare horses from Hell. Eyes burning red, snorting fire from their nostrils and their black manes stood upright and alive. The horses brought the carriage to a halt, guided by a figure dressed in a brown robe and slumped over the reins, so as to be impossible to ascertain the creature's shape.

The door to the carriage flung itself suddenly open, without the aid of the driver. The dark confines of the carriage were also empty. Two steps dropped down to aid their ascension into the dark empty carriage.

This was it. No going back now. Their carriage to Hades awaited them. Nathaniel broke their temporary paralysis and walked two steps towards the carriage, then reached back for Dela's hand.

Dela hesitated, her eyes exploring the carriage, the horses and the driver, then she reached out a wet hand to take Nathaniel's hand, which guided her towards the carriage.

Nathaniel clambered in, followed by Dela and Cerberus bringing up the rear and sniffing the air cautiously. The interior was plush and the seats were of a claret red leather upholstery. Two brass lamps suddenly lit the interior, each one had an ochre colour candle inside. Nathaniel and Dela sat together facing forwards, with Cerberus sprawled across the seat opposite.

A whip-crack of the reins spurred on the Knightmares and began their descent into Hell. Like a rollercoaster's plunge the carriage tipped forward, and it seemed as if their stomachs flew into their throats. The ground cracked asunder again, exposing a fiery gap in which the horses, carriage and occupants plunged.

Nathaniel took Dela's instinctive lead and braced the soles of his shoes against the seat opposite. They clung on to each other as the carriage descended through the Earth and planes and levels of Hell and Hades.

"I wish I had waited for the next one!" Dela yelled, trying not to throw up with fear.

"I'll tell Ashmodaios to put in a lift or something a bit more modern next time."

Stars sparkled outside the windows now and whole constellations and spiral arms flew past at breakneck speed, followed by purple, yellow and orange skies.

Then the carriage jumped, like an aeroplane buffeted by turbulence. They had broken through a crust of earth and a crimson landscape floated below. On rocky islands of cold lava floated the domain of Ashmodaios, Arch-Duke of Hades.

Some of these islands floated freely in the crimson air while their size varied from rocks to the size of football pitches and to the magnitude of the Isle of Wight. Many of these seemingly unsupported landmasses were tethered by chains or golden bridges to the largest Island which contained Ashmodaios's opulent castle and palace of pure alabaster, with basalt walls, towers and keeps surrounding it.

Down the carriage went towards this infernal island. The carriage conveyed them over a vast courtyard filled to the brim with demons. There they stood; oozed; staggered; loped; slithered; in row upon row in every nightmare shape, size and colour imaginable. A vast army ready to invade Earth in a few short hours.

They faced a man-sized seven foot tall arch, raised on a slight dais, with two steps leading to it. The arch either consisted of metal or rock and black as the darkest night. On each side of the gateway were two spikes on which a man and a woman were impaled. Their blood flowed along channels to a copper basin set in the dais on the floor of the archway.

Their route had been designed by Ashmodaios to pass over his army and to give maximum effect. All three of the carriage's passengers' hearts sank. How could Ashmodaios's army be defeated, how could they survive this night, how could Earth stop this invasion?

With the courtyard behind them now they were over the walls of Ashmodaios's castle and they slowly descended before the entrance to his alabaster palace.

The carriage stopped and the door slowly opened on its own, followed by the steps: Hell awaited them.

"Dela, you're going to see a lot of terrible, mind-bending things here. Try not to react, try to think of it as a dream, okay?" Nathaniel held her face in his hands, looked deep into her eyes and kissed her.

"Okay, Nat."

"You ready?"

"No, but let's go anyway," Dela replied.

Cerberus jumped out as his normal earthly size, but landed as his huge three-headed river Styx resident counterpart. Nathaniel came next, followed by Dela, shocked at Cerberus's transformation. The air was warm and sizzled like a holiday she had taken in Tenerife in August three years ago.

A set of rounded steps led up towards the ghastly, but impressive palace. Two enormous copper doors swung open and Ashmodaios, the High Demon Lord appeared in one of his human forms. Down the steps he came and Nathaniel hugged his blanket wrapped sword closer to his chest. A pair of jackals followed him on leashes, ravenous and drooling. They were led (or dragged) by a beautiful raven-haired woman, covered only with scratches and bites from the hungry jackals.

Ashmodaios flung open his arms as he reached the last of the lapis-lazuli steps.

"Welcome to the realm of Gehenna and my humble palace. Abaddon!"

"Love what you've done with the place," Nathaniel stepped forward and looked around, "Neo-Nazi-Gothic style I think."

Ashmodaios laughed off the remark and turned to the others. "It's been a millennia since you last visited Cerberus, I hope the air isn't too rarefied for you."

"Yes, and I would have though you would have re-decorated since then," the left head of Cerberus replied.

Ashmodaios smiled with thin red lips, "And finally, the lovely Miss. Robinson. I hope you will enjoy your brief stay here tonight." Ashmodaios' forked red tongue licked his lips salaciously.

"Don't count on it, freak!" she spat, and moved herself next to Nathaniel.

"Charming." Ashmodaios pointed up the steps to the huge copper doors and slowly they all began to climb them. Nathaniel moved next to Ashmodaios, with Dela at his right and Cerberus flanking her.

Ashmodaios stared down his nose, his nostrils flaring with interest, "What's that King's Paladin? A present for your host?"

"Sort of," Nathaniel hugged the bundle tighter still, "you'll get it later, I promise."

"Oh, I do love surprises." Ashmodaios had reached the huge doors that swung inwards as he approached.

A corridor stretched ahead of them with black marble walls, basalt floor and a gold and copper ceiling. White marble columns lined the walls every ten feet and between each pair of columns were doors, paintings, frescoes and statues.

"If you'll follow me." Ashmodaios led the way.

Nathaniel, Dela and Cerberus followed with the jackal lady behind them with her snarling pets.

The artwork, if you can call it that, represented pain, or pain givers, or acts of unthinkable sadism. There were instruments of torture, a bust of Adolph Hitler, Christ in pictures of depravity with his mother, Mary. Every torture, every sick act, every pain that man could inflict on fellow man was here.

Dela stared at her feet as she walked, the bile rising in her throat. Nathaniel was sickened also and even Cerberus tried not to look.

"Not an art lover then, Dela?" Ashmodaios enquired as they continued to walk.

"That's not art, it's fucking sick and so the fuck are you!" Dela tasted the bile on her lips as she yelled, losing her composure.

"The English language, so poetical. Well said, Dela Robinson, but look again, these aren't acts by demons against men. These are acts perpetrated by man on his fellow man. Not even I, Ashmodaios, Arch-duke of Hades and Demon Lord could have the imagination of evil as are dreamt up by mankind."

"Ignore him, Dela," Cerberus's right head advised.

Dela looked at Nathaniel and drew strength from his resolve and managed to bite her tongue.

"Okay, that was in bad taste, let us change the subject." Ashmodaios played with his long fingers as they walked down the endless corridor.

"Did you see my army as the carriage brought you here? Aren't they magnificent?" he teased, looking back at his guests.

"Very impressive, but doomed to fail Ashmodaios," Nathaniel replied, his voice loud in the long corridor inside the palace.

"Fail? How? There are few on Earth with the skills to stop us and the most dangerous to our plans is you." Ashmodaios stopped to face his guests, "And you three meddlers are here with me in Hades, my humble guests," he added with a bow.

"Not much of a victory if my sword strikes you down after pudding, is it?" Nathaniel managed to find a grin from somewhere.

"I think you are deluding yourself King's Paladin. I've had eternity to practise my sword fighting skills and you've had about a decade. Hardly seems fair does it, Cerberus?"

Cerberus just grunted at the High Demon as he stopped beside a red leather-bound door. Dela hoped it was leather anyway.

"Welcome to my dining halls." Ashmodaios opened the door and led them into a huge cathedral-sized hall used for his feastings.

The small door did not do justice to the room beyond. It was the size and shape of a Norman cathedral, with grey stone walls, high-stained glass windows with unholy images. A huge banqueting table a hundred feet long with wooden arched chairs dominated the centre of the room. To the right of them, as they looked a huge brooding statue sat on a dais, of a goat-headed beast. At its crossed, cloved hooves was a font filled with fresh red blood. The statue and the font were on the same level as the door, but the banqueting area was sunken by five feet and stone steps led down to it.

"Get many wedding reception bookings?" Cerberus's left head asked. Nathaniel laughed and even Dela managed a grin despite herself.

"Only the dark nuns to the Devil himself," Ashmodaios smiled back, "shall we go in?"

They all entered the imposing room, all except Cerberus who couldn't fit through the red door.

"Having trouble?" the jackal handler asked Cerberus.

"None at all," the middle head replied as he vanished and reappeared inside the hall next to the long wooden table.

Ashmodaios led them down to the table and sat down in a mahogany chair inlaid with gold at the head of the table.

"Do sit down, dinner will be served soon." Ashmodaios beckoned them to sit with both hands.

The jackal lady let the leashed animals go, and they each took a bite out of her, then went to lie either side of Ashmodaios's chair. A look of ecstasy had crossed her face as the jackals attacked her. Now bleeding from buttock and thigh, she sat herself down next to her Demon Lord on his left hand side.

Leaving the chair opposite the jackal lady free, Nathaniel sat down to Ashmodaios's right with Dela next to him. Cerberus picked up three chairs in each mouth and tossed them high across the room to smash into the wall, then took his place, sitting on hind legs next to the lady of the jackals.

"Manners," Ashmodaios chided.

"Find Jesus and die," Cerberus's left head replied with a guffaw.

"Menus," Ashmodaios said loudly.

Nathaniel glanced at his watch. Surely it wasn't dinner time yet, but there it was, seven-thirty post meridiem.

A statue in an alcove twirled around and from the secret entrance came what can only be described as an Octopus Demon. Its skin was of the shade of a blood-orange's juice, it walked on two legs, had a potato-dome shaped head and eight arms. To make this image seem even more bizarre, the creature was dressed in a waiter's uniform and had a goatee beard. Its appearance was more humorous than horrible, but Dela had to remember where she was and that everything was a potential killer.

In five of its hands it held menus, two were empty and one had a white cloth draped over it. Down, the Octopus Demon, waltzed to the head of the table and handed over nearly all the menus at once.

Dela couldn't help but feel she was in some deep drug influenced dream. '*No*,' she chided herself, this was real at the moment and Earth, somewhere, felt like a dream.

At the Rectory Nana and Kane sat in the sitting room drinking tea with a nip of brandy to keep out the chill of the storm. Kane was oiling his shotgun which lay next to Nana's on the newspaper covered table.

The radio was on in the background as they waited for twelve o'clock and the invasion. She hoped against hope that

Nathaniel would return to her and stop the demonic plans that lay ahead for the planet Earth.

"Anybody got anything to eat?" Mrs. Dawson asked, her stomach rumbling loudly.

Mr Kenny passed her a Mars bar from the glove compartment of the Zafira, "Here you go."

"Thanks," she smiled. Mr Kenny looked so young; she wondered how many, if any, of her people would survive the night.

She eagerly opened the Mars bar and began eating, watching the rain lash against the windows. Her thoughts drifted off to encompass Nathaniel and his predicament. There was something pure and innocent about the man, with the ancient supernatural knowledge he possessed and the burden he carried alone as King's Paladin. She at least had the Society to back her up, he had Dela and a large hound. She cared for Nathaniel and had lost so many people close to her, she didn't want to lose anyone else. With her Society colleagues she was an icy professional, nobody was let in to see her softer side. Sex with Mr Goldenboy had been an end of the world whim, it was just hard sex: no love involved. Thunder boomed again overhead, waking her from her thoughts. She glanced at her watch again, God, time was dragging on tonight.

Dela chewed her food daintily and slowly, expecting to spit it out at any second. She had chosen curried goat, rice and peas, an old dish her mother used to do to perfection. Dela sipped her red wine, it tasted not of blood, but of good Burgundy.

"Is your food to your satisfaction?" Ashmodaios asked, staring straight at Dela.

"Palatable," Nathaniel answered for her, looking up from his roast chicken meal.

"It will do," Dela answered for herself, knowing it tasted better than her mum's.

"You looked surprised, what were you expecting Miss. Robinson?" Ashmodaios asked, leaning forward on his elbows. "Devilled eggs perhaps, or cold Jackal sandwiches?" Ashmodaios mocked.

"Leave it Arch-Duke," Cerberus's middle head said.

"Yeah, shut the fuck up and eat your chilled monkey's brains," Cerberus's left head guffawed again as its right head bit into a leg of lamb.

"Okay, let's change the subject," Ashmodaios conceded with a grin. "What topic of conversation should we engage in, King's Paladin?"

"Okay. Why is the invasion planned for tonight? Why not any other midnight in the last thousand years?" Nathaniel asked, putting down his knife and fork.

"So many questions in one," Ashmodaios answered. "Okay. I will try to answer them all, only because I'm going to eviscerate and decapitate you later, King's Paladin. Why wait thousands of years to try? I'll answer your planning my dear Nathaniel. Firstly, I had to find the burial ground of a saint, one the world or Church had forgotten or lost. Secondly, that resting place would be on holy ground which had been defiled and tainted by years of sin and evil. Not many of those on the estate agents' books I can tell you!" Ashmodaios sipped his wine and swallowed before continuing.

"Then I had to wait for science to catch up with my vision. I needed demons that could operate during the day as well as the hours of darkness. Mr Telal, my half-human, half-demon son, you have met. DNA splicing, cloning, sperm washing, all these technologies had to be in place to create my demon/human hybrids." Ashmodaios tucked into his steak again. "And the date for the invasion? Vanity on my part: it's my birthday,"

Ashmodaios laughed, followed quickly by the Lady of the Jackals.

Nathaniel and Dela looked at one another and frowned.

"Time for pudding, I think," Ashmodaios bellowed loudly and clapped his hands together.

A huge selection of devilish looking puddings were brought by thirteen hooded human figures that had brought in the previous courses. No faces, feet or hands could be seen, their black habits covered all.

A hooded figure shuffled up beside Dela, a ladle protruding from its long baggy sleeve. Dela pulled her chair back at the same time to reach for a spoon. The hooded servant toppled across her body. The stench of the thing made Dela gag.

"Get the fuck away from me, man!" She shoved the figure away from her as hard as she could.

Ashmodaios smiled wickedly while a concerned Nathaniel rose to his feet. The figure fell backwards, crashing to the floor on his back. His hood and sleeves fell back also to reveal the poor creature who had served them.

"Oh!" Dela exclaimed in revulsion. For there on the floor was a thin man of African descent, but that wasn't the shocking part. The ladle wasn't carried in the man's hands, he had no hands. Just normal forearms that had been severed halfway down. The handle end of the ladle had been hammered into the stumps with painful force.

"You're depraved, Ashmodaios!" Nathaniel shot at the High Demon.

"You sick fuck!" Dela turned to her host and spat.

"You forget, this is Hell, my dear," Ashmodaios replied to her in a mocking tone.

"Are you okay?" Dela looked down kindly at the frightened servant, who hastily pulled down his hood and sleeves and turned to crawl away.

"Don't waste your sympathy, Miss. Robinson," Ashmodaios replied softly. "He had none for the thirty-nine Tutsi men, women and children his soldiers raped, killed and burnt. He died as he lived, violently, and was sent here to be punished and punished he is." Ashmodaios bit into a slice of chocolate cake.

Nathaniel sat down as Dela watched the man scramble to his feet and limp away.

"Dela, this isn't a holiday camp I run here, this is eternal damnation. That is my job. Souls come here to suffer for the evils they commit during life. We are all servants to someone or another." Ashmodaios studied his guests as he licked the chocolate sauce off his spoon.

"If you're a servant Ashmodaios, why do you want to invade Earth?" Nathaniel asked, putting down his spoon.

"After an eternity of service even servants have ambition. There are three Arch-Demon Lords and three Arch-Devil Lords, I just want to be the best of the lot. If I capture the Earth for my Lord, what reward will I be worthy of? To sit at his left hand as his only one true Lieutenant."

"And what of the balance of things then, Ashmodaios? What use is Hell and Hades when you would rule the Earth in darkness?" Cerberus's middle head asked.

"Suffering," Ashmodaios hissed. "Imagine a life full of pain and suffering and then in death eternal suffering. The souls I get here deserve their pain and punishments, there are no innocents in Hell, Cerberus, not even you. To torture the innocent, the wise and virtuous, to make happy families suicidal, to take the virginal or holy and create evil and to blacken their souls would be a power only God possesses." Ashmodaios' eyes flicked red with lust.

"Pride comes before a fall, Ashmodaios, you are not Lord of Earth yet," Cerberus's right head replied.

"I am already fallen Cerberus from Heaven's grace, but at least I'm not the lap dog to a sniff of a boy," Ashmodaios venomously replied.

"I am nobody's lap dog, demon, I am Cerberus, guardian to the gates of Hades and Hell and Nathaniel is not my lord and master, he is my friend," Cerberus's central head spoke proudly.

"Well put, and a fair point I suppose, but master or friend Nathaniel will die by my sword this very night. Nothing can stop this!"

Dela looked at Nathaniel and saw something in his eyes for the first time: real fear. Ashmodaios looked around the silenced dining table proudly.

"Death is always a bit of a conversation stopper. If you have all finished we still have a while until the main event, let me give you a tour of my palace." Ashmodaios stood quickly and the Lady of the Jackals hurried to rise to her master's sudden erectness.

"Anything to kill some time, eh?" Cerberus's left head chuckled, but no one found it very amusing.

The grandfather clock in the hall chimed loudly. Nana had somehow, despite all the anxiety, fallen into a fitful sleep in her armchair.

Kane sniffed and put down his shotgun on the table. He had never felt so helpless in his life.

Outside in the lanes and fields that surrounded the hill, the village undead plodded slowly onwards, loosely encircling the grounds.

# CHAPTER 14

Mrs Dawson sat in the dark pondering as the rain lashed down on her vehicle. The whole world now knew about the attacks on the Idiminu Corporation building and to a lesser extent the warehouse. She knew the Society had been behind them and was both eliminating the threat and covering up the evidence. She just wondered if a tactical strike could happen when she and her team were inside the house to prevent the demonic invasion. The deeper she became involved in the Society, the less sure of its motives she became. The Council of Seven remained a mystery to most members and so her curiosity pushed her on. Hell, she had nothing else to live for! Without the Society she'd have jumped in front of a tube train years ago.

Outside the rain poured, inside Mrs Dawson and her men waited.

They walked the battlements of Ashmodaios's Palace walls, marvelling at the sight of the floating world of Gehenna. They could not look over the battlements for very long, as the blast furnace heat rising up caused Nathaniel and Dela to pull away.

The front courtyard was teeming with jibbering demons, thousands strong and ready to conquer mankind. Dela was very glad indeed that they were thirty feet above the foul creatures. She reached for Nathaniel's hand and he took it.

"If we fail tonight it will be all over for everyone on Earth, won't it?" Dela whispered to him.

"It will be terrible, but others will take up the fight. The human spirit and soul are strong, even in these unbelieving times. Darkness is always followed by dawn eventually, Dela," Nathaniel tried to reassure her, his hand squeezing hers lightly.

It would soon be time for the sword duel. Cerberus's more whimsical head held the King's Paladin's sword in its mouth, the other two heads glad of the silence.

Even though Nathaniel had the worries of the world and its unknowing populace on his mind, all he could think of was Dela. If he failed he wouldn't get to romance her properly, take her to the pictures, bore her to death with Star Wars trivia, take her to Venice, marry her and grow old with her. If he saved the world and lost her it would be no victory at all.

"Okay, let's go!" Mrs Dawson yelled as the dashboard clock in her car turned to eleven o'clock.

The three vehicles, lead by the people carrier, sped off up the hill from their holding positions towards Manes Close. Each of the Society vehicles had four members inside, racing towards their target. Only a minute and a half later they came to a screeching halt outside number three Manes Close.

An artic was parked on the opposite side of the deserted road. Nothing moved apart from the rain in the dark heavens. Everyone exited their vehicles with great alacrity, guns at the ready. Mrs Dawson had a long cricket bag with her and nothing more.

"Mr Goldenboy, take your cell and check out the artic and the other houses, then meet us inside number three," Mrs Dawson barked at the tall blond man. "The rest of you follow me, safeties off and torches on." Mrs Dawson led the other eight Society operatives into the front door of Three Manes Close and the site of the invasion portal.

Mrs Dawson pointed at Mr Atlas, a giant of a man, who shoulder-barged his six foot two frame into the front door, breaking it easily inwards.

Mr Atlas pulled a bowie knife from a sheath on his belt. He never carried a gun, ever. Mrs Dawson followed him into the dark hallway, Mr Green close behind her, followed by Mr Kenny and the rest of her assault team.

"Mrs Jordan, take your cell and explore the downstairs. Once secured make your way upstairs, okay?"

"Okay," Mrs Jordan replied. She was scared witless, but led her cell through a door on the left hand side of the hallway into a large, dark (and, happily, empty) room.

Mrs Dawson, Mr Green and Mr Kenny plus Mr Atlas and his two cell members headed for the stairs and the invoking room Nathaniel had told her about at their last meeting.

The dark, musty house was now invaded with strobes of torch-beams arcing from floor to wall to ceiling. Mrs Dawson crept up the stairs, but the boards creaked loudly however soft her footfalls.

Hands gripped knives, guns and torches harder as they ascended the stairs. Mr Green, protective of Mrs Dawson, moved to her side, then as they reached the empty landing, moved ahead of her and stood guard, scanning the open and shut doors of the first floor.

Mrs Dawson consulted the hand-drawn map that the King's Paladin had provided for her. She pointed with two fingers at the third door along on the left-hand side of the landing, which marked the stairs like a square horseshoe shape. The door was closed, as was the first door they had to pass; the middle door was half ajar and no light could be seen anywhere.

Mrs Dawson heaved the cricket bag on to her back and proceeded across the landing. Mr Green took point with Mr Kenny grinding his teeth in fright behind her. Mr Atlas led his team following the first cell closely behind and guarding the rear.

The boards creaked liked the sun and salt-shrinked decks of the Mary Celeste. Mr Green scanned the inside of the second open door; apart from an old bookcase (empty) the room was completely bare.

They moved on, their torch-beams criss-crossing as they warily kept a look out for demon attack. Mrs Dawson was getting nervous, it was just too damn quiet.

Mr Granby, a Gulf War veteran from Atlas's cell, stepped inside the bare room for a closer look, his weapon held in one hand. His professional eye saw nothing untoward at all, as the lead group reached the third door. This was the room where Nathaniel had found the invoking circle on the floor.

Mr Atlas, the human battering ram, came to the fore again, Mr Green and Mr Granby would go in next with Mrs Dawson and Mr Kenny. Mr Salinger continued to guard the rear in case of a counter-attack.

Mrs Dawson made a thumbs-up sign and everybody nodded they were ready. Mrs Dawson was scared; they had to succeed or else the Earth was doomed. She hoped everyone would hold up. She was pretty sure of Atlas, Green and Grandby, but Mr Kenny, an ex-copper, looked like he was going to shit himself at any second.

"Go!" she cried and smacked Mr Green on the shoulder for good measure. Mr Atlas rammed open the unlocked door with his shoulder and tripped and went crashing to the floor of the room. Mr Green and Mr Grandby jumped over his legs and charged into the large l-shaped room to take up attacking positions.

There was no sound of gunfire as Mrs Dawson and Mr Kenny entered the room. Torch-beams flicked from shadow to shadow across the length of the room. Mr Green, Mr Grandby and Mrs Dawson moved further into the room, swinging torches and weapons from left to right and up and down, seeking out the enemy. Mrs Dawson's torch-beam found the invoking circle on the floor, covered in dust. The room was empty!

"Oh Hell!" Mrs Dawson exclaimed, eyes fixed on the spot where the invasion should be happening.

"Well, that's the grand tour over." Ashmodaios had led them back to the courtyard where the carriage had first arrived. "Now it's time for the real warm up event of the night: our duel, King's Paladin!"

Dramatically the Demon Lord cast off the red cloak that he had been wearing since the beginning of the tour of the battlements. Several familiar imps appeared from a small secret stone door in the side of the steps that led to the Palace. They handed the Demon Lord a curved sword they had been carrying, then collected his cloak and disappeared as quickly as they had arrived.

"You have five minutes to prepare King's Paladin, and say your good-byes." Ashmodaios turned to grab the Lady of the Jackals roughly by the hair and pulled her to him to kiss.

Nathaniel, Dela and Cerberus turned away so they could talk. Dela flew into Nathaniel's arms and Cerberus rubbed at Nathaniel's back with a large paw.

"I don't want you to die!" Dela sobbed into Nathaniel's neck, her tears making his collar wet.

Nathaniel pulled her back, hands on her shoulders, crouching down to look into her sad eyes. "Funnily enough, I don't want to either," he tried to joke, his voice cracking up with emotion.

"Don't forget he's the King's Paladin and what that means," comforted Cerberus's middle head.

"Listen to the big three-headed hound. I was born to slay demons, this is what I do!" Nathaniel smiled and kissed her forehead.

Dela's hands went to his cheeks and pulled him into a long, deep kiss. Cerberus stepped back a little to give them some room.

"I love you Nathaniel." Dela sniffed through her tears.

"Nathaniel? Not Nat or Nath? Must be serious." He winked at her, "I love you with all my heart and soul Dela."

"Make sure you come back to me or I'll fucking kill you!" Dela cried, hugging him so tightly as to restrict his breathing.

"I'll never leave, you Dela Robinson." He held her shoulders and took a step back, a brave smile on his lips. "Cerberus! My sword!"

"With honour, my old friend," replied Cerberus's right head as the left one lowered the bundle into the King's Paladin's hands.

"Are we ready to begin?" came Ashmodaios's sarcastic voice from behind Nathaniel's back.

"Just a mo, old chap, just getting my sword ready." Nathaniel pulled the scabbard from the blanket. He then turned to face Ashmodaios, who stood twelve feet away, his red pummelled sword with a curved copper blade held in front of him.

Dela gasped as flames appeared at the base of the blade and ran up its entire length.

"Let me introduce my sword, "Soul Reaper"," smiled Ashmodaios, the ends of his pointed moustache pointed upwards.

"If we are doing introductions, then this is "Demon Slayer". You may have heard of it!" It was Nathaniel's chance to grin as he drew the golden sword from its scabbard.

Ashmodaios looked wide-eyed and a flicker of worry crossed his brow. "A bold claim King's Paladin, but that blade was lost over half a century ago."

"Not lost Arch Duke, merely hidden for such an occasion as this." Nathaniel nodded, then turned to hand the ancient scabbard to Dela. "Take care of this for a couple of mins, honey," Nathaniel winked. Then he strode purposefully to within six feet of Ashmodaios's blade and whispered, "Quem di diligunt adolescens miritur."

"What did he say?" Dela turned to ask Cerberus.

"Whom the gods love dies young," his middle head replied mournfully.

"Aut vincere aut mori!" said Ashmodaios, raising his sword near his face.

"To conquer or die," Nathaniel replied in English, raising his golden sword to his nose.

Then Ashmodaios attacked, a swift slash to Nathaniel's left-hand side, which he parried as quickly and spun like a dancer to attack the demon's right side. The demon parried low and spun up, pushing Nathaniel back. Yet there was no respite, Nathaniel attacked ferociously again and again while Ashmodaios defended and countered with equal agility.

Dela's hands went up to her face in worry, but she was shocked at the beauty and fluidity of Nathaniel's sword-fighting abilities. She now fully realised who he was and what the title King's Paladin meant. The parries of Nathaniel's golden sword drew sparks from the flame blade of Ashmodaios. The fear in Dela's heart was still there, but another emotion was evolving also: pride. She was so proud that her man was putting it all on the line to save her and the rest of humanity.

Back on earth things were not going to plan.

Mrs Dawson knelt by the invoking circle that Nathaniel and Dela had discovered. It was still there, but smudged and covered in dust. No invasion looked likely in this room tonight.

"Nothing in the room next door either," Mr Grandby reported to her, fingering his sub-machine gun.

Mrs Dawson sucked at her teeth and stood up.

Mrs Jordan entered the room and approached her. "Downstairs check out, no activity at all."

Mrs Dawson felt the walls close in on her as all eyes in the room focussed on her. "Okay, Jordan, take your team and help Goldenboy check out the other six houses. The rest of us will tear this house apart until we find the invasion point. Now go!"

Mrs Dawson strode off to check out the windows of the room, just to give the impression she was in control and knew what next to do. She looked at her watch. It read eleven thirty-one. Less than half an hour to save the world. No pressure at all. She strode from the room to check out each room personally.

The courtyard was getting too restrictive for Nathaniel. He needed to keep Ashmodaios occupied until Mrs Dawson could stop the invasion at Manes Close. Nathaniel spied some steps which led up to the walls of the castle/city and encircled the whole floating rock on which they stood. Nathaniel increased the intensity of his attacking swordplay, forcing the flame-sword wielding demon to parry, defend and retreat.

Ashmodaios was not surprised by the swordsmanship of the King's Paladin. Their skill was legendary, even in Hell. It had been three hundred years since his last swordfight and to a far lesser opponent. Yet he was playing a defensive waiting game, happy to parry and repost until he could find a weakness, or a chance to cheat. He felt the step on the back of his heel and slashed downwards as he edged back up the small set of steps that led up to the battlements.

Dela spotted something and grabbed Cerberus's nearest head so she could speak in his ear. Dela's and Cerberus's three heads whipped around to see the Lady of the Jackals loosening her slobbering wards so they could attack Nathaniel's exposed rear.

She let them go as Dela ran over to her, and the jackals sped off to attack Nathaniel. Cerberus moved also, but he moved through a different dimension. He vanished, then reappeared, both front legs crushing a now dead jackal underneath each mighty paw.

The Lady of the Jackals wailed in despair as her beasts were killed. Then something caught the corner of her eye. She tuned quickly to feel a black fist smash into her teeth and nose, which exploded with a spray of blood and she struck the courtyard flagstones hard, dashing her head. It would be a long time before she got up to mischief again.

"You fucking bitch!" Dela screamed, both for the Lady's treachery and the intense pain emanating from her fingers and bleeding knuckles.

Both Nathaniel and the Demon Lord had ceased fighting, each three steps safe distance from attack. Both were looking down at the courtyard's scene of carnage, mouths agog.

"You have one hell of a woman there, King's Paladin. I shall enjoy breaking her in after she sees you fall." Ashmodaios sneered, advancing down the steps to attack Nathaniel once more.

"Glad she's on my side too, Ashmodaios old mate," and Nathaniel parried the demon's furious attack and pressed him back up the steps once more.

"Now this is fun!" stated Cerberus's left head, looking down at the blood leaking from the jackals' skulls under paw.

It was now a quarter to twelve and panic was biting at Mrs Dawson's icy coolness. She was now downstairs in the once living room of Three Manes Close. A fireplace and a smashed armchair were the only signs it was once a fully furbished family home. A few local newspapers were strewn about the dark carpet for effect. She was alone in the room but could hear her teams searching the other rooms of the house. She did a slow circle of the room then stopped again to think. A drip of liquid hit her head and she hurriedly stepped back, raising her torch to examine the ceiling. Somewhere under the first floor floorboards a pipe had developed a small leak. There was a brown stain on the white ceiling where the water dripped through to the floor.

Another drip sparkled and grew on the ceiling and then fell silently to the mouldy carpet floor. She watched the scene intently now, her mind casting off all other things as if the deeper parts of her brain had had an idea and was striving to push it to the fore. The water drips down, soaking the carpet, then down into the floorboards and whatever was below.

"Maybe even a cellar," she startled herself by speaking the words out loud without even realising. Mrs Dawson spun, scanning to the room. "Where would I get to a cellar? The kitchen normally!" she blurted out as she ran from the room. She knocked into and bounced off Mr Atlas in the hallway and ran into the kitchen.

"We have to find a cellar or something!" she exclaimed to Mr Grandby who had been opening cupboards and drawers.

Mrs Dawson's eyes darted around the room looking for doors or tunnels or trap doors. Mr Grandby pulled at the cupboard doors with more gusto as more of the Society team entered the kitchen.

Nathaniel's continuing ferocious onslaughts had driven Ashmodaios up the steps and on to the battlements. The clash of melee was now going away from the palace, towards the courtyard filled with the demonic invasion hordes.

Cerberus and Dela had followed them up the steps at a safe distance. Cerberus kept one head looking backwards at all times, wary that they might be ambushed.

The swordfight was now on the walls surrounding the vast courtyard. Below the demons yelled and bellowed support for their master.

The arid heat was getting to Nathaniel and was taking its toll on his attacks. Yet Nathaniel knew this would happen and had planned for such an eventuality. The fight suddenly stopped. Nathaniel saw his opportunity with one of Ashmodaios's slashing attacks and took advantage of it. Nathaniel parried the slash, but let himself be moved sidewards. Ashmodaios now aimed an attack at Nathaniel's neck, which Nathaniel parried, but gave him the chance to stagger back a few steps. The two sword fighters had now changed positions and the Demon Lord went on the offensive. To parry and retreat used less energy and still pushed the two combatants to where Nathaniel wanted the fight to go.

Back Ashmodaios pushed him, his demonic army cheering him on. Nathaniel though, was certain he was the more able swordsman and his plan depended on it. He was aware of the plight he was in, his location on the battlements, even Cerberus and Dela following at a safe distance. He just prayed that on Earth the rest of his plan was progressing well.

"I've found it!" Mr Atlas cried with joy. He had pulled away the large stand-alone fridge-freezer from the wall to reveal a large hole in the floor rising to a quarter way up the wall. Demonic claws had tunnelled a passageway leading downwards at a forty degree angle into the walls and foundations of the building.

"Okay, time's running out, everyone in!" Mrs Dawson ordered as she went over to pickup her long bag. "I'll go fir…"

"I got point," Mr Grandby said before anyone could interject and plunged head first into the hole, a torch strapped to his head and machine pistol out front as he crawled down the quite smooth tunnel.

Mrs Dawson angrily followed his boots, pushing her cricket bag in front of her as she held a torch in one fist. Mr Green crouched at the hole to go next as Mr Atlas wondered if he would fit in the hole. The edges of the tunnel seemed baked smooth, like some intense heat had quarterised the house's wound as it went along. Mr Grandby went at quite a speed, military trained for such occasions. The tunnel descended for over twenty feet making it roughly ten feet under the foundations of the house.

Mr Grandby stopped and turned off his Maglite, he could hear the exertions of his fellow Society members behind him.

The tunnel, in its present small state, ended a few feet in front of him. Vague light showed ahead and he saw it opened up into a much roomier tunnel. Grandby slowly eased his way down to the end of the first tunnel. With the nozzle of his machine pistol near to his chin he slowly peeked out of the sloping tunnel.

His head eased out of the sloping tunnel half way up the wall of a larger tunnel heading directly left. The new tunnel was four feet wide and ten feet tall and had a metal ceiling supported by iron braces in the walls. The floors and walls were of heated earth that seemed to flicker like glass. The tunnel only turned right for a yard, while the left way turned about fifteen feet before opening up into a larger chamber. Two braziers, four foot high and two feet in diameter, provided the light. Two fires were lit in each heavy-looking copper brazier.

Between the braziers was a six feet wide excavation. Orange earth had been dug away to reveal an ancient looking grey stone wall. A six feet by five feet hole had been breached in the wall and more naked-flame illumination could be seen beyond the wall's breach. A low chanting could be heard and shadowy silhouetted figures moved around inside.

Grandby could see no sign of demons in the new tunnel or the chamber with the braziers. The former soldier slivered silently down into the new larger tunnel, turning at the lip of the first sloping tunnel to ease his legs from under him. Without making any noise he managed it effortlessly, his machine pistol pointing up the tunnel at all times.

Mr Grandby crouched by the sloping tunnel's exit point as Mrs Dawson's head and shoulders came into view. He put his finger to his lips, then pointed down the tunnel towards the hole in the wall. Mrs Dawson nodded and pointed to her bag, which Grandby lowered to the tunnel floor for her.

Dawson leant on Grandby's shoulder for support as she too lowered herself into the tunnel. Mr Green followed and took his place in front of Mrs Dawson, protecting her. Mr Kenny followed, then Mr Atlas and Mr Salinger.

Mrs Dawson ordered Mr Salinger back up the tunnel to inform Mr Goldenboy and the remaining members of her active cells where they were. Mrs Dawson looked at her watch. It was nine minutes to twelve. She had no time to wait for reinforcements, she would have to attack with the small force she had, and quickly. Mrs Dawson gave the signal and as silently as possible the five Society members crept along the tunnel towards the hole in the ancient wall.

Time was running out and Nathaniel had no chance of looking at his watch to find how much time he had left. Ashmodaios was keeping him busy with his attacking flaming scimitar. Nathaniel was halfway down a flight of steps, parrying and defending with every stroke the Demon Lord had. The steps led down into the courtyard and near to where the obscene portal stood. Massed in front of it was the legion of the demon invasion force.

Cerberus and Dela stood on top of the battlements of Ashmodaios's domain. Dela's hopes faded as she saw where the sword fight was heading. Soon Nathaniel would be fighting with the massed ranks of the Demon Lord's army behind him. She could already see the demons inching towards her man, as the epic duel reached the bottom of the stone steps.

Cerberus saw this too and acted swiftly. "Stay here," his middle head looked down at Dela and spoke. Then he leapt high into the harsh dry air, landing between the demonic hordes and the steps where the duel continued. Several demons moved forward to counter him, but a loud roar from all three heads saw them retreat back to their lines. Cerberus was also a Lord of Hell, which meant he could not interfere with the duel. It also meant that his very presence kept the army back, which inadvertently helped the King's Paladin.

Ashmodaios stood on the last step, "You have fought well King's Paladin, but I have an appointment with destiny to fulfil."

Ashmodaios watched as Nathaniel backed away towards the dais and the invoking portal, as the Demon Lord continued, "You have been a worthy adversary and fair play to you. Yet it is no longer the time for fair play, victory at any cost is the only edict I live by."

Then Ashmodaios's skin split apart coating the steps with blood. Out of his human frame evolved and grew a new demonic form. Over thirteen feet tall, with skin of crimson red, talons of pus-yellow gripped his scimitar, while charred black wings like some humungous bat opened to a wingspan of thirty feet behind him. Ivory horns grew and curved from his forehead and his black split tongue darted though red fanged teeth.

"Your time is over little man. The eternal night of the demons is about to commence." With one cloven-hoofed footstep the demon bore down on the King's Paladin.

"Bugger," Nathaniel whispered and raised his sword high to prepare for the Demon Lord's attack.

Mrs Dawson's group had reached the ante-chamber. Before them was the hole in the grey stone wall. The braziers cast an eerie orange glow around the chamber and the Society members shadows trailed behind them.

The chamber beyond the hole seemed far less illuminated. The light was from two unseen torches fixed to walls either side of the chamber. All the Society team could see was a hooded human shape standing before an invoking circle that had been dabbed on to the smooth plaster-type wall opposite the opening. The chanting in some unknown cant seemed to echo around the chamber beyond.

The Society members braced themselves to attack, getting guns and knives ready. Mrs Dawson was about to reach into her just opened cricket bag when a tall grey and gruesome figure appeared in the hole in the wall to block their path. It had two sets of long sinewy arms with twin sets of talons on each wrist. All this Mrs Dawson noted in a millisecond as the demon bore down on the shocked party.

Only Mr Grandby's army training saved them. Mr Kenny dropped his pistol and ran, while Mrs Dawson and the others took a second to react. Mr Grandby's Heckler and Koch machine pistol startled them into action.

Grandby's bullets hit the demon's abdomen sending it back a step. Then after the initial shock, he re-aimed at the demon's head and fired a shorter, more controlled burst. It was now joined by Mr Green's pistol. Mrs Dawson moved to the right and Mr Atlas to the left to clear the field of fire. Mrs Dawson scooped up Kenny's fallen pistol and began firing, keeping the bag near her at all times, while Mr Atlas inched around the left-hand side of the chamber to flank the beast.

Dawson and Green kept firing as Mr Grandby re-loaded his automatic with special dumb-dumb bullets. The demon wasn't able to attack, but he wasn't falling over slain either.

As both Dawson's and Green's weapon clips clicked empty, Mr Grandby took great aim and fired directly under the grey demon's chins. Great chunks of demon flesh and blood erupted as the ex-soldier emptied the entire clip of dumb-dumb bullets into the creature's neck.

When the small cloud of cordite cleared the demon stood tottering, with its head rolling on its right shoulder. Only a scrap of grey skin held it on, but still it lived and roared angrily.

Mr Grandby swiftly turned the machine pistol around in his hands and used the stock to club what remained of the head right off the demon's shoulder. Mr Green had re-loaded and pumped three more bullets into the demon's chest before it fell to the earth to join its decapitated head.

The Heckler and Koch's stock was now skew-whiff, so Grandby dropped it and pulled a black pistol from his belt. He turned and winked at Mrs Dawson, his eyes so blue and alive. Mrs Dawson's smile died on her lips as three blood-jetting impacts exploded into his chest and he, the hero of the moment, fell to the floor stone cold dead.

Dawson looked up to see a man standing in the hole in the wall firing a pistol. Mr Green cried out and went down, then the pistol swept her way as the man aimed at her forehead.

Mrs Dawson closed her eyes and waited for death. A shot rang out and she fell to the ground, yet only the ringing in her ears caused her any pain. Had he missed? She opened her eyes to see the gunman stagger and fall flat on his face. Mr Atlas's Bowie knife embedded the entire length into the man's right eye socket.

Ashmodaios's dramatic change of appearance and height had thrown Nathaniel's defensive sword skills off kilter. He had to learn how to fight the High Demon from scratch again which caused the odd slip and near miss.

Dela looked on from the top of the steps leading down from the battlements. Nathaniel's plight had her full attention; looking over at the legions of the damned caused her eyes to swim anyway. Even if Nathaniel slew Ashmodaios, how would he escape the demon horde and their swift revenge? Dela watched on as the fight grew closer to the grisly dais and the invoking entrance to Earth.

Mrs Dawson was in mild combat shock. She sat on her bottom staring at the carnage around her.

Mr Atlas was bent over Mr Grandby's lifeless body, feeling at his neck for a pulse. Mr Green groaned and swore, then tried to sit up. At last Mrs Dawson's body and limbs regained the will to move as she hurried over to see to her injured cell member. A bullet had clipped his left side leaving a bloody wound, but he would survive. Still the chanting continued in the next chamber. What was the time?

She was glancing at her watch when Mr Salinger arrived leading Mrs Jordan and her team. It was three minutes to twelve and she had no time for battle plans.

"Right. Mrs Companion look after Mr Green, the rest of you arm yourselves and come with me."

Mr Shaft pulled a grenade from his bomber jacket pocket. Mrs Dawson saw it and pointed at him to use it in the next chamber. The Society members took cover either side of the entrance. Mr Shaft pulled the pin, counted to two and lobbed the grenade into the next chamber underarm. Everyone held their breath as Mr Shaft ran for cover next to Mrs Jordan.

A flash and ear-cracking explosion followed, then, led by Mr Atlas and Mrs Dawson, they piled into the next chamber. Three things hit them at once: the smell of the grenade smoke, the coolness of the stone chamber and the realisation that it was an ancient tomb.

The two flickering torches on the walls to the left and to the right of the hole in the wall cast shadowy light on the proceedings. In the opposite wall the circle of invoking had been dabbed with blood. A copper basin, also half-full with blood, sat against the plastered wall directly beneath the circle. Two frail bones sat either side of the basin, like some fabled trolls' table-setting. On either side of the bones lay two naked, crumpled bodies, their sex unknownable because of their wounds.

In front of the invoking circle stood a hooded and cloaked figure, from where the chanting emanated. It sounded like many voices and added to the eeriness of the tomb. To the left, a foot or so away from the wall, stood an old stone tomb. A saintly figure had been hewn and carved on the lid, yet it and half the side of the tomb had been recently and violently broken asunder, its occupants' ancient bones desecrated to be used to open a portal to hell.

To the right was once the entrance to the saint's tomb. A stone door blocked that exit and had done so for four hundred years. Steps led up behind it, or had. Now it was full of earth and above it concrete. The only remaining thing in the tomb was scrambling towards them now. The grenade had done its work shredding the figure's business suit and had blown some of the skin from its face.

Yet Mrs Dawson recognised it from her surveillance of the Idiminu Corporation building. In front of them was the demon/human hybrid known as Mr John Telal. His blood-red oily demon skin showed in patches on his face and scalp and his hands were reaching for them.

"Welcome to the end of the Earth," bellowed the enraged half-demon. "Now you will perish!" Arms extended and fingers like claws, Telal ran at the group with all hell's fury in his blood and irises.

Mrs Dawson ran right with her cricket bag, tripped on a stone from the tomb and fell behind it. Mr Atlas ran left, a flick-knife in his hand after his Bowie knife had warped inside the skull of the first hybrid they had encountered.

Mrs Jordan did not react quickly enough and Telal grabbed either side of her head in his taloned hands. She managed only one shot from her Sig-Sauer P239 pistol which entered into Telal's guts, enraging him further.

Mr Salinger has fallen in shock to the broken side of the tomb, while Mr Shaft had taken two steps back in fear. He did not have time to raise his Micro-Uzi, such was the swiftness of Telal's attack.

Telal opened his mouth impossibly wide, ripping the skin and lips around his mouth. Mrs Jordan screamed in terror as all hell's fire and heat erupted from the half-demon's mouth. Her hair and head became a ball of flame, her eyes fried in their sockets and her scream died one second before she did.

Mr Shaft staggered back in horror at the grisly death endured by his cell leader.

"You bastard!" he screamed, emptying a full clip from his Micro-Uzi into the demon hybrid's right arm and torso. Telal was pushed back by the ferocity of the impact of the 9mm bullets, dropping the smouldering remains of Mrs Jordan to the floor. Amazingly, to Mr Shaft's brown eyes, Telal staggered, but did not fall. His only response was to let out a mocking, guttural chuckle.

Mrs Dawson blinked and felt her pained head. She must have hit it when she fell.

Mr Salinger scrambled back against the cold sides of the tomb, his Heckler and Koch UPS pistol lay underneath Mrs Jordan's corpse. He had watched helplessly as she died, now he had to do something. He glanced inside the saint's tomb and had an idea.

Mr Shaft clicked in another magazine as the hybrid demon advanced slowly on him. Still the cloaked figure with the many voices chanted away in some demonic cant. Suddenly Telal jerked his head to the left, which would have looked amusing if it was not for the life and death situation they were in.

It was only when Telal raised his hand and drew Mr Atlas's throwing blade from his neck, he realised what had transpired. Telal grunted and dropped the bloody blade and continued his advance on Shaft. Another full burst from his Uzi sent blood and guts flying. Yet still Telal advanced near enough to grab the weapon from Shaft's trembling hands. Mr Shaft thought of his late mother and how he would be going to join her in a few seconds.

Suddenly a jagged shin bone ripped through the half-demon's cheek and down into his cavernous mouth with Mr Salinger being the perpetrator of the attack. Mr Telal screamed, then his whole body exploded across the chamber. Mr Shaft and Mr Salinger suffered a few burns from the death of the hybrid demon/human, but they were alive. More importantly, Telal was gone and they only had the hooded figure left to vanquish.

A quiet descended inside the saint's final resting chamber. Mrs Dawson rose shakily behind the tomb. Mr Atlas ran over to help up the injured Mr Salinger, while Mr Shaft just stared from the smouldering corpse of Mrs Jordan to where Telal had been. Only the hooded figure remained, yet something was different. The chanting had ceased.

Like a pyrotechnic trick the invoking circle on the wall burst into flame. The fire blazed yellow at first then died down until orange fire lined the outer rim of the satanic circle. The wall behind the circle had vanished to reveal a plane beyond the saint's chamber on Earth. Now a permanent portal between Hell and Earth had been opened and all its legions could flow through it.

Mrs Dawson gazed at the red sky that lay on the other side, then at her watch. It was two seconds past midnight. At that moment the hooded monk's garbed figure turned towards Mrs Dawson and threw back its hood.

Mrs Dawson's scream could be heard in the planes of Gehenna and all the seven hells beyond.

A terrible wail of human torture filtered into the combatants ears as they fought. Ashmodaios retreated toward the dais so that he could get a glance at the now open portal between his dukedom of Gehenna and Earth. A buzz went up amongst the demonic horde and only Cerberus's snapping and roaring head kept them back.

Dela rushed down the steps into the courtyard to secure a better angle to watch the action. Even Nathaniel paused his attack to see the open portal between Hell and a badly-lit subterranean room in England. It was endgame time now and everything had to be risked to close the portal, even his life. He lunged forward again to engage the Arch-Demon Ashmodaios in sword-to-sword combat.

Mrs Dawson was rooted to the spot as the many-faced demon oozed itself towards her, more in the motion of a slug than any other human-like being.

Only Mr Shaft had a spare pistol and he began to fire into the fluid, gelatinous demon. The bullets cut holes in its robes, but were absorbed into its jelly-like body and expelled into the floor as it travelled along in search of human flesh. It now cast off its monk's apparel, leaving all in the chamber to gasp at its fluid gelatinous form. Faces of the damned formed and moved along the length of its trunk as it oozed across the floor.

Mrs Dawson was paralysed, not with fear, but with non-understanding; not terrors, but abhorrence at the thing before her and the faces it showed her. She knew she had to get the King's Paladin's secret weapon from her bag and close the portal to Hell, but she could do nothing. It was nearly upon her now, its presence at the edge of the tomb caused Mrs Dawson to lose control of her urethra.

"No, you don't!" cried Mr Kenny as he ran past Mr Shaft into the room at full pelt. The others watched on helplessly as he pulled the pin of the grenade as he ran directly at the gibbering demon. Without word or real thought he punched the grenade deep into the mid-section of the opal-coloured demon. Because of its makeup Mr Kenny's arm disappeared deep inside the slobbering abomination.

Mrs Dawson staggered back, her paralysis broken. She could see Mr Kenny's arm, hand and grenade in the semi-translucent innards of the beast. Not for the first time today she fell back behind the tomb. Then Mr Kenny screamed in terror as he could not pull his arm out again. The acid in the demon's innards began to eat away at the flesh on his arm and hand. Mr Kenny screamed in agony as his arm was dissolved inside the demon and the grenade exploded. The demon vaporised and what was left of Mr Kenny fell to the chamber floor.

Luckily, most of the remains of the demon shot across the corner of the chamber and the tomb. Mr Salinger ran around the saint's tomb to help Mrs Dawson up. Mr Shaft looked aghast and Mr Atlas ran over to the remains of Mr Kenny.

They looked through the portal now as one. All the demons and hybrids this side had been slain. They saw the huge frame of the Arch-Demon Lord Ashmodaios backing towards them. They also saw he was engaged in a sword fight with a tall young man.

"Nathaniel!" Mrs Dawson whispered and reached down, searching behind her to find her cricket bag.

Nathaniel's sword sliced through Ashmodaios's sword hand at the wrist. A turbid jet of fiery blood shot forth as the demon's sword clattered to the floor, sending up a shower of sparks. Nathaniel arched his sword round and spun his entire body around before plunging the golden sword deep into Ashmodaios's loins.

The huge Demon-Lord let out an almighty bellow of pain and staggered back, its wings touching the corpses next to the portal. Nathaniel also took a shuffling couple of steps back without realising it. The demonic legions were silenced, all three of Cerberus' heads turned at once towards the dais and the Demon-Lord. Time, if that existed in Gehenna, stopped.

Mrs Dawson pulled at the cricket bag to retrieve it from behind some masonry where it had got wedged. She carried it with her, letting it drop where she was standing four feet directly in front of the portal.

Mr Goldenboy and his two companions entered the chamber behind her and stopped dead next to Mr Shaft.

She watched the wings and back of the demon take up the whole view from though the portal. She reached down into the bottom end of the bag and grabbed the only thing inside.

Dela watched in horror as from the Demon-Lord's wrists a human-like red hand grew. The hand reached down and pulled the golden sword from its lower abdomen with a howl of pain. Its golden length now covered with a black ichor. Without a sound it thrust the sword down through Nathaniel's left breast and out the lower part of his back. Ashmodaios lifted the sword and Nathaniel from the floor.

"You lose, little man."

The sword wasn't the demon-slayer, yet it still was; holy and burnt at the Demon-Lord's palm. So he threw Nathaniel ten feet towards Dela and threw down the holy golden sword.

"Let the invasion begin!" Ashmodaios cried triumphantly to his legion of minions and raised his arms aloft and extended his wings to their greatest expanse.

Dela looked at her bloody lover's body and screamed. She ran forwards, grabbed the gold sword and raced up the dais to attack Ashmodaios. The Demon-Lord turned and smiled and with a backward swish of his wings, knocked her off her feet and sent her sailing through the portal.

Cerberus raced to his fallen friend as the demonic hordes moved towards the dais and portal. Cerberus put his body between himself and the demons as he looked down at his dying friend.

"Nathaniel," his middle head whispered, "all is lost."

"Not yet," came the King's Paladin's feeble reply between coughs of blood.

Mrs Dawson rose, the steel sword in her hand. She looked on in horror as Nathaniel fell in battle to the Demon-Lord. She had no time to lose and advanced one step towards the portal. Then the image went dark and Dela came flying through the portal, just missing Mrs Dawson and landing in a heap on the chamber floor.

Mr Atlas moved from Mr Kenny's corpse over to Dela. She was awake and breathing hard. The attack and fall had winded her and bruised two of her ribs badly.

"She's okay," he stated to the concerned Mrs Dawson.

"Now to end this," Mrs Dawson whispered as Dela sat up in Mr Atlas's arms, gasping for breath. Dela looked at the golden sword and then the steel one in Mrs Dawson's hand. Realisation hit Dela at once. Nathaniel had sacrificed himself, and given the true Demon Slayer sword to the Society woman.

"Look out!" Mr Goldenboy warned in a high-pitched shout.

A human shape with demonic red eyes was entering through the portal from Hell to the world.

"Oh, no you don't!" Mrs Dawson said through gritted teeth and ran the Demon Lord through with the ancient sword of the King's Paladins.

"No!" Dela croaked, and reached out towards the portal.

A white light brighter than any car headlight appeared around the sword, its circumference expanding every second. The Demon Lord Ashmodaios screamed in terror, for only the second time in eternity. The light spread to cover his entire body until even his eyes were consumed in its encompassing heavenly glow. The light soon filled the entire portal. Everyone in the room could stare at the light, it was blinding light, yet it did not hurt them. Then it was gone, yet still remained imprinted on their irises for ten minutes after.

"Nathaniel, no!" Dela sobbed, realising the portal had been closed forever and Nathaniel was trapped in Hell.

The sword fell to the flagstones with a clatter, waking Mrs. Dawson from her vision. The familiar faces she had seen grotesquely warped in the demon's flesh she had seen again in the heavenly light. This time they were at peace and for the first time in years her soul was full of hope and love.

A car pulled up and stopped ten feet before a gate that blocked the road ahead. The passenger side door opened and a man in a trench coat got out. The full beams of the car's headlights thrust back the darkness and rain to reveal fifty plus rotting corpses lying on the road next to the gate. The Society member looked up and saw the single light visible from one window of the rectory.

"Mr Hogg," he called back into the warm confines of the car, "get a clear-up crew here at once!"

"Did we do it?" Nathaniel coughed. Pain wracked his body which felt cold even in the planes of Hell.

"You did it, King's Paladin," Cerberus's middle head replied.

"And Dela?" he whispered, his eyes closing.

"Safe and sound," replied Cerberus's right head.

"We'd better go," said Cerberus's left head, "The natives are getting restless. The demons had seen the portal destroyed, their Arch-Demon Lord slain for all eternity and the instigator of all this still in their midst.

Nathaniel opened his eyes wide, the pain had now gone. "Let's go."

Cerberus scooped up his old companion in one large, clawed leg and rose up from the realm of chaos. Nathaniel turned to watch the demon's advance and saw his blood-stained lifeless body curled upon the floor.

"Cerberus, where are we going?" he asked as the demons descended on his lifeless corpse.

"Home, King's Paladin," Cerberus's middle head replied. Nathaniel understood his old friend's words.

"Oh, Dela, I'm so sorry," he whispered to himself as the plane of Gehenna faded below him and he passed on into another realm.

Dela crawled to the remains of the portal. Reaching it she sat up on her haunches and touched the cold stone. She butted the stone with her forehead. It was only pain, nothing compared to the pain in her heart. Her soul and stomach felt so empty; Nathaniel, her love, was gone forever.

Mrs Dawson felt Dela's pain, for she had borne it herself. She knelt down beside Dela and embraced her.

Dela sagged into Mrs Dawson's arms and let out wails of anguish. Everyone in the chamber stood motionless, watching. The mournful sobs brought lumps to the throat and tears to the eyes.

The demonic invasion had been stopped at all costs. Now the costs were being counted: Grandby, Jordan, Kenny and the King's Paladin. They had made the ultimate sacrifice and only a few would ever know the real truth.

# EPILOGUE

It was April and the spring sun shone down on the hillside. The dew on the grass and condensation on the greenhouses meant it wasn't quite T-shirt weather yet.

Dela sat on the bench in the Rectory's cottage garden, a picnic blanket wrapped around most of her body to keep out the chill breeze. She was knitting, a re-learned skill that Nana had helped her with. The sun felt good on her face. She smiled, sniffed the fresh air and gazed at the tulips.

From behind the potting shed a shape stirred and moved slowly towards the back of the bench, keeping low to the ground. Dela was blissfully unaware of its presence and the creature that was not of this Earth advanced slowly, within striking distance of the back of the bench.

Dela heard an unhuman footfall behind her and craned her neck around to see who or what was there.

"Oh, there you are," she replied unafraid, "I've been waiting for you; I have a message for you to take to your master."

Dela reached under her blanket and dug out an envelope from her large denim handbag. The creature walked around to the front of the bench and took the envelope from Dela's outstretched hand in its teeth-filled maw.

It looked up at Dela and vanished in a slight puff of green sulphur-smelling smoke.

Dela put down her knitting and stared once again at the deep red tulips.

The creature reappeared in its abode in Hell. It lowered its heads and presented the letter to its master. Eager hands tore at the white envelope. Inside was a square black and white scan showing a human child inside the womb.

The hands flipped the scan picture over and written on the back in black marker pen was:

*To Daddy,*
*Mummy and me miss you so much,*
*Love, your Son xxx*

Nathaniel turned the picture so all three of Cerberus's heads could look at it. Nathaniel beamed at his old friend and went over to his side of Cerberus's house and pinned the picture on the wall. Next to it was a picture of a pregnant Dela standing between Nana and Kane outside the back door of the Rectory.

**THE END**

Peter Mark May
2 November 2005

(Robert's 5th Birthday)